THE DIVIDED
HEART

The American Palace Series

Book 5 1860-1865

The Divided Heart

Book 1: Bless This House
Book 2: Forged in Fury
Book 3: Valiant Hearts
Book 4: A Distant Dream

THE DIVIDED HEART

The American Palace Series Book 5, 1860–1865

Evan H. Rhodes

iUniverse, Inc.
New York Lincoln Shanghai

The Divided Heart
The American Palace Series Book 5, 1860–1865

iUniverse, Inc.

For information address:
iUniverse
2021 Pine Lake Road, Suite 100
Lincoln, NE 68512
www.iuniverse.com

ISBN: 0-595-27297-5

Printed in the United States of America

In Memory of
Isabel Leighton Bunker

Preface

THE WHITE HOUSE...the most powerful office on earth. To Americans, particularly now in our time of trial, it stands as the most visible symbol of our democracy. To the downtrodden of the world, it is a shining beacon of man's eternal quest for freedom and equality.

In October 1792, when the cornerstone was laid—that date chosen because it was the three hundredth anniversary of Columbus' discovery of America, the building was called The American Palace. In 1810, a new name came into popular use, the White House; but no matter what the name, legend surrounds it, for in this house that belongs to all the American people, lives the one man they've chosen to lead them through times of peace and war, adversity and triumph.

As the White House rose, and the tiny village that was Washington, D.C. grew, so did Rebecca Breech grow, from a young girl of thirteen to a woman of extraordinary intelligence and beauty. The Brand brothers, Zebulon and Jeremy loved her, and because of her headstrong, willful nature, she was fated to marry one, but love another. Through the tempestuous years of the young nation's emergence, Rebecca, at the very center of power, discovered her talent as a reporter; but because she was a woman, she was forced to write her fiery, iconoclastic political opinions under a male pseudonym, Rebel Throne. As Rebel Thorne, she became the conscience of Washington D.C., and eventually of the entire nation.

Death and dishonor stalked her, for she was a woman whose passions constantly put her in harm's way, a woman who drew the lightning. But she was indomitable, she persevered and became the matriarch of the Brand dynasty, a family destined to serve the nation and the White House. Rebecca became the confidante of Presidents, often their gadfly, and numbered among her intimate friends the great and the near great in the Executive Office, the Supreme Court, and Congress.

Rebecca imbued her children, Suzannah, Gunning and Bravo, with her own consuming idealism for the United States, the greatest experiment in democracy that the world has ever known. Her children and grandchildren also came to serve the White House and the nation in various capacities, and in their zeal, learned to know the First Families not only as public figures, but as intimate friends privy to their innermost passions and darkest secrets. Over the decades, the Brands and we, learn the answers to some intriguing questions:

Which President had an extraordinary psychic experience that persuaded him he was destined to lead a great nation?

Which President sired five bastard children by his mulatto slave mistress and when it was discovered, was threatened with impeachment?

Which President, whose wife was accused of bigamy, fought two deadly duels to defend her honor?

Which President created a national scandal, when four months after the death of his wife—who'd borne him eight children—he married an heiress thirty years his junior—who subsequently bore him seven more children?

Which President died in office a scant month after his inauguration, lending credence to the curse leveled against the White House that predicted any President elected in a year ending in zero would die in office? In 1840, 1860, 1880, 1900, 1920, 1940, and 1960, that curse proved to be horribly true. In 1980, President Reagan was shot but miraculously escaped death because he happened to be in close proximity to a hospital and the swift response of the surgeons saved his life. Will the curse strike again for President George W. Bush, elected in 2000? It is now believed that the fourth terrorist plane, which was forced to crash in Pennsylvania, had as its target, the White House.

As the generations of the Brand family become more important in the growth of the nation, and as their relationships with the White House grow ever more complex, more questions will be raised and more answers revealed.

Which President and his First Lady participated in seances in the White House to contact their dead son?

Which First Lady had to be put in a mental institution?

During what tumultuous period in our history were there two White Houses in the nation?

All these questions and more will be revealed in this book and in *The American Palace* series.

Now, Book Five, *The Divided Heart,* begins in 1860, when the impassioned, insoluble issues of Union, Secession, States' Rights and Slavery, threaten to tear Rebecca's family, and the nation apart.

Forward

THOUGH *THE Divided Heart* is a novel, the historical events depicted herein are factual.

Two areas likely to generate heated controversy are the seances held in the Lincoln White House, and the Confederate Secret Service's plot to kidnap President Abraham Lincoln, known by the code name, "Operation Come Retribution."

Bizarre as the seances may seem, they are a matter of record; the medium who presided over them, Nettie Colburn Maynard, gives full details in her book, *Was Lincoln a Spiritualist?* published in 1898.

For well over 135 years, controversy has raged over the Confederacy's role in Lincoln's assassination. According to Asia Booth Clark, John Wilkes Booth's sister, John Wilkes was a secret agent for the South as early as 1863, smuggling medicines into Richmond. See *The Open Door*, her memoir written in 1865, right after the assassination, but only brought to public light in 1938, copy in the Library of Congress.

That Booth and his co-conspirators plotted initially to kidnap Lincoln in the hope of negotiating an end to the war, is a matter of public record, and that the plan was funded by the Confederacy is also known. The kidnapping was the South's response to the Union's raid on Richmond in March of 1864; when that raid failed and Colonel Ulric Dahlgren was killed, his handwritten orders discovered on his body exhorted his men to kill Jefferson Davis, President of the Confederacy, and his Cabinet. These details and the workings of the Confederate spy network in Canada and in Washington, are explored in

William Tidwell's book, *Come Retribution* published by the University Press of Mississippi, 1988.

Booth's travels, the dates of his appearances in various cities are fully documented and are not this author's fabrications. It has recently been established through the Confederate war rolls, that Lewis Paine, one of Booth's co-conspirators, and the man who tried to kill Secretary of State William Seward, was a member of General Mosby's Raiders and was assigned to Booth's action team in Washington by the Confederate Secret Service.

Wherever possible, the dialogue spoken by John Wilkes Booth, Jefferson Davis, and Abraham Lincoln has been taken from their own speeches, books, and memoirs.

Though *The Divided Heart* is a novel unto itself, written to stand alone, it is also the fifth book in *The American Palace Series*.

This then is the tale of the most cataclysmic time in American history. In a sequence of interlocking historical events far more extraordinary than any author's invention, the narrative, *The Divided Heart* now unfolds.

THE BREECH–BRAND FAMILY TREE

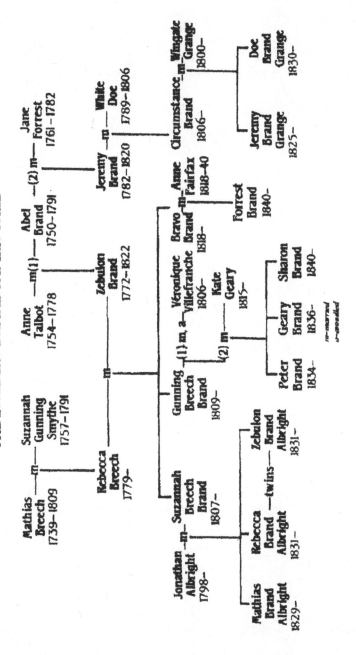

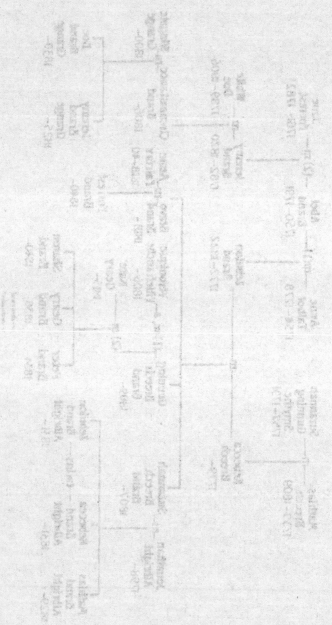

THE RICKEY FAMILY TREE

PART ONE

Chapter 1

"A CATASTROPHE, a damned unmitigated catastrophe!" Rebecca Breech Brand swore as she paced the drawing room of her home in Washington, D.C. "I warned them, didn't I? Every last one of those idiotic Democrats, but did they listen?"

"No, Ma, they didn't, they surely didn't," her eldest son, Gunning, responded with laconic boredom.

She went on, her anger building; "What piece of insanity prompted the Democrats to field four candidates for the Presidency? Split the vote and allow some unknown Republican to win? A rail-splitting country lawyer from a backwater town in Illinois? Elected with the lowest plurality ever in a presidential election? I could scream!" And did. Which brought Rebecca's mulatto maid running, "Who died?" Bittersweet asked.

Rebecca swept to the sideboard and with trembling hands poured herself two fingers of Bourbon.

"Ma, go easy," her youngest son Bravo cautioned. "Doctor Grange said no heavy liquor. Remember your heart—"

He moved to take the glass from her but his older brother Gunning spun him aside. "For chrissakes, Bravo, leave her alone, she's eighty-one, and if indulging in another drink takes an hour or a day off her life, so what? Let her enjoy whatever time she's got left, right, Ma?"

"From your mouth to God's ear," Rebecca agreed, and downed the bourbon. "However, there's no need to push me two years closer to the grave, I'm only seventy-nine."

"Eighty, eighty, eighty," Bittersweet tra-la-laed as she proffered a plate of hors d'oeuvres.

Rebecca glowered at her; "I gave this runaway slave refuge, even freed her, and how am I repaid? The Bible's got it all wrong, it should be 'How sharper than a <u>servant's</u> tooth.'"

"Hush now," Bittersweet ordered, "'n eat some of these crab puffs, you're wasting away to nothing. What man's gonna wanna kiss a bag of bones under the mistletoe?"

"I'm long past the kissing stage, I assure you."

"Never can tell," Bittersweet clucked, "Bible says Sarah had her first chil' at ninety. Eat up now, even President Buchanan says my crab puffs be the tastiest in Washington."

"That Yankee tub of lard would eat anything you stuck under his nose," Gunning snorted. Bittersweet glowered at him and he swept her into a quick two-step; "No offence, my darling, you're the prettiest cook in all Washington, this house smells holiday delicious and if I wasn't married already—"

She squirmed free and as she left, clucked, "You're a scandal, Mr. Gunning and the Lord's gonna get you for it."

"But I'm gonna have one hell of a time before He does."

Rebecca's royal blue taffeta skirts rustled as she moved across the Persian carpet to the Biedemeyer settee. Her posture erect, her stride determined, in the matter of aging, Nature had been more than kind. Her silver hair hinted at the blazing redhead she'd been in her youth; her eyes, huge and hazel remained her signal feature, capable of expressing love and wisdom, or stabbing an opponent with contempt. The doyen of Washington society, Rebecca Breech Brand was still considered a great beauty, an attribute superceded only by her formidable intelligence. Her friends described her as being contumacious, confrontational, and contrary; her enemies used a far shorter word, but one never uttered in polite society.

"That I should live to see this day," she said, looking out of the tall drawing room window to the President's mansion on Pennsylvania Avenue; "I saw them lay the cornerstone of the White House. I've been to every inauguration in Washington, seen every President take the oath of office, but the thought of having to live through four years of this—Illinois ape living in the White House—?" She let out another wounded cry.

"Have another drink, Ma," Gunning suggested, "it blurs the hard edges, makes life just a lit-tle easier to bear—"

"Your solution to everything," Bravo said.

Gunning retorted, "At least I enjoy my life, all you do is bury yourself in your lab and tinker with your toys." He poked him in the stomach; "Look at you, your muscles are going slack, you've got the pallid look of a prissy book-worm—"

"Be quiet you two," Rebecca snapped, "it's almost Christmas, peace and goodwill toward all men—even brothers." Her tone, sharp and commanding stilled her sons—but only for the moment, she knew they'd soon erupt again, fighting the battle that had consumed them all their lives. She tried not to take sides but her scales of justice hung in uneven balance.

Gunning…though she knew his flaws all too well, flaws that had caused her untold grief, nevertheless her eye delighted in him. She thought him the most appealing man in Washington and was secretly thrilled that she'd given heart-beat to such an extraordinary specimen. Over six-foot tall, in any gathering Gunning dominated. He sported a full mane of red-blond hair, graying at the temples, a sweeping moustache and sideburns that angled down to a square, chiseled jaw. His gold-flecked hazel eyes played no favorites but devoured each person in turn, conquering eyes when it concerned women, avaricious when it concerned power. Nature had endowed him with a robust, libidinous body, and he could still outride, outshoot and outfuck many a man half his age; much to the chagrin of his devoutly religious wife, Kate. Indulged shamelessly in his youth by his sybaritic father, Zebulon—God rest his restless licentious soul—rescued from innumerable escapades by Rebecca, he'd grown up believ-ing he was above the law, and now at fifty-two, Gunning Brand had become a law unto himself. He'd been an army officer for years, but a scandal surround-ing the wife of his commanding officer had forced him to resign his commis-sion. Rebecca had heard rumors of Gunning's latest intrigue, but it was so scandalous she dared not believe it.

Rebecca tore her gaze from Gunning and considered her other son, Bravo, some ten years younger than Gunning. Not quite as tall or imposing, if his brother hadn't been in the room he might have been considered handsome—albeit scarecrow handsome. A towhead at birth, Bravo wore his streaked blond hair long, his nose was straight, his lips full, his guileless angular face clean-shaven. A straightforward, honest, reliable face, nothing out of the ordinary, except for his eyes. A legacy of his natural father, his eyes were a brilliant aqua-marine, eyes that looked to the far horizon, eyes that dreamed of yet undiscov-ered mysteries.

Though the two men shared some physical resemblance through Rebecca, they were so unlike in temperament that it was often hard to tell that they were brothers.

Rebecca traced her long tensile fingers across her forehead; "Six weeks since the election and things have gone from bad to worse. Gangs of Northern hooligans roam about Washington beating up Southerners legislators, while a hundred Southern thugs—calling themselves Minute Men, of all things—do the same to Northerners. It's total anarchy. What's going to happen to our country?"

"Ma, you've always been fair-minded," Bravo said. "Why not give this Mr. Lincoln a chance? After all, if Honest Abe's going to be our neighbor, let's see what he's like?"

"If the Ship of State is foundering, I need a seasoned captain at the helm, not some untried political hack. I've seen too many politicians to trust any of them—"

Gunning snapped his fingers; "Ma, here's the solution. Just refuse to attend any of Lincoln's social functions and as the acknowledged arbiter of Washington society you'll put such a pall on his Presidency that he'll _have_ to resign." He placed his right hand on his heart and declared in a flourish of patriotism; "And thus, you, Rebecca Breech Brand, will have single-handedly saved the nation."

She threw her napkin at him. "You are the most infuriating—we're talking about the dissolution of our Union." Yet some tiny part of her glowed with delight that he'd acknowledged her status in Washington. "Gunning, surely you don't believe that the South really intends to secede?"

"It's only a matter of time. South Carolina's on the brink and so are four other states. We should have done it years ago. We've tried every reasonable compromise, but it's only gotten worse; the bloody fighting in Kansas, John Brown's massacre at Harper's Ferry—what next, murdered in our beds? Let's get these damn Yankees out of Washington, send them back to New York or Boston or Springfield or wherever, form our own independent nation of Southern states and go our own way, free at last from the economic dictatorship of the North."

Rebecca stood up shakily; "I won't hear such seditious talk in my house, there's still a chance of compromise—"

"Come on, Ma, I'm only saying what's on everyone's mind."

"Not on mine," Bravo interrupted. "Mr. Lincoln's made it clear that he won't allow the Union to be dissolved."

Like a lion marking his territory, Gunning's roaring laugh reverberated through the house. "Bravo, I always suspected you were something of a simpleton and this proves it. If the South wants to secede, who's going to stop us?"

Bravo clenched his fists, but true to form, controlled his temper. "Before you rush to destroy our Union, _think_. We profess to be a democracy, right? And we exist by the rule of law? Well, Lincoln's been duly elected by our laws—"

Gunning stood toe to toe with his brother. "Exactly the kind of spineless equivocation I'd expect from you. Since the signing of the Constitution seventy years ago, the North's tried to swallow us into the maw of this—Central Government—she's creating, all to further her own ends. We began our destiny as sovereign individual states, and it's time for us to defend our rights or lose our freedom forever."

Rebecca's heart began to pound as her sons confronted each other, fighting the endless battle that had begun the day she'd given birth to Bravo, a battle born of Gunning's natural resentment in having to share his mother's affections, and his overwhelming suspicion about Bravo's legitimacy. She tried to move between them but her head began to whirl and she sat down heavily, brilliant lights flashing behind her eyelids.

Bravo stood his ground; "States' Rights? Freedom? Why don't you call it what it really is? The issue is slavery. Everything else is just an excuse to perpetuate an obscene practice. In this day and age, is it right, or proper, or moral for one man to own another?"

"Since you're so law-abiding, doesn't our Constitution say it is right and proper?" Gunning insisted, his voice rising from aeolian to thunder. "Our laws are defined by the Supreme Court, and in the Dred Scott Decision the Court declared that a slave is property, pure and simple."

"All that decision proves is that Chief Justice Taney is a blithering idiot. On the issue of slavery this country is still in the Dark Ages. The rest of western civilization, including England in 1830—that's thirty years ago!—Abolished slavery, isn't it time for the United States to do the same?"

"Oh, I get it, Bravo, you obey the law of the land—but only when it suits you? Typical Yankee tactic. I don't hold with slavery myself but the law says the Negra is no one's business but his owner's. When the South chooses to abolish slavery, it will, but it will be in our own time, at our own pace and never according to anyone else's dictates. The only answer is secession. And if the North tries to stop us—"

"What then?" Bravo demanded. "Rebellion? War?"

"If it comes to war, then so be it."

"A war the South's bound to lose."

Gunning burst out laughing. "You really are a nincompoop. I've served in the army for decades, from Washington, D.C., to the wild frontier, I've fought Mexicans, Indians, renegades, and any fool knows that one Southern soldier is worth ten Yankee cry-babies."

"Maybe, if we were still fighting with clubs and swords. But these days, wars are fought with modern weapons. Open your eyes, Gunning, industry and invention, that's what wins wars. The South has practically no railroads, no iron works, no manufacturing. How will you move your troops? What will you fight with? Come down to the Patent Office and I'll show you who invented the steam boat, steel plow, telegraph, mechanical reaper, revolver, repeating rifle, sewing machine, lead pencil, friction match, safety pin, typewriter—all invented by Northerners!" He ended on a triumphant note, "And what has the South contributed to the evolution of mankind?"

"Why, the mint julep, sir, and manners, to say nothing of chivalry and a way of life that infuriates all Yankees, why else would they so wish to rob us of it?"

"I'm sure there's right on both sides," Rebecca began—

Gunning boomed; "Ma, the time is long past for you so-called peacemakers with your endless platitudes; the resentments run too deep, the outrages perpetrated against the South too many; you'd best make up your mind, you're either with us or against us."

He jabbed his finger in Bravo's chest; "As for your arguments about the North's greater resources, I remind you that during our own Revolutionary War we took on the greatest power in the world—and won. Victory or defeat is decided by will, and we Southerners have that will in daunting abundance."

All heads turned toward the window as they heard the distant cry of a newsboy, "Extra, extra, read all about it!"

Bravo dashed outside and came back a few moments later with a copy of the *Washington Evening Star*. His face was drained of color. "What is it?" Rebecca asked anxiously.

"South Carolina's just seceded."

"Oh, dear God, it's come at last," she whispered, as Gunning shouted, "Hallelujah! It's come at last!"

Chapter 2

"I SHOULDN'T have come out at all, my rheumatism is killing me," Rebecca complained to Bittersweet as they hurried through the cold January afternoon toward Willard's Hotel.

"Stop fussin', you got on three petticoats; you promised Becky. 'Stead of concentrating on your miseries you should be proud your granddaughter's being honored by the orphanage."

"For your information, I helped found that institution."

"But this be Becky's day so don't go spoiling it, sayin' she should be doin' this 'n that, or getting' married, or—"

"Do you want her to be an old maid? She's twenty-<u>nine</u>." Rebecca stopped short at the sight of soldiers piling sandbags around the public buildings. "All these Yankee soldiers are doing nothing but fouling up our streets, it's a disgrace."

"Us maid folks hear rumors, that this here General Winfield Scott called up eight companies to defend Washington? Cause Southerners be plotting to take over the capital?"

"Ridiculous; Washington's a Southern city already, it's Northerners who are plotting to take it over. When we get to Willard's, they won't let you into the Grand Ballroom so stay at the Colored Entrance and wait, I'll only be a few minutes."

"That's what you say every time, but you're always the first to arrive and the last to leave, and talk, talk, talk."

"I'll be sitting at Senator Jeff Davis' table—"

"Why?"

"What do you mean, why? Because we've been friends for years, that's why. In this town full of scoundrels and idiots, at least Jeff and Varina have integrity and intelligence."

"But they're from Mississippi, right? That's where I ran away from that slave dealer, Harmony Lumpkin. Never forget his mean miserable hatchet face, prays I never see him again."

"What in heaven's name has Jeff Davis to do with that?"

"Mr. Davis, he believes in slavery, don't he? 'N if he knew I was a runaway slave, he'd send me back, wouldn't he?"

"That was twenty years ago," Rebecca cried in exasperation, "Harmony Lumpkin's probably long gone to his Maker. If indeed there ever was a Harmony Lumpkin—"

"You'd believe in him all right if he forced himself on you like he did on me. Miss Becky, she knows how I feel."

Rebecca felt a stab of pain for her granddaughter, then an unbidden memory swept over her. In the long ago her family had a slave named Letitia; Letitia's daughter and granddaughter had been sold to a slave dealer in Mississippi. When Bittersweet came of age, Harmony Lumpkin bought her to breed a flock of slaves. But Bittersweet escaped and ran away to Washington to find her grandmother. Bounty hunters tracked her, but Rebecca spirited her out of the capital via the Underground Railway to Boston. Bittersweet returned a few years later claiming Boston was too cold and even when it wasn't, she couldn't understand the way they talked. Despite the danger of being sent back to Mississippi under the Fugitive Slave Law, she'd worked for Rebecca ever since.

The Willard Hotel thronged with people. The Grand Ballroom had been set up for the charity event honoring the Washington Orphanage and a host of people greeted Rebecca, including President Buchanan, looking trapped by his corpulence and impotence. Buchanan's Attorney General, porcine, scraggly-bearded, squint-eyed Edwin Stanton fawned at Rebecca and she shuddered. Everything about him offended, his appearance, his opportunism, his devious lawyer's mind intent not on justice but on finding loopholes in the law.

Senator Jefferson Davis rescued her and led her to his table. At fifty-two, Davis stood erect as a cadet, one arm crooked behind his back in West-Point-perfect-posture. Five-foot ten inches tall, with a tough spare frame, blond hair going gray, steely blue-gray eyes, and of Welsh ancestry, Davis' voice had a lyric quality. His golden tones, along with his bravery, had served him well as a general in the Mexican War, as Secretary of War in President Pierce's cabinet and now as the commanding Southern voice in the U.S. Senate.

His wife, Varina, cleverly gowned in ivory damask to compliment her olive complexion and brown hair, pressed cheeks with Rebecca in kissin' cousin style. A bit too plump to be considered pretty, her eyes were her best feature, deep brown with a romantic mien. She was eighteen years younger than Jeff; he'd been married to President Zachary Taylor's daughter but she'd died of Yellow Fever. Born in Natchez, Varina had been raised in the North; her paternal grandfather had been governor of New Jersey so she'd sharpened her wits in the political arena. Rebecca suspected that Varina secretly regretted that she hadn't been Jeff's first love; but they had to be doing something right, she'd already borne him three children.

"Miss Rebecca, some punch?" Varina asked sweetly.

"A bourbon and branch will do me just fine."

"A woman after my own heart," said Judah P. Benjamin, the senior senator from Louisiana. Judah was a substantial man, given to fine wines and Havana cigars, brilliant as Solomon, and one of the very few Jews in government. Urbane and witty, Rebecca liked Judah because she always felt challenged by him.

Rebecca toasted the table; "Jeff, if our backroom politicians had any brains at all they'd have nominated you on the Democratic ticket for President and you'd have won."

"My sentiments exactly," Judah agreed, "alas, those hacks think Mississippi too small a state to merit such an honor."

Varina glowed with this praise for her husband. "Rebecca dear, I just saw Gunning, right here in the Willard? Seems he was having quite a contretemps with Veronique Villefranche Connaught." She leaned forward conspiratorially; "Do you know the Connaughts keep a permanent suite at the Willard? Imagine being that rich? Someone told me that Veronique and Gunning were once married, but I said, nonsense, that's impossible—"

Rebecca tried to quell the rush of blood to her face; "One of the many errors of my son's errant youth. They were married, but only for a few months, then it was annulled."

The ballroom filled with politicians, army officers and socialites, and the talk centered on secession. Rebecca said to Davis; "Jeff, of all the voices in the South, yours is the one most respected. What say you?"

He chose his words with care; "There's a growing sentiment that the real value of democracy is not in equality, but in equity, not to press men down into a common mold, but to release them to develop to the full limits of their nature. The Constitution says that we are a <u>compact</u> of states, so it follows that each state reserves the right to secede from that compact, if she feels her interests are being denied."

"Jeff, that sounds so much like a political speech; I want to know what's in your heart. If our Manifest Destiny is to occupy all the land between the great oceans, surely that destiny isn't as two separate countries, but as one nation. Are we to be witness to the Union's dissolution? Become pallbearers for the greatest experiment in democracy that man's ever known? I beg you, use your influence—"

Davis, unable to understand how or why anybody would disagree with him, interrupted, "Miss Rebecca, I cannot comprehend how any intelligent Southerner could deny the most fundamental cornerstone of democracy, our States' Rights."

Judah P. Benjamin nodded in sage agreement.

Rebecca felt her pulse quicken; "Andrew Jackson was a Southerner, yet when John Calhoun threatened to secede Jackson roared, 'Our Union, it must be preserved!' and warned Calhoun he'd send Federal troops into South Carolina and hang him."

Jeff Davis stiffened; "That was twenty-five years ago and since then more injustices have been heaped on us. It's not only the incendiary abolitionist documents that flood the South and encourage rebellion among our slaves; it's not only the unequal and unjust tariff laws. None of those things by themselves are forcing us to contemplate secession." His gray eyes shone bright with his truths; "It's the North's systematic and persistent struggle to deprive the Southern states of equality in the Union. If the South is forced to leave the Union, it will be to escape from injury and strife within that Union, and to find peace and prosperity outside it."

Their argument ceased when officers of the orphanage took the stage. After the usual boring speeches and the financial pledges noted, Rebecca's granddaughter, Becky Albright was presented with a plaque for her tireless service. Rebecca's applause led all the rest, but her heart ached for the girl.

Her manner on stage was so timorous, so self-effacing—and for no reason. She was such a lovely creature, tall, pliant as a stalk of wheat, light chestnut hair and enormous gray-green eyes. Like her mother, Suzannah, she had the disposition of an angel—albeit a wounded one. She'd lived with Rebecca in Washington since her mother died so tragically in Texas thirteen years ago. Now Becky was almost past marrying age, and Rebecca had a melancholy feeling that she was just letting life slip by. If it's the last thing I do before I die, Rebecca vowed, I'll see that precious child married.

After the ceremony, Becky came to the table and Rebecca embraced her; "I'm so proud of you, what a wonderful touch you have with children. I can't wait for you to have your own."

Rebecca looked around for eligible males, when suddenly the hair on her neck stood on end. She faltered; "I don't know what's come over me, I feel as if someone's just walked over my grave." She tossed back her drink, blinked, then saw Veronique Villefranche Connaught glide into the room.

Men turned to stare at her porcelain beauty and all the while Rebecca's heart thumped wildly, I hate her, I don't care if it is unchristian—I hate that hateful bitch.

Veronique's cold dark eyes glittered, acknowledging the compliments strewn like petals in her path. Her artfully made-up face took years off her age, but no amount of rice powder or kohl could mask her decades of sybaritic self-indulgence or her present distress. Then Rebecca saw the cause of Veronique's misery.

A groundswell of approval greeted the entrance of her daughter, Romance Villefranche Connaught. In her twenties, tall and regnant, she looked so imperiously stunning in a gown of widow's black that every other woman in the room faded. Hair so dark it had the raven's purple sheen, jeweled eyes made even more brilliant by thick sweeping black lashes. She seemed to…drift…in a mysterious mixture of innocence and sexual availability. Fires long banked in old men's eyes burst suddenly into flame, while young men and even married men were called to attention by the God Priapus.

Rebecca thought she must faint when she saw Romance's escort; her hand rested lightly in the crook of his arm, her attitude conveying such intimacy that Rebecca knew all the disgraceful, disgusting rumors she'd heard must be true.

She leapt to her feet, a roaring sound filled her head and even as she fainted her mouth was screaming, How could you? Gunning how could you!

Chapter 3

REBECCA OPENED her eyes to find herself in her drawing room, with Gunning leaning over her. "You sure know how to upstage a room, Ma. Becky and I brought you home; I sent Bittersweet to fetch Dr. Grange, I don't like these fainting spells. How do you feel? Are you all right?"

"I was, until I saw you at the Willard."

"Becky's my niece, I adore her, I wouldn't have missed—"

"Yet when I asked you to go with me you pleaded pressing engagements." Let's see you get out of that one, she thought.

"Believe it or not, I do have important things to do. Things change hour to hour; five states have already seceded, South Carolina, Mississippi, Florida, Alabama, Georgia and we're expecting Louisiana and Texas to join us."

"What do you mean—us? What have you to do in this?"

"I told you, don't you remember? The seceded states are holding a convention in Montgomery, Alabama. Some prominent legislators in Virginia have asked me to go—as an observer—and keep them posted."

Had he told her? She was almost certain that he hadn't, but then, she was getting forgetful. She asked irritably, "What's this convention in aid of?"

"We're electing a President of our new Confederacy."

"You never told me that, if you had, I would surely have had another fainting spell. Such a thing is doomed to fail."

"Suppose I told you that we've already put out feelers in Europe about our secession? England not only looks kindly on us, but hints at quick recognition of our Confederacy."

"Then you're a bigger fool than I thought. England's only interest is to see our country divided, the way she tried to crush our revolution, stop the Louisiana Purchase, the way she supplied Santa Ana with weapons in the Mexican War. If we grow too powerful it undermines her influence on our continent. This secession craze plays right into England's hands."

"For a woman whose heritage is English—"

She got up slowly and made her way to the tall window and looked out at New York Avenue, grown quiet in the ice-blue twilight. "Guess I've never forgiven them for burning Washington in 1814…a piece of vandalism that beggars the deeds of the Hun. Forty-five years ago, yet I remember it so vividly it could have been yesterday. From here I could see the White House in flames. Your father had gone to fight the British and you and Suzannah and I were alone in the house."

"And our mammy, Letitia."

"How could I forget Letitia? Maid in name only, more my second mother. When I saw the fire advancing toward our house, I climbed up on this roof, and with buckets of water, tried to put out all the sparks and cinders."

"I remember it too," he breathed softly. "Suzannah and I were, oh, six or seven? We tried to help Letitia carry the buckets, but spilled most of it. I saw someone on the roof outlined against the burning sky, and I thought, God sent this beautiful angel to save us, then I realized that beautiful angel was my mother. I treasure that memory, it will be the winding sheet I'll carry with me to the grave."

His recollection warmed her…what a contradiction he was, capable of the most thoughtless cruelties, the kind you'd expect from a capricious child, but also capable of such kindness that it completely disarmed her.

She came and sat near him. "Gunning, I beg you, don't get involved in this secession madness." When he didn't respond she sighed, "Dear God, where is Andrew Jackson now that we need him?"

"You know, you become positively—girlish when you talk about Old Hickory? Your voice throbs, your cheeks flush—"

Her eyes came alive with the memory of the President—and the man—who'd figured so tenderly in her life. But Gunning's teasing was also edged with approbation.

The vision of Romance Connaught snaked its way back into Rebecca's mind. She cleared her throat; "Gunning, I'd heard these dreadful rumors, I didn't believe them, then today—"

He stood up abruptly. "What would Washington be without rumors? Gossips feed on them like carrion, they gloat when reputations are ruined. Mother, do you realize how very much alike we are?"

"Don't change the subject," she snapped, but he plunged ahead, "We're both rapacious in our zest for life; you may have slowed down a bit but it's still there. We're both intolerant of stupidity, and deny it as you may, we both subscribe to an aristocracy of beauty. After all, you did marry my father, didn't you?" He added softly, "I know he loved you, I saw it all during the years I was growing up."

His words hung in the stillness of the room, sending reverberations down and down through the decades. Passion and obsession and hate and murder, she'd lived a lifetime with the secrets of the Breech-Brand family.

"Then there was your—interlude with my Uncle Jeremy—?"

"Gunning, must you still—I've asked you repeatedly—"

"So you have, forgive me. I'll never mention President Jackson or Uncle Jeremy again. Anyone else I shouldn't—?"

"You are infuriating. You're on the verge of destroying your marriage, alienating your children, and you very adroitly turn the attention away from yourself."

He grinned at her, that maddening, delightful off-center grin so redolent of his father's. "Ma, believe it or not, one of the reasons I went to the Willard was to see Jeff Davis, I had some important things to discuss with him before he leaves for Mississippi. Then you fainted—I've got to go back now."

He started for the door, but with surprising agility she blocked his exit. "Gunning, you're so transparent. I'm old and forgetful, and perhaps I've lived too long. The Good Book tells us three score and ten, so I've lived ten years beyond God's given time. I'm ready to go whenever He calls. But until He does, I will <u>not</u> be played for a fool by anyone, particularly not by my children."

"You mustn't upset yourself, Dr. Grange says—"

"The hell with what anyone says! As sure as we're standing here, you're on the road to perdition. After all that's happened—? The Connaughts have had a hand in every evil that's befallen our family. How could you, a married man—? And with a woman twenty-five years younger, young enough to be your daughter? I beg you, for the sake of everything decent, you must stop seeing Romance Connaught."

The vehemence of her outburst took him aback. As for Rebecca, the Connaught name acted like a cautery on her soul. She sagged and would have fallen if Gunning hadn't caught her. He eased her into a chair, then gave her a glass of bourbon. She took it neat, to drown out the bitter memories.

For generations, since the capital had been moved to the District of Columbia, the Connaught and Brand families had opposed each other, and that confrontation had led to a range of sins that must have turned God's face from them. How else to explain why it had gone on generation after generation? Bringing ruin to both families? Now her son had become ensnared again. Oh Gunning, Gunning, will you never learn?

Outside, a horse-drawn sled sped by, a group of revelers bellowed, "We'll hang Abe Lincoln from a sour apple tree—!" proclaiming just how Washingtonians felt about the usurper.

She took a deep breath; "You don't know how difficult this is for me, but I must speak out, I've an obligation—"

His body tensed, his gleaming golden eyes shone hard as agates. "Your first obligation is not to meddle in my life. I'm a grown man with grown children of my own. I've commanded men in battle, I'm about to embark on the greatest adventure of my life—and if I may be blunt, my personal affairs are none of your business."

"If I've offended you I apologize. But I implore you, think of what you're doing. We all know what Veronique Villefranche Connaught was, and still is. Can you forget so easily that because of her you almost died? Can you forget her family's complicity in the—" her voice caught—"in the death of your sister? My dear, sweet, innocent Suzannah."

"I haven't forgotten," he replied crisply. "No one loved Suzannah more than I did. No, I haven't forgotten at all."

"But Veronique is a novice compared to her daughter. What about that aging financier Romance married? Then drove him into the grave by—?"

"Screwing him to death? What a way to go."

"Joke all you want, but I've lived a great many years, known a great many people, and to my mind Romance Villefranche Connaught is—where can I find words adequate enough to describe her?"

"Beautiful? Desirable?" he offered, then smiled his crooked smile; "I've just had an odd thought, Shall the sins of the mothers be visited on the daughters? I'm not as stupid as you think, Ma, I know what Veronique was, and still is. The wheels of fate grind slow but exceeding small, it's taken me twenty-five years, but I can't tell you what satisfaction it gives me to see that conniving little tart's distress because of my harmless attentions to her daughter."

"Harmless? Don't compound this disgraceful affair by also insulting my intelligence. Even if it were harmless, what about everyone else you're hurting? Have you no feeling for Kate who loves you, stood by you for twenty-five years?"

"What do you know of it? When I married Kate I married her—and God. With Jesus watching, the bed gets awfully crowded; I've been pushed out into the cold long ago. So I'm off to Montgomery, and Kate's staying in Washington."

That news appalled her. "You're separating?"

"I've suggested divorce, but being a devout Catholic, Kate prefers to wear our marriage like a hair shirt."

"What about your children? Have you no shame parading your—proclivities—in front of them?"

His voice grew ominous; "You can play the sanctimonious grand dame all you want with other people, but not with me. Long as we're quoting the Good Book, it also says, 'Let he who is without sin cast the first stone.' And mother, where do you think I've inherited all these—proclivities from?"

She moved to slap him but he caught her hand. "Before you accuse, look at your own life. Are you without sin? Might my father not be alive today if you hadn't—?"

They stood facing each other, decades of unresolved bitterness crackling between them, still fighting the battle that had dominated their adult lives. Your father was a rapist and a murderer! she wanted to scream, but dared not; the less her children and grandchildren knew, the better.

Gunning had lost any vestige of reason, his yellow eyes burned like some predator's. "He worshipped you," he choked, barely able to get the words out. "You were the center of his world, and how did you reward him? By betraying him with his brother. And you have the gall to question my actions? You gave up that right when you bore your lover's bastard."

Overcome with his own anger, he strode out the door and mounted his stallion, Baal, leaving Rebecca standing in the center of her drawing room like a pillar of salt.

Chapter 4

REBECCA'S BITTER confrontation with Gunning left her bedridden with a low-grade fever, compounded with low-grade hopelessness. As Gunning had predicted, Louisiana and Texas seceded; then without so much as a goodbye, he went off to the Confederate Convention in Montgomery, Alabama.

Bittersweet took Becky aside; "Your Grandma's gettin' meaner than cat's meat; Dr. Grange says she's grieving, and grief is poison for the heart, so you grandchildren best do somethin' before she drives all of <u>us</u> into the grave."

The next afternoon, Gunning's daughter, Sharon, paid a call on her grand-mother, and Rebecca, Sharon and Becky sat down to high tea. "Not too strong, dear," Rebecca cautioned, "Dr. Grange insists I mustn't have any stimulants. As one grows older, more and more things are taken away, it hardly makes life worth the living. I look back on my life and what do I see? A crotchety old woman who's barely tolerated by her family—as if I were some down quilt so worn that the goose feathers are beginning to needle through the ticking."

Sharon laughed at that, a melodious laugh inherited from her mother, Kate. Rebecca liked the look of the girl, rich titian hair, pug-nosed with clear blue eyes, eyes as lilting as her laugh. She wasn't nearly as striking as Becky; she was too broad-boned, too buxom to be truly beautiful. The youngest of Gunning and Kate's children, Rebecca hardly knew her, for Sharon had been a babe when Gunning and his family had been posted to a fort on the frontier. She appeared decent enough but Rebecca hadn't yet detected that spark of divine discontent that would set her apart from the herd.

"How old are you now, child? And would you put a tot of brandy in my tea? Just a wee dram, as you Irish lasses say."

"I'm not yet twenty," Sharon said.

"What do you want to do with your life?"

"Marry someday, I suppose. Have children. And why the sour look? Is wanting that so wrong?"

"Heavens, no; my family used to be the comfort of my life—though I hardly ever see them anymore, especially my grandsons, they're <u>never</u> around. But if one feels there's something more, then why settle for just marriage? When I think how corseted my own youth was, trapped as I was by petticoats and flounces and the thousand and one doll-like frivolities that men demand we adorn ourselves in, the better to keep our minds imprisoned. But dear Sharon, as I've told Becky for years, one can have both marriage and a career. There are women who've done it, Abigail Adams for one. In our own day, Harriet Beecher Stowe is a perfect example; *Uncle Tom's Cabin* has had more of an impact on this nation than a hundred ineffectual laws."

Sharon sighed; "Where'd she find the time to write it? Like you say, I'm bound hand and foot by washing and ironing and cooking and cleaning and the thousand and one other drudgeries that make up <u>my</u> life. While my brother Peter rarely lifts a finger to help around the house and my brother Geary can run off and do anything he wants. But in my dreams, ah in my dreams, then I'm at the ball, my gown is spangled bright—"

"No!" Rebecca cried, making both girls jump, "you <u>are</u> in a gown, but it's black and you're wearing it as you preside over the Supreme Court." Her weighted gaze swung to Becky, "If you prefer a different gown, then you're in white in an operating room, saving lives. Those are the gowns you young ladies should be wearing, the dreams you should be dreaming."

Sharon's glance to Becky indicated that she thought Grandma's mind had gone as curdled as last week's milk.

Rebecca hadn't heard the door open and a young man in his mid-twenties with a riot of curly Irish-black hair, a puckish face and engaging hazel eyes stole up behind her and whispered in her ear, "How's my favorite girl?"

"Heaven forefend that I be lumped with that disreputable lot, Geary Brand," and rapped him on the head. "When did you get back to Washington? Why haven't you been to see me?"

"Got back last week. I'm here now. I'll be leaving soon as—don't suppose you could front me train fare, or enough to buy a horse? See, Grandma, before I die, I've made it a point of honor to visit every town and hamlet in our fair country."

"And kiss every girl in each?" Rebecca grumbled.

"Why Grandma, what big teeth you have. Never been so mortified in all my born days. In my defense I can only say I've never lied to anyone, whatever was done was done with free will on both sides, and I hope I left them with a smile."

"Where's Forrest?" Rebecca demanded, "and don't think I haven't heard that you two scalawags have been out carousing—you're older than he, you should be setting a good example—"

"I'm right here, Grandma," Forrest called, and strode into the room and embraced her.

Rebecca's heart melted; whatever discomfort, whatever reserve she felt with her son, Bravo, she lavished all her affection on Forrest. The boy's mother had died in childbirth and Rebecca had raised him. She knew grandmothers weren't supposed to have favorites but everything about him brought her joy. She thought him the best-looking of her grandsons; blond hair worn shoulder length, eyes as pale as the sky, with such an open, innocent expression it pained her for all the hurt he'd have to go through. But it was more than looks, there was something so decent about him, so honorable. How she worried about him, could anyone survive being six-foot and weighing 150 pounds? He'd grown up too coltish, too impulsive and shooting off those thrusts of sexuality that many lean people have. In body, mind, and spirit, he was the image of his natural grandfather, Jeremy Brand, Rebecca's lover.

"Grandma? Why are you staring at Forrest?" Geary asked.

She recovered and said defensively, "I am <u>not</u> staring."

A conspiratorial glance passed between the four grandchildren, then Sharon cleared her throat. "My Dada told us you used to write things, but under a fake name; what's the very first thing you wrote?"

Rebecca shook her head; "I don't recall, my mind is like some musty old root cellar." She pointed to the Lazy Susan, "Turn that to me, dear, I've no appetite at all, but Dr. Grange says I must force myself. Did you know that Thomas Jefferson invented the Lazy Susan? He's the most brilliant man our nation's produced, and to think that he almost lost the election because— that's it—that's what I wrote about!"

The floodgates opened and her recollections came pouring out; "In the Presidential election of 1800—"

"Grandma, that was nigh sixty years ago, is it any wonder that you didn't remember?" Becky interrupted.

"—Jefferson got the majority of the popular vote, but through that peculiar fluke in our system, he and Aaron Burr were tied in the electoral college. The balloting went on for days, thirty-seven ballots, and still no decision. That's when I published my first article, about the unfairness of the system and that the Electoral College should be abolished.

"Finally, Alexander Hamilton who hated Burr, threw his support to Jefferson—he hated him too, but not as much—and Jefferson was elected. It embittered Burr and when Hamilton began spreading rumors that Burr was having an incestuous affair with his own daughter, Theodosia, Burr challenged him to a duel and killed him. It ruined Burr's chance ever being President and that's when he schemed to conquer the West and Mexico and set up a new nation with himself as emperor. Your Grandpa Zebulon got involved in that piece of insanity and he and I were almost thrown in prison—but that's another tale."

Geary put in, "Dada told us that Jefferson had a dozen bastard children by his mulatto mistress? Is that true?"

"Absolutely not. Jefferson sired only five bastards. By his mulatto slave, Sally Hemings, his dead wife's half-sister. She was twelve when they began to—you know. When the opposition party discovered he was living in sin with a slave, it tore the nation apart. Jefferson's enemies brought the case to Chief Justice John Marshall who happened to be his cousin, and also happened to hate him, and impeachment talk began.

"I wrote a few things about that, including that Chief Justice Marshall was sleeping with a mulatto slave of his own. That ended any talk of impeachment." She rapped Geary again; "Is it any wonder that you Southern cads like slavery?"

"Grandma, are you making these things up?" Forrest asked.

"Wish I had that much imagination. I submitted my very first efforts under my maiden name, Rebecca Breech, and sent them to the *National Intelligencer*. But because I was a woman, no one paid any mind. So I became as cunning as the serpent and with the articles I just told you about, signed them Rebel Thorne. The editor of the paper, Silky Milky Sam Smith, assumed they were written by a man and snapped them up."

Without thinking, Rebecca popped a finger sandwich into her mouth. "For the first time in my life, disguised as a man, people paid attention to what I had to say. But I was shrewd enough to realize that if I revealed my true identity, it would end my writing career."

"Dada says you once wrote something that saved him from being thrown in prison," Geary said. "What did he do?"

She debated whether to tell them, then decided that if they knew the truth, they might influence their father. Whatever his flaws, Gunning adored his children and Rebecca needed every possible ally to turn him from Romance Connaught.

"A tiny tot of brandy might just loosen my tongue." After a sip she began; "When your father was very young, serving in Andrew Jackson's Presidential Guard, he became besotted with a French dancer—Veronique Villefranche. This was long before the bitch—pardon my French—married Devroe Connaught and became Veronique Villefranche Connaught. The Villefranches had been nobility in France, then came their revolution and they fled to America. To earn a living, Veronique began dancing on stage in a new-fangled mode; ballet, they called it. When her troupe left Washington, Gunning went a.w.o.l. to be with her. He even married her—"

"—But it was annulled," Sharon interrupted hurriedly, "otherwise Herself couldn't have married a divorced man—"

"—Gunning and Veronique planned to flee to Paris. But she betrayed him to the police. She'd been paid to do that by Devroe Connaught."

"But why? What have the Connaughts to do in all this?" Forrest asked. No one's ever really explained it to me."

"That tale goes back so many generations it would take years to tell. Suffice to say that Devroe hated our family, so he plotted to ruin Gunning and did it through Veronique. Gunning faced court martial for desertion, which meant years at hard labor. Can you imagine your father behind bars? I went to President Jackson and pleaded Gunning's case, but Andrew, being an old army man himself, refused to intervene."

Rebecca popped another finger sandwich. Forrest fidgeted; "Will you keep us in suspense, what did you do?"

"As it happened, Jackson was embroiled in his own mess, one that threatened to destroy his administration, a stupid little scandal centering around a former barmaid who liked to kick up her heels—Peggy O'Neill. She was married to a naval purser named Timberlake, but while he was at sea, Peggy had an affair with Senator Eaton; she became pregnant and had an abortion. Timberlake found out about it and committed suicide. The clergy, those ever-watchful guardians of our souls and bedrooms, denounced Peggy. Nothing is more important to them than who's sleeping with whom; heaven and earth apparently turn on the axis of sex. Though Senator Eaton married Peggy, the wives of many of Jackson's cabinet members refused to speak to her and war broke out, the press dubbed it 'The Petticoat War.'

"Jackson adored Peggy—you do know that Jackson's wife, Rachel, was a bigamist? It was all quite innocent. Rachel had been married to a Louis Robards; she believed Robards got a divorce, so she married Andrew. But Robards hadn't, so Rachel found herself married to both men. Eventually it was sorted out, but when Jackson entered politics the press had a field day. Jackson felt Rachel had been hounded to death by trashy scandal-mongers and now he saw the same thing happening to Peggy. The Petticoat War grew more heated; the government ground to a halt. I'd been trying to find a way out for Gunning and then a glimmer of a plan came to me."

"What?" Sharon demanded as if turning a page, "what?"

"I went to see President Jackson again, and this time I told him what I'd managed to keep secret for thirty years."

"That you were Rebel Thorne?" Becky put in.

"I thought Andrew was going to kill me. Since he blamed the press for Rachel's death he loathed us. He ordered me out of the White House—I said I'd found a way to win The Petticoat War, but I wanted leniency for Gunning—and told Jackson my plan. 'Never work!' he barked, but since he'd tried every thing else, he let me go ahead." She sighed contentedly.

Sharon stamped her foot; "Grandma, what happened?"

"Writing as Rebel Thorne, I excoriated both sides in this silly war, coming down particularly hard on the women, saying that the issues confronting the nation were being slashed to ribbons by these women with razor tongues. I called for the resignation of Jackson's entire cabinet so that the government could get back to governing, instead of peeping into keyholes. As we'd pre-arranged, Martin Van Buren resigned along with other cabinet members favorable to Peggy, and the entire anti-Peggy faction had no recourse but to resign also. Jackson appointed a new cabinet, the United States was saved, and Gunning went free."

"What happened to Peggy Eaton?" Becky breathed.

"Sank into obscurity. But that little ass-kisser, Van Buren did well; for his loyalty, Jackson picked him as his successor and shoved him into the presidency. Curious, though Aaron Burr never became President, his illegitimate son did."

"What?" four voices cried in unison.

"We'll save that juicy tidbit for another time."

"Grandma, you've got color back in your cheeks and you've eaten every sandwich," Becky noted. "It's because you've been talking about Washington. You know so much about the White House and all who've lived here, why not write it down so that all this wonderful information isn't lost?"

Sharon added, "The whole family is saying that you need something to do, instead of just sitting here waiting to die."

"Oh they do, do they!"

"Why so angry? Can't you see it's because we're all so concerned? Think of the tales you could tell—folks would be reading from dawn till dusk, if half of what you say is true."

"It's all true. What's even more shocking is that people are so bored with their own lives they need to be titillated by their leaders' sexual peccadilloes." She shook her head; "At the moment, my concern isn't for the past, but for the present, and whether our Union will survive."

"Then say that why don't you? And for all the country to hear," Becky insisted. "Why not start writing again?"

"Look at these hands, they're so gnarled with rheumatism I can barely put pen to paper."

"Are you just talk then?" Sharon asked. "Easy enough to tell me what to do, but when it comes to yourself—"

"Watch your tongue, missy. I've lived four of your lifetimes and if nothing else, it's earned me some respect."

"Aye, and I'll give you all the respect you deserve, for you're my one and only Grandma, and I'd hug you to bits if I could. To prove it, I'll come every day for two hours and you can dictate to me. I've already cleared it with Herself."

Rebecca's eyes narrowed; "This whole tea party's been one gigantic anti-Grandma plot, hasn't it?"

"It has. What time tomorrow? What's your pleasure?"

"That you not come at all."

Geary nudged Forrest and he said, "Grandma, you always said you wanted to leave us a legacy of the times; might this not be it? Seriously, Grandma, do it. Do it for us."

Rebecca hesitated and Sharon said, "Ten o'clock will be just fine, the mind works best early. Forrest gave me those new things called pencils? They fair glide over the paper."

Before Rebecca could protest further her grandchildren crowded around hugging and kissing her. Then they whirled out of the room in waltz time, leaving behind a breathless void.

Anger and betrayal pumped hugely in Rebecca's breast. So this was what the family thought of her? Someone waiting to die? She looked out the window at the dwindling forms of her grandchildren. She saw herself at that age, head-strong, willful, far more discontented than these girls. But all fashioned from the same clay, woman unrealized.

Rebecca woke up early the next morning thinking she'd sneak out of the house, but her four grandchildren were waiting in the drawing room. "I've nurtured serpents in my bosom," she grumbled, "but I don't have a thing to say."

Sharon handed her a notebook; "Becky and I wrote down all you told us. Maybe you'd like to add whatever we left out?"

Still muttering, Rebecca put on her spectacles and read the pages, jotting notes, correcting errors, inserting dates. "Did I ever tell you about Tenskwatawa? He was a Shawnee Indian shaman who lost the battle of Tippecanoe in 1811? So he leveled a curse against the White House, prophesying that any President elected in a year ending in zero would die in office. We thought he was just a crazy Indian, until General William Harrison, who'd defeated him at Tippecanoe, was elected President in 1840—and after a few short weeks died in office."

"Wait now," Forrest interrupted, "Lincoln's just been elected in a year ending in zero."

"Wouldn't <u>that</u> solve a few problems? Now where were we?"

Rebecca rambled through the decades, anecdote and incident poured forth while Sharon assembled it in chronological order. Always the issue of slavery erupted, like a cancer on the body politic.

Rebecca did experience one major difficulty, every time she tried to recount the personal details of her life she couldn't tell them to Sharon. Yet without these experiences, and the depth of her feelings, the manuscript read lifeless.

In the dark of night, alone with her thoughts, she began to record them in her own diary. She'd often envied Catholics their ability to confess, and soon this diary became her confessional, where she could bare her soul and seek absolution.

She plunged in, her pen furiously whispering secrets that haunted her. She whispered of avarice and adultery, pride and passion, she whispered of murder. Here she could tell the truth about her husband Zebulon, and the base passions he roused in her. Here she could tell the truth about her lover, Jeremy, Bravo's natural father, Forrest's grandfather. Threaded through it all were the Connaughts and their involvement. She wrote until she couldn't hold the pen, wrote as if her soul depended on it. Perhaps one day after she was long gone, the family could read it as a tumultuous record of all that had happened since the building of the White House.

She wondered how they'd react? What if Forrest knew his dear old doddering grandmother had lived such a life? She allowed herself the luxury of believing he'd defend her, be her champion. Thus comforted, she fell at last to sleep.

Chapter 5

GUNNING BRAND bounded up the steps of the State Capitol Building in Montgomery, Alabama. From the balmy weather one would never have guessed it was mid-February; high cumulus drifted across a cerulean sky, a gentle breeze caressed. A riverboat sounded its warning as it navigated the meander of the Alabama River flowing around the town of 8,000; 4,000 whites, 4,000 slaves.

Gunning joined Judah Benjamin in the Capitol's main chamber. A lawyer of considerable brilliance, Judah had been instrumental in forging a Provisional Constitution. Based loosely on the original U.S. Constitution, it was amended so that the President would serve one six-year term, slavery was explicitly defined as legal, but the further importation of slaves was banned, and the Bill of Rights was eliminated.

As to who would lead the new nation, that argument was going on right now; the difficulty lay in thwarting rabid men like Robert Toombs, a drunken blowhard; pompous Howell Cobb; and the bombastic William Yancy, everyone one of them who would have killed to be elected provisional President.

Jefferson Davis had absented himself from Montgomery so it wouldn't appear that he coveted the Presidency but Gunning, Benjamin and other moderates lobbied tirelessly in his behalf, arguing that, "The election of any of the fire-eaters will send the wrong signal to England and France, and especially to staid Virginia. If our new nation is to be successful, Virginia and the seven other border slaves states must join us. They won't unless they see that our Confederacy is led by a seasoned statesman with impeccable credentials."

The moderates prevailed and on February 11, Jefferson Davis was elected President of the Confederacy. In one stroke the new nation had achieved profound validity both in foreign countries and in the South, and it cast a pall over the North.

News of Davis' election went by telegraph to Vicksburg, Mississippi and from there by rider to Brierfield, the Davis plantation twenty miles south. Davis received the news on Tuesday and left the next day for Montgomery. Because the South had few rail lines, Davis had to travel by a torturous, circuitous route and wouldn't arrive before Saturday night.

All during that week thousands of people crowded into the sleepy town until its population doubled. Benign weather and the crush of visitors brought out the slave traders and buyers congregated around the fountain in the Town Square. Gunning watched a smarmy slave dealer put a strapping naked young buck up for sale; "Who'll say a-nine hunnert dollahs for this ebony—Horse, they call him. How much'm I, much'm I, bid? Nary a whip mark on him, never tried to escape, gentle-like, ceptin' for this," the dealer jiggled the buck's attributes, "guarantee y'all have a li'l nigger dividend in a yeah. A-nine hunnert, thank ya suh, but thas a radickalos price—"

"One thousand," called a man with a clipped English accent mellowed by Southern cadences. Gunning thought the voice sounded familiar, but the bidder remained hidden in the crowd. Gunning followed the auction intently; a slave's price was usually the gauge of the South's economic health. Cotton was selling for 10 cents a pound, so a slave should bring $1,000. But euphoria over the new Confederacy had raised expectations throughout the South about its live crop and the buck, named Montgomery, sold for $1,200, reinforcing Gunning's elation over the new nation's prospects.

As the crowd dispersed, Gunning recognized the buyer and muttered, "What in blazes is Sean Connaught doing here?" He'd never liked the dandified snot, trusted him less, but he was Romance's brother, and one of the richest men in Washington. If he had a mind to, he could help the Confederacy.

"Here's yo' bill asale," the hatchet-faced slave dealer burbled, "I sell the best in nigger flesh, anytime yo' in the market, I's at yo' service, the name's Harmony Lumpkin."

After Harmony Lumpkin led Montgomery off, Gunning circled to Sean Connaught; "That's a mighty fine buck you bought."

Sean regarded Gunning down the long slope of his nose. "An investment; I'll get fifteen hundred for him in Washington. Or perhaps I'll keep him; he does have stud potential. No question that selective breeding's produced a stronger strain than the original slaves imported centuries ago. The weaker ones have just died off. Maybe this Charles Darwin is right?"

"Surely you haven't come this far just to buy a slave?"

"Hardly." Pale complexion, pale gray eyes, thinning lank blond hair, Sean looked like he'd been sketched in watery pastels. "I've come to see Jefferson Davis," Sean said. "And you, what brings you to Alabama?"

"Virginia's interest in the Confederacy."

Sean's thin eyebrows arched; "Can it be that for once in our lives the Brands and Connaughts are on the same side?" Then he shrugged irritably; "Why do you keep staring at me?"

"Your resemblance to your father—it's uncanny."

"I take that as a compliment, my father was a remarkable man; who knows what he might have accomplished if he hadn't died so untimely."

Decades before, Sean's father, Devroe Connaught had been a clandestine operative for British Intelligence in America. Since Sean had been schooled in England, Gunning suspected Sean might be following in his father's footsteps.

Gunning asked casually, "Are you here alone?"

"If you're asking about Romance, she came with me. She thought the convention might be amusing, but the damnable trip exhausted her. She's— indisposed—and not accepting any callers." He walked off, posture Sandhurst-straight, riding crop beating in cadence against his supple Bond Street boot.

With hope rising, Gunning went to the Exchange Hotel and left Romance a note, urging that they meet. Midday came and went, then evening, and still she didn't respond. With each passing hour Gunning grew more agitated. Was she really ill? Or was she with someone else? That thought fair drove him mad.

*

Jefferson Davis' train was late; all along the route ecstatic crowds had demanded that he speak. In the four days since he'd left Vicksburg, he'd made twenty-five speeches and was hoarse when he reached Montgomery late Saturday night. Judah Benjamin and Gunning met Davis at the station, as did thousands of others, and a torchlight parade escorted him to the hotel. Though close to midnight, the crowd wouldn't let him retire until he'd addressed them. Negro youths, balanced precariously on the hotel's columns, held torches aloft to hold back the night.

Davis stepped out onto the balcony of his room. "Fellow citizens and brethren of the Confederate States of America—men of one flesh, one bone,

one interest, one purpose and of one identity of domestic institutions. I come...to discharge the great duties devolved on me by the kindness and confidence of the Congress of the Confederate States. I will devote to the duties of the high office...all that I have of heart, of head, and of hand. We have...a prospect of living together in peace. It may be, however, that our career will be ushered in, in the midst of storm." He paused for emphasis; "If war should come, we shall show that Southern valor still shines as brightly as in the days of Seventy-six!"

The crowd went wild; William Yancy, the arch secessionist who'd helped split the Democratic party in the last election and who'd hoped to become the President of the United States or of the Confederacy, swallowed his disappointment and shouted, "The man and the hour have met!"

Afterwards, Davis, Gunning and Judah Benjamin were left alone in the hotel room. Davis asked the question plaguing everyone in the South; "What news of Virginia?"

Gunning told him soberly, "Nothing yet. I've been telegraphing daily reports to Richmond. Had Yancy or Toombs or any of the hell-raisers been elected Virginia would never have joined us. Now there's some hope. All we can do is wait."

Davis said wearily, "I never expected to be elected, but if this is what the people wish, then honor demands that I accept. Suddenly all the demands of office bear down on me. I've had so little time to prepare a speech for the inauguration, I fear it lacks all I must convey."

Judah Benjamin said soothingly, "Just be yourself, all the people want is to be strengthened by your strength."

"Inner strength is what we need, we've little else. If the North makes war, we've little to defend ourselves." He paced the room; "A thousand miles of unfortified boundary between North and South, more than three thousand miles of coastline to defend. Our rivers reach deep into our territories and Federal gunboats could easily navigate them. In the entire South there's not one shipbuilding plant."

"Then we'd better start building them," Gunning said. "New Orleans, Charleston, Mobile, all have fine harbors. We're a resourceful people, and, by God, we're in the right."

"That we are," Jeff agreed, "and would that 'right' could construct rail lines. Four days to get here—for a trip that would take twelve hours if we had the proper railroads. With Lincoln's inauguration set for March fourth, I felt it vital that I be sworn in before then, to present a fait accompli to the Republican administration. We're even more destitute in the matter of armaments; in the

South, there's only one iron mill that can cast a cannon, the Tredegar Iron works in Richmond. That's why it's so vital that Virginia join us."

With his brother Bravo's warnings haunting him, Gunning searched for something supportive to say; "Virginia's given us five Presidents, all of them slave owners, all believing in the sanctity of States' Rights. Inconceivable that Old Dominion would do anything but side with us."

Davis and Benjamin had matters to discuss so Gunning bid them goodnight. Too late to try and reach Romance, so he went to his room. He eased into the bed already crowded with two other men, but in his dreams he lay with Romance.

*

"Monday, February 18, 1861 and the birth of our nation!" Gunning shouted exuberantly. By ten o'clock a crowd of 10,000 lined Dexter Avenue, leading from the Exchange Hotel to the Capitol Building crowning the hill. Tennant Lomax, the town's richest citizen had loaned Jefferson Davis his carriage for the inaugural parade; it was lined with yellow and white silk hangings and drawn by four matched dappled gray horses.

As church bells tolled noon, Jefferson Davis and Alexander Stephens, the Vice-President elect started the parade. Gunning rode shotgun, scanning the crowd; it would take only one bullet to shatter the South's dreams, and John Brown's murderous terrorism in Kansas and Harper's Ferry had proven the North capable of any atrocity.

Maestro Herman Arnold led his marching band in a tune never before heard in Montgomery, a spirited minstrel air, "I Wish I Was in Dixie's Land." Written by a Northerner named Dan Emmet, Gunning thought the song catchy; the crowd thought so too, for knots of slaves began to strut to the music. As the carriage approached, women strewed the road with flowers; the crowd cheered then fell in behind the procession.

After meeting with members of Congress in the Capitol Building, Davis was escorted outside to a stage on the front portico between the soaring white pillars of the western facade. Legislators took seats on the top terrace, facing the speaker's stand. Gunning spotted Sean Connaught in the crowd, but Romance was nowhere to be seen.

As the clock struck one, Howell Cobb administered the oath of office; then Davis delivered his inaugural address.

"...Our present political position has been achieved in a manner unprecedented in the history of nations. It illustrates the American idea that governments rest on the consent of the governed...There can be...little rivalry between ours and any manufacturing or navigating community such as the Northeastern states of the American Union. If however, passion or lust of dominion should cloud the judgment or inflame the ambitions of those states, we must prepare to meet the emergency and maintain, by the final arbitrament of the sword, the position we have assumed among the nations of the world."

Gunning led the wave of ear-splitting cheers.

"We have entered upon the career of independence, and it must be inflexibly pursued...If mutual interest shall permit us peaceably to pursue our separate political career, my most earnest desires will have been fulfilled. But if this be denied to us, and the integrity of our territory...be assailed it will but remain for us...to appeal to arms and invoke the blessings of Providence on a just cause...The suffering of millions will bear testimony to the folly and wickedness of our aggressors."

Nearing his conclusion, his voice grew firmer, "Reverently, let us invoke the God of our fathers to guide and protect us...with His favor...we may hopefully look forward to success, to peace and prosperity."

Wild unrestrained cheers rang out as the ladies threw flowers at the man of destiny. Gunning thought the speech combined exactly the right blend of olive branch and threat.

Then Vice President Alexander H. Stephens, the 100-pound tubercular ex-congressman, looking like he'd been dug up for the occasion, spoke far more bluntly than Davis. "Our new government is founded on the opposite idea of the equality of the races...Its cornerstone rests on the great truth that the Negro is not equal to the white man. This...government is the first in the history of the world based upon this great physical and moral truth."

Church bells pealed, riverboats blew their horns, the band again struck up "Dixie" and the euphoric town celebrated far into the night.

The next day Davis went to work: To insure that all seven of the seceded States felt they were being treated equally, he appointed a cabinet member from each State. Everything had to be improvised; the United States had had a working government for more than 70 years, the South had to start afresh. The first Confederate currency was jobbed out to a New York firm; the South didn't have a printing press equal to that task.

"Where'll I find the State Department?" a visitor asked Robert Toombs, the new Secretary of State, and he boomed, "In my hat, sir, and the archives are in my pocket."

The cabinet met in the Exchange Hotel; at Davis' request Gunning sat in with several other aides. Gunning knew all the cabinet appointees and considered most of them noodles, with the exception of Judah Benjamin, whom Davis had appointed Attorney General. That Davis had the courage to appoint a Jew— Gunning saw that as another sign of his fierce independence.

Robert Toombs immediately began to throw his weight around. "England's textile industry depends entirely on our cotton, so I say, stop shipping our 'white gold' to them, and that way, force England to recognize us. Cotton is King."

Judah Benjamin said quietly, "We do supply eighty percent of the world's cotton, the preponderance going to England. It's why she'll ultimately fall on the side of her own interests and recognize us. But an embargo? On the contrary, I propose we ship several hundred thousand bales to England right now, to be used as collateral against such time as Lincoln's government might declare a blockade."

A blockade? Oh the pooh-poohing that greeted that, especially from Secretary of War, Leroy Walker; "I promise to wipe up all the blood spilled in a civil war with my handkerchief!"

With his cabinet divided, Davis pronounced his final judgment; "We must tread carefully, we know of England's antagonism to slavery, she abolished it in 1830. But this day I've had a meeting with an emissary of a highly placed diplomat in Washington and I've been assured that England believes that secession is our legal right. To antagonize England when we expect her to be the principal source of our weapons is foolish; therefore we'll follow Mr. Benjamin's plan. I'm sending Major Huse to Europe to purchase as many ships as he can and to contract for the manufacture and delivery of weapons."

It had grown late, way past mint-julep time, and the cabinet members stirred fretfully. President Davis adjourned the meeting saying, "Whether we have peace or war depends on what Mr. Lincoln does. We'll know that soon enough; his inauguration is on March 4, less than two weeks away."

Gunning worked furiously to get the administration on track. He had little respect for the legislators in the new Congress—a bunch of pampered lawyer-planters intent on protecting their fiefdoms, but if war broke out it wouldn't be fought in Congress but on the battlefield, and he amassed detailed maps of every state. His energy knew no bounds and within days, Davis appointed him as his special aide.

With the awesome sense that he was about to seize his destiny, Gunning decided there was only one way to celebrate. He strode to Romance's room and knocked; no answer. He went to the roof and feeling much like a schoolboy, lowered himself down to her balcony. He slipped in through the window and stiffened at the bizarre sight confronting him.

Romance sat at her vanity, naked, eyes glazed, staring into a tri-part mirror that cast her reflection into infinity. He called her name softly: she turned but gazed at him without recognition. He knew better than to ask why she hadn't returned his messages; the reason was apparent. He shucked off his clothes and stood behind her. She played with the mirrors until their naked reflections were cast into a bottomless pit. He kissed her and she bit him, drawing blood. Reacting on instinct, he shoved her and she landed on the floor. She lay there, writhing, moaning, "I have a hunger…" and so with lust unbridled, he fucked her back to some small semblance of reality.

At long last she knew who and where she was and lay quiet in his embrace. Passion subdued, a more profound emotion emerged; he felt an overwhelming need to protect her, to cherish her, even to love her.

Suddenly she said, "This Confederacy is doomed, England and France will never recognize a nation whose capital is a stupid little regional village. It's the end of the South."

"No my darling, it's a glorious beginning. In our new nation, anything is possible, a man can rise as far as his imagination. And I imagine the day when Virginia will join us, which will bring in Arkansas, North Carolina, Tennessee, Kentucky, Maryland, and Missouri.

"Eventually we'll incorporate Mexico, then negotiate with Spain to purchase Cuba and turn the Caribbean into an American Mediterranean. We'll open trade with South America, a vast untapped market, and make our Confederacy the greatest power in the world. I'm part of that power now, I plan to rise even higher, I feel my life just beginning, and so I entreat you, my dear sweet beautiful Romance, come and share it with me."

"You are mad," she whispered.

He put her hand on his rising need; "Then come and be mad with me and I'll pledge you my body, my brain, my heart, my soul. Till death do us part. What say you my love?"

Chapter 6

In Washington D.C., March 4th dawned clear and bright, but as the day progressed it turned blustery and cold. Despite a restless night, Rebecca decided she had to go to Lincoln's inauguration.

Becky and Sharon were beside themselves; "Grandma, you mustn't," Becky insisted, "haven't you heard? Southern sympathizers are planning to blow up the Capitol," and Sharon seconded, "The whole city's an armed camp."

"Then you two shrinking violets best stay home," Rebecca declared, "I've been to every inauguration since Washington became our capital and I'm certainly not about to miss the one that might signal the end of our United States."

Still arguing, they hitched Old Glue to the shay and set off. On the ride to the Capitol Rebecca pointed out General Scott's preparations to defend the city. "See how he's sighted the cannons along the avenues? Pierre L'Enfant must be doing pirouettes in his grave."

"Who might this Pierre fellow be?" Sharon asked.

"Pierre L'Enfant designed Washington and patterned it after Paris, with wide radiating avenues that could be defended by strategically-placed artillery. But who ever dreamed it would be used against fellow Americans?" Suddenly Rebecca pointed; "Look there!" They gaped at sharpshooters positioned on top of buildings along the inaugural route. "This should be a day of pride, but instead we're under siege. How can this man's election—with only forty percent of the popular vote—possibly benefit the country if it's led us to this?"

They finally arrived at the Capitol. The building looked half-finished with scaffolding everywhere; the old dome had been dismantled and a new one was under construction, oddly enough, from plans approved by Jefferson Davis when he'd been Secretary of War during President Franklin Pierce's administration. Rebecca had obtained seats close to the inaugural platform that had been erected on the East Portico.

Rebecca spied the Connaught clan; "Look at Sean Connaught gloating; he's going around Washington bragging how brilliant the Confederate convention was." Rebecca had devoured reports of the acclaim Jeff Davis had received everywhere in the South and couldn't help comparing that to Lincoln's reception en route to Washington. In Baltimore, 10,000 hostile citizens had met his train, but Lincoln, warned by Detective Allan Pinkerton of an assassination attempt, had taken a different train and stolen into Washington. General Scott had secreted Lincoln in the Willard Hotel and placed him under heavy guard.

When Lincoln mounted the platform he received a weak cheer from Republicans; Democrats sat on their hands. He hadn't received one vote in the South and Washington was a Southern city. Rebecca studied him; not quite as ugly as rumored, he'd recently grown a beard and that softened his craggy features. But he was long of face, taciturn and peculiar, a stovepipe man wearing a stovepipe hat, looking more like an undertaker than a President. Though he'd served one term in Congress years before, Rebecca had never met him and knew him only through his fiery debates with Stephen Douglas.

She nudged her granddaughters; "Got your smelling salts handy? Look at Chief Justice Taney. He's sworn in eight Presidents, starting with Van Buren, yet now he can barely find his voice, he looks like he may just drop dead on us."

"And Lincoln looks like he's seen a ghost," Becky said.

"Small wonder," Rebecca whispered, "General Scott told me that Lincoln might be shot while giving his inaugural speech."

Rebecca was pleasantly surprised when she heard Lincoln's mid-western twang carry over the moaning wind; whatever his other flaws, he was an earnest, accomplished speaker.

"…I have no purpose, directly or indirectly, to interfere with the institution of slavery in the States where it exists. I believe I have no lawful right to do so, and I have no inclination to do so."

Rebecca took heart at this conciliatory note, but Lincoln refused to sanction any Constitutional right of secession.

"I shall take care that the laws of the Union be faithfully executed in all of the States. The power confided in me shall be used to hold the property and places belonging to the government and to collect the duties…but beyond what may be necessary for these objects, there will be no invasion."

"That's good news isn't it, Grandma?" Sharon asked. "I'm so worried about Dada. We haven't heard a word from him."

Lincoln concluded, "We are not enemies, but friends…Though passion may have strained, it must not break our bonds of affection. The mystic chords of memory, stretching from every battlefield, and patriot grave, to every living heart and hearthstone, all over this broad land, will yet swell the chorus of the Union, when again, touched, as surely they will be, by the better angels of our nature."

The elegance of Lincoln's rhetoric astonished Rebecca, yet somehow angered her. She'd already formed a negative opinion of him and was too old and too cantankerous to revise it. But to his prayerful plea for the preservation of the Union, she could only breathe, "Amen."

Though her heart wasn't in it, Rebecca stopped briefly at the White House for the traditional Open House; protocol demanded she pay her respects to the new President and the First Lady, Mary Todd Lincoln. Thousands of leathery westerners thronged around them in the East Room.

"Grandma, we'd best leave," Sharon shouted above the din, "I've never seen such a mob, I'm afraid we'll be trampled."

"This is nothing compared to Andrew Jackson's first inaugural," Rebecca shouted back. "Sharon, make a note for our journal. Back in 1828, Jackson campaigned as a man of the people and invited everyone to his first Open House. Tens of thousands showed up, every frontiersman, including Davy Crockett and Sam Houston. The crowd smashed every bit of furniture, devoured a thousand-pound slab of cheese sent for the festivities, and what they couldn't eat, they ground into the floor. The place stank for months. Jackson was about to be crushed to death, but his guards smashed out that window and lowered him to safety. Now that was a mob."

But then another unbidden memory came back to haunt her. On that very same day, from that very same smashed window, her daughter, Suzannah, and Jonathan Albright had made good their escape from her, fled to Texas, eloped, and set off a chain of events that had changed all their lives. Poor Becky standing beside her had been one of the innocent victims. Suddenly all the memories proved too much and she pushed her way out.

The moment Rebecca got home she crept into bed. "What a miserable day," she complained to Bittersweet, "I went to the inauguration determined not to like Lincoln, I needed a scapegoat, but now I'm confused. Something about him…he's had no real experience governing, so everyone's convinced that Secretary of State William Seward and the rest of the Republican cabinet will really run the Executive Office. But after listening to Lincoln today…I don't know. I bet we're going to see quite a battle for control of the White House."

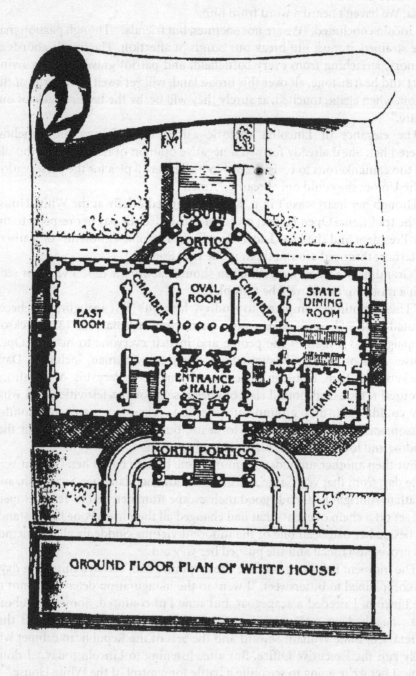

GROUND FLOOR PLAN OF WHITE HOUSE

By evening, a depressing drizzle began to fall, and with rheumatism and memories acting up, Rebecca decided not to go to the inaugural ball.

"You know you just dyin' to go," Bittersweet nudged.

"No, this night is for young people." She'd bought four tickets for her grandchildren; Becky and Sharon were to be escorted by Forrest and Geary. The children stopped by her house before going on to the festivities. She'd had Elizabeth Keckly, a gifted mulatto seamstress who lived in Richmond, make the girls' gowns: Sharon wore Erin green with tiny appliqued rosebuds following the line of her low-cut bodice; Becky in smoke-blue chiffon, appeared to float.

Her grandsons made her brim with pride. Geary, his beaming face framed by impudent curls, looked dashing in one of Gunning's cutaway evening jackets. Forrest, straight as a lance, filled the room with his ready laughter. They looked so fresh, so young, and as Rebecca waved goodbye, she felt as if she'd been stranded in some backwater tidal pool.

Bittersweet started humming "John Brown's Body," and Rebecca grumbled, "Can't you sing something less lugubrious?"

"My maid people hears there's g'wan be trouble at the ball with all them secesh types out for mischief. Pity there ain't no older folks watching out for the chillun, what with Mr. Gunning gone South, and Miss Kate locked away grieving, and Mr. Bravo, he never cottons to these things anyway."

"You really think there'll be trouble?"

"I could drive you over, make sure everything's all right, then we leave right after."

"I know what you're scheming, but it simply will not work…Oh, the hell, lay out my new navy gown."

"It be on the chaise. And your sapphire necklace and earrings, they makes yo' hair shine like silver. Les go!"

A huge structure in the shape of a parallelogram had been built in Judiciary Square for the ball. As they drove up Rebecca clutched Bittersweet; "You were right, will you look at all those armed soldiers patrolling? Hundreds of them."

Inside the building, the walls were covered with white muslin and red and blue bunting to hide the bare planking. The hanging gasoliers made everyone look slightly garish. Scala's Marine Band played the latest waltzes and reels, and the ladies whirled about in their hooped gowns, looking for all the world like careening bells.

After diligent searching, Rebecca spotted Sharon; she was having a glorious time. Having lived on many army posts she'd known lots of soldiers and had the knack of sorting good from bad. The young blades flocked to her, for she was easy to talk to, danced with brio and she gave off an aura that proclaimed, I'll make the best wife that any man could ever want.

Alas, Becky wasn't faring as well. When anyone asked her to dance she accepted with such reluctance, and moved so woodenly, they seldom asked again.

Rebecca's grandchildren spied her and crowded around. "You're to pay no attention to me at all; no, I will not dance; I'm content to sit and watch…and remember."

Suddenly the crowd parted and President Lincoln entered on the arms of Vice President Hannibal Hamlin and Senator Henry Anthony of Rhode Island. Directly behind them, in an attempt to display unity, came Mary Todd Lincoln escorted by the Democrat Lincoln had beaten, Stephen Douglas.

Rebecca flinched when she saw the Connaught clan trailing behind the Lincolns. "My evening's ruined, totally ruined," she grumbled, but couldn't take her eyes off them.

Veronique Villefranche Connaught was escorted by her eldest son, Sean, followed by her daughter, Romance, and Veronique's youngest son, Carleton. Since the First Lady fancied herself fluent in French, Veronique delivered all her compliments in that language; the *bleu* of Mary's gown, the matching *bleu* of her shoes and fan, her coronet of flowers, Veronique's praise knew no limits, and Mary Todd twittered back in her Kentucky fried French, "So *enchante* to have found a kindred *esprit.*"

Rebecca watched with perverse fascination as a cordon of men of all ages and stations surrounded Romance Connaught. Black Belgian lace over black silk shantung proclaimed that she was still in mourning, but tonight her breast smoldered with a river-of-rubies necklace as blood-red as her lips. "At least she's back in Washington and Gunning's still in the wilds of Alabama," Rebecca muttered. Then her heart stopped when she saw her grandson, Geary, ask Romance to dance.

Geary whirled Romance around the floor, double-timed his step to throw her off, but she nimbly followed.

"I suppose everyone's told you how beautiful you are?" Geary declared in an opening gambit and she countered, "Yes, but it will be the first time I've heard it from you."

His grip tightened; "I hear tell you know my father?"

His effrontery, meant to embarrass, only piqued her. "I do know your father—very well indeed, in fact, I've just left him in Alabama. And may rejoin him."

"You do know that he's married? That my mother is Catholic and will never give him a divorce? It's against her religion."

"Religion is so necessary for some people—as is marriage." He flushed and her carmined lips parted in a languid smile; "In a moment I expect you to strip off your white glove and challenge me to a duel."

"I'd love to duel with you, though a whole lot closer than ten paces."

"I might enjoy that, we could parry and thrust all night long before you delivered the coup de grace. But then, dear boy, why duel with the student when one can have the master?"

The dance ended; a new one began and as Romance whirled off in the arms of another man, Geary muttered, "Witch."

Forrest circled to him; "Hey, cuz, you'd best sit down 'cause you're sticking out like a porcupine."

"I meant to shame her, but damnation, she's like Spanish fly. Got to get me to 'Bama, talk some sense into my Dada. I can't bear to see Herself just pining away over this."

When Geary and Romance separated, Rebecca breathed with relief. Maestro Carusi struck up the band and couples formed behind Lincoln and Mayor Berret who were to lead the Grand March. For a brief moment, all Washington paraded in step.

Rebecca's spirits soared when a laughing Becky moved into her line of vision, but then plummeted when she recognized her partner. "Merciful heavens, not Carleton Connaught!" Whatever fears she'd had for Geary were compounded ten-fold for Becky. Geary was worldly, but her granddaughter—had there ever been a creature more naïve? More vulnerable?

Over the years, Rebecca had watched Carleton Connaught grow up, from an absolutely enchanting child, to a young man of startling beauty. But along with his extraordinary looks, came extraordinary rumors.

When Carleton and Becky danced twice more, Rebecca's fears got the better of her. Rescue came in the guise of a young actor she knew, and as he passed by, she called, "John?"

His matinee-idol face lit in recognition and he strode to her. "Dear Miss Rebecca, how wonderful to see you."

"John, am I losing my mind totally, or didn't you tell me that you'd be performing out of town this season?"

"Albany," he answered. "I'm in repertory there, but I couldn't resist seeing this spectacle. The theater's dark on Monday, so I took the train down yesterday and go back tomorrow morning. Miss Rebecca, may I have the next dance?"

"Yes, when they bring back the gavotte. For the moment, you must do me an enormous favor." She pointed to Becky; "Ask my granddaughter to dance, I must get her away from that man. When you're done, deliver her straightaway to me."

John obliged. After the spirited schottische, he brought Becky back. Rebecca saw Carleton lurking and quickly engaged John and Becky in conversation. "Tell us, John, how goes your career? I read nothing but worshipful paeans about you."

With a becoming blush he said, "I could never hope to be as great as my father, nor rival my brother, Edwin. But above all, I want to be loved by the Southern people, I want to be known as the first great Southern actor."

He turned to Becky, his charm working at top power; "Tell me, lovely Becky, if I could wave a magic wand and grant you any wish, what would that be?"

"I—I don't know," she stammered. "I can't think of anything for myself...Perhaps to roll back the years, when my mother and father were still alive...When I was still—?"

Rebecca interrupted hastily, "And you, John? Would being the first great Southern actor satisfy you, or is there more?"

His hazel eyes widened, his smile dazzled; "You've caught me out, Miss Rebecca. I would want to <u>be</u> somebody, somebody so famous, achieve something so extraordinary, that all the world would remember me. Not just for this moment, or in my own lifetime, but down through the generations."

"Such fame is usually reserved for philosophers and saints, kings and Presidents," Rebecca mused.

His voice rang with conviction; "Fame isn't restricted to the great, it can come from many quarters. For example, the Colossus of Rhodes is famous but if a man were to destroy it wouldn't he become famous also? And who is the more interesting character, the despot Caesar or the patriot, Brutus?"

Bursts of raucous laughter kept interrupting and they turned toward a group of politicians surrounding Lincoln. He was regaling them with jokes and they were responding with the sycophantic abandon usually reserved for Presidents.

John glowered; "That man should never have been elected. I have it on the best authority that the votes were doubled to seat him. My home state of Maryland is true to the South, only the Federal cannon on the heights of Baltimore keeps her from seceding; but she will, no matter what desperate measures that man takes. Look at him, his appearance, his pedigree, his coarse low jokes, his vulgar similes and his frivolities—a disgrace to the position he holds. Mark me, other brains will rule the country. He'll be made the tool of the abolitionists, Seward, Stanton and other Republicans of their ilk."

Rebecca saw Carleton circling toward them and said hurriedly, "Becky, I find myself suddenly fatigued. Could you tear yourself away and see me home?"

"Of course, just let me say my goodnights." She curtsied to John, then went off, moving first to Sharon, then to Geary and Forrest, and finally to Carleton, where she lingered.

When Becky returned she asked, "Grandma, that young actor? Who is he? I didn't catch his full name."

"Becky, you <u>must</u> get out more often, I thought everyone in these parts knew John Wilkes Booth."

Chapter 7

"DID YOU have a good time, darling?" Rebecca asked as she and Becky drove home.

"Oh, the best, Grandma, the very best."

Ordinarily this would have thrilled Rebecca but not this night. "Don't you think John Wilkes Booth is charming? So handsome, so manly."

"Oh, he is, but I never quite know if he means what he says. Like all that strange talk about the Colossus of Rhodes? Why would anyone destroy something so magnificent just to make a name for himself? It sounds so selfish."

"He was probably being overly dramatic to make a point." Rebecca shivered under the lap rug and then remarked with forced nonchalance, "I'd no idea that you knew Carleton Connaught. Odd that you never mentioned it to me."

"We met about six months ago when he came to do some charity work at the orphanage. Knowing how you felt about the Connaughts, I was afraid you'd be upset."

Rebecca's mouth clamped into a tight line. When they got home she slipped into her nightclothes and padded down the hall to her granddaughter's room. Becky sat at her dressing table, brushing her hair. Rebecca took the brush and ran it through her chestnut tresses.

"I had hair like yours once, a bit redder, but not as beautiful...you're planning to see him again, aren't you?"

"At the Smithsonian Museum, tomorrow. Grandma, not so hard, you're hurting—"

"You can't be serious, not about Carleton Connaught. Surely you've heard the rumors—"

"I have, and I don't believe them."

"Then open your eyes and look at him. His very nickname describes him. Cotton Carleton. Soft. Fluffy."

"He got his nickname from their slaves; when they tried to say Carleton, it came out Cotton. As for softness in a man, it's a quality I find more endearing than the men who—" she broke off, eyes wide and unseeing, gone back to the day she'd been condemned to relive over and over again.

Rebecca put her arms around her and held her close. After years of nurturing her granddaughter, she couldn't, she wouldn't allow her to slip back into that well of madness. "My darling Becky, if I could take your pain on myself I would. If it would bring back my Suzannah, I'd gladly forfeit my own life."

Becky managed a weak nod, and encouraged, Rebecca went on, "You've every reason to mistrust men. But my angel, don't compound one tragedy by committing another. There are some men who just aren't suited for life with a woman. Carleton is…Carleton is as meek as a lamb."

"But lambs grow up to be sheep, and sheep father sheep, and even the Lord said, 'The meek shall inherit the earth.'"

Rebecca rocked her slowly; "Somewhere between the murdering swine you experienced and the will-o-the-wisp quality of a Carleton, there lies a whole range of men, decent, valuable men, who'd give their lives to make someone like you happy."

"Grandma, I've turned twenty-nine, I've lived with you for more than twelve years, since Ma and Pa died. If not for you I'd have died also. You've introduced me to every available man in Washington…I've tried to like them, I really have, it would've made me so happy to make you happy. But there hasn't been one I could imagine touching me. Could I marry a man just for the sake of getting married, then make him miserable? Every time I thought of it, it was like…reliving that day. Then I met Carleton and for the first time I didn't get sick to my stomach."

Rebecca's head pounded furiously…First Gunning and now Becky? What perverse twists of fate kept her family continually involved with the Connaughts? Were they doomed forever to gouge out an eye for an eye, a life for a life? Was that God's punishment for the way she'd lived her life?

"Becky, I'd be lying if I said I was happy for you. And I'll do nothing to dissuade you…except tell you the truth." She sought the courage to begin. "Many years ago, Carleton's father, Devroe Connaught, planned to marry your mother. This was long before he married Veronique. Devroe was quite a catch, and I had these grandiose visions of my Suzannah marrying into

English aristocracy. So I aided and abetted him, not realizing what his real motives were. On the day they were to be married, your mother eloped with Jonathan Albright, a man I mistakenly believed was beneath her."

"Grandma, I know all this, Ma and Pa used to talk about it, how your mammy, Letitia, helped them elope and how you chased after them all the way to the frontier."

"Devroe and I caught up with your Ma and Pa on a steamboat on the Mississippi. Devroe showed his true colors and tried to kill both of them. During the fight, his arm got caught in the paddlewheel and was mangled. He never forgave us. How stupid I was, I should have trusted Suzannah's judgment, mine always was appalling where it concerned men.

"Despite my interference, your parents built a wonderful life for themselves in Texas. I'll never forget the day Matty was born, my first grandchild. Then when you and Zeb arrived together—I'd always wanted twins, I tell you I preened around Washington as if I'd produced the two of you myself.

"But our dealings with the Connaughts weren't over. Years later, when I visited you all in San Antonio, Devroe turned up. What we didn't know was that for all the years he'd lived in Washington, he'd also been an informant for the British Secret Service, dedicated to impeding the growth of this nation. England was afraid that the United States was becoming too powerful in North America and undermining her influence. To stop that, they aided Mexico in its battle against the Texans, even supplying General Santa Ana with weapons. Devroe was instrumental in all this."

"Grandma, I know that too, Ma and Pa never kept secrets from us, especially if it could affect our lives."

Rebecca bit her lip. She wondered whether to go on, the ground was so treacherous, but the alternative was far worse. "What you may not know is that after you children were grown and Texas had won her independence from Mexico, Devroe re-appeared in Texas. Santa Ana was intent on conquering the territory again and Devroe once more supplied arms to him and to the Mexican and Comanchero raiders."

Becky stood up suddenly; "How do you know that?"

"Your Uncle Bravo told me. Remember, darling?" she said softly, "he was with your Pa when they rescued you?"

Rebecca pressed her fist to her heart to still the pounding. Finally, her pulse quieted. "If any one man was responsible for what happened to you and my Suzannah, that man was Devroe Connaught. Though he's long dead, can you understand my grief when you tell me that you're involved with his son?"

Becky's eyes filled with tears and she whispered dully, "I'm not involved with him, Grandma, I've only seen him casually. But you're right, I'll never see him again."

Rebecca sighed deeply, feeling a reprieve from heaven.

Becky didn't keep her appointment with Carleton nor did she answer his frantic letters. But he kept watch, and one Thursday, cornered her at the Open Market on Pennsylvania Avenue, between 8th and 9th Streets. At first she refused to speak to him but after his persistent pleas, she relented, all the while gazing at him, trying to discover the true man behind the façade of beauty, and beautiful he was.

Slender as a reed, fair complexion, gentle eyes and the other features too perfect to be real. Yet it wasn't looks alone, his manner whispered of kindness and caring.

She pulled her eyes away from him and tried to explain; "There's so much bad blood between our families. I'd be hurting my grandmother grievously if I went on seeing you."

"And I was weaned on horror tales about the Brands. But what's that got to do with you and me? We've done nothing, nothing at all, except like each other."

They talked so long that the greengrocer growled, "Buy something, or make room for paying customers."

Carleton implored her to meet him again; she wouldn't commit herself, but she did leave him with a little hope.

By the time Becky got home she'd gone through a change of heart and tried to explain it to her grandmother. "I know how you feel about the Connaughts and I feel much the same; especially about that bully, Sean. But Carleton's told me stories about how his family feels about us. If the whole truth be known, there are other sides to it, aren't there?"

"I haven't the vaguest idea of what you're talking about," Rebecca replied stiffly.

"That my Grandpa Zebulon was responsible for the death of the very first Lord Connaught, and for driving his wife mad?"

"It didn't happen that way at all," Rebecca blurted.

But Becky plunged ahead, "Don't you see, each family interprets the events the way it suits them. Are we to perpetuate this insane feud for all time? I don't know what will happen to Carleton and me, I doubt I'll ever marry. But he's so gentle and sweet, and—if I'm willing to put aside all that's happened—can't I beg you to do the same?"

Tears spilled from Rebecca's eyes, hot and blinding. "She was my daughter—your mother—and the Connaughts were responsible—how can you ask me—?" She looked up and saw that Becky was crying also, silent, unending tears.

Becky slowly left the room and Rebecca knew she was in mortal danger of losing her, just as she'd lost Suzannah.

Chapter 8

IN MONTGOMERY, Alabama, Lincoln's inaugural address had an unsettling effect on the fledgling Confederate government. The text had been printed in the local paper, and over supper at Mrs. Cleveland's Boarding House, where Judah P. Benjamin had taken lodgings, Gunning worried the speech with Jefferson Davis and Benjamin.

Davis declared crisply, "Nowhere in his address has Lincoln indicated that he'll let us go in peace, all else he professes, trust, friendship, is nothing but political posturing. Why can't Virginia see this? Virginia," he repeated with an edge of desperation, "If only she would commit to us."

Gunning said placatingly, "I've been in contact with Representative Roger Pryor and told him our concerns. His exact words were, 'Give the old lady time, don't press her too hard, she's a little slow and rheumatic. But if you'd bring in Virginia, strike a blow—spill some blood in her face.'"

A considered look passed between the men. A possible solution, but the risks were enormous; the side that fired the first shot would be branded forever as the aggressor. The greatest bone of contention lay in the two Federal forts still in Southern territory, Pensacola, and Fort Sumter in Charleston's harbor. Lincoln's Secretary of State, William Seward, had promised the Davis government that the North wouldn't reinforce either garrison and so the issue remained joined.

After dinner, Gunning drew Davis and Benjamin outside to a secluded corner of the porch. He'd have preferred to speak to Davis alone but in every cabinet meeting Davis had made it clear that he valued Benjamin's opinion above all others. The mid-March air had a pleasant coolth to it, made more intoxicating by the subtle scent of night-blooming jasmine.

Gunning began, "Your Excellency, we have weapons we're not using. There are lots of people in Washington who support our cause, people privy to the inner secrets of Lincoln's government. Like Rosie O'Neill Greenhow, Senator Wilson's mistress; I know first hand that Wilson tells her a great deal about Lincoln's plans. People like that should be contacted and clandestine lines of communication with them established."

Davis looked at Benjamin whose smile broadened; "You're speaking of something that Benjamin and I have been working on for weeks, the formation of a Confederate Secret Service."

"But buried in some innocuous department like the Signal Bureau," Benjamin added. "We've chosen the man to head it, Major William Norris. "I believe you know him?"

Gunning nodded; "Major Norris is an old acquaintance."

Benjamin went on, "What we haven't yet found is the right man to act as liaison between the Secret Service and the President's office. We think it best if nothing can ever be traced back to His Excellency."

Davis regarded Gunning intently; "Might you be that man?"

Gunning's instant reaction was to say no, he'd always been far too direct for the double-dealing needed in such an enterprise. "I've no experience gathering intelligence—"

"But you do have extensive contacts in Washington," Davis noted. "You were born there, you have friends, family…of course, you'd be elevated to the rank of colonel."

Colonel? A rank higher than he'd ever achieved in the Union army. Gunning became aware of being aroused, a sure sign of a deep and primitive interest. Was it the exalted position? The danger? Both? "Your Excellency, If you believe that I'm up to the task—I'd be honored."

"Excellent," Davis said. "The fewer people who know about this the better. Far as possible, stay in the background, as will Benjamin and myself, but rest assured, you'll always have direct access to either of us."

Awed with the responsibility, and the honor, as Gunning strode back to his hotel he muttered to the night, "The Confederate Secret Service drew its first breath tonight, and by God, I'm going to help make it the best in the world."

*

As spring greened Montgomery, the mood in the government grew gloomier; none of the undecided southern states had joined the Confederacy. Davis worried and fretted and was laid low by a blinding facial neuralgia. He recovered when Varina arrived with their children. Congress had leased a house for the Davis family from Colonel Harrison for the huge sum of $5,000 a year. The two-story White House of the Confederacy, on Bibb and Washington Streets, was a 'gentleman's house,' the kind a rich planter would keep in town when he came to sell his cotton. With formidable energy, Varina began renovating it as befitting the President of a new nation and his First Lady.

That afternoon, Gunning was on his way to the Capitol when suddenly two men pounced on him from behind and with bloodcurdling yells lifted him off his feet. He tried to fight them off, only to find himself confronted by the laughing faces of his son, Geary, and his nephew, Forrest.

In a burst of joy, he yelled, "You've come to join the Confederacy?" He looked around; "Is Peter with you?"

Geary shook his head; "Your number one son stayed in Washington, you'll just have to settle for ne'er-do-well me."

Gunning hugged him; "Where are you staying? Never mind, you'll bunk with me." Questions tumbled from him, "What's the mood in Washington? Is there talk of war?"

Forrest shook his head; "My Pa says Lincoln really believes that a compromise can be worked out. Everyone in Washington hopes that Jeff Davis is of the same mind."

Gunning regarded his nephew, wondering, how can he be such a simpleton? Like father, like son. "You rapscallions are in luck; Varina Davis is holding her first levee tomorrow, everyone's invited, even you two."

"That's why we've come," Geary grinned. "We danced at Old Abe's, so we figured we'd try Jeff Davis' and whoever throws the best shindig, that's whose army we'll join."

That evening, Gunning took the boys out for supper. "Forrest, what did your Pa say when you told him you were coming to this hotbed of rebellion?"

"He's so wrapped up with his work I doubt he even knows that I'm gone."

"Sounds like my brother," then asked with a nonchalance he was far from feeling, "what's he up to these days?"

"He's working on balloons."

"Balloons? Are these manned balloons?"

Forrest nodded; "Pa let me go up with him a few times. I can't describe the experience, you've got to do it yourself."

"Exactly the way I felt about my very first cuddle—"

Forrest stuffed a chunk of bread in Geary's mouth. Eyes shining, he leaned toward his uncle; "You see the world in a new way, all blue and green, all the meanness gone. It made me wish...I don't know...I envied eagles...I envied angels."

In their genuine joy at being together, they all got a little sentimental and a little drunk. At one point Geary confided, "Dada, Herself misses you something fierce. I know she'd be willing to come here, if you'd just say the word."

Gunning stared into his glass; "Your Ma's a good woman, the best mother a son could ask for...but something's happened to her. She's lost every bit of her free will, life has to be lived according to the church. Every time she goes to confession she comes back with another 'Thou Shalt Not.'"

"Dada, is that fair? There are always two sides to—"

"Remember all the years she tried to get you to become a priest? It's what second sons do, she kept saying, until one day you finally ran off, because what she wanted for you just wasn't in your nature. Tell you what, my boy, the day you become a priest—that's the day I'll ask your mother here."

With a hiccup and a hapless little laugh, Geary rested his head on his father's shoulder; "How I wish that life was simpler, that there wasn't so much pain in the world."

Gunning rocked his son gently; "Just remember it's not your fault. Most of it anyway, though your Grandma always insisted an ornery imp lived in you. How is your Grandma?"

"The best," Geary exclaimed and Forrest seconded, "the very best, but sometimes I wish she wasn't so strait-laced."

If only you knew, Gunning thought. He was confounded by the way the kids adored their grandmother. Growing up, he, Suzannah and Bravo had rarely gotten along with her; she'd always been after them for some fool thing or other. Though she acted the same with her grandchildren, they worshipped her. Why, he'd never know, it was one of the mysteries of the universe.

The next day a mob from all over the South invaded the new White House. Bouquets of flowers were everywhere, the two adjoining drawing rooms were a riot of color and garlands of wild Cherokee roses twined up the banister to the second floor where the three goggle-eyed Davis children poked their noses through the banisters. Slaves ran between the main house and the unattached kitchen, laden with trays of food and drink.

Forrest and Geary, suffering hangovers, mingled with the crowd, their spirits soon restored by the spike of bourbon Geary poured into Varina's plantation punch. Forrest's hand flew to his forehead; "All these people, all this excitement? Ah do declare ah'm about to have an attack of the vapors."

"Ah don't quite recognize yoah accent, young man," one monobosomed matron said, "where y'all hail from?"

Forrest bowed low; "Washington, D.C., ma'am."

"A Yankee?" she wheezed in a fainting voice.

"Ma'am, Washington is situated on land owned by Virginia and Maryland, which is hardly Yankee territory."

With her fan, she pried Forrest's mouth open and stared at his teeth; she seemed disappointed. "Ah'd heard on excellent authority that all Yankees had hair on their teeth."

"Oh but they do, they do," Geary interjected, "depending on where their teeth have been." Forrest yanked him away.

Southern belles being the most beautiful of women, both boys fell in love at least twice; Geary consummated one of his amours behind an outbuilding, Forrest wasn't so fortunate.

The next day, Varina invited a very reluctant Forrest and Geary to supper; they'd planned to meet their new girlfriends and were twitching with frustration. Varina held forth; "Your sainted grandma would never forgive me if I didn't have you sup with His Excellency. Gunning tells me you've come to join the Confederacy?"

Before Forrest could set her straight, a messenger delivered a telegram. Jeff Davis' face darkened as he read it; "Virginia has just voted not to secede from the Union."

Supper ended in gloom. Forrest said to Gunning, "This about ends it, doesn't it?"

Gunning glowered; "If we have to fight on alone we will."

Jefferson Davis didn't appear at the Executive Office the next day, laid low with an attack of nervous dyspepsia.

Then like a gift from heaven, Gunning received a communication from Rosie O'Neill Greenhow in Washington. He raced to the Davis' house. "I told you we couldn't trust those Yankees! Seward's sending reinforcements to Fort Sumter. This may be the opportunity we've been praying for!"

Davis leapt out of bed; "Alert Charleston. Any Federal ships attempting to land at Fort Sumter must be repulsed."

Within days, Federal supply ships did appear but were driven off by Charleston's shore batteries. On April 12, Jefferson Davis ordered Brigadier General Pierre Beauregard to demand the surrender of Fort Sumter.

Major Robert Anderson, commanding the garrison, followed Lincoln's orders and refused; 4,000 Rebel soldiers opened fire on the 45 Union soldiers and 40 civilians holed up in the fort and in a day and a half, pounded them into submission. Jubilation overwhelmed the South at the news of this glorious victory. The Confederacy had drawn first blood.

Events moved so fast, Gunning could barely keep pace. Telegraph wires hummed with news that Lincoln had called for 75,000 volunteers and a blockade of Southern ports—a clear act of war—this despite the Constitution expressly stating that only Congress had the power to declare and make war.

On April 17th, reacting to northern aggression, Virginia seceded, followed by North Carolina and Tennessee. The celebration in Montgomery knew no bounds. It grew ecstatic when Virginia invited the government to move to Richmond and establish that city as the Confederacy's new capital.

"Now we really have a nation!" Gunning shouted, pounding Geary on the back. "Davis just called for a hundred thousand volunteers—we'll whup those bumbling Yankee shopkeepers. Stay here with me, Geary, I'll get you a commission—"

Geary hung his head; "If I did it'd look like I was siding with you against Herself, and she's sad enough as is. Anyway, I'm not cut out to be an officer. I'd only wind up in some guardhouse for insubordination and you'd get angry with me again, the way you've always been angry. Give Peter the commission, he'll win the gold ring for you, it's what you've always thought anyway."

"What are you talking about? I never played favorites—"

"Come on, Dada, first born sons and all? It's the law of the blood. If I can accept it, why can't you?"

Gunning clenched his jaw, pointless to argue; no one could win this one. "If ever you change your mind, if ever you need me—" They hugged each other, barely able to let go.

Geary collected Forrest and they boarded the train to Atlanta; from there they'd go on to Washington. Geary said, "Forrest, I'm obliged to you for coming here with me, I hoped I could talk Dada into coming back home."

"You tried, that's what counts."

"So I did." Geary slapped his knee; "Now it's time to move on. When we get back we'll hightail it to old Virginny and join up. That way, I'll be able to make sure you don't get your fool head blown off. If anything happened to you, Grandma would kill me. You are her favorite, you know."

"What is all this bull about you and favorites? Geary, you're not serious about joining the Rebs are you?"

"Think we can sit around playin' with ourselves while the rest of the country marches off on the greatest adventure of the century? What's more, the lasses just love a uniform."

"But why the Rebs? Why fight for slavery? That's what this secession's all about, bunch of rich planters trying to hold on to a corrupt way of life. It's just not right."

"I don't think that part's right myself," Geary agreed.

"So let's you and me join the Union army, we can watch out for each other there. If it's adventure you want, Pa's working on these balloons? We could become Aeronauts—"

"Are you crazy? Only time I'm comfortable with my feet off the ground is when I'm making love. "I'm joining the Rebs because anyone with a brain can see that the South's gonna lose. And I've always felt more at home with losers."

"That is the dumbest—? I'm not going to let you do it."

Geary threw his arm around his cousin's shoulder; "I love you, Forrest, couldn't love you more if you were my brother. Tell you what. If ever I get you in my sights, I promise I won't pull the trigger."

Chapter 9

IN THE hills above the Falls of the Potomac, the Connaught plantation house shone with muted light from candles and oil lamps. It would be decades before the gas lines from Washington reached this far into the country, which suited Veronique Villefranche Connaught just fine, for with the passing years she'd learned to avoid harsh light. Kindness began with twilight, then her neck seemed not quite so corded, the crow's feet not quite so deeply etched.

Though over fifty, in her heart she still imagined herself the dancing nymphet who'd captivated audiences throughout America, the glowing creature who'd bewitched the only man who'd ever really mattered to her. And the better to preserve that image Veronique had become a creature of the night.

The Connaughts always dressed for dinner, Carleton and Sean in formal attire, Veronique in evening clothes. Candles in crystal chandeliers threw prismatic light on the medallion ceiling, the heirloom Connaught silver gleamed at each place setting. Sean sat at the head of the table, Veronique at the opposite end; Carleton at Sean's right.

Veronique gazed at her sons appreciatively. Her eldest, Sean, resembled his father right down to his thinning blond receding hairline. If only his lips were fuller, she thought, a thin mouth made a man seem so parsimonious. However, intelligence shone from his pale gray eyes, and Veronique was well pleased that the aristocratic blood of the Villefranches and the Connaughts had commingled with such success in her eldest. She wished that he might be less vitriolic, but if she'd learned anything in America, she'd learned to cope.

As for Carleton, he was simply the most angelic child.

Sean drained his champagne glass. "Maman, did I tell you that Romance and I ran into Gunning Brand in Montgomery?"

"Innumerable times," Veronique answered tartly.

"The besotted old fool still fancies himself a rake. But he may be of some small use to us in the overall plan."

Alerted, she purred, "What plan is that, pray tell?"

"War is coming, that's for certain, but I'm not troubled by it at all. In fact I see it as an opportunity for us and for England. I learned through Romance that the Confederacy's attempting to establish some sort of crude intelligence service with Gunning playing an integral part. That's why I didn't object when Romance went off to Richmond to be with him. I've asked her to funnel information back to me, but so far she won't commit herself. So, Maman, what do you think of Romance's latest—dalliance?"

"Disgusting. He's old enough to be her father."

"Considering you were once married to him, he could be."

That her own daughter had run off with the man once her lover, then her husband—if briefly—Veronique experienced this as a betrayal so monumental it made her gorge rise. Yet along with her rage came a mother's concern for her child. Romance was a fool if she put Gunning in the same category as her other conquests. In her many-faceted career, Veronique had known a stable of men, from the whitest of chargers to the blackest of stallions, and for all his dashing good looks and casual charm, Gunning was surely the most dangerous mount of all.

Veronique hastened to change the subject; "Carleton, news has come to me that you're paying a great deal of attention to this Albright girl? Spawn of Rebecca Breech Brand? How could you so disgrace our family?"

Carleton fought to keep his voice level; "Disgrace? Isn't that rather strong for some harmless meetings?"

Sean lit a cigar, blew a smoke ring and poked his finger through the hole. "Maman, you should be delighted that your precious boy's finally paying some attention to the fair sex."

"But a Brand?" Veronique hissed. "Never!"

"Maman, you're making too much of it we're only friends."

"Your dear father is dead because of such friends," she cried, stoking herself into one of her rages. "I demand that you stop seeing her. If you don't, you'll be cut off without a cent, you won't be welcome in this house."

Sean interrupted wearily, "Must we go through this again and yet again? Under the terms of father's will, this house, this land is mine. You live here at my sufferance, which believe me, grows thinner with each of your outbursts."

"You dare speak to your mother that way?"

"Spare us the histrionics, Maman, you're no longer on the stage, a fact I thought you'd be most anxious to forget. Remember, if in name only, you're now a Connaught."

Veronique sucked in her cheeks; "A Connaught? And what is that, pray? Some clan wearing wolf skins that foraged in slimy bogs? While we Villefranches dined at Versailles?"

"Do tell us about the revolution again, Maman, how the Villefranches lost everything," Sean baited her.

"We did lose everything, but never our spirit. I make no excuses for performing on stage. I did what I had to do to survive." Veronique had detested her husband when he was alive; now that Devroe was gone she loathed him even more for putting her in this hateful position, ever dependent on her son. But she reserved her most reverent hatred for the woman she considered the source of all her woes, Rebecca Breech Brand. The meddlesome mother-in-law of her youth who'd forced Gunning to annul their marriage. Why isn't the old crone dead yet? Her own venom should have killed her long ago.

Drawing strength from her hatred, Veronique turned to Carleton; "My concern is only for you. I didn't tell you about this Becky creature before, because I hoped you'd discover the truth yourself. Alas, my poor naïf, you're not as worldly as your brother, so I must protect you."

Carleton felt his mouth go dry. "Protect me from what?"

"From being deceived about a woman's most precious possession, her virtue. Far be it from me to defame anyone, I leave such judgments to God, but when a son's future is in such jeopardy, a mother must speak. It's common knowledge that in Texas, that uncivilized hell, she consorted with every manner of man, drifters, Mexicans, even Indians."

Carleton paled; "That can't be true."

"Your dear father was in Texas when this girl was but in her teens, and already she had that reputation."

"Stop! I won't hear another word against her."

"But it's true," Veronique persisted. "Every husband has the right to draw first blood, but she hasn't been a virgin since adolescence, if one can imagine such a horror."

Sean smirked; "Carleton, this sounds too good to be true, the perfect experienced partner to goose you over your fears? Remember when I took you to Nellie Starr's House of Delight for your sixteenth birthday and you simply couldn't? Not to mention any number of slaves you could bed right here."

Sean went on, "Maman, the more I think on it, the more I disagree with you. If this woman of the wilderness stiffens Cotton's—spine—why then I say, God Save the Queen! That she isn't a virgin also works in Cotton's favor. If he should somehow manage to produce a bastard, the Brands could never hold him accountable, surely not for goods already damaged."

Carleton wanted to fight back, wanted to smash Sean's smirking face. But the years of his brother's domination, and the deference demanded by the laws of primogeniture, closed like a vise around his throat. He shoved his chair aside, and hand clapped to his mouth, ran from the room.

"How disagreeable, and it's all your fault, Maman."

"What could I do? I had to warn him about her."

"I'm talking about how you raised him. Father recognized his—inclinations early on, knew a strong hand was required, and Spartan measures. But all you did was indulge him."

"Don't you remember how sickly he was as a child? A sensitive plant, all the doctors said, easily bruised. Why, didn't you just see the tears in his eyes?"

"He cries too easily," Sean sneered, "it's unnatural in a man and sets a dreadful example for our slaves. Show them the slightest weakness—they believe that this conflict gives them leave to do whatever they want. Last week I caught one of them trying to escape? That buck I bought in Alabama? God curse that slave trader for swearing he was docile. But he'll escape no more. I plan to ship him off to Richmond and have him work there as a day slave; perhaps Romance will collect his wages for me. Code and usage, that's what sets us apart from the rabble, be they be black, or this white trash that calls itself a government in Washington."

Over dessert, Sean announced, "Mary Todd's invited us to a state dinner for the British ambassador. God spare me another evening with that Kentucky cretin and her idiotic prattle? Forever going on about her family's illustrious credentials? Do Kentuckians have credentials? The poor creature is one step away from being institutionalized."

"She could be locked away for her clothes alone," Veronique trilled. "She's so full of being First Lady she's convinced she must set the fashion for the nation, and winds up looking like a Pekinese in a hoop skirt."

"Maman, Lord Lyons specifically asked if you'd be there. Being a bachelor, he appreciates an attractive woman on his arm. It will be a delicate evening, requiring the utmost politesse, and Lord Lyons expects us to play our part. I assured him that we would."

"Then you'd best instruct me in the finer points."

"Jefferson Davis keeps pressing England to recognize his Confederacy and unless we do, threatens to withhold the South's cotton. Which would be disastrous for our textile industry. So Her Majesty's government must hold out the possibility of recognition, but at the same time, avoid confrontation with Mr. Lincoln and his Union."

"Does England plan to recognize the Confederacy?"

"That depends entirely on whether the Confederacy is about to win the war. Davis and his cabinet don't know that, wrapped as they are in their delusion that Cotton is King."

"Perhaps if the South knew of England's true intent, they wouldn't have been so quick to secede?" Veronique ventured.

"The South would have seceded anyway, they've always been uncomfortable with the Union. Those Northern Puritans are such sanctimonious bores, only the true Southerner knows how to live. But now that hostilities have begun, let these two factions bleed each other dry; a fragmented United States can never be a threat to England. And if we serve Her Majesty's government well, our lands and titles in England and Ireland may be restored to us."

"I've done as you asked and befriended Mrs. Lincoln. But her husband is no fool; we must be very careful, this is a very dangerous game we play."

"As we both know, Maman, those are the only games worth playing."

Chapter 10

THE DAY after Carleton's brutal confrontation with his family he cantered into Washington and reined in at Rebecca's house on New York Avenue. Becky answered the door.

"I must talk to you," Carleton said urgently.

"Who is it, dear?" Rebecca called to her granddaughter.

Torn, Becky hesitated—Carleton mounted up, then lifted her into the saddle. Just then Rebecca came to the door and cried out after them as they galloped off.

As they rode along Pennsylvania Avenue they passed squads of pimply-faced army recruits still wearing civilian clothes and shouldering wooden guns, and trying valiantly to drill. Washington was getting ready for war.

Half an hour later Carleton and Becky had climbed into the hilly country-side; in the distance, Washington lost its outline to May's afternoon haze. They set their horses to graze in a field splashed with wildflowers.

Becky murmured, "We had a meadow like this on our ranch in Texas, with all the dandelions bursting to fly away. Wouldn't it be wonderful to stay here? Away from the city, the threat of war, and all the killing that's sure to come?"

Carleton chanced, "Becky, you've hinted so many times that something awful happened to you back in Texas. Won't you tell me? It stands between us like a chasm."

She reacted as if he'd whip-lashed her across the face.

"Becky, can it do any good to keep it buried? Our darkest imaginings often disappear if brought to the light."

She turned away; "If only these were dark imaginings."

Gently, he turned her to face him. "We've known each other almost a year, a year in which I've come to care for you." She moved like a startled wood's creature but he held her firmly. "There's no reason to fear me, I'd never do anything to hurt you. I know that you care for me—at least a little, you once told me you felt safe with me. Some men might take that as an attack on their manhood, but I cherish the fact that you do feel safe. But Becky, it's as if we're fixed in amber. Are we to remain forever suspended with no hope of going forward because of something that happened years ago? If you tell me, maybe I can help?"

She didn't respond and kept her eyes downcast.

"Does my presence so offend you? If that's true then just tell me and I'll never trouble you again."

"You've never offended me, I was simply afraid that if you knew the truth you'd never want to see me again. But you deserve to know, lest you think my…coldness in any way reflects on you." She paused; "When I've told you what happened, if you choose never to see me again, I'll understand."

She began in a voice so low he had to strain to hear her. "About thirteen years ago, a lifetime ago, we lived on a ranch about fifty miles outside of San Antonio. I'd just turned sixteen. We Texans thought we'd won our independence from Mexico, but not a month went by without some violence, raids from Comanchero bandits, ranches burned, all instigated by the Mexican government. When General Santa Ana returned to power he stepped up the attacks. The dispute was ostensibly over our borders; Mexico claimed the Nueces River as the boundary, Texas claimed the Rio Grande. But Santa Ana's real plan was to reconquer Texas. He'd never given up hope of avenging himself against us, and now he had a secret ally. The British were funding him, they were anxious that the United States not expand its sphere of power.

"Texas is enormous and we were too young a state to have a real militia. That's why Papa and some other men formed the Texas Rangers, to protect ourselves. My family had gotten together for Christmas, Papa, Mama, my oldest brother Matty, my twin brother Zeb, and Uncle Bravo, who was visiting. Uncle Bravo had been roaming Texas for months, we suspected he was on a secret mission for President Polk but he'd never say. One day our neighbor, Mr. Kelly, galloped up to our ranch yelling, 'Been another raid on the Steinhof spread, the murdering bastards killed the entire family!'

"Pa buckled on his holster. 'How many were there?'"

"'Six or seven, from the look of the tracks,' Mr. Kelly panted. 'Headed south, away from here.'"

"'This time, if we ride hard, we'll get them,' Pa swore, and he, Matty and Zeb saddled up. Uncle Bravo saddled his horse also, and Papa said, 'This isn't your fight,' and Bravo shot back, 'The hell it isn't. You're family.'

"Papa said to our hired hand, Lupo, 'Stay here and watch out for Miss Suzannah and Becky. If anything happens, make sure you let the livestock out of the barn, especially Mean Red, that bull is our ticket to a decent life.' Papa called to us, 'Stay close to home, keep your rifles loaded and ready. We'll be back soon as we've tracked them down.'

"Wouldn't it have made more sense if one of your brothers stayed with you?" Carleton ventured.

"They needed every gun. Living on the frontier means taking chances and men and women take those chances together. If you'd known Mama, you'd understand. Nothing could break her, not the frontier, not Grandma and her idea of how a young Washington debutante should live, not bandits, not anything."

"Reminds me of someone I know," Carleton smiled.

"Also, Papa taught me to shoot soon as I was big enough to shoulder a gun. He was considered the best shot in the county, and he'd go around bragging that I was better than he was. That mortified me no end, because it scared off all the boys. He'd left me one of those repeating rifles, and one of those beauties is equal to seven single-muzzle loaders."

She stopped to catch her breath. "The day dragged by, the night seemed even longer. Mama and I took turns keeping watch, four hours on, four hours off. Lupo stayed in the barn and tended to the livestock. We got well into the afternoon of the next day when our hound, Monday, began baying like crazy. She was fifteen, blind in one eye and arthritic, but she still had a nose for trouble. We hoped it might be our men coming back, but all we saw was a lone, swarthy rider.

"'Bolt the shutters!' Mama ordered. 'Cover me, I'll see what he wants. Don't come out of the house, no matter what.'

"I slid my rifle barrel through the gun slit in the shutter, my heart beating fit to burst. Mama went onto the porch. When the rider came within a hundred feet she held up her hand. 'Don't come any closer. What do you want?'

"He was Mexican, with a lot of Indian blood, a Comanchero. '*Por favor,*' he shouted, 'I've been riding for days, my horse needs water.' I called from behind the shutters, 'He's lying, Mama, all the water holes are filled.'

"She yelled sharply, 'I want you off this property, now.'

"He looked around, scanning the house and barn. 'Ah, *muchacha,* you're going to stop me? A lone woman?'

"Mama craned her neck toward the barn and called, 'Lupo?'

"The Comanchero threw back his head and laughed; 'Don't worry about the old man.' Without warning he dug his spurs into his horse and galloped down on Mama, at the same time drawing his gun. Mama raised her rifle but I'd already fired.

"I'd shot marauding wolves and rogue bear, but I'd never killed a man before. But there wasn't time to dwell on that because I saw another Comanche in horrible war paint spring from the tall grass and race toward Mama. I fired; the Comanche clutched his arm and zig-zagged off. 'Mama, get back in the house,' I yelled. She dashed inside and I slammed down the crossbar just as an arrow thudded into the wood.

"'How many of them are there? Did you see?' she asked.

"I counted three, but there may be more. This must be the same band that raided the Steinhof's ranch.

"Mama said, 'Becky, they've got Lupo. When they see they can't get to us, they'll set fire to the barn. I've got to save Lupo and get the livestock out. Can you cover me? I'll stay in your sights as much as I can.'

"Mama, don't! They may have killed Lupo already.

"'That may be, but he's been with us for ten years. What about our livestock? You heard your Pa, I've got to save them. Cover me, and remember, don't come out of the house.'

"Mama lifted the crossbar, watched for a heartbeat, and when we didn't see anything stirring, she started running toward the barn, about two hundred feet away. That's when I started praying, praying so hard, Zeb, Zeb, come home."

Carleton looked at Becky questioningly and she said, "I can't explain it, but Zeb and I being twins, we somehow know when the other's in trouble. It could be in the next room, or miles away, but this feeling comes over us and we just know. It's happened too many times to doubt it, and watching Mama running toward the barn, I never stopped praying.

"Mama was running faster than I thought she could, past our vegetable garden, past the corral where we had a small herd of wild horses waiting to be broken. Suddenly I saw an arrow arch through the air and screamed. But it only ripped through the hem of Mama's skirt and got snagged there.

"Then I saw a thread of smoke rising from the back of the barn. Mama saw it too and I heard her cry, 'Lupo!' She got within fifty feet of the barn doors when I saw a Mexican coming around the side. Mama raised her rifle and fired, but the recoil made the bullet go wide and she only winged him. She didn't have time to reload; she just kept running, clutching the rifle barrel to use it as a club as the wounded renegade came at her. I put a bullet through his brain."

A gust swept in off the Potomac and Carleton shivered, more from the tale than the wind. After what his mother had told him he hadn't expected this.

What disturbed him even more was that the woman telling the story wasn't the Becky he knew. This tormented creature was somewhere back in time reliving the horror. "Becky, I understand now, you don't have to say any more." But his words didn't penetrate, the shutters were shut, no light might pass.

"Mama flung open the barn doors. I could see inside, the raiders had set the hay on fire. I wanted to run and help her, a dozen times I reached for the cross-bar, but she'd warned me not to and I knew she was right. When she screamed, 'Lupo!' I knew they'd murdered him. The livestock had gone crazy, lowing, hooves crashing against the stalls, and Mama ran from one stall to the next, letting them out. Smoke began to fill the barn and I kept praying, Mama, get out, Zeb, where are you, Mama, get out!

"Mean Red was chained in the rear pen and when Mama went there I lost sight of her. Then I saw three men coming around the other side of the barn, pushing an old wagon in front of them for cover. I got off two careful shots and killed one of them. When Mama set Mean Red loose, he charged out the front and the other two bandits scattered. Then Mama came running out after Mean Red.

"Mama, oh faster, I prayed, only a few more yards—Then a gun cracked, Mama clutched her shoulder and pitched forward. She hiked herself to her knees, stumbling toward our door. An Indian sprang forward, grabbed her hair and snapped her head back, his knife at her throat. I couldn't get a clear shot at him without the risk of hitting her. But out of nowhere, Monday leapt and sank her teeth into the Indian's leg. He dropped Mama and stabbed Monday, but it gave me the instant I needed to fire. His face disappeared.

"But a second man, a Mexican, lifted Mama to her feet, twisted her arm behind her back and used her body as a shield. He yelled at me, 'Come out or I kill her.'

"Mama screamed, 'Becky, don't, there's—' I saw her stiffen. 'Don't hurt her, I yelled.' I figured if I opened the door, maybe he'd let his guard down for a second; that's all I'd need. I swung the door open, keeping the rifle out of sight. But I didn't know that a Comanchero had crept onto the porch and was hiding behind the door.

"As I stepped over the threshold, Mama whirled on the Mexican holding her and raked for his eyes. I fired at him just as the Comanchero behind the door swung it back on me, knocking me off balance. Before I could aim again he ripped the rifle from me and threw me down. Close up, his war paint looked even more horrible; he was the one I'd wounded earlier.

"'We were seven when we came,' the Mexican growled, 'now we're only two, but two who know what to do with you, eh? He grinned at the Indian standing over me and they started dragging Mama and me toward the house. That's when I saw the blood staining her side. He'd knifed her when he'd first grabbed her. The Comanchero shoved me into the house.

"I fell against the table and our earthenware water jug toppled to the floor. I hurled it at him, but it bounced off his chest and didn't break. He grinned at me and I remember thinking stupidly, Where did he get such big white teeth?

"Mama kept saying, 'Please don't hurt her, she's only a child—' The Mexican ripped the dress from Mama and before I could help her the Comanchero was all over me, tearing at my clothes. I bit and clawed and screamed, but he punched me. I must have passed out. Then I began to feel this weight on me, this unsparing pain tearing through me right into my heart. The Mexican was violating Mama in the same way even as she was bleeding to death. And I couldn't do anything to stop it.

"But my Mama, there never was another like her. I saw her fingers scrabbling across the puncheon floor, searching for anything she could use as a weapon. Her hand closed around the shaft of the arrow still caught in the hem of her skirt. As the Mexican rose and fell on her with his killing motion, she waited for the right moment and plunged the arrow into his stomach. His full weight came down on it, and a shrieking death rattle tore from his throat.

"The Comanchero rolled off me, sprang to Mama and plunged his knife in her breast. Her body arched in a spasm and fell back. I lost my mind then—"

"Becky, stop, please," Carleton begged.

"—I kept hearing this horrible screaming in my ears, I scooped up the jug again and with all my strength, hit the Comanchero over the head. This time the terra cotta shattered and stunned him. I scrambled to Mama and though she couldn't talk, her eyes were screaming, 'Run!' So I ran, naked and bleeding. To get a pitchfork, a hoe, a knife, anything—

"Outside, the burning barn sent a pall of smoke into the twilight sky, and it seemed to me that the whole world was on fire, Mama in a pool of fiery blood, burning blood all over me, and the only thing I wanted was to die also. But I had to get away from that Comanchero, because I didn't want to die that way, that way was worse than death.

"I stumbled toward the corral, but stopped when I saw the Comanchero in front of me, naked, a knife in one hand, a pistol in the other, his entire body a weapon.

"Spit flecked his lips, I could hardly make out what he was saying, he sounded loco, but his meaning was clear. He looked down at his body with a leer; 'The blood and the fire and the killing, it makes it stand up, no? Afterwards, I take you with me, you live as long as you please me.'

"I scrambled between the corral rails, dodging the horses that plunged all around me. He came after me, describing what he'd do to me, until I'd paid for the men I'd killed. The horses knocked me down, I don't remember how many times. I knew he'd get me soon and I wished I could just lie down and let the horses trample me and be done with it.

"In the growing darkness I could see the white teeth of the whinnying horses, death's heads careening around me, and then the mournful sigh as the burning barn crashed in on itself. Then I couldn't run anymore and collapsed.

"The Comanchero grabbed my hair; 'We have work to do,' he laughed, and his teeth seemed big as the horses'. 'Come, I teach you how to scalp the long-haired woman. Swift, clean.' He'd dragged me halfway to the house when he stopped and peered into the dusk. He cocked his pistol, but Papa came up behind him and near cut off his head with his Bowie knife.

"Papa took off his buckskin jacket and threw it around me. The next was all a jumble, with Matty and Zeb and Uncle Bravo galloping up and everybody running into the house.

"Papa knelt beside Mama and cradled her head in his lap. With each breath, tiny bubbles of blood were coming from her lips. The first thing she said was, 'Becky?'

"'I'm here, Mama, I'm all right.'

"She blinked once, and the tiniest smile lit her face. Papa pressed her head to his chest, as if by holding her close he could cheat death. She looked at him for a long moment, then said, 'I love you...build again...' Her eyelids flickered, and those wonderful brown eyes that had warmed everyone they'd ever looked on went blank and unseeing. 'Suzannah!' Papa screamed, 'Suzannah!' But she was gone."

In the valley below, the setting sun caught the distant spires of Washington, making it look like a miniature fairy tale world. The grazing horse nickered and tossed its mane to shake off the oncoming night mist. Shaken out of self, Carleton murmured, "We should go back."

Becky nodded. "Now you know why...and if you choose never to see me again—"

"Never see you again?" he repeated in a flash of anger, "you make it sound as if it was your fault. What you've been through would've killed a lesser woman. You said your mother was wonderful? What were her last thoughts? Why for you, that you were safe. When she said, build again—"

"She meant the ranch, everything we'd worked for."

"And your lives," he insisted. "Your life, Becky. And you do her and her memory a dishonor if you don't rebuild."

She looked into the darkness. "Don't you think I yearn for someone to love? To hold children of my own...but if a man so much as touches me, I see the

burning barn, the whinnying horses, I smell the sweat of the killers and see my
Ma bleeding to death."

Night had cloaked Washington when they got back. A few times Union
pickets challenged them in frightened voices, beardless youths shouldering
arms they hadn't yet learned to fire. Whatever fears of invasion plagued
Washington during the day were magnified a hundred fold after dark.

When Carleton took Becky home, they made plans for the next day, even
growing excited about what they'd do, but both knew they were lying. For after
hearing her tale, Carleton realized how inadequate he must appear to her. She
who'd killed to defend her home and honor, while the crack of a gun still made
him wince. Before he'd be worthy enough to win her, he had to conquer his
own cowardice. Only then could he offer her a whole and complete man. War
was coming, anyone with half a brain could see that. At dawn tomorrow, he'd
leave the Connaught plantation forever, Maman and Sean and their mean,
ugly, cruel lives, ride hard for Richmond and find his soul in battle, or die in
the attempt.

For Becky, reliving the horror had prized her out of herself. She took a deep
breath and for the first time in years felt it filling her lungs, quickening her
blood. She looked out her window for Carleton, but he'd disappeared.

Chapter 11

"HURRY UP with that shovel," Rebecca urged Bittersweet as the two women continued to dig a hole in the basement.

"Crazy old lady," Bittersweet mumbled.

"Crazy am I? Don't you read the newspapers? On May sixth, Jeff Davis declared that a state of war existed between his Confederacy and the Union. The Confederate capital is now in Richmond, that's only a hundred miles from here!"

She babbled on, "General Beauregard—he's the one who conquered Fort Sumter?—Is commanding the Rebel army and he's at Manassas, only twenty miles away. Any moment I expect to see the Rebels come pouring down from those hills and engulf Washington. Everyone's in a panic, Union Station is mobbed but no trains are running in or out, we're surrounded."

Bittersweet let out a piercing scream as a shadowy form suddenly appeared in the basement.

"It's me, Ma," Bravo called out. His eyes took in the shallow hole; "What are you two loonies doing?"

"Burying the silver and other valuables. If I should drop dead suddenly, you'll know where it's hidden."

"Why don't you use our bank vault?" Bravo asked as he herded the women upstairs and into the drawing room.

Rebecca sank to the settee; "Long as Lincoln reigns in the White House, I trust no institution in Washington. If that man had the unmitigated gall to levy an <u>income</u> <u>tax</u>? At the astronomical sum of three percent of any income over eight hundred dollars? Never in all my life—!"

"It's only a wartime measure," Bravo said soothingly.

"It better be, the country will <u>never</u> tolerate a permanent tax on income. And what about suspending the Writ of Habeas Corpus? If he could do that, then robbing a bank would be as nothing to him."

"Ma, he had to do it to protect the government."

"The opening gambit of every despot," she declared, then was struck with her son's somber, hollow-eyed look. "Something's wrong—what is it? Is it Forrest?"

"He's okay, but he's hurting bad about Geary; he just found out Geary joined Colonel Thomas Jackson's brigade."

"Oh Geary, Geary," Rebecca sighed, "a wilder creature never drew breath. I begged, pleaded with him not to join the Confederates, now the idea that he might be in that very army poised to attack Washington—have we all gone mad? Bravo, you seem to have Lincoln's ear, why don't you urge him to appoint Bobby Lee to defend Washington?"

"He's already tried, even offered Bobby Lee full command of the entire Union army, but Lee turned him down."

"Lee's no secessionist; Mary does own two hundred slaves, but they're phasing it out at their Arlington plantation."

"Bobby Lee said he could never raise his hand against his own people, so he went with Virginia. Pity, the Union's lost a damned fine soldier. If Jeff Davis knew how vulnerable we were, he'd attack now and he'd get an awful lot of help from Southerners here. Ma, I want you to leave Washington."

That caught her attention. "Are you telling me that Lincoln plans to abandon the capital?"

"Not on your life. Say what you will about him, he's no fool. He understands the value of symbols, and the Capitol and the White House, those are the abiding symbols of our nation. If he gives them up, the Union's lost. He's called for reinforcements from every Northern State to come defend the city. But the Rebels in Baltimore have torn up the rail lines leading in and out of Washington. Our only hope is to bring in reinforcements via Annapolis."

Bittersweet came in with a tray of cold chicken and ham; "Whatever happens, best we die on a full stomach."

Rebecca watched her son wolf down a thigh. "You forgot to eat again, didn't you?" He shrugged and she shook her head in exasperation. With the current crisis she saw him hardly at all and knew even less about what he was doing. Bravo had been affiliated with the Patent Office for years and held a number of patents, including some involving firearms. Though he'd never said anything, she suspected he was serving the government in some mysterious capacity to develop new weapons.

"Bravo, I can't leave Washington, when you get to be my age you need your creature comforts around you, and I refuse to be forced out of my home by either Rebels or Yankees. When the British burned Washington in 1814—"

He rolled his eyes; "I know, Ma, I know—"

"If I managed to survive that, I'll survive this also. We'll just have to hold our breaths and see who gets to Washington first, North or South."

After another desperate week, Federal regiments finally did arrive from New York and a host of other northern states. Rebecca saw Washington filling with a polyglot of uniforms and regimental flags and fresh-faced lads eager to put down what Lincoln called an insurrection. Since the city had no adequate housing for such a horde, the soldiers were bivouacked in every conceivable place. Some found rest in the aisles of the Patent Office, others were put in the Capitol building, where disingenuous rural youths admired the indoor plumbing, and others commandeered the congressional chambers and played at being pompous politicians.

By mid-May, all Washington marched to a new drummer, up with reveille, the daily roll call and drill, then to bed with taps. Rebecca hated this invasion of Yankees, hated the incessant harangue of vitriolic abolitionists clawing their way to power over the issue of slavery, though many didn't give a damn about the Negro. Most of all, she loathed the bellicose posturing of politicians too old to fight themselves but eager to send young men to their deaths. Each day she found it more difficult to walk the tightrope of neutrality; having to choose between North and South was anathema but she knew the choice would soon have to be made.

*

In Rebecca's garden, the delicate lilacs of May had surrendered to the vibrant lupine and poppy of June. She planted and pruned and weeded and worried, about the war, about her kin, for a great battle appeared to be immanent.

Tuesday, the 18th of June, Bittersweet ran into the garden, crying, "Be the end of the world! Look up there!"

Rebecca squinted against the sun and her mouth fell open. "My nerves!" An enormous balloon floated in the sky.

"What is it, Miz Rebecca? What's it doin' up there?"

"Run get my telescope, it's in my desk drawer."

"Uses it to spy on neighbors," Bittersweet muttered.

"I do not!" Rebecca objected, but blushed furiously.

Bittersweet returned moments later and Rebecca trained the telescope on the balloon. "I see a little basket contraption hanging on the bottom—mercy, are those people in it? I can make out its name, it's the *Enterprise.*"

Bittersweet clutched her cheeks; "Gonna get caught on the Washington Monument."

"Don't be silly, we only got the monument up to a hundred and fifty feet before we ran out of money; the balloon's at least three times as high. Look, it's coming down!"

The balloon descended, slowly growing larger. By now a goodly crowd had gathered and their vigorous cheers gave it all a carnival atmosphere. Rebecca and Bittersweet hurried to intercept the *Enterprise* being hauled through the streets by teams of horses and men hanging on to the tethering lines. The crew maneuvered the colorful gas envelope to the White House lawn where a growing mob gawked at the curiosity.

Rebecca saw President Lincoln stick his head out of a second story window; for a moment she thought the addled fool was going to climb into the wicker basket, but reason prevailed. The entire contraption was staked to the South Lawn and a cordon of armed guards stationed around it.

Bittersweet grasped Rebecca's arm; "There's Bravo, and Forrest too. Standing right next to the balloon, see?" The women pushed their way to Bravo and Forrest.

Bravo's eyes sparked with excitement; "Hi, Ma."

Rebecca, arms akimbo, demanded, "What is this all about?"

"I'll explain later, Ma. Right now I'm due at a meeting with Mr. Lincoln." With a wave, he loped away.

Rebecca hooked her arm firmly through Forrest's. "You are not going anywhere, not until you tell me everything."

They sat on the South Lawn and listened raptly to Forrest who couldn't stop twitching with excitement. "Pa's too modest to tell you himself but he had an idea that if we could combine a gas balloon with a telegraph it might make a formidable weapon. He buttonholed every general he could, even talked to Stanton, the new Secretary of War, but no one would listen. So Pa went straight to Lincoln. He's damned smart, he saw the potential and had money appropriated to develop the idea."

Bittersweet fidgeted. "What makes it so forma-?"

"On the battlefield, you could send a man up in a balloon; from high up it's easier to spot enemy positions. Then he could telegraph that information down to the officers at the ground command post."

Rebecca told Bittersweet proudly, "Bravo was Samuel Morse's assistant for years right here in Washington, and Morse taught him everything about the telegraph."

Forrest went on, "Pa corresponded with a lot of balloonists, but the guy who really jumped at the idea was Thaddeus Lowe, said he'd been thinking along similar lines. Lowe was in the gondola, dark hair, late twenties? The *Enterprise* is his craft. He used to barnstorm at carnivals but now he's got a contract to work as a civilian aeronaut for the army."

"How many mens gotta blow in that thing to fill it up?"

Forrest laughed; "We filled the *Enterprise* up at the Colombian Armory, there's a gas main at Independence Avenue and Fourth Street. Pa hooked up the telegraph line on a reel, running from the gondola to a telegraph station he set up in the White House. So there'd be no suspicion of fraud, Lowe took up an officer from the American Telegraph Company and an impartial telegraph operator who sent the message to Lincoln."

Forrest read from a scrap of paper, "To the President of the United States. Sir: This point of observation commands an area nearly fifty miles in diameter. The city, with its girdle of encampments, presents a superb scene. I have pleasure in sending you this first dispatch ever telegraphed from an aerial station, and in acknowledging indebtedness for your encouragement for the opportunity of demonstrating the availability to the science of aeronautics in the military service of the country. Signed, T.S.C Lowe."

"It certainly is long-winded," Rebecca commented.

"Deliberately," Forrest explained, "to show that even the most complex message could be sent and understood." Unable to contain himself, he did a series of cartwheels on the lawn. "Don't you understand? With this experiment, we've ascended into a whole new age, the Age of the Aeronaut!"

Rebecca frowned; "Am I missing something? If the balloon needs to be filled from a gas line, where are you going to find <u>that</u> on the battlefield?"

"That's Pa's next big surprise. But it's top secret."

Bittersweet then asked the question that Rebecca had been too frightened to even consider; "You ever been up in a balloon?" Forrest hemmed and hawed and Bittersweet grunted, "I don't care whose side you on, Reb or Yankee, this thing be the devil's work and no good can come of it."

That night during her fretful sleep, Rebecca dreamed a dream...of Icarus and Daedulus ascending toward the sun, only the faces of father and son looked achingly familiar.

*

The blossoms of June gave way to the wilting heat of July; Washington choked in a cloud of dust created by tramping feet, the hooves of cavalry, the rolling caissons. From northern newspapers came strident demands for Lincoln to put down the rebellion. But as Rebecca appraised the motley army, she had her doubts. It took more than pompous editorials from pompous asses to win a war. Nevertheless, Lincoln remained under tremendous pressure to capture Richmond before the Confederate Congress convened there on July 20.

One afternoon, what Rebecca feared most came to pass. Bravo and Forrest arrived at her house and her heart shriveled when she saw her grandson—wearing the uniform of a second lieutenant. She kept a brave front but all the while wanted to scream, No, you can't take him from me! The dark blue uniform made him appear taller, thinner. Was this the babe she'd taught to walk? Whose skinned knees she'd kissed when he'd fallen? The grandchild whose every expression brought back aching, joyful memories of her lover, Jeremy Brand?

"Grandma, get rid of that hound dog look," Forrest commanded, "I came here to show off and I won't have it spoiled by tears." He turned round and round, so self-conscious in his blue and brass that she almost smiled.

She sighed, wiping her eyes. "First Gunning, then Geary, then my own Doctor Grange—that traitor—abandoning me to go off to Richmond—? And now you? How will it all end?"

"With a smashing Union victory. One good battle and the South will have enough sense to return to the Union."

"Ah, youth; I wish I could be so sanguine. You haven't told me about your assignment."

"It's a special unit that's being kept sort of secret."

"But dangerous enough to give me a heart attack?"

Forrest swept her in his arms and waltzed her about; "Oh my lovely, let's not talk of war, let's just dance the night away and not worry that tomorrow I face the jaws of death—"

She cuffed him; "When do you leave?"

"All units are prepared to march, but just exactly when—or where—we haven't been told."

"Then you're the only ones who don't know. Rosie O'Neill Greenhow told me that Senator Wilson told her that you're headed for Manassas, for the big showdown battle."

Forrest hunched his shoulders; "Beats me, but then I'd best be going, I wouldn't want to be late when Rosie O'Neill Greenhow bugles the call for reveille."

Forrest held his father's shoulders, then impulsively hugged him. "Goodbye, Pa, be careful." He kissed his grandmother; "I know I can leave Washington safely in your hands, you're more than a match for Rebels and Yankees put together, because when the British burned Washington, you stood on this very roof and—" He dodged away as she swatted him. His voice caught, "I love you both so much, you're the blood and the bone and the heart of me." With a stiff salute, he left.

Rebecca and Bravo watched Forrest ride off. Bravo said glumly, "I begged him not to enlist, told him I needed him, that he could work with me, but—"

"What is Forrest's assignment? Please, God, don't tell me it has anything to do with those infernal balloons?"

"I don't know," Bravo said, but she knew he was lying.

The next day, Rebecca visited the family plot in Rock Creek Cemetery. The prospect of the upcoming battle brought her to the gravesites to commune, to pray for guidance. The tombstones cast elongated shadows across the mounded earth. Here Zebulon lay in uneasy sleep; alongside him, his half-brother Jeremy. A bit apart was the grave of Anne Fairfax Brand, Bravo's wife. She'd died at twenty-two giving birth to Forrest. Bravo had never remarried, and probably never would, Rebecca thought. There were some men like that, who mated for life. And some ducks too, according to this strange scientist Charles Darwin, so monogamy wasn't purely a human aberration.

She gazed at the plot where she would eventually lie and thought without the slightest bit of fear or sentiment, sooner or later it must all come to this.

Stooping to weed Jeremy's site, she whispered, "You'd be so proud of your grandson, he's the image of you. Every time I look at him…I remember how much I loved you."

All at once her legs betrayed her and she fell heavily to the loam. Her inept attempts to stand soon gave way to uncontrolled laughter. "To think I'd be reduced to this," she giggled, "I, who could out-run, out-climb any boy my age."

She had a sudden thought and exclaimed to the sentinel stones, "God, you've arranged it all wrong. We should be born old and infirm, then grow younger as we make our way through life. So by the time we reach our most productive years we'd have the advantage of all our experience and the energy to make our last years the most romantic." The more she thought about it, the more sensible it seemed. I really must tell Him about it, she mused, then struggling to her feet, added wryly, "You'll have your chance—and sooner rather than later."

She had no fear of dying. Her life had been full of joy and figured with tragedy. More than enough for any lifetime. Her fears weren't for herself, but for her children and their children, and all the children of the nation. She closed her eyes and prayed for guidance but the Shades remained mute. Whatever peace she'd hoped to find at the gravesites eluded her and she returned home, weary, and discomforted.

Late than night, when fatigue and pain held her in their grip, she would have welcomed release. But she could no longer afford the luxury of thinking only of herself and of her comforts, be they the comforts of living or dying. She had an uncanny feeling that she was being saved. But for what end?

Forrest, off to fight for the Blue, Bravo in Lincoln's inner circle, planning God knows what. Gunning in Richmond on Jefferson Davis' staff. Geary gone also. And what of her other grandchildren, scattered all over America? She repeated their names in a litany of prayer.

"Dear Lord," she breathed into the night-filled well of the room, "if it's your plan to take any of them, then take me first, for I couldn't bear that pain."

In the darkness, she became convinced that the Lord was saving her, to fight for the lives of those she loved. Not to confide her complaints to some old moldering journal, but to speak out as she'd done in the past, to sound a clarion call for all to hear. To raise such a cry against this war, that all men, North and South, would see the madness and stop it.

"Time enough to die when your work is done," she muttered, "and not one moment before." With trembling hands she lit the oil lamp; took pen in hand and began.

"Would that I had two hearts. One to grieve for the injustices done to the South, and another filled to the overflowing for my Northern brothers. But the Lord, in His infinite wisdom, has given me but one, and so I must write to you from a heart divided.

"As I write this, my children and grandchildren face death at the hands of their own countrymen. And it may be that in choosing opposing sides, those of my blood may even now be raising their hands against each other. Father against son, brother against brother. And what are we to do? Wring our hands and resign ourselves to the notion that this is God's will? I say this is madness, a madness concocted by men, and a madness that must be solved by men.

"But I'm told by politicians on both sides that this is a 'just' war. Think! How 'just' can it be if it devolves into killing our own people, our own brothers?

"What is this curse that's afflicted mankind since Cain raised his fist against Abel? Is war, as Thomas Hobbs claims, the natural state of man? Can it be that the Christian principles we so piously proclaim are the thinnest crust on a seething insurgency of violence? Along with the good, can there also be evil, an evil which figures in each of us like the graining in a piece of marble? Oft times it's this very graining that gives the stone its beauty. But let us not be deluded, for if it results in murdering each other, then it is evil. And where is God in all this? Doesn't Jefferson Davis pray to the same God as Abraham Lincoln? Is God on the side of the South <u>and</u> the North? Or is it just that He's leaving the solution to us, his benighted creation?

"We must call on Abraham Lincoln and Jefferson Davis—no, we must <u>demand</u> that these two leaders arrange a truce immediately. Let them sit down together, and with mutual trust and forbearance lead us away from this brink of insanity. We must heed the injunction of the prophet, Isaiah, 'Let us reason together.' It's not too late, it's never too late if men can reason together. We must bind up our differences as we would bind up our wounds, until our people, our nation, is divided no longer but beats with one heart."

PART TWO

PART TWO

Chapter 12

"A HEART DIVIDED", created a firestorm in Washington. Hate mail poured in and Rebecca was vilified by Republicans for her pacifist sentiments and cursed by secessionists as a traitor to the South. Her situation was further exacerbated by the impending battle at Manassas.

On Friday, July 19, the Union army probed the positions held by the Rebels at Manassas, some 25 miles from Washington. The Confederates were woefully outnumbered and outgunned, they had 25,000 men and 13 cannon; the Federals had 35,000 troops and hundreds of cannon. Sunday morning, Republicans brimming with confidence, drove out to Manassas to witness the end of what they derisively termed 'the rebellion.'

"This has to be one of the most macabre things I've ever done in my life," Rebecca clucked to Becky as they joined the stream of carriages driving along the road to Manassas. "But I had to come, Gunning and Geary and Forrest— they may all be fighting at Manassas, or Bull Run, or whatever they call it."

Senator Charles Sumner of Massachusetts, a vengeful and vitriolic abolitionist, sped by in his carriage and shouted, "Did you bring your gown, Miss Rebecca? We'll be dancing in Richmond tonight! So much for your misguided, divided heart."

"Pompous twit," Rebecca muttered, "ever since Charlie got caned on the Senate floor for calling the South a whore, he thinks only of revenge. He'd immolate the South if he could."

The carriages reined in on the crest of a hill, looking down on the two armies confronting each other on farmland owned by a William Mclean. The battle began with a thunderous cannonade, then see-sawed back and forth. Every time the Union forces made a strategic advance, the Rebels seemed to anticipate it and beat them back. Under constant pressure from the Rebels, the Union army of unseasoned volunteers finally broke and fled for their lives and what should have been a smashing Union victory turned into a disaster. The panic spread to the watching Republicans and they whipped their horses to get away from the floodtide of deserting Blues. People screamed, carriages overturned and only Becky's expert handling of Old Glue prevented them from being crushed.

Once more Senator Sumner's carriage sped past Rebecca's, this time fleeing back to the safety of the capital. She couldn't resist shouting, "Charlie, are you dancing your way back to Washington?" After a bit she said to Becky, "That was stupid of me. If the Rebels continue their attack they'll take Washington, and the war and the Union will be over. Is this what our Forefathers fought and died for? The dissolution of our nation? I wish I'd never lived to see this day."

But the Rebel troops were too exhausted to pursue their advantage. They planned to go on the offensive the next day but that night a torrential rain made the roads impassable and they lost their golden opportunity to capture Washington.

All that next morning Rebecca and Becky stood in front of her house ladling out water to the bedraggled Union soldiers slogging back from the battlefront, defeat written on their dazed faces. One lad, close to Geary and Forrest's age, had hands so badly burned he couldn't grasp the ladle and Rebecca held it to his lips. His simple, "Thank you kindly, ma'am," left the two women close to tears.

The bucket was almost empty when Bravo came running down New York Avenue. "Ma, I just heard what you did! How could you? Going into a battle zone as if it were some Sunday picnic? You belong in an institution!" Her hapless little shrug softened him; "Come inside before you get sunstroke."

She allowed him to lead her into the house. "In all my years in Washington I've never seen such despair, not even when the British invaded. Then there were perhaps three thousand residents, but now with a hundred thousand people jammed into the city—Washington reminds me of a giant ant hill that's been destroyed and all the ants are rushing about in aimless panic. To make it worse, the press keeps fueling the despair. Every hour there's a new headline calling Manassas the 'Great Skedaddle,' 'the Bull Run Run,' and claiming that one Southerner is worth ten Yankees. Is it true, Bravo, are Southerners better soldiers?"

"Most of the army's career officers are from the South, Lee, Johnston, Jackson, Jeb Stuart, Jubal Early, and they're all fighting for the Confederacy, so the Rebs do have better leadership. Manassas has been a bitter blow; some members of Lincoln's cabinet are demanding that he put out feelers for a negotiated settlement before the Rebs capture Washington."

"Will he?" Rebecca asked softly.

"Never. I was in the cabinet meeting when Lincoln told them, 'I'll pursue this rebellion until the South is brought back into the Union—or die in the attempt.'"

"An empty promise—unless he can field a better army. And an army led by better generals—"

"Lincoln just named General George McClellan to command the Army of the Potomac and defend the capital."

"That's a name I don't know."

"West Point grad, second in his class. Served in the Mexican War. President of a railroad for a bit. He's won a few skirmishes in western Virginia, nothing significant."

"From your tone I take it you don't like him?"

"Everyone's touting McClellan as the Union's great hope—and no one's doing more touting than McClellan. He goes by the nickname, Little Napoleon, a name he doesn't discourage. I find it tough to like someone like that."

Rebecca sighed; "This is too much to bear, all I wanted was to live out my last years in peace, and instead—"

Bravo chuckled; "You may find this hard to believe, Ma, but this war isn't personally directed against you."

"Are you sure? After my last article I received sacks of letters threatening my life. From both sides. Speaking of which, was there any reaction from the White House?"

"Lincoln hasn't discussed it with me, he's too much of a gentleman. But Mary Todd's busy braiding a hangman's noose."

"Of all people you'd think she'd be the most sympathetic, after all, most of her family is fighting for the South, including her brothers. Bravo, I'm truly sorry if I caused you any trouble with Lincoln."

"Nothing I can't handle; if it comes up I'll explain that the entire family's been trying to muzzle you for years—to say nothing of any number of Presidents—but you consider it your bounden duty to bedevil anyone within earshot."

"What a comfort to know your own children will spring instantly to your defense. Will you stay for supper? Rosie Greenhow's coming, she always asks what you're doing."

Bravo tensed; "And what have you told her?"

"How can I tell her anything? I haven't the faintest idea of what you do for this administration. Since you're not in uniform, can I assume that you're not in the army?"

"I'm not; it would limit my freedom; I'd always be answering to higher ups, like our Little Napoleon McClellan. So the President decided that this would be best."

"But what exactly is <u>that</u>?"

He clasped his hands over his mouth like the Speak-No-Evil monkey. "Much as I cherish and adore you, you are a gossip. Look, Ma, this is going to be a long war and ugly things are bound to happen. I beg you, for your own safety and protection, don't see too much of Rosie Greenhow."

Her brows arched in surprise; "But she's been a friend of our family's for years."

Just then Becky came home from the orphanage and after a brief, melancholy little greeting retired to her room.

"She looks so sad," Bravo commented, "is anything wrong?"

"She's been this way ever since Carleton Connaught went to Richmond to join up. When I found out I did a jig. To add to her mood, all the killing at Manassas affected her badly."

Bravo stood up; "Got to go, I've an appointment with the President. Remember, not a word to Rosie Greenhow."

*

Several days later, Rebecca was riffling through the newspaper when she cried out, "Bittersweet, quick, my smelling salts!" Bittersweet came rushing into the drawing room and Rebecca choked, "I just read that Rosie Greenhow's been arrested. As a spy! My nerves! Quickly, Bravo will know."

She hurried to her son's house and found him in his basement laboratory tinkering with some infernal invention.

Bravo confirmed the shocking news. "Pinkerton arrested her; she's been smuggling the Union's strategy to the South."

"How in the world—?"

"You know how. She's been Senator Wilson's mistress for years—among others. She wheedled our entire battle plan out of him then passed it on to the Confederacy. It's one of the main reasons we got the hell beat out of us at Manassas."

"What an extraordinary achievement," Rebecca exclaimed, feeling a rush that a lone woman had accomplished that.

"Perhaps," Bravo replied soberly, "but just remember that your grandson Forrest might easily have suffered from what you so casually call an extraordinary achievement."

That effectively shut Rebecca up.

They climbed the narrow flight of stairs to Bravo's drawing room. Spare, cluttered with papers; the home of a bachelor. "How's Becky doing?" Bravo asked, "any better?"

"Worse, if such a thing is possible. Matter of fact, I haven't seen her all day. I wonder where in the world she's gone?"

Chapter 13

WITH A great deal of trepidation, Becky entered the War Department building on the southeast corner of 17th Street. Inside the cavernous building, she found the office of Miss Dorothea Dix. The anteroom was crowded with women a good deal older than Becky, and dressed in very plain clothes. Surreptitiously, Becky unpinned the cameo of her mother she'd worn for luck.

While she waited, Becky's thoughts drifted to Carleton. Two months since she'd received his letter saying that he'd joined the Confederate cavalry. She had no address for him and could only hope he'd write again. But with each passing week hope had evaporated. She didn't fault him. No matter how kind a man might be, what man would want damaged goods?

If a husband and a normal life were denied her, so be it. Her mother's dying word had been, "Rebuild". For so many years she hadn't, but now, especially after seeing the dead and dying at Manassas, there were too many worthwhile things she could do. And so she'd come to see Miss Dorothea Dix.

"Next," the clerk called, and Becky entered the inner sanctum of the woman in charge of all the nurses in the Union.

Dorothea Dix was about sixty years old and fragile as a cracked porcelain bowl. The way she wore her hair made her head appear too large for her slight body; her severe black dress was the height of dowdiness. Without taking her eyes off Becky's application, she waved to the supplicant's chair. A born crusader, this Massachusetts spinster had done much good reforming the treatment given prisoners and inmates of insane asylums. With the war she'd become Superintendent of Female Nurses serving in Union hospitals.

With a voice as sharp as her features, Dorothea Dix asked, "Have you had any nursing experience? No? And I see you've never married? Why not?"

"I—I don't know. I haven't fallen in love."

"The qualifications for a nurse are very strict. You must be over thirty, preferably married, able to read and write, strong enough to turn a wounded man in his bed, and be of unimpeachable character."

"I'm literate, I'm strong, and I'll be thirty in a few months. As you requested, I've included letters of recommendation from two clergymen; one is from Reverend Pyne of St. John's where I worship."

"You look far younger than your age and far too pretty for this kind of work. You'd be thrown into constant contact with young men, men far from home, vulnerable men—are you a virgin?" Becky gasped and Dorothea Dix repeated icily, "Are you a virgin? Yes or no?"

"I can explain—"

Dorothea Dix stood up; "No explanation is necessary, your private life is your own. But it doesn't suit me. Good day."

With cheeks burning, Becky went home and cried all afternoon. That night she lay awake sinking deeper into her dark mood. "Am I going to let an dried up old prune stop me?" The answer came back a resounding no. "If the Union won't have me, it's their loss."

That week she quietly made arrangements for someone to replace her at the orphanage. She wrote out her will. One last detail remained and she put pen to paper. "Dear Grandma, How can I tell you that I must leave? I couldn't do it in person, for I knew just one of your tears would melt my resolve. I tried, but the Union won't have me as a nurse, so I plan to go to Richmond, to Chimborazo Hospital where Dr. Jeremy Grange is working as a surgeon, and pray that he can find a place for me there. In this time of killing, saving lives is what's important and North or South, they're all Americans. I feel strongly that I'm being directed to a new path, one that will lead to my salvation, and it's a path I must follow. So I must say goodbye with the fervent prayer that when this madness is over you'll forgive me enough to welcome me home. Long ago you gave me this cameo of my mother and I treasure it above all things. Please wear it for me. With so much love, Becky. P.S. Don't forget to take your medication."

She slipped into a pair of overalls and an oversized shirt; with her hair tucked under a cap, she could reasonably pass for a young man. She secreted what money she had in her boot and tucked her revolver in a band around her waist. She led her horse from the stable and in the dark hours, rode south, away from the concentration of Union forces. She paid a sympathetic farmer to ferry her across the Potomac; a brisk ferrying business had sprung up all along the river, it was impossible for the Federals to patrol the entire area and people left and entered Washington at will. As the rim of the sun appeared in the east, she'd crossed safely and stood on Rebel ground, feeling that her life was just beginning.

Richmond lay a hundred miles south. The Virginia landscape was enthralling, especially at dawn, when the dew-diamonded grass sparkled with first light, and at dusk, when the mauve mists of autumn cloaked meadow and hill and gentled the land to sleep. Having lived on the frontier, the lore of the land returned. Stay clear of red insects, she warned herself, bright snakes, shiny berries; nature often used color as a warning, and she smiled, wondering if painted women fell into that category.

On the fourth day, Richmond rose before her, sprawled across its seven hills and energized by the James River.

The tangy odor of tobacco hung in the air, tobacco growing in the fields, drying in the kilns, glowing in the mouths of the citizenry. Tobacco had made Richmond rich and its smell was the sweet smell of success. She rode across the 14th Street Bridge toward the city and became aware of other smells: of flour being ground at the Gallego flour mill, the largest in the nation; of sulphurous gunpowder from the arsenals; of coal fueling the furnaces of the Tredegar Iron Works at 7th Street and the river. Shifts worked round the clock to forge the weapons of war. Richmond had a population of 40,000 but war had swollen that to 70,000. Becky felt the pervasive excitement; these people believed they were right, believed they'd win. After all, they were Virginians. Bid farewell to uncouth log cabin Presidents, Southern aristocracy had fashioned this new Confederacy, this new nation destined to rule in the New World.

She headed east on Main; it dropped precipitously for a mile, then climbed again for half mile to Old Church Hill. There atop a high commanding bluff, stood Chimborazo Hospital. The 40-acre complex spread before her; hundreds of slaves hammered away, constructing hospital buildings. She saw a few women on the grounds and took heart. At the Administration Building, she asked for Dr. Grange and was directed to his ward. The one-story structure was 100 feet long, 30 feet wide and white-washed with lime; with 20 beds on each side of a center aisle, the ward could hold 40 patients.

Still wearing overalls and with her hair pinned under her cap, the wounded soldiers paid little attention to her. Her heart quickened when she saw Dr. Grange working on a mortally wounded patient; he glanced up, "Just in time, Becky," as if it was the most natural thing in the world for her to be there. "Hold him down. Gently, if possible."

Thrown into the breech Becky had no time to react to the gore. In his delirium the soldier flailed about, knocked off her cap and her hair cascaded down.

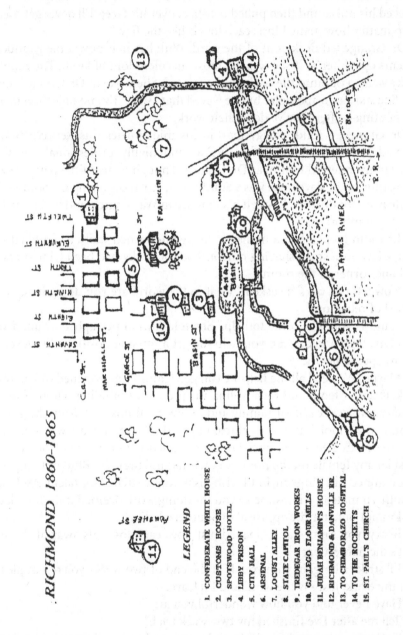

RICHMOND 1860-1865

LEGEND

1. CONFEDERATE WHITE HOUSE
2. CUSTOMS HOUSE
3. SPOTSWOOD HOTEL
4. LIBBY PRISON
5. CITY HALL
6. ARSENAL
7. LOCUST ALLEY
8. STATE CAPITOL
9. TREDEGAR IRON WORKS
10. GALLEGO FLOUR MILLS
11. JUDAH BENJAMIN'S HOUSE
12. RICHMOND & DANVILLE RR.
13. TO CHIMBORAZO HOSPITAL
14. TO THE ROCKETTS
15. ST. PAUL'S CHURCH

A spasm shuddered the lad's body, then he lay still. Dr. Grange stiffened, checked his pulse, and then pulled the sheet over his face; "I'll never get used to it, no matter how many I lose, each loss is like the first."

Dr. Grange led Becky out of the ward. With her hair down, the gauntlet of patients ogled her as if she was the most succulent loin of lamb. The moment Becky walked out into the cool air, she fainted. She woke in Dr. Grange's quarters. She started to apologize but he waved that aside; "I've no objection to anyone fainting—<u>after</u> they've done their work."

Dr. Grange, a solid, craggy man in his mid-thirties was Rebecca Brand's adopted grandson. Thoughtful, serious and highly professional, everyone, even family, referred to him as Dr. Grange. Though he had little patience with the institution of slavery, he was a Southerner, and recognizing the South's desperate need for doctors, he'd left his practice in Washington and had joined the staff at Chimborazo.

His room looked like a monastic cell, whitewashed walls, a scrubbed pine floor, a lavabo, a small shaving mirror. The cot Becky had been lying on occupied one corner of the room.

"Now tell me, cuz," he asked, "what in the world are you doing here in this hotbed of rebellion?"

"Same as you, I've come to help." She told him of her ugly encounter with Miss Dix, then asked, "Can you help me get a nursing position? I'll never ask for any special favors."

"Maybe. We need all the help we can get. Chimborazo opened officially last week, October tenth and we're still in the process of building. Though we're a military unit, we're self-sustaining and receive no funds at all from the government. I won't fool you, it's backbreaking work. We've only a few women here and they're treated—well, the slaves are treated better. Some of our doctors consider any female on the premises their natural prey. Dr. Blutkopf, in particular; damned fine surgeon, but I wish his morals matched his talent. And many a Southern matron will ostracize you for doing work deemed unfit for a lady."

"I'm not here for the approval of Southern ladies."

"Becky, you saw what happened just now, each loss eats away at the soul. That's the hardest part."

"I'll strike a bargain with you. If at the end of two weeks you're not pleased with my work, just say the word and I'll leave."

"Have I ever told you how wonderful you are?"

"Tell me after I've finished my two-week trial."

Dr. Grange arranged for Becky to be assigned to his division at a salary of ten dollars a month. There were five divisions at Chimborazo, each under a surgeon answering to Dr. James McCaw. Thirty wards, each in its own building (to prevent the spread of disease) comprised a division. A corps of hospital stewards assisted fifty assistant surgeons. Wounded soldiers from the same state were put in wards run by doctors from that state. In a section-conscious people, this greatly helped morale.

Becky lived in a tiny cubicle in a building set aside for the few other females working at the compound, and supposedly off-limits to the male staff. One night, after a backbreaking day's labor, Becky stumbled upon a young laundress lying on the grass and weeping piteously.

Becky knelt beside her; "Whatever's the matter?"

"I told him, no, I'm promised to another. But Dr. Blutkopf swore he have me fired, and my family needs the money I earn." Becky comforted the simple girl by telling her that since it hadn't been her fault, God would forgive her.

Becky got up at 5:00 to help cook breakfast, unfailingly hash. Most of the wounded were grateful for any kindness, but a few acted as if they were paying guests at some grand hotel.

"This hyar ain't nothin' liken my mammy cooks," a cracker from Georgia griped. "When are we gonna git some sour soup? I'll nevah heal proper without mah sour soup."

Dinner at 1:00: patients on a full diet got beef, corn bread and vegetables, those on half diet got soup and toast, or rice and milk. "Call this hyar beef?" the cracker whined. "My mammy wouldn'a feed this to a hog. I want mah sour soup!"

The afternoon spent writing letters for the illiterate or for those severely wounded. Sour Soup had 200 cousins who had to be told, "I jinned up to fight the Yankee anti-Christ but I'm bein' poisoned-kilt-dead by these hyar hospital slops."

Finish in time to serve supper at 6:00. The washing up done, preparations made for the next day's meals, and so the rhythm went on day after day. There simply wasn't enough time for Becky to get tired. By week's end, Becky's chores had taken her to every place in the compound, more akin to a village than a hospital; 5 soup houses, 5 icehouses, a bakery capable of making 10,000 loaves of bread a day, a dairy, and a brewery making 400 kegs of beer at a time. In the hillside toward the south were fresh springs of water. A large farm owned by Franklin Stearns pastured the hospital's 200 cows and 400 goats, and Becky was able to board her horse there.

Becky soon discovered that all the men considered working woman 'easy meat.' She had to slap several with greedy hands; a slave master named Harmony Lumpkin proved particularly obnoxious, and she assiduously avoided Dr. Blutkopf. She never went out without her revolver.

Her duties weren't without its brighter moments; while serving dinner one afternoon, Sour Soup kept gawking at her. "Ah declare, you're purty fine breeding stock, and so am I, so let's get hitched." He shucked off his blanket to expose his attributes as if showing off his best pointer.

The other patients waited avidly for Becky's response. Realizing that this was the test that would make or break her in the ward, she gingerly replaced his blanket; he ripped it off again to exhibit his staying power. Whereupon Becky dumped a pitcher of ice water on the offending member. With a hoot and a holler and a rousing cheer, the ward was hers.

A month flew by. Late one night, unable to sleep from fatigue, Becky sat outside and listened to the cicadas lull the complex to sleep. She felt the presence of someone and looked up at the face of Major Blutkopf. He was in his early forties, Teutonic in ancestry, with a thick powerful body and a manner to match. Without being invited, he sat down beside her. His cologne overpowered; he used it heavily to mask the smell of death but it only reminded her of it.

"Tired?" he asked gruffly.

"Yes, but it's a good tired, as if I've gotten all the chicks into the hen house and we're safe for the night."

"Did you know that Chimborazo's named after a mountain in Peru?" Blutkopf said. "Dr. McCaw once served there and said this bluff reminded him of it. He's my dearest friend."

She found his manner as cloying as his cologne and moved to stand, but he gripped her wrist; "Don't go, you're not like these other women. Will you not show a lonely doctor the same tender solicitude you show your patients? I'm in a position to do you a great deal of good—ease your workload—"

"If you don't release me, I'll be sick," and forced her stomach to heave; he relaxed his grip and she scrambled to her feet. He clutched her leg and she kicked his hand away. With a curse he grabbed for her again and she whipped her revolver from her waistband and smacked him hard across the head.

Stunned, he sat down heavily. She cocked her revolver; "Make another move toward me—"

"Unnatural woman," he cursed.

"Unnatural man," she retorted, "to try and seize by force what the Lord meant to be won through love?"

He choked on his rage; "You'll leave this place, tonight, or I'll have you thrown out!"

"Try that and I'll have every woman here testify against you and your lechery."

"You threaten me? One night, when you least expect it—"

"No! It's you who'll sleep with one eye open. Now get out of here, or my first shot will make it impossible for you to ever molest another woman again."

She watched him slink off. When she reached her room, she barred the door. She thought she might feel fear, or panic, or revulsion, but she felt none of those things.

"What's happening to me?" she wondered aloud.

In truth, something curious was happening; thrust into a position where she had some control over men, she was gradually losing her fear of them. She knew she'd made a dangerous enemy in Blutkopf, but that didn't matter.

"What matters," she whispered to the darkness, "is that in deed or thought, I'll never have to be a victim again."

Chapter 14

ON A SUNDAY in late November, Dr. Grange strode into the ward. "Becky, you've been slaving away here for six weeks without one day off. Come on we're going into town."

"I can't, I've so much to do—"

"This is an order from the President of the Confederate States of America. I saw Jeff Davis yesterday and when he found out you were in Richmond he insisted on seeing you."

"Me? Why?"

"We'll know soon; we're due at the White House at three."

Becky freshened up; put on a simple dress and a woolen cloak she'd bought and they set off. Once in town, they headed to Capitol Square. She gazed at the State Capitol Thomas Jefferson had designed; it stood on the crest of the hill surrounded by 12 acres and with its plateaus of steps and massive marble columns, it looked like a classical temple.

"Don't you find it extraordinary that Grandma used to know Thomas Jefferson?" she asked.

"Grandma will be the first to tell you that she's known every single one of our Presidents," he waggled his heavy eyebrows, "including one very personally."

"Do you really think that she and Andrew Jackson—?"

"Our grandmother? Heaven forfend! Grandmothers wear dimity caps, smell of lavender and swoon at the very notion of copulation."

They continued on through the quiet residential neighborhood, tree-lined with poplar and sycamore. On 12th and Clay they turned onto a cobble-stoned street and stopped before the White House of the Confederacy. The substantial three-story structure, stucco over brick, was painted a gray-blue so pale it appeared almost white. A simple, hip-high wrought iron fence surrounded the grounds.

Becky balked, but Dr. Grange led her up the front steps to the oak door. A Negro butler greeted them and they entered a small elliptical entrance hall; two niches on either side housed large bronze-painted statues of Tragedy and Comedy. An ornate gasolier hung from the ceiling. The canvas rug, painted in a blue and beige geometric design, was lacquered to prevent wear. The drawing room hummed with guests.

The main room was spacious, with a 14-foot ceiling, floor-to-ceiling windows, and decorated in the ponderous Victorian style; maroon and black flocked floral wallpaper, green and maroon floral rug, and black horsehair settees.

The Davis' Sunday levees drew Richmond's finest: Most of the men were in uniform, Confederate gray emblazoned with gold braid and epaulets; the women, gowned in a rainbow of satins and silks, made Becky conscious of her Quaker-plain blue woolen dress. Perhaps she could slip away—

"Becky!" sounded the alarm, cutting off all hope of escape. Varina Davis advanced on her, leaning back for balance, so pregnant Becky could barely embrace her. Varina wore her omnipresent white with a red hibiscus in her hair, which made her look rather like a large dish of vanilla ice cream topped with a cherry. But her face glowed, and after they'd pressed cheeks, Becky remarked, "You've never looked more radiant."

"Bearing a child does that, you'll see when you have your own. I'm very cross with you for not calling on me the instant you got to Richmond, whatever will your Grandmama think?" Leaving Dr. Grange to fend for himself she led Becky off. Varina obviously adored her position as First Lady of Confederate America. Sociable by nature, outspoken to a fault, she moved through the crowd and seemed to have exactly the right comment for each guest.

"His Excellency is upstairs at a meeting," Varina told Becky, "he never stops working even when he's ill, that's why in addition to his official office at the Customs House, he insisted on having an office here at home. He'll summon us when his meeting is over."

"Do you know why he wants to see me?" Becky asked.

"I don't, but while we're waiting, you must see the house, providing you promise to write every detail to dear Miss Rebecca." Varina kept up a running commentary; "The mansion was built by Dr. Brockenbrough in 1818 in the neo-classical style; it passed through a number of hands, then in 1857 became the property of Lewis Crenshaw. He added the third story and changed its appearance to its current Victorian style. The City of Richmond bought the house and wanted to give it to His Excellency, but he insisted that the Confederate government pay a yearly rental. It came completely furnished so we brought very little of our own possessions."

Varina led her through the rooms on the first floor, the Main Drawing room, the adjoining Ladies Parlor, both decorated en suite; a tiny study called the Snuggery; the State Dining Room, and in each room she introduced her to a host of guests, most of whose names Becky missed.

Varina shepherded Becky to the rear of the mansion. A huge two-story columned portico that faced south ran the entire length of the house and opened onto the garden. They stepped outside; there was a 15-foot drop from the portico to the ground. Varina pointed out the brick outbuildings; the kitchen, greenhouse, carriage house, and servants' quarters.

The land sloped in terraces to the valley below, affording a glorious view of the city and of the James River.

The complex didn't have the grandeur of the deep-South plantations nor was it isolated within its own acreage like the White House in Washington. But it was one of the finer residences in Richmond, scaled to human beings rather than to grandiose state functions and Becky thought it a more livable home than Lincoln's White House.

An aide of Davis' signaled Varina; "His Excellency is ready to see you." Inside, Varina began the arduous climb up the tight spiral staircase to the second floor and was panting when they reached it. She suffered from a heart condition exacerbated by attacks of nerves and tended to retain fluids. She'd married Jeff when she was seventeen, but for the first seven years she'd been unable to conceive, a terrible blow, so ingrained was child-bearing to the psyche of Southern womanhood. But now Varina had three children, and by the look of her, another due within the hour.

A tiny outer office, with a pass-through cut into the wall, guarded the President's study. Varina knocked, went into the study and announced, "See whom I've brought?"

"Becky! My darling Becky!" Gunning Brand exclaimed, and bolted from the conference table to embrace his niece.

Becky tried to absorb everything; the large sun-lit office that faced the garden, bookcases and armoires, maps, Jefferson Davis, thinner, haggard almost, but with that same steely determination she associated with him. In a cloud of Havana cigar smoke, Judah P. Benjamin, exuding energy and optimism. And the forceful presence of Uncle Gunning, looking more vital and appealing than she remembered.

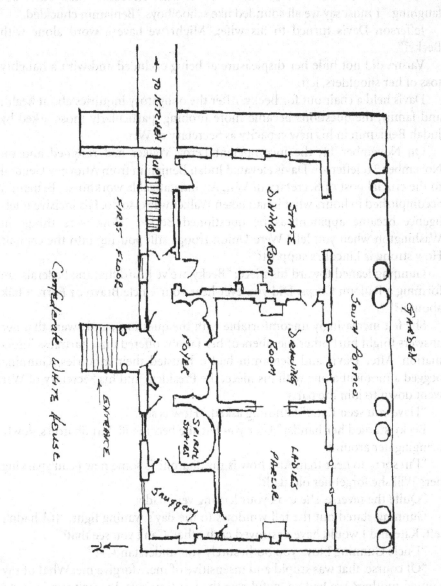

All three men asked in chorus, "How is Miss Rebecca?" then burst out laughing. "I must say we all sounded like schoolboys," Benjamin chuckled.

Jefferson Davis turned to his wife; "Might we have a word alone with Becky?"

Varina did not hide her displeasure at being excluded and with a haughty toss of her shoulders, left.

Davis held a chair out for Becky. After the obligatory inquiries about health and family, the questions became more probing, particularly those asked by Judah Benjamin in his new capacity as Secretary of War.

On November 11, the incompetent Leroy Walker had resigned and on November 21, Jefferson Davis elevated Judah Benjamin from Attorney General to the crucial post of Secretary of War. An indefatigable workhorse, Benjamin accomplished in hours what it had taken Walker weeks to do. His incisive intelligence became apparent as he questioned Becky; "How were things in Washington when you left? Were Union troops still pouring into the capital? How strong is Lincoln's support?"

Gunning leaned toward his niece; "Becky, we've heard that the Federals are forming a Balloon Corps. Did you ever hear your Uncle Bravo or Forrest talk about it?"

She felt increasingly uncomfortable with the questions, and aware that her answers might hurt other members of her family, offered only harmless information. After Davis and Benjamin had exhausted their inquiries, Gunning begged a moment alone with his niece; the President and his Secretary of War went down to join the party.

"Have you seen Kate?" Gunning asked. "How is she?"

Becky studied her hands; "After you left she became ill, but Sharon's slowly bringing her around."

"I'm sorry to hear that. And how is my Sharon? Is some new beau sparking her? Will she forget her old dad?"

"Quite the reverse, she took your leaving very badly."

Gunning stared out the tall windows to the day's waning light. "If I hadn't left, Kate and I would have destroyed each other. Can't you see that?"

"Uncle Gunning I love you both, surely you understand—?"

"Of course, that was stupid and insensitive of me…forgive me. What of my sainted mother? We had an awful row the last time out. I wasn't very nice to her; anything she's said about me is probably true."

"Grandma's never says anything but the most wonderful things about you. Everyone knows you're her favorite."

Gunning snorted; "Your mother was her favorite. When I was born I might have held her attention for a bit, but then Bravo came along…"

Becky pushed her next question forward carefully, "Do you know of any way I could get a letter to Washington? I want so much to let Grandma know I'm all right."

"This is strictly confidential. We've got couriers going to Washington regularly, but if one got caught it might compromise you and Grandma. There is a man named Burns, he runs a gambling house down on Main Street and also operates the best underground mail system in Richmond." He told her the address; "Tell him I sent you. Now we'd best join the party."

The levee had grown in size and intensity. The burning topic on everyone's tongue was the Trent Affair. To Becky's surprise she saw Jefferson Davis and Judah Benjamin in vigorous conversation with Sean Connaught. "What in heaven's name is he doing here?" she asked her uncle.

Gunning regarded Sean with disdain; "The little blowfish comes to Richmond often, puffed with his own importance. He's really a glorified errand boy between the British consul here and Lord Lyons, the British ambassador in D.C. Still, he's useful; we count on Sean for news of the official reaction from England, especially now that the Trent Affair is coming to a head."

Gunning took Becky's hand and pushed his way toward President Davis. Becky, along with everyone else in America hung on the outcome of the Trent Affair. In early October, Davis had appointed John Slidell of Louisiana and James Mason of Virginia, as ministers to France and England respectively. They'd sailed from Charleston, managed to elude the blockade and made it safely to Havana. There they'd boarded the British packet boat *Trent* bound for England; since they were on a neutral vessel they believed they were safe. But a Union warship, the *San Jacinto*, intercepted the *Trent* and despite the vehement protests of the English captain, U.S. Marines forcibly removed Slidell and Mason, then transported them to Boston where they were now imprisoned.

Gunning and Becky reached Davis just as Sean Connaught proclaimed, "Prince Albert was penning the official British protest when he suddenly died. Queen Victoria was devastated, she did so adore him," his brows arched, "eight children, need one say more? But now that the official mourning period is over, Great Britain is preparing to act forcibly."

Benjamin and Davis leaned forward and Sean continued, "As we all know, England demanded that Lincoln abide by international law and release Mason and Slidell. When the Illinois Ape refused—? Well! I'm pleased to inform you that Her Majesty's government has ordered two troop ships to Canada carrying eight thousand of her most seasoned soldiers. War between England and the North appears immanent."

That news swept through the White House on the crest of Rebel yells. Bets were made, the consensus being that if England would just grant recognition to the Confederacy, the war would soon be over. Becky winced at the cacophony of shouts: "She <u>must</u> commit." "Her mills hunger for our cotton, without it, her economy crumbles, and with it the Empire." "Victoria may be Queen but Cotton is King!"

As the hue and cry continued, Becky studied Sean Connaught. His eyes glistened, his lips parted in the barest of smiles, as if pleased with the turmoil he'd created.

"But what if Lincoln gives in to the British and frees Mason and Slidell?" Becky asked, and asked it again, but everyone was too intoxicated with the prospect of victory to hear her.

Dusk gave way to evening, conversation grew more animated and then a sudden hush fell over the room. Romance Connaught had entered. Her hair was piled up in the style affected by Princess Eugenia of France. Her gown of shimmering peacock peau de soir exposed an expanse of roseate flesh; an amethyst big as a pigeon's egg nestled in the swell of her bosom, sparkling hypnotically with her every breath.

Becky stared at her in wonder. How must it feel to be so beautiful that every man in the room desired you? She watched as Uncle Gunning pushed his way through the cordon of Romance's admirers and in a move that signified ownership, led her back to their group.

"*Alors,* my brave brother, in Richmond again?" Romance cooed to Sean, "you've come to join the Confederacy at last?"

Sean colored to the roots of his thinning hair. "Not quite; Maman insisted I come and see how you were faring, after all, it isn't as if she doesn't know Gunning."

It was Gunning's turn to blush, but Romance smiled languidly; "Tell Maman that Gunning and I have never been better."

Gunning drew Becky forward and presented her with glowing affection; "Romance, do you know my niece?"

The tiniest frown creased Romance's forehead; "No, I—oh, but of course, for a moment I didn't recognize you, though my dear brother Carleton has mentioned you—in passing."

"Have you heard from him?" Becky asked eagerly.

"Constantly." Then she asked solicitously, "My dear, have you been ill? You must take the fresh air more often, get the color back in your cheeks."

Becky's face flamed—had an insult been buried in her kindness? Impossible to tell, Romance was that consummate an actress.

Sean grasped Gunning's elbow; "There's a rumor in Washington that Congress is planning to free the slaves in the District of Columbia. Rather than risk losing all my property, with some judicious bribes and a very avaricious slave master—remember that oaf, Harmony Lumpkin? I managed to smuggle twenty of my slaves to Richmond. I plan to hire them out and Romance has agreed to collect their wages for me. Whom shall I see about it?"

"Josiah Gorgas, our Chief of Ordnance. He'll put them to work in the Tredegar Iron Works," Gunning said.

"Is Montgomery in the coffle you brought?" Romance asked.

Sean nodded; "To be rid of him. No matter how hard I punished him, he's turned into an inveterate trouble maker."

"Sometimes a civil word can do more than a cutting whip. I'll have him, indulge me. I'll pay you the fair market rate. Is it still fifteen dollars a month?"

Four dollars more than a Confederate soldier's wages, Becky thought. Are our soldiers less valuable than slaves?

"Done, dear sister." Sean said to Gunning, "Remember him? He's the strapping young buck I bought at the slave mart in Montgomery; the one they called Horse? Romance always had a penchant for things heroic."

Gunning brushed this aside then in a burst of joy lifted Becky and hugged her. "You darling girl, I'm so glad to see you!" He turned to Romance; "Why don't we all have dinner—?"

"That's not possible," Romance said abruptly. "I've other plans," and started toward the door.

"Another time then, Becky," Gunning called over his shoulder as he went after Romance.

Dr. Grange joined Becky and they watched their uncle leave. Becky said quietly, "I believe he loves her."

"Besotted, obsessed, bewitched, those might be better words," he said. "The biggest surprise is that from what I've seen, it's not all one-sided."

"Are they living together?"

"Officially, no. Gunning's taken quarters in a house Judah Benjamin rented on Foushee Street, a mile from here. Romance rented the guesthouse behind the Valentine mansion. Richmond society is far too proper to discuss it, but it's common knowledge that Gunning's a very frequent visitor."

Becky shook her head; "I know it's their lives and none of my business, but I've a terrible feeling about this." She went to the window and watched her uncle and Romance climb into her carriage. Then Romance's whip cracked with the report of a gunshot and the horses bolted forward.

Chapter 15

AGAIN AND AGAIN Romance whipped the horses, the carriage careening over the cobblestones as it tore through the streets. "Romance, stop!" Gunning shouted, trying to tear the reins from her. As she tried to fight him off, they narrowly missed a crowd of parishioners emerging from evening services at St. Paul's Church and heard their fading shouts, "You'll wind up in hell for blaspheming the Sabbath!"

"Don't they know we're in hell already?" Romance cried to the wind. At last Gunning eased the lathered team to a trot.

"What the devil's got into you?" he demanded.

She didn't respond but said as if in a trance, "I'm in desperate need of diversion. Take me to Johnny Worsham's."

"Are you out of your mind? That gambling den's in the roughest part of town. Do you want to be raped? Murdered?"

"God protects fools and madmen. If you don't take me I'll go alone," and started to get out of the carriage.

He grabbed her arm; "All right, but only for a bit." And all the while he cursed inwardly, Damn her, if any other woman had acted so he'd have booted her the hell out of his life.

They drove past the Marshall Theater on 7th and Broad, and Romance said casually, "The last time I was in this theater—two years ago—I saw John Wilkes Booth in *Richard the Third*. You know him, Gunning, don't you?"

Gunning tried to hide his alarm; "Why do you ask?"

"My brother Sean told me an amusing tale about Booth. At Lincoln's Inaugural Ball he saw Booth and your mother having a frantic tete a tete. It seems your niece Becky is besotted with my brother Carleton—simply will not leave him alone—and your mother tried to use Booth as bait to lure Becky off."

Gunning said nothing but his eyes changed from hazel to a smoldering gold; though the Brands might fight like idiots amongst themselves, they closed ranks against outsiders.

The land sloped east and south to the James River. There was a heavy concentration of slave markets in this section; except for New Orleans, Richmond boasted the largest slave market in America and the Confederate government was its biggest customer. Gangs of shackled blacks were being marched through the streets by overseers; they were on their way to work the night shift in various war industries. The Tredegar Iron Works alone employed 20% of Richmond's labor force.

The riverfront had always been Richmond's demimonde and war had given it pulsing new life. It abounded in every type of watering hole from the grandest hotel bars, like the Ballard, the Exchange, and the St. Charles, to the lowest dives. The most evil dens ran east along Main and Cary Streets for a mile to the wharves of the Rocketts. As they drove deeper into the area, drunken soldiers, black marketeers, and female and male prostitutes accosted them, shouting lewd offers that made Gunning blush and Romance sing out with laughter. They clip-clopped past Locust Alley, famous for its bawdy-houses. Less famous but more numerous, were the dingy establishments around Ram Cat Alley which, many claimed, had given rise to the name, Cat Houses.

Johnny Worsham's wasn't the poshest of Richmond's forty gambling houses but it was the liveliest. Two gigantic Negro bouncers stood guard at the door. The place was enormous, filled with cigar smoke, piano music, absorbed customers and powdered women, who strolled about to lubricate the action at the gaming tables. On the large stage, scantily clad girls whooped and high-kicked for randy soldiers on furlough.

Johnny Worsham's attracted a mixed clientele, gentlemen and government officials sat alongside professional gamblers, pimps and blockade-runners. A bar jammed with patrons ran around all four walls, under a balcony of upstairs rooms designed for more private pursuits. Women stood on the balcony like Loreleis, they'd catch the eye of someone who'd just made a killing, then motion them upstairs.

Gunning snorted; "What fools. A man wins a small fortune, then squanders it for a few minute's pleasure?"

"Better to face death with such a memory than die with a pocketful full of money," Romance retorted. She ordered champagne and drank two glasses in quick succession. Suddenly, she gripped Gunning's arm. "See there at the poker table? Now there's a man who knows how to balance duty and pleasure."

Gunning spied Judah Benjamin who'd just arrived. Johnny Worsham's had a room reserved for important guests, but tonight Judah played with the hoi poloi.

"How do you rate our indefatigable Judah Benjamin?" Romance asked. "Will he be a successful Secretary of War?"

"Far more than LeRoy Walker, he's already proven that. But the generals mistrust him because he's not a military man. And he's a Jew."

"Then why did Davis choose him?"

"Jeff needed somebody to carry out his own war policies; Davis uses Judah as a sounding board, sometimes as a hatchet man, and Judah is thick-skinned enough and devoted enough to do his bidding without really questioning his policies. The Confederacy would be better served if a professional military man headed that office, someone who'd challenge Davis if and when he believed that Davis' battle strategies were flawed."

"Like you?"

"Davis could do worse."

"It will never happen; you're too strong a personality and Davis doesn't like to be challenged. He'd do best as dictator of some duchy, or master of a plantation where his word was absolute law. Or better still, commanding the Confederate army. That's where his true genius lies, fighting, inspiring men, not in some dungeon of an office where he has to cope with the never-ending demands of stupid politicians."

"You forget that Jeff's had a long and distinguished career as a politician—"

"Must you always settle for the obvious? It demeans your intelligence. A man may be many things in life but I'm talking about what fulfills him, and being fulfilled draws out his true genius. For example, take Judah; he knows that his success depends solely on Davis. Look at him, he acts so sure of himself, what a pity it masks such hellish inferiority."

"Judah? Inferior? You're dead wrong there."

"He's a Jew, isn't he? Davis' pet Jew, so the *Richmond Examiner* calls him. No matter what his triumphs, for the Gentile majority, it will never be good enough. To my mind he serves the same function as the old court advisers in medieval Spain; a brilliant counselor but the ultimate decision is never his. Without Davis he'd be torn apart by the mob."

"I thought you liked Judah?"

"I don't like him—I adore him. He's the only cosmopolitan man in the entire government, the only man who knows which side of the cracker has the caviar. You've a lot to learn from him for he's a born survivor; whatever happens in this war, Benjamin will survive. Next to him, Davis is little more than a feudal overlord. Yes, yes, Davis is the President of the Confederacy but the Confederacy is doomed."

"It is not! The moment England recognizes us—"

"England will never recognize you," Romance retorted scornfully. "The institution of slavery was finished when Great Britain declared it illegal in the 1830's, and the rest of Europe followed suit. Can England or France now turn around and say that slavery is to be condoned? The South has cotton balls stuffed in her ears, she simply hasn't caught up with the world."

He interjected hotly, "But the Trent Affair—"

"Imbecile! Do you really believe Lincoln would be stupid enough to keep Mason and Slidell imprisoned in the face of England declaring war? That's the trouble with your government, it's totally reactive, depending on the North's mistakes without really having an agenda of its own."

His anger got away from him; "If you're so convinced that we're doomed, why do you stay in Richmond?"

She drained another glass of champagne then looked around the smoke-filled hall...at the near-naked women dancing on stage—had an oblique thought that her mother had once performed in this way and wondered what it might be like to be up there herself. She caught the glance of some soldiers slavering at her, heard the whir of the roulette wheel that presaged fortune or poverty, thrilled to the pulse of life lived at the edge where every emotion was intensified under the magnifying glass of war, and then she lost herself in Gunning's eyes, golden as a lion's, the tawny hair that curled to his shoulders, his powerful, overwhelming body that could bring her to such a peak of passion she could momentarily forget the deadly feud that existed between their families...

Gunning shook her gently; "Romance? Come back to me?"

In answer, she rose and joined Judah Benjamin at the Poker Table. She kissed his cheek; "For luck."

"Then consider me the luckiest of men." As Judah played the game he told her, "I've always preferred poker or faro. Games of pure chance, like roulette or dice, don't use the brain. When I risk, I need a deeper involvement."

He won a hand then another and soon had a pile of chips before him. The other players folded and left the banker and Benjamin facing each other. The crowd sensed blood and thronged around the table. The musicians stopped playing, the girls stopped dancing, people stood on tiptoe.

It all devolved into one last hand. The slight smile never left Benjamin's lips as he weighed and measured, then bet everything on one final draw of the cards. And lost.

A deflating sigh came from the crowd. Romance pressed her fist to her breast.

"Don't distress yourself, my dear," Benjamin soothed, his demeanor unruffled, "think only of the pleasure we had."

For some reason Gunning was furious; "Damn it, Judah, you've just lost a small fortune. How can you be so cheerful?"

"So I've lost, what matter? I believe that Fate operates in one's destiny. Useless to distress yourself about something that's already been foreordained."

Romance asked quietly, "This destiny, does it apply to everyone…or only to those who believe?"

He considered her question; "To all, or only to those who believe…? Of that, I'm not quite so certain, but if I had to wager on it, I'd say to all, believers and non-believers."

Romance took off her amethyst necklace and placed it on the green baize table. "Dealer, one last draw, all you have in front of you, against this gem; the jewel is worth a hundred times more. Judah, will you play the hand?"

His mouth opened in shock; "Your pendant? I couldn't."

"If you don't, I'll play it myself and will most certainly lose. Besides, the gem means little, it was given to me by my mother. Play, I beg you. Play."

The crowd watched breathlessly as the cards snapped on the table. This time Benjamin won. Amid the gasps and cries, the dealer shoved all the chips to Benjamin. Judah put the pendant around Romance's neck, then pushed the chips to her.

She shook her head; "You've returned the loan, the winnings are yours. Others may not give you the full measure of your worth but I know your true value. Don Quixote may appear the hero, but he's nothing without Sancho Panza."

Gunning thought he saw tears start to Benjamin's eyes.

"Then Madam," Benjamin declared, "help me make this a truly memorable night," and began handing chips to everyone.

Romance scooped up fistfuls of chips, tossing them to the dancers, to the musicians, to every soldier, until everyone in the room shared in the good fortune. Johnny Worsham recognized the remarkable nature of the moment and broke out free food and liquor. The band struck up a Virginia reel, the Rebel yell resounded as everyone sang at the top of his lungs,

"We'll hang Abe Lincoln from a sour apple tree!"

The evening ended on a rousing, brilliant note.

Because Sean was staying with Romance, she and Gunning had to go to his quarters. "I've never seen where you live," Romance said, "I'm sure it will be very amusing."

As they drove home Gunning said, "That was an extraordinary thing you did, I believe it's the first time I've ever seen Judah Benjamin genuinely moved."

Her words appeared ghostly in the frosted air; "He's an outcast and I know a kindred spirit. Dismissed by my father because I wasn't the male heir he wanted. Barely tolerated by a mother who felt threatened as I grew up. Tormented by a brother who knows I'm brighter than he is. And what of all the men who think only to use me, without knowing who I truly am?"

They arrived at Davenport House, the three-story house that Judah Benjamin had rented on West Main Street near Foushee, where Gunning had taken quarters. Gunning smiled his crooked grin; "Romance, you do know it's not seemly for a Southern belle to visit a gentleman's quarters without a chaperone?"

"Seemly rules are for seemly people," she sang out. "People will talk anyway, so why not give them reason?"

Gunning unlocked the door to his suite. He'd converted his sitting room into an office, its salient feature a wall-length map of the Virginia and Maryland area, and the two capitals, Richmond and Washington. Colored pins were stuck in the map, many along the Potomac River.

Romance studied the map; "You'd be wise to cover it when you're away, else your plans could be compromised."

"The place is always locked. No one's allowed in here."

"I'm here. How do you know I'm not some secret spy for the Union, seducing you with my wiles?"

"I'd break your pretty little neck if I thought that."

"Shiver, shiver," she breathed. She poked her head into the bedroom; a bed so ugly it could only be intended for sleep. And something she hated even more. On a bureau stood a daguerreotype of Gunning's three children with a matronly woman whom she took to be Gunning's wife; next to it a miniature of a stunning girl who bore a striking resemblance to Gunning. Romance picked it up and studied it. "She's very beautiful. Your sister?"

He shook his head; "My mother. She was beautiful, wasn't she? My father had it painted when they married. He carried it with him everywhere. He had it with him when he died."

"Hmm, no wonder Maman hated her. Your father loved her?"

"Beyond reason. Difficult to imagine that frosty old lady could generate such passion, but in her youth she did."

With a deft motion Romance turned the pictures face down. "I'm not yet so free that I enjoy people watching." They were out of their clothes in moments, kissing wildly. Romance pulled away; "Tell me about your wife. After being married to Veronique how could you bed a woman so plain?"

Her question made him uneasy. "If you'd seen Kate in her early years you'd understand. She was passionate but so shy she always undressed in the dark. Once I insisted that we make love in daylight? That engendered God knows how many Acts of Contrition."

Romance murmured, "Then let me give you something to really confess about," and her kisses cut off any other recollection. She reveled in her body and in all the pleasures of sex. She was even more adept than her mother in Veronique's special French art, except she insisted that Gunning reciprocate, and soon they were a tangle of spooned bodies. She reached fulfillment before he did but he wouldn't stop; she tried to push him away, but he pinned her arms and continued, and when she thought she must faint, he entered and rode her as if repeating their abandoned steeplechase ride. When he climaxed he buried his mouth against her bosom to muffle his cries. He held her in a death grip as wave after wave of aftershock shuddered their bodies.

Quiet, return, to the dark room and dark thoughts. "Tell me," he asked quietly, "what happened to you when we left the White House? I thought you'd kill the horses and us."

She propped herself on an elbow, midnight hair cascading across his chest. "Your niece, Becky. When I saw how you looked at her, I knew I'd never command such love from you."

"But that's madness. I adore you, since you, there's been no one else."

"*Tiens!* And we've been together how long, seven months? Darling, your constancy amazes me. Surely you know that your reputation has preceded you?"

"So has yours."

Her eyes flashed; "Whatever my sins, I can honestly say I've never been involved with more than one man at a time. Whereas you—well, dear heart, two can play at that game."

"If I caught you with another man I'd kill him and you."

"I believe you would; but you'd have to catch me first, and as you well know, the Villefranche-Connaught combination makes for a very wily mix."

He stroked her cheek; "Why are we fighting? Don't you know that I love you?" He reached into the bedside table and took out an oblong package. "I bought you a little present."

She opened it and gasped when she saw a silver stiletto letter opener whose handle was crusted with semi-precious gems. "It's magnificent," she cried, "oh do you love me? Really love me? If I asked you to go away with me, tonight, right now—Paris, London, anywhere—would you go?"

"Romance, you know that's not possible."

She rolled away; "See? First the Confederacy, then me."

"That's an absurd comparison. We're at war."

"Always the same excuses. Duty, honor, freedom, words to mask the real reason that men make war, because they thrive on it. Each generation seeks its own justification—"

"Now you sound like my mother."

She slipped from the bed and went to the window, her sinuous body blending into the darkness. "We'd go tonight. Leave everything behind. Your family, mine, all the memories of trying to squirm out from under the thumb of my warden-mother, to say nothing of my brother Sean. I've enough money so we'll never have to worry." She grew excited; "I'll show you joyous, heady Paris. We'll climb the ruins of the pyramids, worship in the temples of Jerusalem, see all, know all. Glory in everything we do. Tonight, my love."

He had an overwhelming memory of a time thirty years before when Veronique Villefranche had made the same demand, give up all for love. He had…and had lost everything, including love. Yet he did adore this creature, who could be as pure as the flame in a votive lamp…or as wanton as a Magdalene. And each time they made love she gave him back life's most precious gift…

He murmured, "I've something even more glorious for you. When we win this war I'll give you a life such as you've never known. I'll be part of this new Southern Empire, and I'll build a city for you, a city that will beggar any in your wildest imaginings, and we'll call that city, Romance."

Night had claimed her and he could barely hear her soft reply, "If we leave, right now, tonight, we may have a chance. If we stay, I fear we'll destroy each other."

"Ah, Romance, that's what I love most about you, the surge and clash of drama in your soul."

She came back and ran the tip of the bejeweled stiletto along his body, prickling it with gooseflesh; "Make fun if you like, but in your soul you know I speak the truth."

Chapter 16

BECKY STRUGGLED to make New Year's Day dinner at her ward festive. The women of Richmond started arriving that morning with covered dishes and pitchers of eggnog. Outside the wards, slaves sang spirituals and patients and visitors joined in. Eyes shone with memories of happier times and for a brief moment the war seemed far away.

But the reality was very different. Days before, December 26, Lincoln had done a stunning about face over the Trent Affair, apologized to England, and released the two Confederate ambassadors, Mason and Slidell. England accepted Lincoln's apology, the War Between the States continued.

As Becky was clearing the plates, someone stole up behind her and whispered huskily, "Am I talking to the most beautiful belle in all Richmond?"

"No, but I'm talking to the wickedest wildest reprobate in the entire Confederacy—Geary!" she cried and turned to embrace her cousin, crying for joy at the sight of him. He looked thinner, subdued; he looked…caged. She hugged him again. "How in the world did you know I was here?"

"Grandma, God bless her; she managed to sneak a letter through Union lines; I got it months late, but I got it."

"Are you on leave?"

"In a way; winter's brought hostilities to a standstill. Camp was so ornery dull and so cold I decided to slip away for a bit, find out how all my kin in Richmond were doing."

"But if you're with Stonewall Jackson's army—that means you must have traveled at least—a hundred miles?"

"No distance at all for a wandering man like me. A uniform and a bit of blarney will get you a ride on any farmer's wagon, or a night's sleep in his barn."

She clutched his arm; "You haven't deserted?"

"Good heavens, what do you take me for, someone of intelligence? I've every intention of going back, but for some odd reason, I've got a hunger to see my Dada."

"Geary, I'm scared for you, General Winder's got military police all over the city, scouring for deserters."

"Don't I know it, being only one step ahead of those Plug Uglies, that's what we call them. I found out where Dada lives but he wasn't there. They did tell me he was going to be at President Davis' New Year's levee. Would you come with me? If I've got a pretty girl on my arm, the military police would be less likely to stop me."

"Oh, I couldn't. Look at me, exhausted, no clothes—"

"Becky, this may be the last chance I'll get to see him."

His voice sounded so plaintive that she called to her patients, "Unless someone really needs me, I'm taking my half day off and going into town."

"Ah needs ya," Sour Soup bleated, "how can ah see the New Ye-ah in without mah sour soup?"

Arms akimbo, she came at him; "See here you malingering cracker, got shot four times, did you? And isn't it a wonder that each bullet went exactly through the same hole?"

"Oh Lordy, forgive this cold-hearted woman, if she was lyin' here adyin', I'd cook her up some sour soup to ease her pain. Ya start with buttermilk brought to a bile—"

Giggling, Becky and Geary fled, with the recipe pursuing them; "—Add leeks if you got 'em, but scallions'll do, lots of coarse ground pepper 'til ya cain't stop sneezin'!"

On the long walk to town Becky said, "I'm exhilarated and scared all at once and I don't know why. Did you ever feel that something momentous, something wonderful was about to happen? That's the way I feel right now. But what?"

At the White House, the New Year's Day levee was well on its way to being a roaring success. Richmond's Three Hundred, the top echelon of families in all America, rubbed elbows with the common man. Varina Davis had given birth to a boy on December 17, and didn't attend the party, but Jefferson Davis greeted the guests with his customary charm.

Geary and Becky caught sight of Gunning and pushed their way toward him. Gunning and Judah Benjamin were doing a post-mortem on the Trent Affair, their voices carrying.

"It's only a momentary setback," Benjamin kept insisting.

Gunning retorted angrily, "I say the hell with England's endless teasing, we'll win this war on our own. The North's so damned pleased with its blockade of our ports? Operation Anaconda they call it, meant to squeeze the life out of us? But with the Norfolk Navy Yard now in our hands, I guarantee, they won't feel so cocksure for long."

"Got yourself a new secret weapon, Dada?" Geary asked.

Gunning whirled, then with a bellow of delight, swept his son up in a bear hug. "Let me look at you, boy! I'm so glad to see you! Are you all right?" then crushed him close again. "Are you on leave?"

"Yeah, old lemon-sucking Bible-thumping Stonewall Jackson gave me permission to come to Richmond—make sure you were all doing your duty. At least I think he gave me permission."

"God, I love you—what do you mean you think Jackson—?"

"See why I could never be an officer? Sure there's duty and all, but a hug from you is worth a week in the stockade."

Romance, who'd been watching the encounter with growing envy, called from across the room, "Gunning, come rescue me from these officers, my defenses are about to be breached!"

Gunning fidgeted; "Geary, come meet—" but Geary shook his head. Gunning nodded, "Okay, I understand. I'll be back shortly. You'll bunk with me tonight," and went to Romance.

Geary breathed; "Will you look at her? What chance does an ordinary old wife have against a Jezebel like that?"

Becky touched his arm; "Sooner or later he'll come to his senses and see her for what she is. I just know he will."

Geary pulled his gaze away from them. "Dada's head seems to be filled with some secret weapon. Know what it is?"

"Not the vaguest."

Into the room swaggered a man in his late twenties. He wore garb as swashbuckling as any pirate's, sported a full ginger beard, a dancing plume in his slouch hat, a wide yellow sash around his waist and thigh-high leather boots. Rebel yells greeted Brigadier General J.E.B Stuart. Crowding behind him stomped a group of his equally flamboyant officers.

All at once, the exhilaration and fright Becky had felt earlier came to fruition—there stood Carleton. In that tremulous moment jumbled impressions crowded in on her: He'd changed greatly, weather-beaten, lean as a strip of jerky. And he'd grown a moustache. His once diffident manner had given way to a prideful swagger. Clearly, he'd taken on the rough spirit of his cavalry corps. Everything dictated that she should have been pleased with his new-found confidence, yet his boisterous cavalier attitude struck at her heart.

Romance cornered Carleton first and engaged him in spirited conversation. Then Carleton saw Becky. His face lit, he rushed to her and with an effortless motion whirled her around, discommoding several people. In their rush of joy they stumbled over their questions. He was thrilled to hear that she'd cast her lot with the South, but taken aback when he learned, "You're a nurse? Is that proper work for a lady? Men can be—so rough."

She hadn't expected that reaction—not from him—and her color rose. "They are rough, but they're also sick and wounded; they're our men, they deserve to be cared for."

"Of course," he agreed, eager to make peace. He held her at arm's length. "You look so different."

She heard herself making excuses for her appearance, yet knew it was impossible for her to compete with Richmond's beauteous debutantes. These bejeweled belles, bathed, perfumed, coddled and cinched by their slaves were being treated as national treasures by the gallants of the Confederacy.

"How long will you be in Richmond?" Becky asked.

"Until midnight, then we go back into the field. Word is that General McClellan's gathering a huge army around Washington. He plans to capture Richmond come spring and it's my job—the cavalry's job—to find out which route he'll take."

Jeb Stuart clasped Carleton's shoulder; "Can you tear yourself away for a moment? President Davis wants a word."

Carleton squeezed Becky's hands. "Be back soon."

Geary, who'd been watching the exchange, whistled long and low; "Can it be that our Becky's finally found a beau?"

Before she could reply, one of the officers in Carleton's regiment, a Captain Beacroft, descended on Becky and Geary.

"So you're the Becky that Cotton always talks about?" He had an innocent habit of pinching her when he spoke. "When Cotton first joined our regiment some of us thought he was so fine-looking—why he's got eyelashes longer than my wife's—and being deprived of the fair sex, come nightfall we'd go to his tent and serenade him. Just as a lark, nothing mean intended. But Cotton did-n't cotton to our hi-jinks, punched me in the nose. I do believe that's why he grew his moustache."

She felt a flash of anger at the old derogatory nickname. "Why do you insist on calling him Cotton? You know his name."

He blinked his guileless blue eyes; "Most officers have our body slaves with us and the darkies just can't say Carleton, it comes out Cotton." Pinch. "He told us that's how he got the nickname. But since cotton is the South's most valuable commodity, that's the way we think of our own Cotton. He's the most reckless daredevil? First in every charge, if one of us is in trouble, count on Cotton to fight at his side. He's our regiment's white gold." With a final pinch, Beacroft joined the circle of officers drooling over Romance.

"Becky, Becky," Geary exclaimed, "will you look at that blush in your cheeks?" He grew serious; "Do you love him?"

"I...I think so."

"You think so? Think means that you've never—?"

"Certainly not! Geary Brand, you are a scandal. Have you no respect for the marriage vows?"

"None whatever. Do you really believe that God cares if you say 'I do' in front of a priest or parson? Or is that little lie something invented by those wily critters so they can crush us with all their rules? But if your vows come from the heart...I believe that's all He cares about."

"And have you loved all the girls you've sparked?"

"Passionately. At least for the moment. But then we all know that I'm a sinner and will come to no good end. I've been told that so often I feel I don't dare disappoint anyone." He grinned and for a moment the old, irrepressible Geary shone through. He took her hands; "Becky, this day, this hour, this moment, these are the moments of your life, and once spent, they never return. This is not a dress rehearsal for real life, this is it. If you love this man, then love him with all your heart and soul, right now, this moment, and seize all the joy you can. That, is what pleases God."

"But Grandma hates him and his family."

"Grandma's had her life, time now for you to live yours." With a tender touch he wiped away her tears.

Then he glanced out the window; "Can those be General Winder's Plug Uglies I see lurking in the street? Who can they be looking for, I wonder? Is there a back way out?"

She took him to the staircase that led to the basement. Down they went to where the favored house slaves had quarters.

He kissed her cheek. "Say goodbye to Dada for me? Tell him I had to leave suddenly. And remember what I told you."

Then he dashed through the garden, vaulted the stone fence and disappeared. Some womanly instinct told Becky that he'd get away. She went back to the main drawing room. Carleton returned and they fell into a conversation so comfortable it seemed that they'd never been apart.

Then somehow Romance had insinuated herself between them. She flicked Carleton's epaulets; "Remember, dear boy, seven o'clock sharp. I've already invited every young beauty in town, and they're besotted with you. You'll have your pick."

He pushed Becky forward; "Romance, do you remember Becky? I haven't seen her in ages, I want her to come."

A tiny furrow creased Romance's brow, companion to her tiny look of alarm. "But that's impossible, the seating—"

Carleton fixed his sister with a hard stare. "I'm sure you'll manage—or I'm afraid I won't be able to come."

Never having seen this side to her younger brother, Romance was astute enough to backtrack. "I have it, I'll invite dear Uncle Gunning to balance the table. It will all be so intimate. The Connaughts and the Brands supping together, what could be more civilized? Carleton, my throat is so parched I can barely speak. Do be an angel and bring us some champagne? Dear Becky and I must make plans."

Carleton went off. Romance studied Becky as if trying to figure a way to make a silk purse out of a sow's ear. "*Alors*, my dear, to work. I'm sure I've a more suitable gown in my wardrobe, and I'll insist that my hairdresser do your hair; Dusquesne is a genius, he can spin gold out of straw. In a room full of swans, we mustn't waddle in like a little duckling, hmm? The poor little duckling might be pecked to death."

"Have no fear, my dear, it's the heart of the duckling that counts and I'm sure Carleton's wise enough to know that."

"The heart indeed. But that being the case, perhaps it would be wise not to mention that you work as a nurse? We hear those women have <u>such</u> reputations, and there <u>were</u> those wild tales about you in Texas—"

Becky swung back and slapped her so hard it resounded like a shot through the room. Everyone turned to stare at them. Gunning started forward but Carleton reached them first. "Becky, what in the world—?"

"If you want to see me, I'll be at the hospital," she snapped, "I've sick and wounded to care for," and stormed off.

Romance stared after her, the barest smile on her lips and triumph huge in her breast.

Chapter 17

"MIZ REBECCA, you think this here 'Operation Anaconda,' is working?" Bittersweet asked.

Rebecca turned from her vigil at the window; "All too well; we hear these dreadful reports that the South is hurting for all sorts of supplies, but particularly medicines. That is so inhuman I could scream." She rubbed her temples; "Bittersweet, the mailman's awfully late today, isn't he?"

"He's come 'n gone and no mail, told you that ten times."

"I'll never forgive Becky for leaving me, never. And not a word from her since. I worry so about her, and Sharon never visits anymore, what with her new job clerking at the War Department. I'm all alone."

"You forget there's a war on? I gives up," Bittersweet said, "no reasoning with you today, not when you in this cantankerous mood." She began dusting Rebecca's desk; "How come all these newspapers be opened to the Obituary Page?"

"It's the first thing I turn to in the morning; to grieve over the friends I've lost and to gloat over the enemies I've outlived. I see that former President John Tyler just died in Richmond. Did you know he had fifteen children? By two wives? Seventy-two and still going bump in the night—the old goat."

"What you wearing to this reception at the White House tomorrow?" Bittersweet asked. "Your yellow satin's nice."

"It's By Invitation Only. I've no interest in going; who cares about Mary Todd Lincoln's new decorations? Congress is screaming that she spent seven thousand dollars more than the twenty thousand they appropriated. How can she be so irresponsible in a time of war?"

"Didn't get invited, huh? That's 'cause you're so mean to Mr. Lincoln. Writin' all them articles in vinegar and gall."

Bravo called from the front door, "Anybody home?" He came into the drawing room and Rebecca greeted him sourly, "What new killing machine have you invented today?"

Bittersweet rolled her eyes; "Didn't get an invite to Miz Lincoln's fancy party, so she's drivin' everyone crazy."

Bravo winked at Bittersweet. "Ma, one of the reasons I stopped by—President Lincoln gave me two invitations—"

"If Mary Todd got down on bended knee—"

"Know who's behind this 'Invitation Only' nonsense? Veronique Connaught. How many times have you told me that the White House is the people's house? Are you going to let a Connaught shut you out of what rightfully belongs to you?"

"Bittersweet? I'll be wearing my yellow satin!"

The next evening, February 5, as Rebecca and Bravo walked to the White House, she said, "I've just met this enchanting young woman—I'm going to have the two of you to tea—"

"You're an incorrigible busybody and matchmaker to boot."

"Show me a mother who isn't? It's part of our job, it comes with the womb. Bravo, I only want your happiness."

"I am happy."

"You can't be. If you were sixty, seventy years old, I might understand. But you're only forty, it's unnatural for a man your age to be so alone."

"Ma, I'm forty-three. Why is it that anytime a woman sees an unattached man she feels compelled—?"

"Because, 'Two by two they were led into the ark.'"

"Right. I'll consider it—come the next flood." His mood turned somber. "I know what it's like to love…but when Anne died, that part of me…seemed to die also. Having Forrest, helping him grow up, that helped me too, maybe even saved my life. Will I fall in love again? I hope so, but I'll never marry just because I'm afraid of being lonely. I hope I'll never be that much of a coward."

A cold miasmic mist rose from the flats of Tiber Creek and enveloped the White House. Edward McManus, the ancient doorkeeper who'd guarded the portals since Zachary Taylor's brief tenure, tipped his hat. "Why Miss Rebecca, how good to see you. You haven't crossed this threshold in a bit."

"If Mary Todd Lincoln had her way, I never would."

"But I miss our little talks," Old Ed complained. "First Ladies can be contentious, and we've got our hands full with this one. Won't stick to a budget, wants a <u>salary</u> for playing at being First Lady. Hope you had a belt of bourbon before you came, 'cause there's not an ounce of liquor here tonight. This First Lady insists she can't afford refreshments, not even wine at state dinners. How can she, when most of the household funds wind up on her back? This past month she bought three hundred pairs of gloves."

"Three hundred?" Rebecca repeated incredulously, "does she think she's a centipede?"

"Guess I shouldn't gossip about the poor soul—"

"Nonsense, Ed, gossip is society's horse manure, let's you and I just keep spreading it around."

Rebecca and Bravo joined the crowd in the East Room, much to the surprise of Mary Todd and the chagrin of Veronique Connaught. Mrs. Lincoln wore a white satin gown with an embarrassingly low neckline and a floral headdress with a huge cabbage rose stuck smack in the middle of her forehead. One disgruntled bluenose complained to Rebecca, "Mrs. Lincoln has her bosom on display and a flower pot on her head."

Lincoln looked miserable in white gloves and a black claw-hammer evening jacket. Both Lincolns appeared distressed and several times during the evening Rebecca saw Mary Todd hurry upstairs to check on her two young sons, Willie and Tad, who'd come down with severe cases of bilious fever.

The Marine Band played, 500 invited guests milled about while Mary Todd took groups on a tour of the newly re-decorated rooms. Rebecca positioned herself in the curve of the grand piano and surveyed the East Room; the crystal chandeliers sparkling with gas light, the muted green velvet wallpaper and sea-green rug, the huge gilt mirrors on opposite walls that reflected the revelers on into infinity. "Much as I hate to admit it, Bravo, Mary Todd's done a fine job."

An attractive woman curtsied to the President, whereupon Mary Todd interposed herself between them. Rebecca raised her eyebrows; "Bravo, do I see jealousy rearing its Hydra head? Does the President give her cause? Is he a philanderer?"

"Mary Todd's jealousies are all in her tormented mind."

At one point in the evening, Rebecca caught Veronique glaring at Bravo with such baleful hatred she felt her heart contract. She cornered her son; "I know that bitch loathes all the Brands but she seems to reserve a special hatred for you. You don't admire her very much either, do you."

"I do admire her—the way one admires Clytemnestra."

Rebecca's face came alive; "Are you telling me, after all these years, that she did kill her husband? You were there, you know if she shot Devroe Connaught—"

"It was an accident."

"I didn't believe you then, I don't believe you now."

"Ma, Veronique had three young children, what good would it have done to take their mother from them? Besides, if ever a man deserved justice it was Devroe Connaught. I'd have killed him myself if—if the accident hadn't happened. Vengeance is mine, sayeth the Lord, so let's put it behind us and as the good Bard says, 'leave her to heaven.' Now let's go home, these parties bore the bejesus out of me."

The next morning, the newspapers gave the reception mixed reviews; some praised Mrs. Lincoln for her skill as a hostess, others castigated her for such extravagance in time of war.

"I don't much like Mary Todd," Rebecca told Bittersweet, "but I do feel sorry for her. The White House can be a maddening place especially for a woman of her nervous temperament. In fact, the only First Lady who ever thrived there was Dolley Madison, the country just couldn't keep up with her."

"Aunt Mary, colored maid I knows workin' there, says Miz Lincoln does good works, visits all the hospitals, and gives to Negro charities and such, but she's a mite tetched, sweet as wine one minute, vinegar the next. With both her boys taking a turn for the worse, she's all vinegary with worry."

"It's a wonder anyone survives in that cold damp house, it just breeds pestilence."

"Aunt Mary says Tad's a bit better today, but Willie? It will take an act of God."

But God chose not to act and on Thursday, February 20, Willie Lincoln, age twelve, died. The President was desolate and walked endlessly around the small coffin in the East Room. "My poor boy, he was too good for this world, too good."

Grief robbed Mary Todd of her senses and she fell into a delirium. Along with hundreds of other mourners, Rebecca came to pay her respects, but Mary Todd responded to no one, intermittently breaking out in paroxysms of heart-rending cries.

Doorkeeper Ed McManus, confided to Rebecca, "Secretary of War Stanton had Dorothea Dix assign Nurse Pomroy to care for the First Lady—round the clock lest she do herself harm. But when she wouldn't stop screaming, Lincoln took her to the window and pointed to the insane asylum. 'Mother, if you go on this way, that is where you're going to end up.'"

The funeral was held on the following Monday but Mrs. Lincoln, still mad with despair, couldn't attend. Rebecca ached for her; having lost her own daughter, Suzannah, she knew how this poor woman must feel. No words could heal, not even time could heal the loss of a child.

*

About a month later, in early March, Rebecca was preparing to go out when Bittersweet careened into the drawing room, screeching, "War's over! South won! Hide!"

"Stop being so ridiculous. Now sit down, catch your breath and we'll daydream together."

"Even when I tells the truth you don't believe me; Confederate Navy just sank the whole Union fleet!"

"In whose bathtub? There is no Confederate navy."

"The Rebs are steaming to Washington right now, I just came from the White House. Aunt Mary told me so herself."

"Did she also tell you that the sky was falling? If I listened to every tall tale you told—look, I've invited Bravo to tea at the Willard Hotel. A charming young lady joining us, though Bravo doesn't know it yet. Bravo and the President are like that," she crossed her fingers, "if there's any truth to your tale, Bravo will know."

A short while later, Rebecca and Bittersweet were hurrying along Pennsylvania Avenue; Bittersweet whispered, "There be a man followin' us, doggin' us since we left the house. He's not tall, not short, kinda medium—"

Rebecca glanced about; "I don't see a soul. Are you having your Bumpkin, Pumpkin, Lumpkin delusions again?"

"Couldn't rightly see his face, but he's young, and white. Watch the crossing, carriages coming, cow too. Shoo, bossy, shoo," Bittersweet waved her arms and in response the annoyed cow left her a pie in the middle of the dusty road.

When they reached the Willard, Rebecca looked uncertainly at the two Greek Revival porticos, one on 14th, and the other on Pennsylvania Avenue. When war broke out, Henry Willard had been confronted with a grave problem; both Northerners and Southerners frequented the hotel, and since he didn't want to lose the business of either, he assigned the avenue entrance to Northerners, the street entrance for Southerners.

Rebecca hesitated; "Oh dear, which entrance shall I use?"

"Dumbest thing I ever heard, they'll find you froze solid 'afore you makes up your mind. Since you're meetin' Mr. Bravo best use the Pennsylvania. Bye, pick you up at six."

Henry Willard greeted Rebecca; she glanced around the jammed dining room. "Has my son Bravo arrived?" He shook his head and she said, "Henry, I realize that etiquette and all ten of the commandments dictate that I wait for my escort, but if I promise not to flirt with any of the patrons, could you seat me now? I'll need a banquette, and a double bourbon."

He led her through an obstacle course of tables; reporters, politicians, lobbyists, financiers, contractors, anyone of any consequence patronized the Willard. The clientele was predominantly male, though with the war, more women were frequenting the dining room, some of dubious reputation.

"You've done wonders with this place, Henry," Rebecca said as he seated her, "it's a far cry from the decrepit old City Hotel that Benjamin Tayloe used to run."

"Surely you're much too young to remember that?"

"Ah, that inimitable Willard charm, no wonder you're such a success. As it happens, I remember when this plot of land was nothing but a mud hole, and when the Potomac flooded, fish were stranded in the pools."

About ten minutes later Bravo came in and sank into the banquette; "Sorry I'm late, cabinet meeting all day."

"Bravo, the most attractive young lady is meeting us—"

"Not today, Ma, I can't stay long, this has been a grim day for the Union. The Rebels let loose an iron monster and it's already sunk three first class U.S. warships."

"My nerves!" She bolted her bourbon. "Where in heaven's name did the South get a navy?"

"Where they're getting most of their armaments—from beating the hell out of us. When the Rebels captured Norfolk we had a number of warships there, including the *U.S.S. Merrimac.* Gideon Welles ordered the fleet scuttled to keep it from falling into Rebel hands. But Stephen Mallory—he's the Confederate Secretary of the Navy—had the *Merrimac* raised and refitted as a new ironclad warship and renamed it the *Virginia,* but it's still the *Merrimac.* Slanted superstructure, oak hull twenty-four inches thick sheathed in four-inch iron plate, and mounting ten guns. Saturday, the *Merrimac* steamed to Newport News where she engaged five Union ships. The Federals thought it would be a turkey shoot, they had a combined total of a hundred and twenty-four guns, more than ten times the firepower of the *Merrimac.* She went after the *U.S.S. Cumberland* first and sank her. *Merrimac* then engaged the *U.S.S. Congress,* which had fifty guns, and sank her also. Then she forced the *U.S.S. Minnesota* aground. The *Merrimac* retired for the night, but our navy expects her to come out today and finish off the *Minnesota*."

"I need another bourbon."

"Lincoln's cabinet is in an uproar, especially Stanton. What a mean little coward lurks in that fat bully's belly. He kept blubbering, 'The *Merrimac* will change the whole character of the war. She will destroy seriatim every naval vessel; she will lay all the cities on the eastern seaboard under contribution. A cannonball from the *Merrimac* may very well crash into this room before the cabinet adjourns!' Even Seward, who's usually unflappable, caught Stanton's hysteria."

So had Rebecca, for she half-rose in her chair, her mouth working as she struggled to speak.

"Ma, what's—?" he rummaged through her reticule, found her heart medication and put it to her lips. "Swallow."

She swallowed several times, struggling to regain her composure. At last she managed, "I need some fresh air." She left a note for her lady friend saying she'd become indisposed but hoped they could all meet at some future date.

On their walk home she murmured, "When you told me about this monster steaming toward Washington, fifty years flashed before my eyes. It was like reliving the day during the War of 1812 when I saw the British invasion fleet sail up the Potomac. To have it happen again—"

Bravo looked at the river; "Until today, I never actually realized how vulnerable Washington is from the sea." Bravo led her into her house. "Ma, are you all right now?"

"I will be when you tell me our plans for defense."

"Gideon Welles straightened out Stanton in short order. I love that man, he may look like a dyspeptic Santa Claus, but before he'd finished he really shamed Stanton. From our naval reports, Welles estimated that with its new heavy armor, the *Merrimac* had a draft of twenty-three feet, and sat so low in the water she'd never clear the channels and reach Washington. Furthermore, she only has a top speed of five knots an hour, about as fast as a man can walk. Welles ordered the chain barriers reinforced and that a flotilla of canal boats loaded with stone be sunk and obstruct the channel—if the *Merrimac* should come into sight."

Bravo paced the room, growing more agitated. "Do you realize that this is the end of naval warfare as we know it? In this one battle, every wooden fleet, England's, France's, has been rendered obsolete. It's the dawning of a new age, and damn it, the South did it first. This could well mean the ruin of General McClellan's entire invasion plan."

"What invasion plan?" When he didn't respond she repeated insistently, "What invasion plan? Bravo, why won't you answer? I'm your <u>mother</u>."

"That you are, but you're a reporter first."

She threw up her hands. "You say that the *Merrimac* has a deep draft and therefore Washington's safe? But isn't it conceivable that a ship with a shallower draft could be built, and <u>that</u> ship could attack us?"

Bravo kissed the top of her head; "You're a whole lot smarter than I give you credit for."

"To think it only took you forty-three years to recognize that. If George Washington were here I'd wring his neck. He insisted the capital be built here, <u>below</u> the Falls of the Potomac, rather than above. Why did he, a surveyor and a general who should have known better, do that, you may ask?"

"Ma, you've told me a hundred—"

"Because he owned huge tracts of land around here, rather Mary Custis did, George was dirt poor before he married her—and he knew that if the capital was built here, their property would appreciate tremendously, which it did. But it allowed the British access, and fifty years later we're confronted with the same threat. All because of greed."

"Where is it writ that one can't be President and a good business man to boot?"

"Hopefully, on a man's conscience. If your business affects the country adversely, then business be damned. I won't close an eyeball tonight, and all because of George."

"If it'll help you sleep, I'll tell you a little secret. You talked about a ship with a shallower draft? Well, we're the one's who've built that one, it left New York two days ago, it may have already engaged the *Merrimac*."

"Are you telling me that the Union <u>anticipated</u> what the Confederacy was doing?"

"You're a sophisticated woman, surely you realize that information gathering is a two-way street?"

It took several moments for his meaning to penetrate, then she realized he was talking about a spy network, one operating for the North. That sent chills through her.

"Even if we hadn't had an inkling of what the South was doing—I've been involved with the Patent Office for twenty years and I've noticed that inventions come in bunches. If the need is there, people at opposite ends of the earth can come up with the same solution, sometimes simultaneously. And war seems to open up a floodgate of ideas; we've never been so inundated with inventions, some crackpot, some visionary."

"Are you involved in this—this information gathering? Is Forrest?" He shook his head, but she said, "Why do I get the feeling that you're lying through your teeth? A mother knows these things. As I said, it comes with the womb."

"Okay, you're right, I'm not telling you everything. I can't, on pain of your safety and well-being."

"Bravo, you're frightening me."

"I hope so. Months ago you told me you'd sent letters to Geary, Becky and Gunning. Under no circumstances must you write to them again. You insist on visiting Rosie Greenhow in prison; you write articles attacking this administration, and all that's brought you to the attention of Secretary of War Stanton and General Lafayette Baker, head of the War Department's Secret Service. Both men are ruthless; they've imprisoned people for less; contact with the enemy is a crime. If you get caught, I won't be able to protect you. I beg you, be discreet. Now I've got to get back to the White House."

"Bravo, what invasion plans were you talking about?"

But he was already out the door.

All that night, Rebecca punched her pillow, unable to sleep. Bittersweet had claimed they were being followed; had she been right? She'd have to keep her wits about her. But as for being muzzled, she always been contrary and just the fact that they demanded her mindless obedience would demand that she resist, especially if it concerned her children and grandchildren. And if the opportunity presented itself to smuggle a letter to Richmond, she knew she would.

Any doubts Rebecca had about Bravo's tale of a new Union warship evaporated the next day when news swept Washington that a great naval battle had been fought on Sunday at Newport News. She devoured the newspaper report. "The ironclad *U.S.S. Monitor*, its deck just a foot above the water and with a revolving turret housing two eleven-inch Dahlgren guns, engaged the ironclad *C.S.S. Merrimac*. At 900 tons, the *Monitor* was far lighter than the 3,500 ton *Merrimac*, but being faster, could outmaneuver the larger ship and with her revolving turret, fire at her from every angle. The *Merrimac* tried to ram the smaller vessel but the *Monitor* continually eluded her. Shells bounced and slid over both vessels, neither sustaining serious damage, though the men in the *Monitor* suffered deafness from the bombardment against its turret. After four hours the fight broke off with neither ship able to claim victory."

But with the *Monitor* now standing guard, the *Merrimac*, with her poor engines and heavy draft was virtually imprisoned in Hampton Roads, and Rebecca and all of Washington breathed a collective sigh of relief.

The South's secret weapon, designed to break the Union's blockade and allow desperately needed food, weapons and medicines to come into the South had failed. And Operation Anaconda tightened its deadly stranglehold on the Confederacy.

Chapter 18

WITH THE latest intelligence reports tucked firmly in his breast pocket, Gunning Brand bounded up the circular staircase to Jefferson Davis' study. Davis had been gravely ill for several days and the affairs of state were being conducted from the Confederate White House. "What a time for Davis to get sick again," Gunning muttered under his breath.

He found Davis at his desk; a debilitating attack of facial neuralgia had caused him to lose sight in one eye, and a nervous affliction had immobilized his arm. "How are you, Your Excellency?" Gunning asked encouragingly.

"The doctors tell me that my loss of sight is temporary, and I am getting some movement back in my arm."

"We can thank the Good Lord for that," Judah Benjamin said softly as he stepped out of the shadows.

Gunning bit his lip pensively; he'd noticed that Davis' ailments seemed to flare up whenever he was burdened with bad news. Let Robert Toombs attack the administration—or that little worm, Vice President Alex Stephens, rail against a strong central government—which is exactly what they needed to win this war—and Jeff was laid low. "I have the intelligence reports you asked for," Gunning began—

Davis interrupted, "Before I hear your report, Brand, Judah Benjamin and I are faced with a serious problem, one in which you may be of some help."

It was part of Davis' nature that his ordered mind found it necessary to recount the many crises leading up to the most current one and he listed those that had befallen the fledgling nation since the beginning of the year. Fort

Donelson in Tennessee lost to Ulysses S. Grant; Roanoke Island in North Carolina overrun by Federals. Secretary of State Hunter resigning after a violent policy disagreement with Davis. Davis concluded, "Now we're faced with the gravest internal emergency of all, one that may well destroy our Confederacy."

Gunning, along with everyone else in the South was aware of the emergency. Judah Benjamin, in his capacity as Secretary of War, and General Stonewall Jackson, had clashed on a matter of military protocol. It hadn't been an issue of any importance, just two men of dissimilar backgrounds having a difference of opinion and Gunning had thought the silly mess would blow over. But when Jackson submitted his resignation, a howl of rage rent the South, for Jackson's victories had elevated him to an icon. In Congress, in newspapers, and in the court of public opinion rose the cry, How dare anyone desecrate an icon? Particularly a Jew? Even if he happened to be Jefferson Davis' pet Jew?

Davis turned to Gunning; "Since you're a military man and objective in this, Benjamin specifically asked for your input. How may we best handle this crisis?"

Gunning chose his words with care; "Had it been any other general except Jackson, the situation might have been salvaged. But we all know Jackson's odd, and opinionated, and uncompromising—hell, gentlemen, he's crazy."

Davis nodded; "He truly believes he's been 'called' to lead an army of the living vengeful Lord here on earth. Once a man believes that, then he thinks himself above any constraints, be they mine, or Benjamin's."

Benjamin interjected, "Yet it's this very belief that makes him successful, our only general who's been consistent in his victories. The Confederacy cannot afford to lose him."

"Nor can I afford to lose you," Davis insisted.

Gunning mused, "If we hadn't lost Roanoke Island—the generals complained that they begged for ammunition, that the War Department promised it, but it never arrived. It's left such a legacy of ill will in the army—"

Davis' piercing gray eyes held Gunning's for a long moment. "What I'm about to disclose mustn't go beyond this room; Benjamin didn't send any ammunition to Roanoke because we had none. None whatever. Rather than reveal our dire straits to the Federals and risk immediate invasion, Benjamin took the blame on himself. And is still taking it. But if the good people of the South knew the truth—"

"They must not be told," Benjamin interrupted passionately, "we're still in the same predicament. Time enough for the truth to emerge after the war's won. But this doesn't solve our dilemma with General Jackson. If I remain as head of the War Department I'm convinced it will tear our government apart and defeat our greater cause. Therefore, Your Excellency, I've written an apology to Jackson, and I'm submitting my resignation to you."

A stab of pain contorted Davis' face.

Gunning regarded Benjamin with grudging respect; to have kept silent when all the abuse had been heaped on him...He wondered, would I have had that kind of strength?

Benjamin went on, "Your Excellency, do not for a moment think I intend to abandon you or our cause. I'll continue to work with all my heart and soul, wherever you choose to place me, be it in the lowliest of positions."

Davis rose shakily, his thin mouth thinned even further. "You shall work for the Confederacy. With Mr. Hunter's post vacant, I plan to submit your name to the Senate as my new Secretary of State." In the stunned silence that followed he added, "And the Senate will confirm you, this I swear. All that's lacking is your acceptance. Will you accept?"

Benjamin's glowing look said it all.

Gunning couldn't quite roll with this punch; one moment Judah Benjamin faced political oblivion and the next he held the second most powerful post in the Confederacy? He couldn't recall a similar situation in all of American politics, one man serving in three separate offices within the same presidential cabinet? Romance was right, not only had Judah made himself indispensable, he was a born survivor.

Gunning pumped Judah's hand; "Heartiest congratulations," and was surprised to discover that he meant it.

"We're now without a Secretary of War," Davis said.

Benjamin replied, "Your Excellency, may I suggest that you need look no farther than this room?"

In the palpitating silence that followed, Gunning's entire being sang in anticipation, yes! And again yes! At last my life and fortune finally converge, I'll show you what I can do, I'll move mountains—be the best—

Davis hesitated; "Under ordinary circumstances Gunning would certainly be a candidate, but Virginia guards her prerogatives jealously; she demands that her sons have a voice in how the war is conducted. For that reason, George Randolph, who's related to the most powerful families in Virginia, would best serve our overall need. In addition, Brand, I cannot spare you from the very necessary function you now serve."

Gunning clenched his jaws lest his disappointment show. "As you wish sir, as always, I serve at your pleasure."

"I'll hear your report now. Good news, I trust?"

"I wish it were. My agents along the Potomac and Chesapeake Bay confirm our earlier intelligence; an enormous invasion fleet is about to set sail, hundreds of ships carrying an estimated one hundred and twenty-five thousand men. Their destination, Yorktown peninsula."

"Are you absolutely certain?" Benjamin asked.

"As certain as I can be. All our agents report the same thing. Apparently, the Yorktown plan is General McClellan's strategy, he absolutely insisted on it. It's common knowledge that everyone, including Lincoln, defers to him. As far as the army's concerned, McClellan's become a virtual dictator."

Davis limped to a large map on the wall. "His plan has tactical merit. The peninsula is the most direct route to Richmond and McClellan's flank can be protected by Union gunboats on the York River. But that leaves Washington vulnerable to Stonewall Jackson who's operating in the Shenandoah Valley. This may be our opportunity to capture Washington."

Gunning burst that balloon; "Unfortunately, Lincoln's aware of that danger. He agreed to McClellan's plan on one condition, that a strong Union force be left to protect Washington—forty to fifty thousand men."

Gunning stabbed the map; "McClellan's first objective will be the city of Yorktown."

Davis blanched. "We've less than ten thousand men defending it; perhaps a dozen cannon. Facing a force of a hundred and twenty-five thousand? If only the *Merrimac* hadn't been neutralized by that infernal *Monitor*! She'd have wrecked havoc with the Union fleet, stopped the invasion."

Benjamin interposed softly, "Your Excellency, you know this man McClellan, what's your opinion of him?"

"When I served as Secretary of War under President Pierce I sent him to the Crimea to study that war; he values his reputation above all and won't do anything to risk it."

Gunning added, "From his interminable delays, he appears to be a general who'd rather drill than fight, who won't move unless the odds are overwhelmingly in his favor."

Davis stroked his chin whiskers; "But now the odds are overwhelmingly in his favor. If Richmond falls and Virginia loses heart, the Confederacy is lost."

"Your Excellency, what if we use McClellan's flaws to our own advantage?" That caught Davis' attention and Gunning went on, "Plant false information among Pinkerton's spies operating in Richmond, spread the rumor that Yorktown is heavily defended. That might stall McClellan and buy us some time."

Davis considered this, then ordered, "See to it."

They spent another hour going over other theaters of war, including the deteriorating conditions in Tennessee and Kentucky. In New Orleans, a Union fleet commanded by Admiral Farragut was massing to attack the critical port through which the majority of war supplies came into the South. But the men agreed that New Orleans was impregnable; nothing could get past Forts Jackson and St. Phillip guarding the approaches from the sea and nothing that walked could survive the swamps surrounding the city.

When Gunning finally left the White House, a penetrating mizzle had begun to fall. Cold and miserable, but he thought, Let winter linger, we need more time. His mood turned darker. Though Davis had tried to placate him about his value to the Secret Service, he knew that Major William Norris, head of the Signal Bureau, could have assumed his duties; he held that titular position anyway. Gunning Brand, Secretary of War...what a prize that would have been, for himself and for Romance. To have been so close, only to lose out because of family pedigree? It was unconscionable, undemocratic. But then the planter class had never been known for its democratic practices. He felt betrayed, and by the man he'd idolized.

"Enough of this self-pity, you've work to do."

Pinkerton's spies would be loitering in the gambling halls. A staggering invasion fleet with a monstrous army would soon land on the Yorktown peninsula. Richmond was in peril, and with it, the fate of the Confederacy.

Chapter 19

GUNNING'S FEARS about the strength of the Union's invasion force were beggared by reality.

On March 17, McClellan's fleet set sail from Alexandria, steamed down the Potomac into Chesapeake Bay, then landed unopposed at the tip of Yorktown Peninsula. The size of the fleet alone should have made the Rebels sue for peace: 113 steamers, 188 schooners and 88 barges transported 125,000 men, 25,000 animals, 44 gun batteries, and the other multitudinous supplies of war. The largest amphibian assault ever mounted on the continent, Lincoln had given McClellan everything he'd asked for to end the rebellion in one swift, punishing blow.

With his right flank protected by Union gunboats in the York River, McClellan prepared to march up the peninsula, then on to Richmond. But he'd been warned by Pinkerton's spy network operating in Richmond that the Rebels had formidable defenses at Yorktown, so he proceeded at a snail's pace. The delay allowed the Confederate army, commanded by General Joe Johnston, to race south to reinforce the South's paltry troops at Yorktown before McClellan could overrun it.

The Yorktown defensive line, stretching for 12 miles between the York and James Rivers, had been built by Robert E. Lee months before. From years of experience as an army engineer, Lee had realized that Richmond was vulnerable via the peninsula route and had taken these judicious precautions.

By April 5, McClellan's ponderous army had crawled to the outskirts of Yorktown. The next day, a mile from the battle line, Union soldiers stared in amazement at a procession of wagons hauling bizarre machinery never before seen by man or beast. Thaddeus Lowe and his Corps of Aeronauts had arrived.

Lieutenant Forrest Brand rode in the lead wagon. There were four balloons and nine aeronauts to man them. Seven wagons were required to transport the crafts, and additional wagons carried the generators, washers, iron filings and glass carboys of deadly sulfuric acid needed to create the hydrogen gas that would make the balloons airborne.

With the exception of Forrest, all the aeronauts were civilian balloonists who'd worked in carnivals barnstorming all over the country. War had given their profession a serious dimension; Lowe and his men operated as independent civilian contractors attached to McClellan's army, but the support system of drovers, linemen, mechanics and guards were all regular army. As the only officer in that group, Forrest answered to both Lowe and the regular army chain of command.

Forrest nudged Private Timothy Aikens, driving the wagon. A twenty-year-old bible-thumper from Indiana with an asthmatic wheeze, Tim complained about everything, yet got his work done better and faster than anyone in his platoon.

"Our big test is coming up, Tim," Forrest confided eagerly. "If we help McClellan beat the Rebs, there's no reason why we couldn't establish a permanent military Air Corps—a corps like the cavalry, with officers and technicians and balloons, and whatever aircraft we might one day invent."

"Forrest, you're a decent enough guy—for an officer—but just plain locofoco. If God meant Adam to fly would He have given him Eve? I just want to go back to Elkhart and my Emmaline, get hitched, and start begatting right quick."

The Balloon Corps had become a front-line reality with the invention of the portable hydrogen gas generator, a contraption 11 feet long and 5 feet high. Forrest recalled how hard his father had worked with Thaddeus Lowe to perfect it. With President Lincoln's support they'd built the first model at the Washington Navy Yard. When it worked well enough, Lincoln ordered five more portable generators built.

Forrest scouted around and found a running stream, water being an absolute necessity for the production of hydrogen. McClellan had demanded every bit of information about the Rebel fortifications and the aeronauts were eager to prove themselves. The crew worked far into the night to set up the operation. Forrest caught a couple of hours sleep then woke before dawn to find winds gusting with gale force. Thaddeus Lowe refused to sanction a flight, but Forrest volunteered.

"Gotcha brains in your britches goin' up in a gale like this?" Tim grumbled. "Didn't nobody never teach you the army's First Commandment? Thou Shalt Not Volunteer?"

With extreme care, a technician poured a carboy of sulfuric acid into the funnel atop the generator; the acid trickled down onto iron filings distributed on the inner shelves and in some mysterious alchemy turned base metal and acid into the gaseous gold of hydrogen. The gas was fed through a limestone washer and cooler to remove any residue of sulfuric acid and to bring the volatile gas to a safe temperature. Then it was hand-pumped into the envelope of the one-man balloon.

Forrest fretted impatiently as the *Eagle* gradually took shape; 15,000 cubic feet of highly flammable gas—one match, one bullet—Three enlisted men clung to the braided manila ropes tethering the *Eagle* to the ground; the 5000-foot ropes were rigged to pulley blocks used in releasing and hauling in the balloon. The men tried to maintain a triangulation pattern to give the craft greater stability, but the gusting winds were giving them hell.

Forrest yelled, "Hold steady now," and climbed into the wicker basket. Securing his instruments and paraphernalia, compass, telescope, maps, paper, pencils, Forrest took a deep breath and shouted, "Let's fly!"

"You take care up there," Tim called to the rising craft, "and don't piss down on us like you did last time."

As Forrest ascended, he scanned the area. The most dangerous time would come when the craft cleared the tree line and became visible to Rebel gunners. "Like right about now!" he shouted as the whine of enemy bullets flew past. He estimated the nearest Rebel positions to be a mile away, too far for rifle accuracy. Then he saw puffs of smoke in the distance, took them to be cannon fire and ducked inwardly. Rebel gunners had learned to raise their angle of elevation by dropping the rear of the cannon into holes and were ramming their guns with grape and canister. A direct hit on the bag—

Two hundred feet now, the horizon took the lifting light of dawn and the slice of molten rising sun banded the sky with vibrant reds and yellows. Forrest felt a thrill at the base of his spine, the same primal thrill he felt each time he went up. Silence now, only the wind strumming the rigging like a lyre, singing of the ancient legends…singing of the dream that had transfixed man since the dawn of time…in every age, be it that of Ra or Apollo or Icarus, man had turned his eyes to the heavens, and now he, Forrest, was ascending and his entire being vibrated with the wind and the song.

A sea gull startled him with its haunting cry. Mesmerized by its joyous loops about the craft, he yelled, "One day I'll get up enough nerve, cut the ground ropes and soar free, and race you to heaven!"

The morning mists burned off and Forrest snapped from his reverie. "To work." The *Eagle* wasn't equipped with telegraph equipment so he recorded his observations on paper. He swept the area with his binoculars: to his right, the York River, on the left, the James River; Richmond lay at the headwaters of the James, the heart of the rebellion, the rebellious heart that must be ripped from the Confederacy to end the war.

Some Rebel encampments were visible, with knots of soldiers pointing up at the balloon. "For all I know Geary could be down there," and the thought that he might be doing something to harm his cousin made his stomach knot. He sketched the position of all the artillery emplacements he discovered.

Something about the cannon bothered him; some of the gun barrels glinted in the sun, others looked dull. Suddenly, experience and intuition met and mingled in his head—"The dull cannon aren't real, they're wooden dummies!" He felt a growing excitement; this discovery couldn't have been possible without aerial reconnaissance. Yorktown wasn't as strongly defended as they'd been led to believe. With a bold attack, McClellan might break through the thin defenses and sweep on to Richmond.

After hours in the buffeting winds, Forrest signaled that he wanted to come down. The ground crew began the laborious task of hauling in the *Eagle*. Once again Forrest came within range of Confederate guns and bullets and balls hurtled toward him like meteorites. Then he was safe on the ground.

After he'd thawed, Forrest reported his findings to Thaddeus Lowe. Lowe went aloft, corroborated Forrest's observations, then forwarded their report to General McClellan's command post. Two days later, on a mean muddy morning, Forrest received an order to appear before the Supreme Commander of the Army of the Potomac.

"This is it," he told Tim Aikens excitedly, "McClellan realizes the truth now. Why else would he send for me?"

Field headquarters lay five miles to the rear, well out of danger from a Confederate counterattack. Immaculate white tents in precise rows boxed in McClellan's tent, big enough to accommodate a dozen men without crowding. The general traveled with 18 wagons filled with personal possessions, gourmet foods, fine wines, ceremonial uniforms, field beds, cooks, waiters, and whatever else McClellan believed imperative to wage war. An administrator par excellence, McClellan found his true bent in presiding over strategy conferences.

An immaculate aide ordered Forrest to clean his boots on the mudguard. McClellan sat at his campaign desk penning communiqués to the press. He didn't acknowledge Forrest who stood at attention, his sodden trousers and boots forming little puddles. His eyes widened at the table set for the noon meal, fine china, silverware, crystal glasses, decanters of wine opened to let the grape breathe. Savory odors came from a nearby mess tent and Forrest wondered, Where's the war?

McClellan put down his pen and launched into a blistering attack; "I've read your report, Brand, and it troubles me greatly. You claim the Yorktown defense line is thin? That the cannon are wooden? What if it's a ruse to deceive us, and once we've committed our forces, spring the trap? Pinkerton's intelligence reports state emphatically that the Rebels are entrenched at Yorktown with an army far greater than ours."

Forrest shifted from leg to leg, trying to stay sharp under the assault. He responded stiffly, "Sir! Pinkerton's spies are far from the front lines, reporting information that may be inaccurate. The Balloon Corp doesn't have to rely on second-hand information, we can <u>see</u> the enemy's positions."

McClellan drummed his stubby fingers in irritation. "Your name is Brand? Are you related to a Bravo Brand?"

"My father, sir!"

McClellan compressed his lips, his sour expression saying I should have known—another troublemaker. "Your report is inaccurate, you've made a grievous error, admit it."

"With all due respect, sir, I know what I saw."

When Forrest refused to repudiate his report, McClellan curtly dismissed him.

A day later Thaddeus Lowe told Forrest, "Just got a communiqué from McClellan, says he's going with Pinkerton's information. Insists they're much more detailed than anything we've given him, and since Pinkerton's a <u>real</u> detective while we're still wet behind the ears—"

"Our Supreme Commander's got his supreme head up his supreme—" Forrest swore.

Instead of a direct attack, McClellan opted to bring his huge siege guns to Yorktown and pound the Rebels into submission. It took a month to transport the guns up the York River then build platforms so they could be fired with any accuracy. A month during which incessant rain turned the Yorktown Front into a pestilential sinkhole, and left the disease-afflicted Union army totally demoralized. And in that same month, General Johnston moved his army south to reinforce Yorktown, while General Robert E. Lee, called back to Virginia, furiously built a series of defensive lines around Richmond.

The only cheering news for the Union occurred on April 24, when they learned that Admiral Farragut's fleet had fought its way past the supposedly impregnable forts defending New Orleans and captured that vital city. "Know what that means, Tim?" Forrest asked excitedly. "Now the Mississippi's plugged at New Orleans and our blockade can really tighten."

"All I care about is, how soon can I go home and see my Emmaline? I'm hornier than a horned toad."

One night when the men were bedding down, Forrest read a copy of a Washington newspaper that McClellan had ordered to be distributed to all units. Forrest bolted upright.

"Listen to this, Tim," and read aloud from an article; "Isn't it time for Citizen Lincoln to keep his nose out of military matters and allow professionals to wage this war? As General McClellan has told my fellow reporters and me, his strategy is to get as close to Richmond as possible without needlessly sacrificing lives. Once within range, he'll level Richmond with his siege guns. Mr. Lincoln, if you're unhappy because it's taking a bit longer than you planned, then speak to any mother whose son's life may have been saved, listen to any wife whose husband will return home. Finally sir, when will you learn that splitting rails and telling jokes does not a military strategist make?"

"That reporter's got brass balls," Tim declared. "If we had him back in Elkhart he'd be tarred and feathered."

Forrest groaned; "That article wasn't written by a man but by a sweet old lady, who happens to be my grandma."

"Your grandma?" Tim hooted, "you're funnin' me, right?" Forrest shook his head and Tim repeated in awe, "Your grandma? The way she took off after the President of the United States? No offense, but she sure sounds like a pis—a humdinger."

"No offense taken. But she'd dead wrong this time. If McClellan had attacked a month ago we'd be in Richmond by now and the war might be over. He just gave the Rebs a chance to bring up their own forces and dig in."

"Imagine, your grandma? Mine just makes jam and things."

*

At long last McClellan's siege guns were in place. At dawn on May 4, Thaddeus Lowe went up in the *Constitution* and came down with the news that scores of Rebel wagons were on the move, soldiers milling about, more gun batteries visible. McClellan interpreted this to mean that the Rebels were preparing to attack, and reinforced his gun batteries.

Late that same afternoon Forrest ascended. For hours he studied the procession of wagons moving in and out of the encampments. Reinforcing, or retreating? He couldn't tell. Twilight gave way to night; he could see little save

for the activity around the campfires. He trained his telescope, searching for
the truth…then he noticed in the light of the campfires that the wagons going
out appeared to sink deeper into the earth, those that came in, rode higher.

"They're evacuating," Forrest shouted to the night, "packing up, but if we
move fast—" and couldn't get down fast enough to report that the Rebels were
escaping from Yorktown.

But McClellan discounted this, demanding positive proof. Another day
dragged by as he sent in probing patrols; when they met no resistance the truth
finally dawned on the Union brass, but by then the Confederate army had
made good its escape. When the Federals occupied Yorktown they discovered
most of the artillery left behind was of the Quaker variety.

"Did McClellan really believe the Rebs were just going to sit on their butts
and wait for his siege guns to blast them to pieces?" Forrest demanded. "The
minute the guns were in place they just upped and moved out. And what have
we got to show for it? A whole month wasted."

"The army ain't calling McClellan Little Napoleon any more," Tim wheezed,
"now he's The Virginia Creeper."

Like a slug leaving a trail of slime, the Army of the Potomac continued its
slow march toward Richmond. McClellan remained convinced that his strategy was bearing fruit, for General Johnston wouldn't commit his troops to battle but just kept retreating. By the first week in May the Federals had reached
Harrison Landing, twenty miles from Richmond.

"This is it," Forrest told Tim soberly, "time to do or die. Far as I can see,
McClellan's got every advantage. Bigger army, more guns, better equipped. All
he's got to do is keep from making a mistake and this war's over."

Chapter 20

GUNNING BRAND fought his way across Main Street to the Customs House. The streets roiled with wagons and horses and people and hysteria; a dray heaped with furniture broke an axle and spewed its contents across the roadway, to be trampled under the hooves of oncoming horses and wagon wheels. The boom of cannon nine miles away signaled the approach of McClellan's army and Richmonders were fleeing their capital.

Gunning gained the Customs House and bounded up the stairs to Jefferson Davis' office. Clerks scurried about, packing archives bound for Columbia, South Carolina. Most members of the Confederate Congress had already fled, so had Varina Davis, taking the children with her; she'd begged to stay, but Davis had insisted she leave, her presence would only distract him and prevent him from doing his duty.

Gunning heaved for breath; "I've just returned from the field, General Johnston's retreated to Seven Pines and the Federals are in close pursuit. McClellan is moving up one hundred siege guns, unless he's checked, we can expect him to start bombarding Richmond in a few days."

Davis paled but didn't respond and Gunning's control evaporated in the heat of his anger; "Will Johnston never stand and fight? Your Excellency, isn't it time to—?"

Davis cut him short; "Disgusted as I am, I cannot replace him. Johnston is a Virginian, with powerful advocates in Congress, in the press, in the army, and unless we give him his chance we'll be fighting on two fronts, both the Federals and the dissenters in our own ranks."

Gunning threw up his hands. In most cases he'd seen Davis act with an iron will—except when it came to Virginians. With the privileged sons of Old Dominion, he tiptoed on eggs, as if recognizing that he was but a first-generation planter, scrub aristocracy from a minor state, whereas Virginia, with its 200-year history had already produced the greatest men in the nation. Johnston had refused to divulge his military strategy to Davis, claiming there were leaks in the cabinet; the truth was that Johnston was a sloppy thinker and a sloppier soldier and probably had no plan at all. That Davis accepted such gross negligence from his commanding general—wars had been lost for less. Now if I'd been Secretary of War, Gunning thought, I'd have booted Johnston the hell out of there and taken on the Virginians myself.

After giving his report to Davis, Gunning went directly to Romance's where he tried again to persuade her to leave the city. But in some perverse way she seemed energized by the immanent danger. Tonight, she couldn't get him into bed fast enough. Her mouth ranged over his body; "Who knows how much longer any of us have? On the brink of death, one savors life even more. Colors are brighter, the smell of fear stronger, the taste of your body sweeter," and devoured him rapaciously.

He lost himself in some mindless place made up only of sensation when suddenly she raised her head; "McClellan's plan calls for the forty-eight thousand additional troops now defending Washington, to join him in the siege of Richmond."

He sat up abruptly, dislodging her; "How do you know that?" and she replied firmly, "I know, take my word for it."

Her information so matched that sent by his own agents in Washington that he became unnerved. "Romance, I know you go to the gaming halls, been seen mingling with known spies."

She reached for her bejeweled letter opener and pricked his loins; "Have you been spying on me? I cannot, will not stay home alone night after night while you're locked away with your interminable meetings. None of them amount to anything anyway, witness the wolf at our door. Besides, Montgomery always accompanies me, he's quite protective."

"Have a care, with the Yankees this close lots of slaves have run away. Montgomery could be next."

"I think not," she remarked, and with such casual assurance that his skin crawled.

He grasped her wrist; "Romance, for your own safety you must stop, it's far too dangerous. I absolutely forbid—"

She ripped free; "Forbid? I'm not your chattel to be forbidden anything by you. I'll go where I want, do what I—"

He threw her onto the bed and she tried to stab him. He knocked the letter opener from her hand and she sprang for his throat with her teeth. The violence roused them and anger gave way to demanding, breathless sex, lustful, primitive, an affirmation of life to fight off the impending disaster, in Richmond and in themselves.

After they'd exhausted each other and she lay sleeping, he gazed at her. In repose she looked so angelic one might never guess the tormented soul that lived within. He wondered if the Connaught curse had surfaced in her...was she mad? And for continuing to be with her, was he mad as well?

During the next frenzied days Gunning made repeated inspections of Richmond's defenses. Under the forceful supervision of General Robert E. Lee, thousands of slaves had constructed redoubts, artillery emplacements and enfilading entrenchments around the capital. Lee had also pressed soldiers into the labor force and those who resented doing 'nigger's work' derisively labeled him the King of Spades. As impressed as he was with Lee's fortifications, Gunning doubted they could withstand the pounding of one hundred siege guns.

Friday, May 30, at a somber cabinet meeting attended by Lee and Gunning, Davis raised the dreaded question; "If Johnston doesn't act soon and McClellan moves his siege guns into range, Richmond may have to be abandoned. If so, where should our next line of defense be?"

Shock registered on Lee's patrician face; "Give up Richmond? Lose the Tredegar Iron Works and more than half the armaments produced by the Confederacy? That's tantamount to committing suicide." Tears started to his eyes; "Richmond must not be given up, it shall not be given up."

The meeting ended in gloom. But later that day a torrential downpour brought the Confederacy new hope; the Chickahominy River breached its banks, flooded many square miles of that vital area, and divided McClellan's forces.

"This opportunity is heaven-sent," Davis told Gunning as they galloped out to Seven Pines. "If Johnston attacks now, he can outflank the Yankees."

But Johnston was nowhere to be found and Davis declared contemptuously, "I can only conclude that our commanding general still has no idea of what he's doing. If only I could don a uniform, I'd do it this instant, that's how I could best serve our nation."

Their search took them close to the front lines. As they cleared a thicket, Gunning's arm shot skyward, pointing to a balloon hanging in the sky. He trained his telescope on it; "I believe this particular abomination is the *Eagle*. Damnable contraptions, we can't seem to hide anything from them."

Gunning's spotters had reported that other balloons, the *Constitution* and the larger *Intrepid* spelled each other, keeping a 24-hour surveillance on Rebel positions. Studying the craft, Gunning recalled the talk he'd had with Forrest in Alabama. Who'd have thought that within a year his nephew's prophecy would come true with such a vengeance? The South had tried to build its own gas balloons but lacked the technology.

A Rebel sharpshooter took aim at the *Eagle*, but Gunning sprang to him and deflected his rifle. "You're out of range and we don't have ammunition to waste. And you'll give away our position to the aeronaut; I can't have that with His Excellency here." But long after Gunning left the field he mulled his real reason for having stopped the sharpshooter.

The next day, May 31, General Johnston had run out of excuses and finally attacked the Union's position at Fair Oaks. But he'd neglected to share his plan with his field commanders; confusion reigned in the Rebel ranks, men fought in the treacherous Chickahominy swamp until it colored red, and many of the wounded drowned. What should have been a smashing Confederate victory devolved into an inconclusive draw. In the midst of the battle, Fate, acting in the guise of an exploding artillery shell, accomplished what Jeff Davis had been unable to do; Johnston suffered a severe head wound. Davis couldn't have been more solicitous to his injured commander but instantly replaced him with Robert E. Lee.

Gunning confided to Benjamin; "Judah, let's find out the name of that Union gunner and give him a medal. With Johnston out of the way, we may have a chance. But is Bobby Lee the right choice? So far his record's hardly been distinguished. Will he fight? I mean, what about all this trench digging?"

Benjamin rallied to Lee's defense; "Whatever his apparent failures, they were created more by ineluctable circumstances than by him. Having been Secretary of War, I know this for a fact. Believe me, given half a chance the man will astonish."

Whatever doubts Gunning had about Lee evaporated in the energy of his command. Outnumbered and outgunned, Lee knew his army would lose a defensive war and opted for an offensive policy. He devised a series of bold strokes, which involved all elements of the Confederate Army including Stonewall Jackson's 'foot cavalry,' now rampaging around Washington D.C.

On June 12, Lee dispatched Jeb Stuart and his cavalry to determine McClellan's real strength. In a daring foray, Stuart led 1200 men in a sweep around the entire Union Army. For three days Stuart wreaked havoc with the Federals. He returned to Richmond on June 15, laden with a trove of captured supplies and weapons and the information Lee had prayed for.

"McClellan's right flank is weak and with a little luck and a lot of daring it can be turned," Jeb Stuart reported.

The audacity of Stuart's raid embarrassed McClellan to the quick and further convinced him that 200,000 Rebels were defending Richmond. He screamed for reinforcements, demanding that the 48,000 Union troops he'd been promised join him at once. Only to be told by Secretary of War Stanton that they couldn't be spared, they were too busy defending Washington.

Acting on Lee's orders, Stonewall Jackson continued to confound the Union; at all costs, he was to keep Lincoln from reinforcing McClellan. Though outnumbered three to one, Jack-son routed three separate Union armies and chased them all the way back to the Potomac. Washington braced for an attack. But Jackson, implementing the next phase of Lee's daring plan, stole away one night, turned south and marched to join Lee.

Gunning knew that his son Geary was fighting in Stonewall Jackson's army, and beset with an uneasy premonition, tried to locate him whenever he went into the field. To no avail.

Gunning wasn't an easy man to impress but on June 26, he witnessed the military genius of Robert E. Lee. With the trenches and redoubts he'd constructed around Richmond completed, Lee was able to protect the capital with a small force of 10,000. With the rest of his army, a scant 50,000, he struck McClellan hard at Fair Oaks. The Federals outnumbered Lee two to one, but Lee mauled them.

On June 27, with Stonewall Jackson's forces now joined with him, but barely effective because of fatigue, Lee struck at Gaines Mill; on the 29th, Savage's Station; on the 30th, Frayser's Farm and White Oak Swamp; and on July 1, Malvern Hill. For several days the battle for Richmond raged, for seven horrendous days blood flowed. Casualties on both sides were staggering, 15,000 in all, but in the end Lee's smaller force had savaged McClellan's numerically superior army.

Gunning was convinced that if not for the Union's balloon corps, McClellan's army would have been destroyed. But the aeronauts, with their bird's eye view of the battlefield, provided invaluable information about Lee's tactical position, enabling McClellan to retreat with some degree of order.

Outmaneuvered and outfought, on July 2, McClellan bleated that the Republicans in Washington were responsible for his debacle. He was forced to withdraw to the safety of Harrison's Landing where he could be protected by Union gunboats.

Lee had decisively broken the siege of Richmond.

*

Throughout July, both armies licked their wounds and regrouped. McClellan had written to many northern newspapers extolling the brilliance of his retreat. But the judgements against him were harsh. Many Republicans now believed that McClellan was a traitor to the Union. How else to explain why the Peninsula Campaign, which had been his strategy alone, and which he'd touted with such fanfare, had devolved into such an ignominious failure?

Rumors began to abound that McClellan, a Democrat, had never intended to wage an all out war against the Confederacy. He wanted a negotiated settlement, for such a settlement would insure that the South returned to the Union—with slavery. Everyone would save face and in the next presidential election, McClellan, viewed as a hero by both sides, would be invincible against any candidate.

For his 'brilliant retreat', Lincoln placed McClellan under the direct supervision of General Halleck. Halleck ordered McClellan to withdraw from the peninsula; McClellan objected vehemently, withdrawal was tantamount to admitting his error, but Halleck insisted for General Lee was no pussyfooting Joe Johnston and after several weeks respite, Lee had now gone on the offensive. Forget Richmond, Halleck ordered, the entire Army of the Potomac was now needed to protect Washington.

For Lee had started a drive to invade Maryland and bring that state into the Confederacy. "Washington, thus surrounded by hostile states, must surely fall of its own weight," Lee told his staff, sending a thrill through them all, but none more profoundly than Gunning. In the boldness of his military genius, Lee had not only lifted the siege of Richmond, but had changed the entire nature of the war.

Chapter 21

IN EARLY AUGUST, General John Pope was rushed in from the Western Theater to counter Lee's invasion. Pope intercepted Stonewall Jackson at Manassas and on August 30, a terrible battle was fought in the same area as the first battle of Manassas. Ambulance wagons groaning with wounded began to roll from the killing fields back to Washington.

A horrified Rebel Thorne wrote, "At the First Battle of Manassas in July, 1861, North and South were appalled at the 5,000 lives lost. Now, 14 months later, both sides have perfected such techniques of slaughter that more than five times that number are listed as wounded, missing or dead. My Fellow Americans have we all gone mad? We're killing our brothers!"

Stunned Washingtonians lined the avenues watching the endless cortege of ambulances slowly moving toward their assigned destination in one of the city's forty hospitals. Johnny Reb and Billy Yank lay side by side, the lucky ones in wards, others in corridors. In the sharply divided city and sharply divided hearts, the battle between the States was put aside, there was no North and South, just wounded Americans, desperate and dying.

Even as the wounded streamed into Washington, citizens heard the faint booming of cannon as Stonewall Jackson, following up his victory at Second Manassas, continued to drive the demoralized Federals back. He was now attacking Chantilly, a scant twenty miles west of the capital. Union reinforcements were rushed to the ring of fortresses protecting Washington and every inch of ground was contested.

*

Kate and Sharon Brand were at Rebecca's house, rolling bandages when they heard a knock on the door. "Bittersweet, will you get that?" Rebecca called. She leaned toward Sharon and Kate; "Remember how she hated to answer the door? She was always so terrified it might be some slave bounty hunter, come to drag her back to Mississippi. Thank God that's all over."

Several months before, on April 16, 1862, Congress had passed a bill that ended slavery in the District of Columbia. At long last, Bittersweet was safe from bounty hunters—providing she remained in the capital.

Rebecca pursed her lips knowingly; "A few weeks ago Bravo let slip that Lincoln's planning to do something even more drastic about the slaves, this time in the entire country."

"Free them, maybe?" Sharon offered.

"Not very likely, that would be political suicide. He'd lose the Democrats, the Border States—and the war."

Bittersweet brought in a bedraggled soldier. "This here soldier-boy says he's looking for Miz Kate Brand."

Kate rose, her high coloring paling with apprehension; "I'm Kate Brand. Something's wrong, I know it."

The private, an affable young man of medium height and weight, doffed his cap. "Name's Private Sam Stockwell, I was helping out with the wounded—got a message for you. Went to your house, ma'am, they said you might be here." The broad 'a' of his accent marked him as a New Englander; Boston, probably.

Kate crossed herself; "It's my son, isn't it? Merciful Jesus, don't tell me something's happened to Peter?"

Stockwell blinked; "Peter? This is about a Reb name of Geary? Geary Brand. Wounded at Manassas. He asked if I'd get a message to you, let you know he was here."

Kate swayed and collapsed onto the settee.

"How badly is he hurt?" Rebecca demanded. Stockwell's noncommittal shrug cut across her heart. "Do you know where they've taken him?"

"Dropped that batch at the Main Navy Yard Hospital. Got to go, I'm due back with my unit."

Rebecca took his hand; "Bless you for telling us, young man. Will you come back and see us soon?"

Sam Stockwell's hopeful, covetous brown eyes lingered on Sharon; "That would be my great pleasure."

Soon as he'd gone Bittersweet grumbled, "Don't trust that Yankee no how. I think he's the one followed us that day at Willard's Hotel? 'N why'd you ax him back? Mark my words, he be a spy, and you writin' all that meanness 'bout Lincoln—"

Rebecca clutched her temples; "Are you crazed? He came out of the good-
ness of his heart. Now hitch up the shay."

Rebecca, Kate and Sharon drove, as fast as Old Glue would take them, to the
Navy Yard Hospital in southeast Washington. At the confluence of the Potomac
and Anacostia Rivers the waterfront hummed with activity, arms and munitions being offloaded from ships onto supply wagons, other ships sailing to
join the blockade of southern ports. The rutted roads were heartbreaking
reminders of the ambulance traffic; many hospitals had sprung up here
because the wounded could be transported from the Virginia battlefields down
river to the Sixth Street docks.

After a long despairing search they finally found Geary. He was lying in the
hospital corridor in a semi-coma, a gray pallor over his boyish features. He'd
been shot in the abdomen and Rebecca didn't have to be a doctor to know he
was gravely wounded. After a bit Geary opened his eyes, blinked, and smiled
weakly when he recognized them.

"How are you, my darling boy?" Kate murmured.

"A mite beat up, Ma, but you should've seen the other guy." His attempt to
act with his usual quirky humor was made all the more poignant by intermit-
tent spasms of pain. "Hi, Grandma, well, here I am again, causing you all nothing but grief. How'd you know where to find me?"

"That nice private you spoke to told us," Sharon said.

A puzzled look crossed his face; "Don't remember any private, only thing I
do recall is being questioned by some brass buttons I took to be intelligence
officers. Asked me where I lived, and like a dunce I told them, not realizing it
might get you all in trouble, me being a Reb and all."

Rebecca grimaced at the corridor, crowded with wounded men, the specter
of death in the air. She took Kate aside; "If we don't get him out of this pestilential place and into a clean bed—" Kate nodded and Rebecca went on, "I'll
see if I can't get some help right now and we'll move him."

Rebecca hurried off to see the surgeon on duty and when she told him she
wanted to take her grandson home, he gaped at her. "Madam, have you lost
your mind? He's a prisoner, there is no way on God's earth that he's going to be
released." Nothing she could say or do could budge him, and as she left she
heard him mutter, "The only good Rebel is a dead Rebel."

Shaken, she returned to Kate and Sharon. "We'll have to care for Geary here,
at least until I can speak to someone in the government. Bravo can help—
damn! He's gone into the field. Why is he never here when I need him? Well,
my girls, it's time for the Brand women to roll up their sleeves."

While Rebecca made the rounds of legislators' offices, Kate, Sharon and
Bittersweet divided the day into shifts so that Geary was never alone. Bittersweet

brought hampers of food that he liked, and oh their joy when he managed to eat something. Soon the women were lending a hand with other patients and the overworked hospital staff was grateful.

Late one night while Rebecca was standing watch, Geary suddenly became lucid; "Grandma, know who's winning this war?"

"Who, child?"

"The lice. They're getting their fill of blood. War's a crazy business, you need crazies to run it and there's none crazier than old Stonewall Jackson. Sucks on lemons all the time. Doesn't use pepper because he says it makes his left leg ache. Won't sit because it throws his organs out of balance. Religious as a saint, but what a genius for killing. He truly believes he's been called to command God's army on earth, fighting for the right. The South's right. Lord, the excuses we make to get around 'Thou Shalt Not Kill.'"

"You shouldn't be talking," Rebecca soothed.

"It helps to talk, keeps my mind occupied. How that man drove us, forced marches, thirty miles a day, until everybody called us Jackson's 'foot cavalry.' But the men worshipped him; I confess I got caught up in the madness too because we kept winning. You know he used to be a schoolteacher? He'd lecture us as if we'd all grow up to be generals; 'Always mystify, always mislead and surprise the enemy…never fight against heavy odds if you can hurl your own force on only a part of your enemy and crush it. A small army may thus destroy a large one, and repeated victory will make it invincible.' And that's what we did, every single time. End of June, we took on that cockadoodle do, McClellan, at Richmond and pulled his tail feathers for seven days. Did I tell you that's when I saw Forrest?"

Rebecca clutched her heart; "You saw him? In the flesh?"

"Almost as good. In a balloon, floating lazy like on the clouds. I tried to scare up a telescope but nobody had one. But I knew it was him. He followed me everywhere, Seven Pines, Savage's Station, Gaines Mill, I'd jump up and down waving my arms and yelling like mad, Hi coz!"

He motioned for water and Rebecca held the glass to his lips. "After we drove McClellan from Richmond, Bobby Lee decided to invade Maryland. That's when Old Abe sent west for his next big-mouth, General John Pope."

"Geary, please, you can hardly catch your breath."

He pressed on, fever burning bright in his eyes. "Pope announced, 'From now on my headquarters will be in the saddle.' Funny, we thought that's where his hindquarters should be. Just couldn't keep his mouth shut for the bragging."

"I read his communiqués," Rebecca said, "they were about as idiotic as McClellan's, and speaking of that pompous windbag, I surely was taken in by him—to my everlasting shame."

"Stonewall made out like he was real scared of Pope, but then we tore up his rail lines, looted his supply depot at Manassas Junction, then slipped away. It took Pope two days to find us. By then we'd dug in on Stony Ridge, overlooking the same battlefield where we'd whipped the Yankees the year before. Pope, thinking he had us trapped, attacked.

"But we held; when ammunition ran low we hurled rocks down at the charging Union troops. If Bobby Lee orders you to hold, you hold. Stonewall must've sucked a bushel of lemons that day. Seeing we had nothing but rocks, Pope was convinced we'd cut and run, and announced to reporters that he'd pursue us relentlessly until he'd bagged the whole lot, General Lee and all. 'May God have mercy on Lee, for I shall have none.' But then Bobby Lee sprang his trap, and sent the other wing of our army, five divisions strong, storming into the Union flank along a two-mile front. Pope had a nervous breakdown, so did his army. Now Lee's going after Maryland, that state's just itching to secede and if they do then Washington falls and the war's over. And here I thought I was fighting on the side of the losers?" With a satisfied grin, Geary drifted off.

Having failed to get any help from her friends in Congress, Rebecca decided she had no choice but to go directly to President Lincoln. But he was unavailable, for Lee had slashed through every Union force thrown against him and was fighting his way deep into Maryland. Lee seemed invincible.

Then, in one of the unaccountable vagaries of war, as Lee was overrunning Maryland, two Union soldiers accidentally discovered his battle plans; they'd been wrapped around some cigars, which had been discarded by one of Lee's couriers. With this foreknowledge, McClellan was able to counter Lee's moves. On September 17, with his vastly superior army, McClellan intercepted Lee at Antietam and fought him to a stalemate. More than 26,000 casualties on both sides made Antietam the bloodiest single day of the war.

Lee couldn't afford such devastating casualties and withdrew to Virginia. Washington was saved. For the moment.

Chapter 22

IN THE midst of the Union's celebration over Lee's defeat at Antietam, a political bombshell exploded that threw the capital into violent turmoil and further prevented Rebecca from getting any help for Geary. For months she'd heard rumors that Lincoln was planning something momentous and was only waiting for some decisive victory to make it public. On September 22, Lincoln acted; it proved to be more stunning than anything that she, or the nation, could have imagined.

"This is the most outrageous, hypocritical—pure snake oil—who in the world does Mr. Lincoln think he's fooling?" Rebecca cried, rattling the newspaper at Bittersweet.

"Hallelujah, Lincoln g'wan free the slaves!"

"This Emancipation Proclamation frees the slaves—but only in the <u>South</u>. However, Lincoln doesn't control those territories, so what good does it do? If he's so altruistic, why doesn't he free the slaves everywhere?"

Bittersweet regarded her mistress in genuine distress; "Then you ain't for this here 'Mancipation Proclamation?"

"I'm certainly not for all the grief it's causing, riots in the streets, fistfights in Congress." Then she added grudgingly, "I suppose it does elevate the cause of this damnable war. It sounds a whole lot more humane than Jeff Davis' brittle abstractions about States' Rights. Well, in a few months we'll see what happens; the Emancipation Proclamation becomes law on January 1, 1863. I just wonder if our wily President is motivated by a genuine sense of humanity or if this is just another shrewd ploy by a canny politician."

Rebecca had little time to dwell on it, for Geary's condition worsened. Desperate to see Lincoln, she petitioned his secretary, John Nicolay for an appointment. Nicolay seemed surprised to see her, for Mary Todd had made her dislike for Rebecca quite public. He checked his appointment book. "The President's in conference all day today. Saturday he won't be at the White House at all. The casualties at Bull Run and Antietam were staggering and he's obsessed with this notion that he must visit every hospital in Washington. What about Sunday afternoon?"

"Yes, thank you, yes." Armed with that hopeful news Rebecca went back to the hospital. She discovered that Geary had been moved to a ward; as the wounded died, beds became available. She found Sharon sitting at his bedside holding his hand as if to keep him from slipping away as he slept.

"He gets weaker by the day and I don't know what to do." Sharon watched two orderlies heft a body onto a stretcher and carry it out. She shuddered; "It goes on all day. First they lay them on top of the bed, then they pin their socks together so the orderlies will know which ones to take. Oh, Grandma—"

Rebecca gripped her shoulders; "It is terrible, but hysteria won't help us. Go home, get some rest. I'll stay here until your mother comes. Do as I say, I need you strong, go."

Recognizing the tone, Sharon did as she was told. Rebecca took up the vigil, watching Geary drift in and out of consciousness. Once, he bolted upright, crying weakly, "Forrest?" He pointed at the gaslight globe in the ceiling. "There he is, up in that balloon. Forrest, it's me, Geary."

Rebecca felt her body go numb. Then Geary blinked his fevered eyes, "Grandma? Been meaning to ask you…can't tell Herself, she wouldn't understand. One of these days some fair lass—or two—may come to your door carrying a sprout with a mop of curly brown curls? Mind you, take a good look, you'll know by the curls…then might I ask you to be kind to them?"

"You listen to me, Geary Geary Brand, if you think you're going to shirk your responsibility that easily—I want you up and working to support all your curly kin."

"One last thing, I don't have much in the way of possessions, never believed in them, the more you got the more you worry, but I want Forrest to have my gold pocket watch." At her quizzical look he shrugged, "I know I don't own one, but if I did, I'd want him to have it." He settled back, closed his eyes then opened them; "Almost forgot, I do hereby bequeath all my slaves to Harriet Beecher Stowe."

Rebecca's burst of laughter sounded so out of place in the sad and barren ward that she immediately shut up. "Geary, would it be any comfort if you…?"

"A priest?" he finished. "Why would I do that, seeing as how they scare me half to death anyway? Herself has been after me to confess, but I'd be an old man by the time I finished. Whenever it is I'm called, I'll go as I've lived, believing that no man needs another to intercede for him. God knows my sins, but He also knows where my heart is."

At that moment she was overwhelmed with a rush of love for him, and the melancholy knowledge that throughout his life she and Gunning and Kate had given him such short shrift. She leaned forward to tell him, but he'd lapsed back into his secret hiding place where there was no pain.

She had a sudden image of this imp running madly around her drawing room shouting over and over, "My name is Geary Geary Brand, I'm the only one who has two last names for two first names," then breaking into peals of enchanted laughter as she tickled him into submission. When she stopped, he caught his breath, then said, "Again."

"I'll make it up to you," she whispered. "Only live, and I'll prove how much you're loved."

She became aware of a boy across the ward staring at her. He couldn't have been more than sixteen, with peach fuzz on his cheeks and the saddest expression in his enormous china blue eyes. When he continued to stare at her she crossed to his bedside and asked, "Can I get you anything?"

His voice sounded even younger than he looked; "I'd be obliged if I could have a drink of water, ma'am, but the doctor won't allow it, not even a swallow. Some Yank got me in the gut with one of them Minie balls? Doc claims that if he squints he can see clear through me to tomorrow. Says if I drink, the water will run out for sure."

"I know a little trick," she confided, "one that can't possibly hurt you." She got a tumbler of water, dipped her handkerchief in it and gently swabbed the boy's lips.

He licked the droplets eagerly, moistening his parched mouth. After a bit he looked under his blanket; "Nothing's run out either. You his kin?" he asked, indicating Geary. Rebecca nodded and he sighed, "He's might lucky to have his folks around him. Wish I could see mine, my Ma especially. Don't rightly know why but I miss her something fierce."

"Then you must write and tell her."

"Would if I could but where we live in the Smokies, ain't a school nigh for fifty miles. Never did learn my letters."

"Tell you what, you dictate it to me and I'll write it."

"Why that's right neighborly of you." His brow creased in concentration, "Can't think of what to say."

"Why not tell her what every mother yearns to hear, that you miss her. And that you love her."

The china blue eyes grew brighter. "All right. Dear Ma, I miss you. I love you. Your son, Johnny." He propped himself on an elbow, looked in wonder at the note, made a large X after his name, then lay back down. "Thank you kindly, ma'am."

The effort exhausted him and soon he fell into a fitful sleep. He's dying, Rebecca thought, the way so many were, simply because there were too many wounded and not enough doctors to tend them.

Kate arrived an hour later and kept the watch all through Friday night; Sharon relieved her Saturday morning. Saturday afternoon Rebecca returned to the hospital. "How is he?" she whispered to Sharon.

She rubbed her eyes, red-rimmed from weeping. "No better. If only we could get him out of here!"

Rebecca put her hand on Geary's forehead and felt the slow fever burning the life from him. "Geary? Look what I got you." She dangled an elegant gold watch on a long gold chain. She'd gone to Galt's Jewelers on Pennsylvania and Eleventh St. and bought the finest pocket watch they had.

His eyes widened as he watched the sunlight glinting off it. "Thanks, Grandma. Would you hold it for me?"

"I will, but only until you're up and about. Tomorrow I see the President. I just know he's going to let us take you home. And you'll get well." But he'd slipped away again.

"Speaking of Lincoln," Sharon said, "we keep hearing rumors that he's visiting every hospital in Washington."

"John Nicolay did mention something like that."

"The entire staff, the patients, even the Rebs, are very excited that he might come here. You've never seen such tidying up. An orderly told me Lincoln started out early this morning at Georgetown University Hospital way out in the western part of town and he's working his way east."

Is he coming to gloat over his handiwork or is he just driven by guilt? Rebecca wondered. After Sharon left, Rebecca sat by Geary's bedside, watching the last rays of the autumn sun lance through the windows; sometimes it would touch the bed of a wounded man, then move inexorably on, leaving it in shadow. The sounds of the ward became muted as she slipped into a reverie where the ghosts of her past, Jeremy, Zebulon, Suzannah, beckoned her to join them in their dance macabre, while the spirits of the living entreated her to remain.

After a time she became aware of a growing bustle in the ward, a nervous hum that prized her into awareness.

She saw him then, the President of the United States, all six foot four of him towering over the bedside of Johnny X. He spoke briefly to the Confederate youth with the china blue eyes, then moved on. Many of the men in this ward were Rebels but the President acknowledged every one of them.

Then he stood before Rebecca, his probing eyes searching hers. "Mr. President, I am Rebecca—"

"I remember you well, Rebel Thorne," his words had a mock sternness, but how his eyes twinkled when she blushed.

In a rush, she explained that she had an appointment to see him tomorrow, but since he was here, might she—his nod gave her leave to speak and she hurried on, detailing the desperate need to get Geary out of the hospital.

"But he's a prisoner, isn't he?" Lincoln asked.

"I give you my solemn word that as soon as we've nursed him back to health I'll bring him to any prison you name."

Lincoln shook his head slowly; "I cannot go against the regulations of my Secretary of War, why Stanton would put me in the dock." His weary smile indicated he was only half-joking. "And you yourself, writing as Rebel Thorne, have given Stanton so much ammunition."

Rebecca plunged on, "Mr. President, may I remind you that Rebel Thorne has never spoken out against the Union, I am now, and always will be for Union. If I've seemed unduly harsh—it's only about certain policies of your administration—surely in a democracy every citizen has a right to dissent."

"Unfortunately, rules change in time of war. Devotion and loyalty can be more constructive to the cause."

"My son Bravo is on your staff. Is there anyone more loyal than he? And though I agree with you about loyalty and devotion, I believe there are qualities even greater than these. Compassion, mercy, forgiveness."

Unbidden tears rolled from her eyes. Taut with embarrassment, President Lincoln handed her his handkerchief. She rushed on, knowing that if she lost this moment, Geary's life was forfeit. But how treacherous the path she had to tread, for this was a man of iron determination and nothing had yet moved him from his vision of a united nation.

"Mr. President, I know that in your own house, there are divided loyalties."

He stiffened; it was common knowledge that four of Mary Todd's brothers, and innumerable other family members were fighting for the South; that Achilles heel had hobbled Lincoln, particularly with the more vitriolic members of his cabinet. He started to move away but she clutched his hand between hers.

"If the situation were reversed and this poor lad lying here was your flesh and blood, wouldn't you plead for his life even though he was a Confederate? Is life itself not more important than sectional affiliation? Your proclamation frees the slaves, a merciful and humane act, but won't you extend that same mercy to a fellow American? Can we ever be reconciled without that quality of mercy which you've so eloquently stated reflects the better angels of our nature?"

In quoting from his own speeches, in effect asking, Were those merely the words of a politician or do you truly believe them? Rebecca had opened the tiniest path to his conscience.

She saw his mind work, saw the delicate balance tremble and sway as she repeated, "The better angels of our nature…"

He cleared his throat; "I'll talk to the surgeon in charge. But this must remain our secret."

Unable to speak, she nodded her thanks and through swimming eyes watched the tall gaunt figure leave. She bent over her grandson, her entire being singing in elation; "Did you hear that, Geary? You'll be going home, just as soon as Kate gets here and we can make the arrangements."

She dried her eyes, then noticed Johnny X beckoning weakly to her. His gaze was so wounded she could barely stand his pain. "What is it, child?"

He gulped; "I want so bad to pray, I know my Ma would like it…she taught us our prayers, but I don't exactly know which one?" A thought lit his eyes; "Strikes me that a Presi-dent should know that kind of thing. Could I see him again?"

"He's already left." He looked so crestfallen that she said, "Let me see if I can catch him."

She hurried through the corridor to the entrance and saw Lincoln leaving. "Mr. President?"

He turned and shook his head; "Not another prisoner?"

She laughed aloud; deny it as she might, the man had the one ingredient essential for every successful politician, a sense of humor. "Mr. President, the young boy you spoke to, the Confederate lad who's dying—he so very much wants to see you again. I think it would mean a great deal to him."

He nodded, then escorted her through the ward to Johnny X's bedside. "What can I do for you, my boy?"

Johnny X gazed up at him; "You seem so far away, like on a hilltop…I'm so lonely, sir, and 'ceptin' for this lady, without friends here. I used to pray every night but I don't know which one is right for now, and I was hoping that you might tell me what my Ma would want me to say."

"Yes, my boy," Lincoln murmured, and knelt beside the lad whose life was ebbing even as they spoke. "I know exactly what your mother would want you to say and do. And I'm glad that you sent for me to come back. Now as I kneel here, please repeat these words after me."

Lincoln kneeled and cradled the boy in his arms, the lad's innocent eyes opened wide. The last rays of the dying sun transfixed and transformed them as the lad and the President of the United States prayed together.

> "Now I lay me down to sleep,
> I pray the Lord my soul to keep,
> If I should die before I wake,
> I pray the Lord my soul to take…"

The boy closed his eyes, a beatific smile on his face, and through her tears, Rebecca saw the haunted face of the President, lined and weary and bearing the suffering of the divided nation.

"They are all our sons," he whispered, "North and South alike, all my sons." Then bowed and weighted, he left.

The moment Kate arrived, Rebecca told her the news; Kate fell into her arms, her embrace more eloquent than words. They hurried downstairs to see the assistant surgeon. With his authority countermanded by Lincoln, he'd become even more obnoxious and surly. Yes, the President had talked to him, he said, but there were forms to fill out—

They fretted over the interminable delay, but finally the paperwork was done and the surgeon accompanied them upstairs.

Geary was lying on the top of the bed, hands folded across his chest. "Why is he uncovered?" Kate cried, her voice rising hysterically. "Why are his socks pinned together? Why?"

The assistant surgeon glanced at an orderly who nodded soberly. The surgeon chortled; "Of course you can take him home, ladies, I have no objection. He's a good Rebel now."

PART THREE

PART THREE

Chapter 23

THOUGH KATE BRAND was devastated by her son's death she bore it far better than Rebecca, for Kate had her all-encompassing faith to sustain her; special masses, church morning and night, helped fill the terrible void. Rebecca had no such crutch; all she'd feared that long ago day in the cemetery had come to pass, this insane immoral war against fellow Americans had claimed one of her blood. Nor could she overcome the preternatural feeling that more disaster lay ahead.

Aware of his mother's need during this punishing time, Bravo came to see her whenever he could. Bittersweet told him, "Hardly eats at all, she's grieving herself to death."

Rebecca's first questions always concerned Forrest, and though Bravo had scant news about his son he tried to reassure her. "He's fine, Ma, he's in winter camp at Falmouth."

She wrung her hands; "But Falmouth's less than ten miles from Fredericksburg where Bobby Lee's army is entrenched."

"Ma, I hear you've been pretty short with Kate; go easy, she's suffering too, you know."

"I suppose I'm so foul-tempered with Kate because I really envy her," Rebecca confessed. "How much easier life would be if I had her faith. How much easier death would be if I could believe in an afterlife."

"I thought you had long-standing reservations up there?"

"No need to be facetious, you'll face this mystery yourself some day. What makes us believe that the Lord involves himself in our daily affairs? First off,

He'd find it much too boring. And if we are His creations, shouldn't we be able to solve these trials—which we've created ourselves—by ourselves? I'm so confused, so desperate to believe in anything—please don't think I've lost my mind, but I've recently met this young spiritualist in Georgetown? Nettie Colburn is her name, and I've been to one of her seances."

Surprise lit Bravo's face; "What an odd coincidence, I've just had a nasty encounter with a medium, Charles Colchester."

"Really? I've met Charlie; he's quite dashing and very popular in certain social circles, and especially with the Bitch. She's the one who sponsored him in Washington."

Bravo's eyebrows shot up; "Veronique Connaught?"

"Is there another bitch in my life? But you, a scientist involved with a medium? Is the world coming to an end?"

"My intent was to prove Colchester a fraud." He paced the room, his mind working. "Veronique and Colchester? So that's how the miserable cheat found out the personal details about Mary Todd and President Lincoln."

"What in the world are you talking about?"

Thinking it might take his mother's mind off her grief, Bravo began; "There's a wave of spiritualism sweeping the country. It seems to happen in times of great trial. People can't cope and become involved in irrational things like dreams, astrology, palmistry, seances. Well, some six months after Willie Lincoln died, the Lincolns were staying at Soldier's Home for the summer and Mary Todd, egged on by Veronique, begged Colchester to conduct a seance. She was desperate to contact her little Willie, make sure he was all right. Apparently, Colchester was brilliant and amid tinkling bells and bumping tables, he received several messages from Willie, telling 'Maw' not to fret about him and 'Paw' not to work so hard. Since the Lincoln boys called their parents Maw and Paw—well, you can imagine Mary Todd's bliss."

"So Veronique was feeding Charlie Colchester those intimate details?" Rebecca noted. "But for what end?"

"Who knows? Power, to gain control over Mary Todd, and thus influence Lincoln? Colchester held several more seances, but even though Lincoln's given to dreams and premonitions, he isn't naïve and finally asked me and Dr. Henry—"

"Joe Henry? How is Joe? Is he still the superintendent of the Smithsonian?"

Bravo nodded. "We held a private seance at Dr. Henry's office. We suspected that the eerie sounds coming from different parts of the room were caused by Colchester, but damned if we could find out how the devious bastard was doing it. We told Lincoln our suspicions, and he warned Mary Todd but she refused to believe it. Until the second incident, a seance attended by myself and Noah Brooks, who's a friend of Lincoln's. Brooks caught Colchester red-handed."

"My nerves! How was Charlie doing it?"

"Colchester had strapped an instrument around his upper arm, it allowed him to produce tappings by flexing his biceps even while his hands are being held by others. Confronted, Colchester tried to blackmail Mary Todd. Lincoln gave him an ultimatum, leave Washington or be thrown in prison. You'd think that would be enough for Mary Todd, but she was desperate to believe that there might be other mediums who could contact Willie. Enter your Nettie Colburn. Mary Todd discovered Nettie through Congressman Soames and being an elected official, presumably his motives are above suspicion."

Rebecca interrupted, "That's how I met Nettie, Soames and his wife are very active in things occult. But Nettie's nothing like Colchester, she's a sweet little girl in her teens and she actually believes in the spirit world."

"Nettie was in Washington on a visit and we hoped she'd go back to White Plains, New York, but Mary Todd got her a job at the Department of the Interior—to keep her here. Mary Todd wanted Nettie to conduct a séance at the White House immediately, but she consulted her guides on 'the other side' and they've all concluded the best time for a seance would be April twenty-third, two months from now."

Rebecca put forward tentatively, "Who'll be there?"

"So far, the Lincolns, Soames and his wife, Nettie Colburn, myself, and Mary Todd insisted that Veronique and Sean Connaught be there. Why, Ma, do you want to go?"

"Me and the Connaughts holding hands at the same table? I'd sooner send them to the Great Beyond. The first question I'd ask the spirits is when is this damnable war going to end? Tell me the truth, Bravo, not a politician's truth, or a medium's, but the real truth. How much longer?"

His shrug had a hint of despair. "Lee's proving what we knew all along, that he's a military genius. McClellan's no match for him; after they fought to a stalemate at Antietam, which surprised everyone including McClellan, Lincoln ordered him to pursue Lee and crush him. McClellan had overwhelming manpower and weaponry. Lee crossed the Potomac and got back to Virginia in one night; it took McClellan four weeks to accomplish the same thing. That wasted time allowed Lee to regroup and entrench his army at Fredricksburg."

"And Forrest is ten miles from there? Good Lord."

"Lincoln was so disgusted, he removed McClellan from command. McClellan's mad as a rabid dog and he's consolidating his political base in the Democratic Party. He swears that his destiny is to become President and save the country."

"Thank God we won't have to confront an election for another two years, and, please God, by then this war will surely be over. Does Lincoln really intend to carry out his Emancipation Proclamation? Or is it just a political ploy? You know how crazed the planter class is on the question of slavery. He may just harden the South's resolve to fight on."

"He told me he made a vow to God that if we were victorious at Antietam, he'd free the slaves. His original intent may have been politically motivated—to deprive the South of manpower—but that's long gone, he feels that if ever he's judged by history, it will be for this one act."

"Judged and cursed, I imagine." She handed him a smuggled copy of *The Richmond Examiner*; "Read the editorial."

The editorial labeled the proclamation, "The most stupid, heinous act ever committed by one civilized government against another; the North's nefarious purpose is clear at last: Not Union but Abolition. Deprive the South of her wealth, black flesh and white gold, and bring her under the control of Northern capitalists. To prevent slaves from escaping, President Jefferson Davis is forced to continue his earlier edict that those who own twenty or more slaves are exempt from military service. This has created deep dissention among our gallant soldiers who grumble that our struggle for freedom has now become a 'Rich man's war, poor man's fight.'"

Bravo threw the paper down in disgust.

Rebecca said, "There's also an article in the paper that claims France, England and Russia offered to arbitrate a settlement between North and South. Is that true?"

"Jefferson Davis told London that the South was amenable to mediation, with the proviso that there be two separate nations. But Lincoln refused; the Union <u>had</u> to be preserved."

"But is the country behind Lincoln now? In last November's election the Republicans lost so many seats—every day more people are calling call for peace at any price."

"Lincoln will never give up the Union, never."

"What a curious contradiction the man is. Though I detest certain of his policies, like suspending the Writ of Habeas Corpus, I don't feel the same animosity I once did. At the hospital, he acted with such compassion, for Yankee and Rebel alike. Can it be that after years of mediocrity we've finally got a man of conviction living in the White House?"

"I believe that, I hope one day you'll believe it also."

"Bravo, how can we let Gunning know about Geary?"

"I'm trying through official channels. But remember, Ma, Secretary of War Stanton's made it a capital offense to have any contact with the South. He's furious that we can't keep Confederate spies from infiltrating the capital." He rattled the Richmond newspaper; "Getting caught with this could land you in jail."

After Bravo left, Rebecca tried once more to write to Gunning; no matter what the consequences she had to risk it. She began by describing Geary's last days, the angelic way that Kate, Sharon and Bittersweet had behaved, and concluded with, "So I grieve for you, dear Gunning. Our last meeting, so fraught with anger, seems so unimportant when gauged against Geary's passing. Someone wonderful slipped from our lives, I didn't realize how wonderful until he was gone, and I weep for every harsh word I ever said to him. To have been taken from us when his song had not yet been sung, and what a beautiful song it was, had we but listened.

"Who else will to make us laugh in that same madcap way? Who else will infuriate us with his will-of-the-wisp manner, when all the while we were really angry because we envied him his freedom? He had the gift of love, and used it to bring love into the lives he touched. My dear sweet Geary Geary Brand. I'll light a candle for the repose of his soul, and one for your safety, Gunning, for though I've often been unable to express it, I do love you, my dear son. I embrace you, I wish I could be there to comfort you. Ma."

Chapter 24

FROM HIS vantage point two thousand feet in the air, Forrest Brand scanned the terrain; the winter camp of the Federal army, 135,000 strong, spread for miles around the town of Falmouth. The camp was a scant mile from Fredericksburg where Robert E. Lee had built his line of defense.

A gust of fierce March wind buffeted the *Eagle* and Forrest rolled with it; storm coming, black clouds racing in from the west, as bleak as his mood and he thought, got to finish my work fast or get caught in the storm. He trained his telescope on the Union army's advance posts near the Rappahannock River; across the river lay an impenetrable terrain called The Wilderness.

Though both armies had gone into hibernation and snow lay on the ground, the Federals had become so wary of Lee that the balloon corps had been ordered to keep constant tabs on him. General Joe Hooker had taken command of the Union army; 'Fighting Joe' was no bumbling equivocator like McClellan and he'd brought new energy and spirit to the Army. At the first sign of decent weather, Hooker planned to mount an offensive and sweep Lee from Fredericksburg. Once that was accomplished, the road to Richmond and victory lay open.

A blast of wind moaned through the rigging, seeming to sound a dirge…Forrest's hand moved reflexively to his breast pocket where a letter from his grandmother had lain these past weeks. Written back in November, it had only recently reached him. Work, the harder the better, was the only way he could keep his mind off Geary's death. He had flashes when he wanted to kill every slave owner for starting this war, and other moments when he just wanted to run away to clean places like the sea…or the sky. Here, unseen, he could allow his tears to wash away some of his grief.

He was so preoccupied, he didn't noticed the frantic tugging on the guy ropes. Minutes later the storm hit, snapping him from his reverie. Hail the size of filberts tore at him and battered the gas envelope. The crew tried to haul him down but the wind increased, swinging the craft in wild, erratic arcs. He'd have to help his crew, release some gas in the envelope, and fast, before the *Eagle* was torn apart.

He struggled to open the gas valve. Frozen solid. A gust shot the *Eagle* skyward and Forrest heard a rope snap. Now only two guy lines tethered him to the ground—unless he acted the other lines would break—he'd be swept away.

He tied a rope around his waist, secured the other end to the gondola, then clambered into the rigging to get at the valve from above. Again and again he hammered at the valve, feeling his strength ebbing in the icy blasts, while the *Eagle* careened crazily through the roiling sky. He shouted, "I'll never get it open, got to break the valve off!"

With a desperate blow he bludgeoned the valve off and the gas escaped with a suspiring sigh. The *Eagle* slowly enfolded on itself and without its buoyant bulk the ground crew was able to haul it down. Even then it took them more than fifteen minutes to moor it and by that time Forrest had lost consciousness from the cold.

"Get him inside fast, or we'll lose him," Tim Aikens shouted to the crew. They carried Forrest into the crude wooden shack they'd built to ride out the winter. A simple room, ten foot square, pallets ranged around the walls, the bare planking covered with risqué posters of scantily clad women. The men had built a low stone hearth in the room's center, and barrels with their ends knocked out and stacked on top of each other, acted as chimney and flue.

Tim stripped Forrest down to his long johns, and then two men carried Forrest to the fire and held his arms around the barrel chimney, pressing the front of his body against it. In moments he started awake, thrashing; "I'm burning up!"

Tim clucked, "Can't have that, I already wrote my sisters all about ya, what a manly specimen you are? How'd it look if I brought you home with fried pecker?"

The crew jumped to attention as their new commander, Captain Cyrus Ballou Comstock, entered. In early March, Comstock, a West Pointer with a reputation as a stickler for regulations, had been put in charge of the corps. Thaddeus Lowe and the other aeronauts, though still employed as civilian contractors, no longer had a free hand but answered directly to Comstock.

Lowe, a man of soaring ego, found this galling and pouted, sometimes even refusing to fly.

Comstock declared, "I've just received word from General Hooker, we're expecting important visitors tomorrow."

"Lincoln?" Tim whispered, "'cepting he just visited."

Comstock ordered that every tent, shack and latrine be policed. As they worked, the men took bets on who might be visiting; they ranged from the King of Siam, who'd offered to supply Lincoln with war elephants, to Queen Victoria.

After a meager dinner of salt pork, cornbread and coffee, the men lay about, guzzling their contraband moonshine. "Can you believe how lucky we are?" Tim asked. "We get this sumptuous meal, including mystery guests, and the grand sum of thirteen dollars a month? That comes to, lessee, 'bout forty cents a day. Is it any wonder so many men are deserting?"

Forrest groaned; "Not that again. When this war's over don't you want to brag to Emmaline and your dozen kids that you won it single-handed? Instead of being a miserable little coward who got shot for deserting?"

Tim smacked him on the rump. "Forrest, m'boy, you'd best go get your ashes hauled, 'ccount of you're getting' meaner 'n cat's meat. The washer-women over to Hooker's headquarters only charge two bits—and they wash your underwear to boot. Hooker's got so many girls there, the men are callin' 'em Hooker's whores. Go plank one of them hookers, maybe it'll make ya human again?"

The jaunty twang of a harmonica began, followed by a banjo backed by the rhythm of two clacking spoons. The soldiers bellowed, "Yankee Doodle," and "Pop Goes the Weasel" then proceeded to serious patriotic fare like "John Brown's Body." Tim claimed he'd read that some lady had written new lyrics to that tune, she called it, "The Battle Hymn of the Republic," but he hadn't learned those words yet. The camp fires burned low, a young lad, his haunting tenor mellow with Irish accents, led them in "All Quiet on the Potomac Tonight," and ended with "Home Sweet Home."

Taps sounded, the fires were banked, Forrest burrowed under his blanket and whispered, "G'night, Geary, rest easy," and hurt so badly he drew in his breath a few times.

"Forrest, that you cryin'?" Tim murmured. "Felt like a good cry myself when we sang "Home Sweet Home"….Who'd ya think is coming to visit tomorrow?"

"Don't know and don't care, now go to sleep, damn it."

Forrest fell into a deep reverie where he and Geary played tag through cerulean skies, higher, higher, their laughter twining as from one throat, ever higher until Geary suddenly flew off in a burst of speed into the blackest night.

Ten o'clock the next morning, Captain Comstock ordered all platoons to fall in for inspection. Forrest and his crew stood at attention in front of the deflated *Eagle*. Tim jerked his head toward the inspection team moving slowly down the line toward them. "Who are them dillies? No uniform I ever seen before, looks like a foreign circus to me."

Forrest could hear sonorous French phrases punctuated by clipped British accents and guessed that the officers might be from the French and British embassies in Washington. The delegation stopped in front of Forrest's unit. There was something familiar about the ramrod-stiff man muffled in his greatcoat, but it wasn't until he spoke in his precise, authoritarian voice that Forrest recognized Sean Connaught.

Sean Connaught stopped in front of Forrest, his crisp tone sounded like an order; "I'm told that you're something of an authority on these observation craft? Be good enough to explain the workings of the balloon and generator."

Forrest glanced at Captain Comstock—surely he wouldn't want him to reveal any vital information—

"Proceed, Lieutenant Brand," Comstock ordered, "these men have clearance from Secretary of War Stanton; he wants them to see just how powerful the Union is—lest they make the foolhardy mistake of recognizing the Confederacy."

Having been raised with a profound mistrust of all the Connaughts, Forrest gave the group a simplified explanation of operations. But Sean's pointed questions revealed that he had a fair knowledge of the discipline. When Forrest finished, Sean said to Comstock; "These delegates have come all the way from Europe, they're most anxious for a flight demonstration."

"Sorry, sir," Forrest said, "but the *Eagle* isn't operational. We lost our gas valve yesterday. It's impossible to make an ascent without it."

Sean sighed with world-weary annoyance; "My dear friend Stanton assured me, as did General Hooker, that we'd receive full cooperation. Now I discover that Thaddeus Lowe's left the field and is sulking in Washington, that a craft is supposedly inoperative—Captain Comstock, can nothing be done? I assure you, it's of the utmost diplomatic urgency."

"What about it, Lieutenant Brand?" Comstock asked.

"Even if I had parts for the valve, it would take several days to get the system operational."

"Perfect," Sean exclaimed, "we'll be inspecting these winter quarters until week's end. I'll see if I can't persuade General Hooker to be on hand."

Comstock said, "Mr. Connaught, rest assured, we'll have the *Eagle* in work-ing order by the end of the week."

"Let's hope so." What passed for a smile thinned Sean's thin lips, then he and the delegation continued down the line.

When the men were dismissed, Tim piped, "Jeez, what a nasty piece of work that Connaught is. Acts like he's got a poker up his pokey. Bet he doesn't even know Stanton. But he sure acted like he knew you."

"Yeah, we know each other. Our families have been at each other's throats for years. My Uncle Gunning was once married to his mother. It was annulled. Now my uncle's living with Sean Connaught's sister—"

Tim slapped his leg; "I swear, I never met a body who could make up tall stories like you. First there was that fib about your grandma, and now this? Best wait till I'm a little drunk, I'm sure I'll understand it much better. But that doesn't mean you're going up in this foul weather?"

"You bet I am," Forrest answered grimly. "No way a Connaught is ever going to get the best of a Brand."

They worked for days, and by week's end Forrest had gerried a valve that worked well enough to risk an ascent. He made one last check; "It's as good as we're gonna get it. When Sean Connaught gets here, I'm going to take that pompous bastard up—bet you a silver dollar he wets his pants."

Then Forrest sensed something wrong. He felt the reverberations in the ground first, heard the nervous nickering of the horses in the corral, then saw a covey of grouse flush from a stand of trees, followed hard upon by the gray-coated riders breaking from the forest and charging straight toward them, sabers flashing in the fading twilight.

It all crowded in on Forrest simultaneously, Jeb Stuart's cavalry—they'd captured or killed the Union pickets—the camp was wide open—good God, the generator and the *Eagle*!

He drew his Colt and got off two fast shots to alert the camp as the Rebs thundered closer. The Federals ran from their tents only to find their stacked arms trampled and scattered by wave after wave of horsemen—at least two hundred—coming from every direction, slashing tents, their piercing Rebel yell straight from hell as sword and bullet ripped through Yankee flesh.

Forrest whirled as a Reb rider charged down at him; he fired his Colt—missed. Only three bullets left. Blood splashed irrelevant patterns in the snow, the smell of gunpowder and fear, tents being fired, the whinny of stampeding horses, the curses of the wounded, the screams of the dying assaulted Forrest as he raced across the clearing toward the wagons that held the generator and the *Eagle*.

A dozen supply wagons had already been captured by the Rebels and had disappeared into the safety of the forest. But the flatbeds holding the balloon equipment required a two-horse team; several Confederate cavalrymen had already hitched up the *Eagle*'s wagon to a team of horses they'd brought with them and were turning the prize toward the distant line of trees when Forrest leapt onto the wagon.

He punched a cavalryman off the flatbed, then fought the driver for the reins. The wagon lurched across the meadow, Reb riders galloped alongside the careening cargo, trying to get a clear shot at Forrest without killing their own man.

Behind them, Forrest's crew had realized what was happening and was giving chase.

Forrest yanked back hard on the reins—Got to slow the wagon down—the *Eagle* mustn't be captured—with General Lee's vastly superior knowledge of the terrain, he could use the observation craft with devastating effect. The Union could lose its edge.

The driver punched Forrest's head and face. Three bullets left—shoot one of the horses and the whole team will go down—He scrambled to free his revolver from his holster, took aim and missed when the flat of a saber caught him on the side of the head and pitched him forward.

He fell onto the wagon tongue, his head ringing with the blow and the thundering sound of the horses' hooves just inches from his head. The ground sped by beneath him while the driver gee and hawed the team trying to shake him off.

Forrest hooked his legs and one arm around the wagon tongue. With his free hand, he held his Colt against the wooden tongue and fired. For an instant he thought he'd missed, then the tie-bar shattered, the flatbed tore itself from the traces, the horses galloped free, yanking the Rebel driver to his death. The flatbed gradually bumped to a halt. Bruised and battered, Forrest dropped to the ground.

Within moments, Forrest's men had galloped up and after a fierce saber fight, they drove off the remnants of the Confederate cavalry.

When they got back to their camp they found the site wrecked. More than a score dead, at least fifty wounded, a herd of horses and two dozen supply wagons captured.

That night, Forrest and his crew, in hushed and sober tones relived what had happened. Forrest chewed his lip; "Don't you guys think it's weird that the Reb cavalry knew exactly where the *Eagle* and the generator were? They went right to them, even brought their own teams of horses to cart them off. So they must have known. Their spy system has got to be awesome."

Chapter 25

GUNNING BRAND slammed the report down on his desk. "Damn and double damn! Almost had it."

Jeb Stuart's raid on the Union camp at Falmouth had captured a wealth of supply wagons, scores of horses, and hundreds of rifles. But the principal reason for the raid had eluded them, capturing one of the Union's infernal balloons.

The intelligence Gunning had received via Sean Connaught had been uncannily accurate. Sean had implied that more information of this nature would be forthcoming, and the South needed every bit of help it could get, even if it was from as slippery a source as that poisonous bastard.

Gunning put the report in his desk drawer, as he did he saw the letter from his mother. He'd gotten it several weeks before and the news of Geary's death had devastated him. The only thing that brought the slightest relief was throwing himself into work, or losing himself in Romance's arms. Why death should have intensified his need for sex he couldn't understand, but it had—much to Romance's amusement.

He'd tried to get the news to Becky but quarantine in the city had prevented it. Smallpox had raged in Richmond since the first of the year; over 500 cases had been diagnosed and there'd been 100 deaths. The citizenry had been banned from visiting any hospital lest they bring the scourge to the vulnerable patients, and hospital staff was forbidden from coming into town. The city had instituted free vaccinations and a major health catastrophe had been avoided.

By the third week in March no new cases had been reported. With the ban on visiting lifted, Gunning saddled Baal and rode to Chimborazo.

The first day of spring was hidden in a numbing blizzard; snowflakes big as silver dollars continued to fall, adding to the nine inches on the ground and the Chimborazo complex was barely visible. Construction on the final compliment of its 105 wards had been completed—not a moment too soon—every bed was filled. Gunning tried to see through the swirling storm. How long, oh lord? We're consigning the best of our youth to the grave, what will our country be made of save the halt and the blind, the indigent and the aged?

He found Becky in her quarters, her coat wrapped tightly around her. Firewood had become so expensive that she burned it only when absolutely necessary. Her face lit when he entered and Gunning felt warmed by her genuine joy in seeing him. Lest he lose heart, he plunged right in; "I'm afraid I've some bad news."

"Carleton," she blurted, half-rising from her chair.

He handed her Rebecca's letter. After she'd read it they sat silently, their tears growing cold on their cheeks. "We see so much death I didn't think I had any tears left," Becky sighed, "but when it's your own family...I can't imagine never seeing him again," and broke down once more.

Gunning sat with her a bit longer, comforting her. Finally he rose to leave. "One last thing, trouble is brewing in Richmond. People are starving, threatening to storm the granaries, there's no telling what will happen, I've warned Dr. McCaw to double the guard out here. Be careful."

*

Twelve days later, on Thursday morning, April 2, Jefferson Davis convened an emergency cabinet meeting at the Custom's House. "I've just received some catastrophic news. General Lee's collapsed at his winter quarters."

Exclamations of shock were followed by anxious questions.

Davis went on, "Lee's been suffering from exhaustion; he lives a Spartan existence in the field just a cut above the ordinary soldier. Hard enough for a younger man, but Lee is fifty-three. He came down with a severe throat infection that settled into an inflammation of the pericardium, the membranous sac that encloses the heart. If he recovers, and I emphasize if, the doctors say it will be at least two weeks before he's out of bed and another two weeks before he can take command. Until then our spring offensive is on hold."

A pall fell over the room. With his stunning victories over a phalanx of Union generals, the gentle, brilliant Virginian had become even more popular than Stonewall Jackson and the South looked to him to gain her independence.

After an hour of indecisive talk, the meeting broke up. At Davis' request, when the others left, Gunning and Judah Benjamin remained in the office. Davis glanced out the window to Main Street, the snow had melted, buds were visible on the trees. "Lee planned to go on the offensive at the first sign of good weather, catch the Federals off guard. Now our opportunity is gone," and began recapitulating what he'd already said a dozen times, driving Gunning up the wall.

Davis' tendency to repeat himself had grown more pronounced as the South's fortunes waned. A series of defeats in the West, particularly Grant's assault on Vicksburg, had begun to fragment the Confederate government. Once hailed as the South's savior, Davis had now become its scapegoat and was being pilloried everywhere. He reacted by tending to lose sight of the overall picture, burying himself in excruciating details better left to clerks. The work was crushing him, further undermining his fragile health; thin to emaciation, Gunning feared that at any moment Davis might also collapse.

Exasperated, Gunning interrupted, "Sir, we're faced with a groundswell of anger in Richmond. The complaint is that the common man goes hungry while our warehouses are full of food."

Davis near-shouted, "Don't they understand that we must keep those stores in reserve for our army?"

"Difficult to tell that to a mother with a hungry child, especially when Lee himself complains that his troops aren't getting enough to eat."

Davis' eyes welled with compassion; "Never in the history of the world have there been such monsters as rule in Washington. They deprive us of medicines for our wounded, food for our starving, they make war on women and children. But they shall not prevail. If we have to fight until there is not one Southerner left standing, they shall not prevail!"

With Richmond's population swollen to 100,000 with soldiers, wounded, refugees, prisoners, prostitutes and spies, inflation had become so rampant that even the privileged suffered, while the poor were literally starving to death. Judah Benjamin observed, "It takes five times more money for a Southerner to live now in 1863 than it did in 1860."

"But a few shrewd operators are making millions from war profiteering," Gunning spat, "and our Congress does nothing to stop it. I lay the blame for every ailment that afflicts us squarely at the feet of Congress. Every one of them deserves to be shot for treason. They play at governing in the Capitol, loving the sound of their own voices, gorging on peanuts and swilling bourbon, every legislator protecting his own fiefdom while our sons go without shoes, without guns, without ammunition, without everything necessary to fight a war—except their own courage."

Benjamin quickly agreed; he and Davis both realized that Gunning's despair stemmed from his son's death and treated him gently, tolerating his outbursts.

"Something bold must be done, something that will take our destiny out of the hands of Congress and win the war," Gunning insisted. "Your Excellency, as we've discussed in the past, I propose that you dissolve Congress, and for the duration of the war declare a military dictatorship."

Davis squared his shoulders; "My answer is the same now as it was then. The Confederacy has always operated from the strictest code of honor, I accepted the Presidency on that basis, I'll do nothing to betray that trust."

Benjamin spoke up, "Even if His Excellency did declare a dictatorship, what's to prevent the Southern states that objected to such a move, from seceding from our Confederacy? Our own Vice President Stephens, and Robert Toombs, and Governor Brown of Georgia are panting for just such an excuse; they'd break away in a shot, and the entire game would be up."

"We're caught on the horns of a dilemma," Davis said. "To conduct a war, a strong central government is absolutely necessary; yet that undermines our doctrine of States' Rights. I urged Congress to establish a Supreme Court to arbitrate our legal problems? But the states refused to give up their individual powers. North Carolina hoards ninety thousand uniforms in her warehouses while our soldiers fight in rags. Georgia commissions men into her own militia so they can avoid serving in the Confederate army. If we fail, the epitaph on our gravestone should read, 'Died of a Theory.'"

Gunning rubbed his temples, vaguely recalling that his mother had argued this all along, that the very nature of this rebellion, that each state remains autonomous, made it a political and practical impossibility. Damn it, he thought, I wish she wasn't so right all the time.

An anxious rapping on the door interrupted; John Jones, the fifty-year-old clerk of the War Department, stuck his balding head in and exclaimed breathlessly, "Your Excellency, there's a riot in the city. Mayor Mayo's declared a state of emergency and Governor Letcher's mobilizing the militia!"

Davis grabbed his pistol, equivocation vanishing in an instant as the soldier took command. "How many rioters?"

"Hundreds. Perhaps thousands. And growing."

Davis dashed out with Gunning right behind him. They ran along Main Street, leaving Judah Benjamin far behind. A captain of the militia ran alongside them and told them what had happened. "A group of women met at the Belvidere Baptist Church on Oregon Hill. They begged the government for food. They marched to Capitol Square and by mid-morning, several hundred women had gathered. Groups of men joined them until there were more than a thousand. A pistol-wielding Amazon named Minerva Meredith and her crony, Mary Jackson, incited the crowd to riot."

"We know those trouble makers," Gunning panted, "we believe they're in the employ of Federal agents—there they are!" he cried, as they turned onto Cary Street.

All along Richmond's market hub, the mob milled about in front of locked food shops, chanting, "Bread, give us bread." "Our children starve while the rich roll in wealth."

Some of the mob looked disreputable, others were ordinary citizens, housewives and workers, many carried knives, clubs, and some brandished hatchets and axes. A flying wedge of women attacked the stores of the worst speculators; these places were heavily guarded but they were no match for the ravening crowd who fell on them like locusts and stripped them bare. Drays and carts were stolen and loaded with flour, corn meal and slabs of meat, while famished people crammed food into their mouths. The rioters, swirling about in a feeding frenzy, broke into other stores and looted them.

The city's fire brigade galloped up, and with hoses hooked to the horse-drawn tanks, battered the crowd with powerful streams of water. Gunning hustled Davis into a doorway, shielding him. The drenched crowd fled from street to street, drawing more people until the mob had quadrupled.

Davis declared grimly, "Unless it's checked, we'll have a full-fledged insurrection on our hands."

Confronted by a company of militia that Governor Letcher had called out, the mob doubled back to Capitol Square where they stood their ground, defiant, shouting for food and always the insistent chant, "Rich man's war, poor man's fight!"

As Davis and Gunning approached, some emboldened youths threw crusts of bread at them. Gunning growled, "Give this mob a few more minutes and it'll be rocks, then bullets."

Davis jumped up on a cart, one of a jumble that the mob had thrown together as a barricade. He held up his arms for silence and his commanding presence quieted the crowd. Gunning peered about anxiously; anyone in the mob might be aiming a gun at the President.

"My friends, my fellow citizens," Davis began, "no one is more sick at heart at your plight than I am. I'll gladly share my last loaf of bread with those in actual need." He turned out his pockets and threw coins at the crowd, who grabbed for them. "But I remind you that many of you have stolen jewelry and finery as well as food. Such criminal acts cannot, and will not, be condoned."

"Food! My baby is starving!" came a plaintive cry.

Davis pointed his finger at the woman; "Such unlawful acts as you've committed, looting, and rioting, may actually bring more famine down on our heads, for country people and shop owners will hesitate to bring food into a city ruled by a mob. I urge you, return to your homes so the soldiers now ranged against you may be sent against our common enemy. I trust all you patriots to bear our current privations with fortitude and remain united against the Northern invaders, who are the authors of all our sufferings."

Cowed by Davis' fearlessness, the crowd quieted somewhat and Gunning breathed a bit easier. He saw Minerva Meredith towering over everyone, a stiff white feather rampant in her battered hat. A man next to her raised his arm and sunlight glinted off the blade of a butcher's cleaver.

Davis saw it also, and his voice rang out, as he called to the militia, "Make ready!" Rifles were aimed and cocked. Davis' gunmetal eyes hardened; "My friends, I will give you five minutes to disperse. If at the expiration of that time you remain here, I will order this command to fire on you."

He took out his watch and held it up so all could see. He continued to survey the crowd, staring directly into any eye he could catch. After a time he looked at his watch again; "My friends you have one minute more."

Gunning, hand on his revolver, caught himself holding his breath, overwhelmed by Davis' bravery. Some of the crowd started backing away, others began to run. When Davis put his watch back in his vest pocket, the crowd had dispersed.

Later that day, Gunning circulated a report claiming that the 'Bread Riot', as it was now called, had been instigated by northern spies and agitators. But the truth was that the war profiteers had the fear of a mob-driven God drummed into them and dropped their prices. The cost of flour, coffee and butter plummeted; best of all, beef returned to a $1 a pound.

Though the city returned to a semblance of normalcy, a persistent fear grew in Gunning: unless conditions improved, rebellion could erupt again. Not only did they have to contend with the Federals poised to begin their spring offensive—and Lee bedridden! Not only did they have to keep fractious Southern states in line, now an enemy lurked within the ranks of their own starving people. Only the iron will of Jefferson Davis held the Confederacy together. If anything happened to him...

Gunning's worst fears were realized that evening when Davis was felled with an attack of facial neuralgia so severe, his physician warned that it might attack his good eye and leave him totally blind. Gunning wondered, How long could the Confederacy last with a bedridden Robert E. Lee, and a blind President?

Chapter 26

THE BREAD RIOT sent shudders throughout Richmond and its environs. At Chimborazo the guard was doubled again, lest starving citizens take it into their heads to raid their facilities. The situation gradually quieted but the bitter memory of the insurrection remained.

After an especially depressing day in Surgery, Becky and Dr. Grange were cleaning up when she said, "We've almost no chloroform or quinine left. What are we going to do?"

Dr. Grange let out a long low sigh. "Uncle Gunning said he had a shipment being smuggled in from a new source, but it hasn't arrived yet."

With the memory of a patient who'd just died in agony, Becky lost her head. "Why won't Lincoln lift the embargo? At least on medical supplies? It's inhuman! We wouldn't treat any other wounded enemy that way, why fellow Americans?"

She began to tremble and he held her close. "We'll do the best we can. We're discovering new remedies every day; green persimmon juice is working as a styptic, we're experimenting with wild cherry to replace digitalis, and hemlock helps dull pain. We're asking every one in Richmond to plant poppies this spring…" He lifted her chin, "All right now?"

She nodded. After a moment she said, "I'm going into town to see Uncle Gunning. He's trying to act bravely about Geary's death—but—he shouldn't be alone. Will you come?"

"I can't, I've—Becky, there's something I've been meaning to tell you but didn't have the guts—"

"You're leaving Chimborazo. Going into the field." She said it without thinking, without knowing what she was saying.

He stared at her in dumb amazement. "How did you know?"

"I didn't, it just came to me. But why are you leaving?"

"I'm convinced that we could save many more lives if we treated the wounded sooner. By the time they get to us they are so weak from loss of blood, the trauma of travel—men treated in the field have a much higher rate of survival. So I asked Dr. McCaw to release me from duty here, and the Surgeon General's put me in command of a field hospital."

The room, the moment disappeared…Becky stood in a wind-swept void, hearing Dr. Grange's voice, but also hearing deeper truths, truths that seized her in their grip and wouldn't let go. "I've got to go with you—"

"That's impossible. I'm assigned to Lee's army and we'll be in the thick of battle. A woman—"

She cut him short, "I read in one of the newspapers that Clara Barton is serving with the Union army in the field. You remember her; she was Uncle Bravo's friend when they both worked at the Patent Office? Then she became an independent contract nurse. Are you telling me I'm not as good as some Yankee from Massachusetts?"

"You're the best nurse here, but Clara Barton's a fortyish spinster, you're a beautiful young woman. Surrounded by all those lonely men with only one thing on their minds? I'd worry myself sick. I wouldn't be able to do my job."

"No need to worry about me, I loved only one man and since that's not possible I no longer think of men that way." Her shoes left footprints of blood as she paced the room; "How can I make you understand? Just as I knew you were going into the field, so I absolutely knew I had to go with you. When I was young, I'd get these premonitions, most times they involved my twin brother, Zeb, but sometimes things just came to me. I haven't had a feeling this strong since the day my Mama…" She broke off.

"Becky, premonitions or no, it's just not possible."

The set of his jaw, his stern tone warned her not to pursue it. Instead she asked, "When do you leave?"

"With Lee's illness, everything's on hold. However, he's getting better, so hopefully, in another two or three weeks."

She put on a bright face. "I know you'll be wonderful."

They parted, and she thought, and so will I be wonderful. For in the next two weeks she intended to wear him down until he found a place for her in his field unit. If he didn't, she'd follow him anyway, that's how overwhelming her premonition had been. She struggled to divine the reason, but couldn't. She'd just have to let Fate unravel its skein.

Still bemused by her experience, she rode the two miles to Uncle Gunning's house. Her uncle had always looked a decade younger than his real age, but it was no longer true. His hair, shot through with gray, had only a vestige of its leonine tawniness; deep lines scored his cheeks and he had the haunted look of a parent who'd lost a child, but somehow hoped to find him again.

After a spate of reminiscences and commiseration Gunning got to his feet. "The best way to honor Geary is to win this war, that way his death will have some meaning."

Knowing how Geary had really felt—that North and South were both crazy, Becky remained silent.

"We've got to show the best possible face to the world, laugh and be merry, that's how Geary would have wanted it. Tonight, I'm exercising an uncle's prerogative; I'm taking you to a starvation party at the Memmingers'. Our Secretary of the Treasury rarely entertains, he's a tight-fisted Teutonic cuss so a starvation party suits him just fine."

"I shouldn't—what about Romance? Our last encounter—"

"Romance and I had a small—contretemps, as she calls it. She's otherwise occupied tonight." His lips parted in his delightful off-center grin; "So when I appear this evening with a lovely young lady on my arm and claim that she's my niece, this time I won't be lying."

His eyes, so wounded, begged her to go and she didn't have the heart to refuse him. The Memmingers had rented the Valentine mansion on Clay and 11th Street; built in 1812 in the neo-classical style, Becky thought the residence every bit as grand as the White House of the Confederacy. A strapping stable hand with shackled feet took their horses.

"Evening, Montgomery," Gunning greeted him offhandedly. He told Becky as they entered the house, "That's Romance's house-boy, she rents him out by the day and with the shortage of manpower makes a pretty penny on him."

Becky thought the slave a fine-looking young man, but couldn't shake off an uneasy feeling about him; his deferential manner couldn't quite mask the smoldering resentment in his eyes, and the continual clink of his leg chains sounded a ghostly knell in the night.

"Curious," Gunning mused, "I was in Alabama when Sean Connaught bought that buck; now to find him here, serving Romance…sometimes I wonder at the twists and turns of fate. Can it only be coincidence? I keep thinking, if only Geary had let me get him a commission, maybe he'd still be alive? If only I'd paid more attention when he was growing up—my whole life seems to be made of 'if onlys.'"

Becky pressed his arm; "Didn't he come looking for you in Richmond? He risked prison—even his life—to find you. That's how much he loved you. You must take comfort in that."

He nodded absently; "That I do. These past weeks I've thought of little else but my boy. That's what Romance and I fought about, she complained that I was becoming too morbid."

Becky didn't answer, furious with this self-centered wretch who couldn't bear to have any attention taken from her, even if it was for mourning.

In the Memminger's salon, determined merriment reigned, news of Lee's recuperation an undeniable tonic; reports had it that he'd felt well enough to ride his horse, Traveler. The guests congregated around the Sheraton sideboard, picking at the radishes, carrots and turnips; the more substantial food brought by the guests had long since disappeared.

Gunning excused himself to talk to Memminger. Becky felt a bit more comfortable at this gathering. Even though she looked slightly moth-eaten in her shabby blue dress, so did everybody else. Very little was getting through the blockade and every bit of cloth was going into the war effort.

Becky felt a strong arm circle her waist, felt a tall rigid body behind her, and the murmured, "Hello, Becky."

She turned to face a man who looked like Carleton Connaught, yet somehow was not.

Chapter 27

CARLETON'S FACE had hardened, his eyes, once so innocent had turned inward. He moved woodenly and his hands were callused where they'd gripped rein and sword…she shuddered with the thought that his soul had died.

Yet all she'd so carefully buried deep within herself, hidden from the world these many months, came flooding back. Why then could she only mouth polite platitudes when all she wanted to do was scream, I love you!

He gripped her hand; "Let's leave. We've no time for a starvation party, you and I have been starving for too long."

"I can't, I'm with my—"

Carleton nodded in Gunning's direction; "I don't think he'll miss you." He and Romance were deep in conversation and oblivious to anyone else. "If the truth be known, we've been used, so they wouldn't have to confront this party alone. They had a fight but Romance was praying that he'd be here, she told me so. Becky, the last time we met I got trapped in my sister's agenda, let's not make that mistake again."

He led her out the door. When Montgomery brought their horses, Becky told the slave, "I noticed that your ankles were rubbed raw. Cut the bark off some slippery elm, rub it on the sores and on the insides of the leg irons, it may help."

"You do that for yo' slaves?" he asked.

"I don't own slaves, I've never owned any," she answered, feeling oddly relieved that she could say this.

As they rode off Carleton asked, "What do you think of Romance and Gunning? In the beginning I was against it. But they do seem well-matched, and that's a first for Romance." He saw her start and asked, "Are you shocked at the way I talk about her? Remember, my mother is French, my father English, both highly sophisticated people. We were taught to confront the truth about the sexes. Though I was always uncomfortable about it. My concern is that there doesn't seem to be any future for Romance. Your uncle's married to a Catholic with no hope of a divorce, even if he wanted one."

"Maybe Romance doesn't want a future?" she offered. "In these times, living day to day may be all one can hope for."

He shook his head vehemently; "I don't believe that. Hope for a future was the only thing that kept me going."

So many vital questions churned in Becky, but she heard herself mouth the inane and obvious; "Are you on leave?"

"Jeb Stuart's orders, he says I'm wound too tight. My last chance before the spring campaign starts."

"How long do you have?"

"A week. I arrived this afternoon. Went straight to Chimborazo; your cousin, Dr. Grange, told me you'd gone to see Gunning, I stopped off at Romance's; you know the rest."

Her heart leapt when he said he'd gone to Chimborazo first. "You look thinner, a bit sad. How are you really?"

"Thinner, a bit sad," he chuckled. "But as good as can be expected after wading in blood for two years. I took a bullet in the shoulder, my left arm's not much use."

They rode aimlessly, allowing their horses to wander, their eager questions interrupted by the melancholy warble of a whippoorwill and the lunatic laugh of a loon. Soon they'd exhausted every topic except the most pressing one. He reached for her bridle and drew her horse toward him.

"What now for us?" he murmured. "Will we go on as we were, unable to break free of this crazed St. Vitus dance we're in? Becky, when you first told me what happened in Texas, I thought you the bravest, most wonderful woman in the world. I felt unworthy, felt I had to prove myself to you. That was one of the reasons I enlisted. Since then I've killed so many men, I try not to think of how many."

She started to interrupt but he stopped her; "Let me finish, I'll never get up enough courage again. In battle, the biggest fear any man has is that he might be a coward. I've seen what happens to men who desert their posts, or mutilate themselves to get out of serving. Some deserve the punishment they get, because they're cowards in their souls, and worse, put their comrades in jeopardy. But some unlucky men simply break and they're punished as examples. When you see a man branded with a C for coward on his palm and cheek, then half his head shaved and thrown out into the world—marked—"

He shuddered; "And the fear was always in me that in the next battle maybe I'd break. You see, dear Becky, I'm a coward, plain and simple. I've always known it, from the time Sean bullied me and I was too weak to do anything but give in...Or worse, when Maman tortured me mentally and I didn't know how to fight back. A coward right up to this moment. Yet my men think I'm rash and daring and brave. So who's right?"

"Both," she answered softly. "Sometimes, when we fight against the thing we fear most, we overcome it. I think I have...just a little."

"Perhaps. But then I became drawn to the killing, as if each man I dispatched proved me the better man, and gave the lie to the whispers of my youth."

"Surely you can't kill every man just to prove your own manhood?"

"No longer; I know who I am. For two years, while other men were out carousing, womanizing, I thought only of you, wanted only you. In the army everyone gets reduced to the lowest common denominator, yes, even in our gallant cavalry, a man's measured by his swordsmanship on the battlefield—and in the bedroom. How men boast, but to me it was ugly. What does any of that have to do with love?"

The heady scent of night-blooming jasmine reached them on the night breeze. "I love you," he said simply. "I want to be with you. Body and soul. Right now."

Though she'd sensed this was coming it still shocked her. Everything in her life screamed that she didn't dare. Decent girls didn't, corseted as they were by the Shalt and Shalt Nots of society, clergy, family. How then to explain that she also heard Geary whispering, "If you love him, then love him with all your heart and soul, that's all God ever wants."

Carleton hefted his wounded left arm with his right. "Before I say anything else, you must know that the doctors tell me there's nerve damage and I may never have the use of this arm again. Could you stand being with a cripple?"

"We're all of us crippled, it shows with some, with others the wound goes so deep that it's hidden. But I have arms enough for both."

His face lit with a radiant smile. "Becky, dear, sweet, wonderful Becky, just as there was only one Eve for Adam, so there's only one Becky for me."

The moon flirted with the cloud cover, limning its edges, emerging briefly to cast its pale light over the hills of Richmond, then disappear, returning the world to darkness. Somehow, Becky's horse had led them back to the bluffs of Chimborazo. Before they reached the hospital complex she turned onto a path that took them down and down past gullies to the base of the cliff, where no one lived and hardly anyone ever ventured. They dismounted, tethered their horses in a thick copse of silver buttonwood.

Her hands moved with a will of their own and her clothes fell away until she stood naked. She whispered, "We have been in a mad St. Vitus dance, but my dance has stopped."

He moved to her, the brass buttons of his uniform cold on her skin. His lips found her, gently, then more urgently as his own urgency rose. He stripped off his clothes and they lay down on the cool dark grass.

Her fingers recoiled from the welting sword and bullet scars on his bone-thin body and she shed tears as she kissed them. She felt as if she'd never experienced any man and in some strange emotional leap, her thoughts went back to the day before she'd been violated, when everything new and fresh and womanly loomed before her.

Her lips pulsed with blood, her soul was dry no longer, she ached for him, and when he eased into her, she thought she would never let him go. They lay quietly for a bit, he sparing her the full weight of his body, until she reached up and drew him to her, and then their motion began, the ageless motion the moon had borne witness to throughout time…only both were convinced that no one before them had ever experienced such joy. Rise and fall and rise again, in their dance of love, she fell away to a place where time had no meaning, the only thing that mattered was that she loved him, for he'd erased every evil that had befallen her, shown her what love could mean and had given her back her life.

He climaxed before she did, and she cried out with him as he muffled his joy…quiet, return, to a place of whispered words, of promises made for the ages, and when he murmured huskily, "Becky, I love you, I'll never love another," then his words shuddered through her, resonating again and again with his vow until she reached an unbearable peak of ecstasy.

She hardly remembered getting dressed, hardly heard him whisper that he'd come to see her tomorrow, hardly remembered her promise to try and get some time off. She watched him ride away, fighting her every impulse to run after him. In her room, she leaned against the rough wall planks remembering everything that had happened, his closeness, how they'd become one, his gentle motion…and relived it all again.

Before drifting off to sleep, thoughts of her mother and father flitted through her mind. She and her brothers had grown up in a household figured with love. Shortly after her mother died, her father had gone off to fight in the Mexican War. Whether by accident or by putting himself in harm's way, she knew that she'd never see him again. She'd resented him bitterly for abandoning them, but now she understood him completely. For if Carleton were to die, yes, she'd go on, but she had no desire to live without him. She wondered if God had given her lover the same feelings. A lover, she thought in childish wonder. Me, Becky Brand Albright, I have a lover!

By nine the next morning Becky began to fear that Carleton would never show up; by eleven, she was convinced of it. At noon, he arrived at Chimborazo. Becky had already made arrangements to have a few days off, her first real vacation since coming to work at the hospital.

"I've all sorts of surprises," Carleton cried, galloping off, then wheeling to come charging at her with abandon, only to veer away at the last moment.

"You'll frighten the horses," she scolded.

"Only if we do it in the streets!"

He took her to the Rocketts, an area of warehouses on the James River at the base of Chimborazo cliff. Before the war, tobacco had been shipped from here to all parts of the world. Now most of the warehouses were given over to the demands of war, but there was a group of buildings so derelict they'd been condemned. Carleton dismounted.

"I got up with the first cock," he began, then blushed so furiously she could barely keep from kissing him. "I searched for a place for us, away from the crowd, but close to the hospital." He climbed the rickety staircase to the top floor and led her into a small living space under the eaves. "It used to be the watchman's quarters, but he's dead. The owner fled to Europe when the war broke out; I've rented it from his agent and it's ours, all this week. What do you think?"

"Divine. Far grander than Varina's White House, even grander than Mary Todd's White House. Will you look at this fireplace? I love aged brick, so what if they're crumbling? And the floorboards have such a comfortable sag." She put her finger to her chin; "But where shall we put the grand piano?"

"Why, right next to the crib."

They made love then, less hurried this time, paying more attention to pleasing the other, reveling in the wonder of discovery. When they were done, they lay on the floor, her head nestled in the crook of his bony shoulder. They dozed off for a bit, and when they awoke, made love again.

That afternoon they scoured the shops where people had pawned their furniture to buy food, and bought an old bed, a table and chairs, and a small compliment of kitchen equipment. Food proved harder to come by, but they finally found a loaf of crusty bread and a chunk of cheese.

That night they had their first meal at home. "I've never tasted better," he swore, "not even at the grandest dinner at the Connaught mansion."

Afterwards, they stood at the dormer window. The warehouse faced the James River and the moonlit ribbon of silver meandered off into the darkness. "Have you ever been to Europe?" he asked. She shook her head. "We used to go every June to escape the heat. Maman insisted that unless we did we'd turn into savages like all Americans. I dreaded it."

"Have you ever been to Texas? No? I'll take you; you'll see some real savages, but you'll love it."

He drew her to the bed. She bounced up and down, exclaiming with each bounce, "A bed! A bed! Do you realize we've never made love in a bed? The first time happened on the ground, the second time on this floor. But a bed? Dear God, can we stand the luxury of it all?"

For the next week they played house with desperation born of knowing it would end all too soon. They left home only to search for food. They never stopped talking; he wanted to know everything about her and her family, while he shared everything he could about his. Becky experienced his growing up as a loveless existence, with Sean, Veronique, and Romance always jockeying for power. She found it a wonder that Carleton could love anyone at all.

But he could, and oh, the places that fingers and mouths discovered, no spot, however intimate, was sacred, and oh, the protestations and the rollicking laughter that always gave way to the ultimate coupling, where they became one, safe from everything and everyone.

One day she broached the subject of his arm. "The wound is pretty bad, so bad I think you could be mustered out."

He considered that. "So many of our men are wounded far worse, without arms, legs, and they keep on fighting. I can't abandon my men, I must see this through to the end."

She knew better than to fight his resolve, but asked soberly, "How do you think it will end?"

"In the beginning we all believed that the Yankees were nothing but shop-keepers, worthless fighters. But I've seen such acts of bravery—for instance, a few weeks ago we went on a mission to raid the Union's winter quarters at Falmouth? They were using a weapon we wanted to capture—one of those damned observation balloons? Jeb Stuart received information giving us its exact location. We took the Federals totally by surprise and were about to get clean away when one Union officer leapt onto the wagon, fought the driver—one man against my entire unit! But he slowed us down long enough so we had to abandon our prize. Funny thing, this man looked so familiar, and I've wracked my brain but I can't place him—"

"My cousin Forrest is in the Balloon Corps—"

Carleton smacked his head; "Of course! What a fool I am. I met him with you at Lincoln's inaugural ball. I was so jealous of him—until I found out he was your cousin."

"Merciful heavens, you could have killed each other."

"Well, we didn't. But to answer your question, how will it end? With such determination and bravery—on both sides—only God knows."

She swayed on her feet and he caught her before she fell. "Becky, what's wrong?" he asked anxiously.

"I—I don't know. I've been having these strange feelings, and when you mentioned balloons—and Forrest—I don't know. I'm probably just overworked."

Try as they might to grasp each moment, the week slipped away. His last day, he went off for a bit and returned at twilight. "This is our last meal for awhile," she said, trying to keep up a brave front.

For dessert, he feasted on her. Later, they stood at the window, staring out into the darkness. "Becky, marry me."

"I will, if you promise me one thing."

"Anything."

She kissed him fiercely; "Come back, and I'll marry you."

He took her hand and pressed a key into it. "I saw the agent and paid the rent on this place for a year. I'll be back by then and though one day we may live in a fine mansion, I'll always think of this as our first home. Will you take it? I'd be comforted knowing you had it as a retreat."

She stifled a sob and he kissed away her tears. "I also bought you a little going away present." He slipped a wedding band on her finger.

The moon painted a window on the floor and she stepped into its light. "Come kneel with me and let the moon be our witness."

Her voice sounded husky and oddly akin to tears as she murmured, "I do wed thee of my own free will, and in the eyes of God," he picked up the cadences and repeated the vows with her, "To have and to hold, in sickness and in health, till death do us part. Forever and ever, amen."

*

In the days after Carleton left, Becky became obsessed with wanting a child, his child; in the face of death, she wanted to throw down her gauntlet and produce life, to proclaim to all the world just how much they loved each other. She made a vow, if she became pregnant, she wouldn't go into the field with Dr. Grange, she'd stay in Richmond and have the child under safer conditions. "There you are, God," she whispered, "it's all in Your hands."

Chapter 28

REBECCA AND SHARON were in the kitchen helping Bittersweet bake several pies, including one for Corporal Sam Stockwell who'd become a very frequent caller. Bittersweet grumbled, "Don't know why I'm bakin' that Stockwell a pie, I'm tellin' you he's a spy and up to no good."

"He is not," Sharon cried, "just because he's a Yankee you don't have to be so mean."

Rebecca slapped the dough down on the counter. "Hush, the two of you. I've got far more important things to think about than some silly moon-struck Yankee. Nettie Colburn just told me the most astonishing news. She's going ahead with her séance—and in the White House. Has President Lincoln lost his mind? If this leaks out to the press—Lincoln's committing political suicide."

"You goin' to this here séance?" Bittersweet asked.

"I wasn't invited. Unless the invitation was written in invisible ink and delivered by a spook." With a hand dusty with flour, she tapped Bittersweet's nose; "Spook, spook!"

Bittersweet rubbed her nose furiously and mumbled several voodoo incantations to ward off evil. "Sharon, your Grandma communes with spirits, the ones locked in the liquor cabinet."

"Lies, lies, in my own house I'm so viciously maligned."

"Must be a spook drinking it then, since you the only one with the key," Bittersweet humphed.

The mantel clock chimed six and in a reflexive motion, Rebecca handed Bittersweet the keys to the cabinet. "Seances at the White House, what next? The only thing that will calm my nerves is a <u>teeny</u> tot of sherry." As the three women sipped the heady liquor the kitchen filled with the tangy aroma of cinnamon and apples.

Rebecca said, "Bravo once mentioned that Lincoln's given to dreams and omens, the Emancipation Proclamation came about because of a vow he made. Matter of fact, Lincoln's not the first President to believe in the mysteries of the unknown."

"Oh tell, so I can put it in your journal," Sharon said, feeling the first effects of the sherry. She'd learned early on that using the journal as a blind was the best way to pry gossip out of her grandmother. "Who else believed, Grandma?"

"Andrew Jackson kept a Bible at his bedside. Every night he'd let it fall open wherever it would and read that passage, convinced that it held a special message for the day."

Bittersweet nudged Sharon; "At his bedside? How'd she know it was at his bedside?"

"George Washington had several other-worldly experiences, I remember him talking about one as if it were yesterday. We were building the White House—or the American Palace as it was called in those years—and Washington and Jefferson took a stagecoach down from Philadelphia where the capital was then located, to inspect the progress. Both men were very imposing—over six foot tall, unusual for those days. James Hoban, the architect, was giving the men a guided tour; I was wandering about, making a general nuisance of myself."

"How old were you?" Sharon asked.

"Thirteen, or fourteen, something like that."

"They just let you wander about?" she asked dubiously.

Bittersweet refilled Sharon's glass; "Have another, the more of these here teeny tiny tots, the more believable the story gets."

"No, I didn't just wander about," Rebecca retorted. "In the first place, my father, your great grandfather, Mathias Breech, supplied the bricks for the White House and I kept a sharp eye on the accounts. Second, there were less than two hundred people living in what's now the entire District of Columbia and we all knew each other. Third, your great uncle, Jeremy Brand, who was a few months younger than me—"

"Few <u>years</u> younger," Bittersweet hiccuped.

"—Was apprenticed to James Hoban, who not only designed the White House, but was in charge of building it. Jeremy had a little crush on me and used to sneak me into the mansion to show me the progress; he was so proud of everything." Her thoughts went back to the long ago. "I can smell the wet plaster even now, the curlicue wood shaving, see Jeremy carving our initials on a beam in the East Room."

"What was George Washington like?" Sharon asked. "Was he handsome?"

"How could any man be handsome wearing that silly powdered wig and a set of false teeth made from a hippopotamus?"

"Oh Grandma, nobody wears false teeth from a hippopot—"

"He most certainly did. He alternated them with a wooden pair, made from the cherry tree he chopped down when he was a lad; he wore the wooden ones to remind him that even if he was a politician, he must never lie through his teeth."

Sharon giggled; "You are so mean about Presidents?"

"Nonsense, just truthful. I feel it my bounden duty to reveal our leaders as they truly are, mere mortals, like the rest of us. Just because a man is elected doesn't automatically endow him with divine wisdom. We as a people would be much better off if we realized that. Where was I?"

"Powdered wigs and 'potamus teeth," Bittersweet chimed.

"Right. Now Thomas Jefferson was very good-looking. He and George were inspecting the East Room and in that vast empty chamber, their voices were clearly audible." Though some alchemy of mind and memory, Rebecca discovered she was repeating almost verbatim everything she'd overheard some seventy years ago.

"Washington said, 'One wonders at the ways of the Almighty, for if we'd lost our war for independence against the British, then this American Palace would never be rising here. The low point of the war came on Christmas Eve when our army was encamped at Valley Forge. My men were freezing, bleeding, starving…had the British and Hessians attacked then, we would have been finished. I knew my men's lives would be forfeit if we fought on. Despair overwhelmed me and I lay down on the cot that my dear Martha had sent me. I passed into a state—not sleep, more like a reverie. I decided the only sane thing to do was to surrender. I tried to get up to give those orders, but a great weight pressed down on my chest, holding me immobile. Then a voice from an invisible world called, telling me that I must fight on.'

Rebecca continued, repeating Washington's words, "'This voice reminded me that during my army career, many, many horses had been shot from under me, and <u>seventeen</u> times had bullets passed through my coat and hat. I thought I'd merely been lucky, but as I lay there I was made to realize that with each bullet, Providence had spared me, for I was to become the leader of a great nation, a nation destined by fate. I got up, all signs of despair gone and gave orders to attack Trenton. After that victory we fought on, the rest is history...who can ever fathom the mysterious ways of the Almighty?'"

"I've got goose bumps all over me," Sharon declared.

Bittersweet shuddered; "Won't close an eyeball tonight."

Suddenly the back door swung open and the three women shrieked. In bounded Bravo. "You scared the life out of us," Rebecca panted.

"I've been banging on the front door—say, what's going on here? Are you three just a little tipsy?"

"Certainly not," Rebecca declared grandly. "Furthermore, for someone who claims everything can be explained by science, is it true that you're taking part in this evening's séance? You'd never catch me going to anything so juvenile."

"What a pity, I've just come from the White House where Nettie Colburn's preparing the event. When President Lincoln found out that you'd been to a few of Nettie's spiritualist meetings—why mother, what a becoming blush, or is just too much sherry—? Anyway, Lincoln asked me to invite you."

"Me you say? Me? Why?"

"Enough talk, Ma, enough questions. Yes or no?"

"Bittersweet? My green gown, the matching coat, no jewelry—spirits find the glitter distracting—"

An hour later, Rebecca and Bravo were walking briskly to the White House. "Bravo, does Mary Todd know I'm coming?"

"I'm sure Lincoln told her—or will at some point."

"This may not be wise, Mary Todd hasn't exactly made me feel welcome at the White House."

"That's why I was so glad when Lincoln requested you...well, I confess I did make a case for your presence. First off, if the newspapers find out about this, they'll try to crucify Lincoln. But since you're so sympathetic to seances—"

"Ah, I understand, I'm being used; you want me to write about it and explain it all away in some bland politically-correct fashion?"

"Only if the news leaks. But this séance may not come off at all. We've got to avoid another Colchester disaster. So, with Lincoln's approval, I've prepared a secret little test for Nettie, if she doesn't pass it—finito. And that will be the end of this séance insanity once and for all."

"What sort of test?"

"If I tell you, it won't be a secret."

"Outrageously used—and by my own child."

Rebecca felt somewhat comforted when Old Ed McManus greeted her at the front door with a wink; "Heard all about the goings-on tonight; it sure is going to be a dilly."

President Lincoln, who happened to be passing through the entrance hall with Edwin Stanton and Gideon Welles, stopped to greet Rebecca. He took her aside; "May I be candid?"

"Always," she replied, "but if your concern is that I may write something derogatory about this, put your mind at ease. Having lost a child and a grand-child of my own I'd never trade on a parent's grief. Whatever happens tonight, I promise I won't publish a word of it without letting you see it first."

"Thank you," he said, and went upstairs to a meeting.

The seance was to take place in the Red Room; a fire burned merrily in the fireplace, a pyramid of flowers and palms occupied the center of the room. A marble bust of Lincoln stood before a large pier glass, seeming life-like in the shifting play of firelight.

Nettie Colburn greeted Rebecca warmly; Rebecca felt protective toward lit-tle Nettie…nineteen and alone in these halls of power. Nettie had straight eye-brows that sloped downward, a short nose and an unblemished complexion. Brown hair falling in rolled curls framed her delicate face. Hardly the precon-ceived notion of what a medium should look like.

Rebecca braced herself when Veronique and Sean Connaught entered with Mary Todd. The three of them froze when they saw her, then huddled franti-cally. Then Mary Todd rushed to Nettie Colburn, who was busy lighting a series of strategically-placed candles, and let loose a flood of invective.

Nettie explained gently, "But Mrs. Lincoln, your husband asked that she be invited and I agreed. I thought it best to have another woman, otherwise the table would have been unbalanced with men, who tend to be notoriously unreceptive."

Rather than risk a scene, Rebecca prepared to leave when she heard Nettie say, "I'm so terribly sorry, Mrs. Lincoln, I had no idea—perhaps it's best if we didn't—when there's dissension—another time—"

Mary Todd rushed back to Veronique, and after a hasty conference, she returned to Nettie with the grudging agreement that the seance should go for-ward. Mary Todd sent her waiting woman, Mrs. Cuthbert, to fetch Mr. Lincoln; he came down shortly thereafter with Stanton and Welles. Mary Todd glared balefully at her husband, but he remained affable and serene.

After greeting the group cordially, Lincoln said, "I'm very busy and must forgo the pleasure of conversation and ask our little friend here to see what can be given us tonight as briefly as may be."

The slip of a girl arranged the group of twelve around the table. Nettie sat at the head, then clockwise, Lincoln, Veronique, Bravo, Mary Todd, Secretary of the Navy Welles, Rebecca, Secretary of War Stanton, Sean Connaught, Congressman Daniel E. Soames from Maine, his wife, and Parthenia Hannum, a young friend of Nettie's. Mr. and Mrs. Soames and Parthenia Hannum were all long-time devotees of spiritualism.

Rebecca thought Lincoln looked vaguely uncomfortable, but she also believed that he'd been politically astute in inviting two of his cabinet members. By including them, it made the strange occasion more informal, with less approbation falling on Mary Todd. Rebecca could imagine the two cabinet members saying to other government officials, or to the press, "Oh, yes, we went to a seance last night, what fun we had."

And, he had invited her, a member of the press.

Bravo cleared his throat; "Miss Nettie, before we begin, I believe Mrs. Lincoln has something to ask you."

Mary Todd's forehead wrinkled, then remembrance lit her face. "Nettie, please understand that nothing personal is intended, but we've had several unfortunate incidents where unscrupulous men have tried to prey on the President and me. To avoid any such feelings, would you be willing to undergo a little test?"

Rebecca held her breath, Nettie took her gift very seriously; she'd leave at the slightest insult. But to her relief, Nettie answered, "I'd be happy to oblige."

"It's a simple enough experiment," Lincoln said softly, whereupon a figure wrapped in a long cloak that completely concealed his face and body, entered the Red Room. Outside of being a male, there was absolutely no way of determining who this man might be.

"Can your spirits identify this person?" Lincoln asked.

Rebecca saw a penetrating look pass between Lincoln and Bravo. So this was the test they'd prepared? How unfair, how in the world could anyone possibly identify this individual?

Nettie asked quietly, "Please put out the lights?"

Bravo complied; only the flickering glow from candle and hearth remained, casting shadows over the expectant faces. Silence descended over the room.

"Would everyone please join hands?" Nettie closed her eyes and with a gentle sigh settled into a deep trance. Rebecca felt her skin prickle. A breeze lifted the edge of the curtains and the candle flames danced madly. Nettie began to speak in a voice not quite her own.

Having attended several of Nettie seances, Rebecca recognized the voice of Pinkie, Nettie's teenage Indian spirit-guide. She thought she made out the word, "Army?" Yes, there it was again, then, "Murder...Insane...Key," then the word "General", and finally the words "Crooked" and "Knife." Nettie put it all together and repeated, "Pinkie says that the man hidden beneath the cloak is General Crooked Knife."

Sean Connaught burst out laughing; "General Crooked Knife indeed," and started to get up, but Rebecca asked, "Who is it really? Don't we at least deserve to know that?"

Bravo stripped the covering from the man. The gathering stared at him, recognizing the notorious General Daniel Edgar Sickles.

Several years before, Washington had been scandalized when Sickles had shot and killed Philip Barton Key in Lafayette Park, just across the street from the White House. Key, the son of Francis Scott Key, who'd written "The Star Spangled Banner," had been having a torrid affair with Sickles' wife. Sickles was brought to trial for murder. Stanton, a Washington lawyer at the time, had defended him and gotten him off with the novel defense of temporary insanity, the first man ever to be acquitted on those grounds. The outbreak of the Civil War had given Sickles a new start and he was now serving in the army with distinction.

The gathering had fallen silent; not one of them had to be reminded that a sickle was a crooked knife.

The identification correctly established, the seance proceeded with awed respect for the little medium. Once again the group joined hands. "Don't let go or you'll break the circle," Mary Todd twittered, "the concentration of energy enables the spirits easier access to our world."

Minutes passed, the room seemed to grow warmer, and Rebecca felt her eyelids growing heavier. How much was real and how much her own imaginings...The aureole around the candle flame, was it be some phantasmagoria, or a trick produced by her slight cataracts? The sounds she heard, were they really moanings, or were they a product of her impaired hearing?

Once again Nettie was taken over by her guide. Pinkie talked of the plight of the Black freedmen in Washington and urged the 'Chief' to appoint a commission to aid them. Then came stern warnings, "The Chief is too gullible, he's being led astray by envious warriors seeking their own glory."

Suddenly, Stanton cried out, "Ouch! Stop that. Who pinched my nose? Stop, I say!"

"Willie?" Mary Todd moaned, "is that you, Willie?"

"Everyone, hold your partner's hand tight," Bravo ordered. "Has anyone let go?" The circle was still complete.

Then Gideon Welles called out in wonder, "Someone's pulling my beard. There it is again."

For a moment, Rebecca thought the two men were trying to make a joke of the affair, but she did see Welles' chin jerk.

Pinkie's voice rose in near-hysteria, "Danger! Danger all around the Chief—he won't heed—so many threats—"

"What of the war?" Sean Connaught interrupted impatiently. "What of the spring offensive at Fredericksburg? When will it commence? Can you tell us the outcome?"

With her eyes still shut, Nettie's head swiveled to Sean and held him transfixed in her blind gaze. "A father untimely taken," the voice of Pinkie whispered, then another word that seemed to echo through the Red Room, "Murderess…"

Mary Todd cried out in hysteria, believing the spirits were talking to her, but Veronique dug her fingernails into Bravo's palm and fainted dead away. "Lights!" Sean shouted.

Bravo turned on the gas jet. Rebecca blinked at the light then saw Nettie trembling and slowly coming out of her trance. Veronique lay sprawled on the floor.

After Sean revived her, Veronique apologized profusely to Mary Todd. "Dear Mrs. President, I don't know what came over me, just the thought that we were about to contact Willie…the child was so precious to me, my heart couldn't bear the pain."

But terror of another sort was written on her face. Mary Todd had to be helped from the room. The group disbanded with everyone much chastened.

On the walk back home Rebecca said to Bravo, "Well, my Doubting Thomas, what do you think about the spirit world now? And what about your Clytemnestra? Veronique's not the sort to faint easily."

Bravo didn't respond, absorbed by his own confusion. "Someone could have told Nettie about General Sickles, though only Lincoln and I knew whom we'd chosen. Could it be just coincidence? Of course, that's it, coincidence."

"'There's more in heaven and hell, Horatio…'" Rebecca quoted quietly. "Bravo, tell me the truth, have there really been that many threats against President Lincoln's life?"

"More than you'd believe, and what's worse, he won't take any precautions. He thinks he's safe here in the capital, but he keeps forgetting that Washington is, first and foremost, a southern city."

Chapter 29

FORREST BRAND galloped along the line of wagons, shouting to the drovers, "Close ranks, keep a sharp eye, these woods are full of snipers." He fell in alongside the flatbed carrying the *Eagle*, his rifle at the ready; he still had nightmares about the Rebel raid the previous month.

A bramble lashed Tim Aikens across the face, drawing blood. "Never seen such mean country. Like the Good Lord despaired of ever making it livable and gave up."

"They don't call it The Wilderness for nothing," Forrest answered. He continued to scan the impenetrable thickets along the overgrown, rutted road. Moments later, the crack of a rifle sent the men diving for cover.

"Get down, Forrest," Tim yelled and yanked him into a ditch beside him. Tim swore, "No one I hate more than sharpshooters, Yank or Reb, they don't give a man a fighting chance. If I had my way, I'd string 'em up by the balls, southern balls or northern balls, makes no never mind to me."

Long minutes passed while they waited for their squad to reconnoiter and flush out the snipers. The April sun felt warm on Forrest's shoulders, a relief from the cold rains of March and early April. By mid-April the rains had slackened, and like some great beast wakened from hibernation, the Union Army, 135,000 strong and with 'Fighting Joe' Hooker in command, had shaken off its lethargy had gone on the offensive.

On Monday, April 27, in a surprise move, Hooker sent General Sedgwick with 30,000 men to pin down the Confederates at Fredericksburg. Hooker led the rest of his 105,000 men, on a forced march from Falmouth up the

Rappahannock to Kelly's Ford, where he began crossing the river to the Rebel side.

Hooker was moving to outflank Lee, and at the Confederate stronghold at Fredericksburg, the bells at the Episcopal Church rang out the tocsin, calling man and God to battle. By Wednesday, the major part of Hooker's army, including Forrest and the wagons carrying the *Eagle* had crossed the Rappahannock and plunged into the Wilderness, clear of Lee's left flank.

Faced with immanent disaster, Lee had no alternative but to split his already inferior army of 55,000. He left General Jubal Early with 10,000 men to defend Fredericksburg; with his remaining 45,000 men, commanded by some of the best officers in the Confederacy, including Stonewall Jackson and Jeb Stuart, Lee raced to intercept Hooker before he could deliver the coup de grace.

The squad sent out to search for the Reb sharpshooters came back empty-handed and the column moved on. At dusk, they reached General Hooker's headquarters set up at the Chancellor family home, from which the tiny village of Chancellorsville took its name. At the quartermaster's compound, each man was issued 60 rounds of ammunition, 30 hardtack biscuits, and 5 days' ration of salt pork.

"This has got to be the big battle coming up," Tim said. "We're gonna do it, Forrest, ain't we? Smash Lee once 'n for all and take Richmond? Hell, we out-number the Rebs two to one—with triple the arms."

Forrest tried to tamp his own excitement. Given the vastly superior strength of the Union army, Hooker's plan appeared foolproof. "I keep warning myself not to get carried away, Lee's as wily as a fox, but this time, yeah, I think we got him trapped."

"Lord 'a mercy, we might be home in time for harvest? My sisters will be buzzing all over you like flies on piss."

Hardly a man slept that night, for on the eve of battle Hooker had galvanized his men with a stirring address. "The operations of the past three days have determined that our enemy must ingloriously fly, or come out from behind their defenses and give us battle on our ground, where certain destruction awaits him. Splendid success awaits."

Friday night, Forrest woke at midnight and his crew began the arduous task of gassing up the *Eagle*. By 4:30 A.M., it was fully inflated. Forrest double-checked the telegraph equipment, which he'd recently inherited from a defunct two-man balloon. The line would go from the Eagle directly down to Hooker's headquarters.

At 5:00 A.M. came the call to arms; Forrest heard a major ordering his men, "Pick off their officers, especially the mounted ones. A wounded Reb is more of a hindrance to his comrades than a dead one, but wounded or dead, let's whip Lee, then on to Richmond."

With dawn approaching, the *Eagle* went aloft; a hundred feet, five hundred, a thousand, and as he rose, Forrest felt a thrill at the base of his loins. Then the sharp jolt as the tethering lines held. The gray of the sky gave way to a nascent blue, with pale yellow bands broadening in the east. It was a calm cloudless morning with excellent visibility, at least ten miles, Forrest estimated. He took in the panorama of the Wilderness…an hour passed…then two, and then he spotted movements.

With a bird's eye view of the battle area, telescope trained, he was stunned when he made out two distinct Rebel armies converging on The Wilderness. One army was deployed to confront Hooker's major force around Chancellorsville. The second Rebel army—"What in hell are they doing?" Forrest shouted. It was hard to tell because many of the battalions were using the tangled forests for cover, but they appeared to be sweeping wide around the Union emplacements and moving to attack Hooker's right flank.

Forrest took the telescope from his eye, blinked—"This can't be, I'm just tired,"—and trained them again. His eyes had not deceived him.

Furious dots and dashes clicked out the alarm; "Saturday, May 2. 2 P.M. Two distinct Rebel armies. Repeat two armies.

One positioned to attack Chancellorsville. The other moving to attack Hooker's right flank."

He watched as the Confederate flanking force moved past Catherine Furnace and plunged deeper into The Wilderness. "It's got to be Stonewall Jackson," Forrest breathed, "no one else would be crazy enough to try something so crazy."

With his blood pounding, he waited for Hooker's headquarters to react to his message. "Why don't they counter the Rebel move?" he shouted to the wind. A half-hour passed, then an hour, while he frantically telegraphed the same message. Still no response. The Rebels continued their encircling movement unopposed.

"God, what if the telegraph's broken and they're not receiving me? I've been wasting time up here while—" He signaled the ground crew to haul him down, his entire body like an exposed raw nerve.

When the *Eagle* got within twenty feet of the ground, he hooked his legs around one of the guy ropes, slid down the rest of the way and ran like hell for headquarters. "General Hooker!" he shouted, as he barged into the command post.

"The general isn't available," a colonel with impeccable social and political credentials told him, "he's gone into the field."

Forrest saw his crumpled telegraph messages scattered on the floor and had the sinking feeling that no one had even looked at them. Forrest leaned his lanky frame across the desk, "Sir, my communiqués, didn't you read them?"

The colonel stared at him as if he'd gone mad. "Lieutenant, watch your mouth. I read them—" then chastised Forrest like a schoolboy, "you can't see the overall picture. We know Lee's army is dangerously split, he's only got maybe forty-five thousand against our hundred thousand. Like any good tactician, Hooker is consolidating his position until he's ready for the major battle. If you were grounded in military tactics, you'd know that with our superior force, there's no danger whatever of Hooker being outflanked."

"I tell you I saw them!" Forrest shouted. "There's an army of Rebels moving through The Wilderness, God knows how many, I can't tell because they're hidden by the forest. They're circling around our right flank. You must have gotten ground reports? Haven't our patrols seen them?"

"Of course we've had ground reports," the colonel yelled, "but from seasoned scouts who see things as they really are, instead of floating in the air and making wild assumptions. What you saw were the Rebel forces being flushed out by us and retreating, just as General Hooker anticipated."

The three commanding generals, Hooker, Meade and Sedgwick were in the field and there were only some desk officers left at headquarters. They gathered around Forrest as he kept repeating, "I swear, they're not retreating. If you don't believe me, then one of you come up with me, I'll show you."

But regimented minds found it impossible to believe that even as reckless a gambler as Lee would dare a maneuver so dangerous. Against a numerically superior force, to divide his army a second time and try to outflank the outflankers?

"Preposterous," one captain declared, "Lee's a West Pointer, he knows military history and strategy, and the one cardinal rule drummed into us is never weaken your forces by dividing them. Nowhere in the annals of warfare has anyone committed such a tactical blunder."

"I hope Lee reads the same textbooks you fools do."

"One more word out of you and I'll put you on report," the colonel shouted. "What we have here is another example of how misleading aerial reconnaissance can be, and how worthless the balloon corps really is."

If I don't get out of here I'm going to kill every one of these stupid bastards, Forrest thought, and bolted from the room. He tried frantically to reach Thaddeus Lowe, maybe Lowe could persuade them, only to discover that Lowe had gone off also, exactly where, no one knew.

By late afternoon, Stonewall Jackson's main columns had reached Orange Turnpike, within striking distance of the unsuspecting camp of the Eleventh

Corps of the Union Army. At 6 P.M. the Rebels attacked. The swiftness, the fury of the onslaught overwhelmed the Union outposts and they fell back or succumbed. Jackson's forces continued to smash forward. The Federals, in growing disarray, retreated to Chancellorsville.

At the same time, Lee struck Meade's corps so hard, they had to fight for their own lives. This prevented Meade from going to the aid of Hooker, who'd now been outflanked by Stonewall Jackson. The result was a growing panic that infected the entire Union army.

Sunday morning, May 3, Lee and Stonewall Jackson's forces joined up and attacked the ever-constricting Federal army. The Rebels seized a hill, Hazel Grove, and opened up an artillery barrage, firing directly down into Chancellorsville.

"Let's get the hell out of here," Tim Aikens yipped as shells exploded all around them. "Stop messing with the balloon, Forrest. Leave it. Nobody's listening to you anyway."

"We've got to save the equipment," Forrest shouted. "After this stupid disaster—which could have been avoided—maybe now somebody will pay attention to us."

Amid the booming cannonade, the crack and whine of rifle fire, he helped load the last of the equipment onto the flatbeds. He slapped the horses' flank, "Go!" The drovers whipped their teams mercilessly and just managed to slip through the Rebel forces before they closed their trap.

Disbelieving, and wounded, 'Fighting Joe' Hooker ordered a retreat and the defeated Union army withdrew and took up defensive positions on the Rapidan and Rappahannock Rivers. Lee's army occupied Chancellorsville at 10 A.M.

By Tuesday May 5, Hooker had abandoned his position on the Rebel side of the river and retreated across the Rappahannock. Hooker suffered a total collapse, so shaken by Lee's audacity that he no longer had any confidence in himself. His despair reflected itself down the entire chain of command and throughout the Union Army, immobilizing it.

Lee, with only a third of the manpower of the Federals, had achieved the greatest Confederate victory of the war.

Chapter 30

JOY UNRESTRAINED in Richmond! Citizens danced in the streets and in the Confederate White House Jefferson Davis, Judah Benjamin and Gunning devoured Lee's communiqués and the newspaper reports that blazoned the astounding victory.

Gunning read aloud: "Generals Lee and Stonewall Jackson's victory will be studied by military strategists for generations. The Federals had 135,00 men in the field and suffered 17,250 casualties. The Confederates had 60,000 men and suffered 12,750 casualties, a higher percentage, but we inflicted a terrible defeat on the invaders."

Gunning broke off, "Damn our press for releasing those statistics. Do we really want the enemy to know how few men we were able to field? Your Excellency, I implore you, stop the papers from releasing the news about Stonewall Jackson."

"Impossible," Davis said, "such terrible news cannot be hidden for long. But thank God Jackson was only wounded."

The next day the South learned that their victory at The Wilderness had been gained at a dreadful price. *The Richmond Examiner's* headline blazoned: "Stonewall Jackson Wounded!"

"General Lee gambled and won at Chancellorsville. But the Confederacy also suffered, for during the battle last Saturday, Jackson went on a reconnaissance foray. In the twilight gloom, his own men mistook him for a Yankee officer and shot him. His left arm had to be amputated. But God is merciful and Stonewall Jackson appears to be out of danger."

That evening, while dining at Romance's, Gunning vented his outrage; "To be shot by his own men? Of all the stupid—"

"Calm yourself," Romance soothed, "he's recovering."

"If only that was true. Davis just got word from the surgeons. Complications have set in, infection, pneumonia—Jackson doesn't deserve this, the South doesn't deserve this."

"I'll never understand men," she sighed, "you flock to war as if it were some bacchanalian orgy, but complain bitterly when someone's hurt? What did you expect?"

"Sometimes you can really be a cold-hearted bitch. Don't you understand his importance to our cause? Jackson may die."

"And if he does? What better way for a man of his stripe to fulfill his destiny? In peace he was little more than an eccentric, with such a myriad of bizarre habits and beliefs he could have been institutionalized. But if he falls in war? Overnight he becomes a martyr; children will revere his name, poets will sing his praises."

"There are times when I could strangle you. I'm going to do what I haven't done in years; go to church and pray."

The entire South did pray for Stonewall Jackson but their prayers went unanswered. On Sunday, May 10, he bolted up in his bed, his fanatic-blue eyes burning as he shouted to his men, "Attack!" then sank back and breathed his last…"Let us cross over the river and rest in the shade of the trees."

On May 12, the South held a huge state funeral. Davis and Lee led the cortege and generals fought for the honor of being a pallbearer. Tens of thousands wept openly as they paid homage to 'The Fist of God.'

Afterwards, Gunning and Romance returned to her house. At the door she faltered and pressed her fists to her temples. "What's wrong?" Gunning asked anxiously.

"I loathe funerals. Though I was quite young, I remember my father's vividly…how my mother wept, such tears, crocodiles would have envied them. My father never liked me very much, he'd wanted his first-born to be a son, to continue the Connaught line. But I set my cap to win him over. Dying untimely as he did, I never got the chance. Now with all the men I meet…you may have noticed that I have a penchant for older men? Men old enough to be my father? Ah, poor Maman, retribution has so many guises."

Gunning's ears pricked, for years he'd heard dark whispers about the circumstances surrounding Devroe's death. "Are you implying that your mother—?"

"I'm implying nothing," she answered abruptly, and with mounting distress, hurried into the bedroom and threw herself on the bed. Gunning drew the curtains and applied cold compresses to her forehead, feeling her pain as her body contorted in agony.

"Has any more of the medication come?" she moaned.

"No, but I'm hopeful that a new shipment will slip through the blockade."

Through a young and extraordinary agent in the North, Gunning had been receiving precious supplies of morphine and heroin. He gave it all to Surgeon General Sam Moore who distributed it where needed. But on several occasions Gunning had kept a vial of morphine for Romance. When one of these episodes overwhelmed her, it was the only thing that prevented her from going mad.

*

Though stricken by Jackson's death, the South couldn't afford the luxury of prolonged grieving, faced as it was with growing threats on many fronts: in the Carolinas, two of the South's remaining open ports, Charleston and Wilmington were under siege by the Federal navy. But it was at Vicksburg, Mississippi that a disaster of monumental proportions loomed.

On May 15, Davis called an urgent meeting at the Customs House to determine the future conduct of the war. Cabinet members, generals and several aides attended. Always alert to the President's health, Gunning studied him; victory had always proven a tonic and he'd recovered from his critical illness of the previous month; the inflammation in his good eye had subsided and total blindness no longer threatened.

Davis told the group, "Ulysses S. Grant is tightening his siege of the strategic river port of Vicksburg." His lips thinned contemptuously; "Grant's record during the Mexican War was woefully undistinguished. Though he was a West Pointer, I considered him mediocre; so did the army, and forced him to give up his career. A failed soldier, a failed farmer, a failed tanner, a failure at everything he touched—and a drunkard to boot. One would think that General Johnston could crush him easily, yet—" Davis shrugged in disgust.

General Johnston now commanded the Confederate armies in the western theater and Davis' dislike for him had grown to contempt. Davis considered Johnston lack of leadership the principal cause for the current crisis. Johnston consistently refused to engage Grant, complaining to his champions in Congress that Davis wasn't sending him enough men.

True enough, Gunning thought, but Lee didn't have enough men either. Lee and Johnston shared many similarities: both were Virginians, both aristocrats, both career officers, but there the similarities ended. Johnston equivocated and lost; Lee dared and won.

Davis continued, "Each day, Grant's noose grows tighter. Vicksburg is the linchpin of the Confederacy, holding our western and eastern states together; if it falls, supplies flowing in from Texas, Louisiana, and Arkansas would be lost to us, causing untold hardship. Vicksburg must be rescued."

Gunning squirmed impatiently; Get on with it, Jeff, order Lee to get his army to Vicksburg and lift the siege.

Postmaster Reagan of Texas, bluff and outspoken, pushed the case for Vicksburg and Gunning also lent his voice. "We can't afford to lose the thirty-five thousand men besieged there, nor can we afford to lose the herds of horses vital to our cavalry that come from the Trans-Mississippi."

Lee sat immobile; he was totally gray now, with a full gray beard, but his patrician features still reminded everyone of the name given him at West Point, 'The Marble Ideal.' Lee said quietly, "Given the South's meager rail facilities, I see no way I can transport my army to Vicksburg in time to save it. We must also ask ourselves if we're willing to sacrifice Richmond. The moment I move my army west, the Union will surely attack the capital." He paused; "Which loss would prove the greater blow to our cause, Vicksburg, or Richmond?"

The cabinet members stirred uneasily. Gunning thought, There we have it: President Davis wants to save his own state of Mississippi, General Lee wants to save Virginia.

With the attention of the room fixed on him, Lee said, "Chancellorsville proved that the South has a better fighting soldier than the North—" A chorus of huzzahs seconded that, and Lee warmed to his plan. "Given the Union's superior numbers and supplies, in a war of attrition we're doomed to defeat. So I strongly urge that we go on the offensive again. This time there'll be no unforeseen accidents to alert the Federals as happened at Antietam. I want to mount our largest offensive ever and invade the North."

Lee went to the large map on the wall; "We must carry the battle out of Virginia, away from the Shenandoah Valley, so our crops can be planted and harvested and our soldiers and people fed." He made slashing motions across the territories; "Washington is too strongly defended, so I propose we bypass it, strike through Maryland and into Pennsylvania, capture Harrisburg, then press on to Philadelphia. Philadelphia ours, Washington must fall from its own isolation."

After two grinding years of fighting the invader on Southern soil, the sheer audacity of Lee's plan thrilled the cabinet. "Yes," came the cries, "let the North witness destruction on its own soil!" "With Harrisburg, Philadelphia and Washington ours, they'll have to sue for peace!"

Even Gunning found himself catching fire. Lee's reputation was so secure after his miraculous victory at The Wilderness that the cabinet voted for his plan and Davis acquiesced. If it had to be, Vicksburg would be sacrificed for the greater goal of invading the North and ending the war in one terrible stroke.

Chapter 31

ON LEAVING the cabinet meeting, Gunning and Judah Benjamin repaired to the State Department where a courier for the Secret Service awaited them. He was a thin, twenty-year-old native of Maryland with fair hair, a budding moustache, and a rogue pimple here and there. His boyish face reflected both innocence and intelligence, characteristics that served him well in his dangerous forays through Union lines.

Gunning considered young John Surratt one of the best couriers that intelligence employed. "How goes it in Washington, John?" Gunning asked.

"My task will be a whole lot simpler as soon as my family moves in from the country. My mother plans to open a boarding house in Washington; I figure that the comings and goings of the boarders will help mask my comings and goings."

Benjamin gave Surratt several coded messages, which he hid in the false heel of his boot. He was to deliver them to the spy network that Confederate Intelligence had established in Canada. The messages asked for arms and supplies to support the upcoming invasion of the North.

After John Surratt left, Judah pointed to an old battered horse collar lying in the corner; "That just arrived today."

Gunning slit the seam—"Hallelujah!"—and took out a treasure trove of medicines. They'd been smuggled into Richmond, once again by his most reliable agent. Usually agents tended to be nondescript, preferring not to call attention to themselves, but this man was the exception. His profession, flamboyant though it was, enabled him to move all over the country without arousing any suspicion.

He'd even wangled a pass from General Grant to travel in the Border States and this shipment of medicines had arrived via Nashville by way of St. Louis.

Gunning pocketed a vial of morphine for Romance and mused, Wonder what my sainted mother would say if she knew that one of my most trusted agents was also one of her intimate friends?

When the day ended Gunning started for Romance's house, then recalled she'd told him she'd be occupied tonight; that annoyed him. Rumors always swirled around her and though he'd never been able to unearth anything, the suspicion lurked that she might be cuckolding him. Footloose, he wandered about and soon found himself at Capitol Square standing before Thomas Jefferson's beautiful and imposing Capitol building.

Gunning paused; how would you have viewed this war, he wondered? You who owned and sired slaves and never freed them, even though they were your own children? Whose side would you have taken, you who warned us of this fire bell in the night? The questions continued to haunt him even as he discovered himself loitering in front of Romance's house.

He found her in the drawing room with Montgomery. She wore a simple calico dress, hair loose and falling below her shoulders. Without her elaborate maquillage she looked very young and very innocent. The slave stood barefoot, breathing hard, sweat plastering his thin homespun clothes to his powerful body. The tableau, so domestic, yet so intimate, made Gunning tense and he asked sharply, "What are you doing?"

If Romance felt any embarrassment it didn't register. "Darling, how divine to see you. Look at these exquisite pieces, I just purchased them at a bankruptcy auction. These chairs are genuine Bellanger. I practically stole them."

With his uneasiness building, Gunning jerked his head at Montgomery; "Send him away."

"But we haven't laid the new rug. It's an oriental; I fantasize that it's like the one Cleopatra used when she stole into Caesar's presence. "Montgomery, lay it—"

Gunning growled, "If you don't get rid of him, and right now, I'll have him conscripted. Think you'll enjoy doing all your household chores yourself?"

The room crackled, then Romance said, "I never argue in front of servants." With a wave of her hand, she dismissed Montgomery. But the moment the buck went down to the basement she turned on Gunning, her fingernails clawing at his heart.

He fought her off, then toppled her backwards onto the sofa. He pressed his mouth to hers, she caught his lip and bit hard, drawing blood. With an oath, he bit her back, and her cry of pain arched up and blended into a moan. Hate and desire spilled from her violent violet eyes as he tore at her clothes. They rolled onto the floor, thrashing about. He ripped off her dress and undergarments until she lay naked—fighting him desperately, yet somehow pliant and accepting as he thrust into her in one sure swift motion. He bucked and bucked, faster, until her body moved with a primal need of its own and she responded, faster, mouths locked, faster, and his outcry ended in her scream.

She fled to the water closet. He knew she had a terror of becoming pregnant and given his marital status, he couldn't blame her. But he often day-dreamed about what a child of theirs would be like...beautiful probably, but what other miracle might the mix of Brand and Connaught blood produce? He stared at the chandelier whose crystals chimed in the breeze and cast mesmerizing prismatic patterns on the ceiling. He closed his eyes and saw those same patterns on his eyelids...opened or closed, she had him hypnotized.

She returned holding a compress of arnica to her lip to reduce the swelling. When she offered it to him, he declined with a grin; "I wear my battle scars as badges of honor."

She served a delicious supper of cold duck. As he devoured a drumstick, he asked; "What is this genius you have for getting food when all about us, people are starving?"

"People give me things," she replied sweetly.

Having given her his heart he knew well what she meant.

Later, lying in bed, he recounted his confusions about Davis. "I cast my lot with the Confederacy not because of any passion to protect slavery—not because I champion States' Rights,—who's to say where a man's allegiance should lie, state or country? I got involved because of Jeff Davis and his uncompromising honesty."

"Not quite accurate," she corrected him, "you thought to advance yourself tied to his star. You were also searching for a hero, and now you suspect that the emperor's feet might be fashioned of the same clay as your own?"

He considered that. "Today I saw Davis knuckle under to rule by committee, when, right or wrong, he should have been more forceful, acted as Commander-in-Chief."

Romance stretched languorously; "You've imbued Davis with virtues that reside more in your own wishes than in his character. This is Virginia, where bloodline counts for everything, else you'd now be Secretary of War. Lee not only comes from one of the First Families of Virginia, he's also married to George Washington's great granddaughter. Every new country develops its own mythology and Lee and Virginia are part of that mythos. How can you expect a provincial planter, from a backwater state like Mississippi, to stand up to that?"

She grew pensive; "Long ago I begged you to leave this country, for I had such a fear. Away from everything that tormented us, we might have found peace. But you insisted that we commit ourselves to this…this hell. Now we can do nothing but await the judgement of Fate."

Mercurially, her mood changed and she poured him a snifter of brandy. She deliberately spilled some of it on her body, shivering as the rivulets of alcohol ran into crooks and crevices, cooling and burning all at once. "Rescue me," she gasped. When the cat had licked the platter clean, she asked with a contented purr, "What do you know of Cleopatra?"

"That's the second time you've mentioned her. Why?"

"I read an ancient legend about her; what a woman, what cunning. Queen Elizabeth of England chose virginity as the means to protect her crown from the designs of men, but Cleopatra faced a far more perilous task. A Greek ruling a land of Egyptians; forced to pay homage to Rome; and under constant threat from a conniving brother. Yet she denied herself nothing, certainly not the pleasures of the flesh. I'm not speaking of Caesar or Marc Anthony or of her brother, those were political alliances. I'm speaking of her excursions into pure sensuous pleasure. To preserve her throne, whomever she took to bed would spend just one night on her barge; come morning, she have his throat slit. That way, there'd never be anyone who could gossip about her or challenge her rule. Yet she was so desirable that men gladly gave their lives to spend one night with the Queen of the Nile."

"Do you imagine yourself Queen of the James? Are you planning to take a paramour to bed then kill him in the morning? If so, how is it that you haven't yet killed me?"

"But I am, my darling, I am. Your demise is to be slow and painful, on you I'm using the arsenic of love. At the moment, we seem a perfectly matched nymph and satyr, but we both know that can't last. There'll come a moment, next month, next year—whenever—when I'll want more, and you'll be too fatigued to oblige. Why, see how pale you've become? As if you'd seen your end? For as we both know, my darling, for you, such an end is far worse than death."

Challenged, he laughed uneasily, then rolled over and took her, without a kiss in preparation, dry, abrading, causing a pain so exquisite it could have been love…or hate.

Yet even in the act of rutting, an unbidden thought overtook him, We've done this before, will again, and to what end?

When they were done she asked, "Why so moribund?"

"I was just thinking, wouldn't it be wonderful if we had a product of our love? A child to replace the one lost, another chance to prove that I can raise a son without making the same mistakes…" He then asked with the barest hint of hope, "And you? What were you thinking?"

"Not that, I assure you. Do you think I'm some brood mare you can use to correct your own mistakes? We'll talk of a child when you're free of your wife. Until then my thoughts are on Nubians in chains, and long journeys down the Nile."

Thus obsessed, she neglected to go to the water closet and take the necessary prophylactic precautions.

The next morning Gunning walked briskly to his own quarters to get a change of clothes. The evening's encounter had revitalized him and the morning's lovemaking had made him feel even more secure. He was startled to see Becky sitting on his front steps. She seemed subdued, a bit lost.

"I wanted to say goodbye, my train departs at noon," she explained. But she didn't explain that a few weeks before, she'd had her period. After that profound disappointment, she'd decided that if she was destined not to bear life, the least she could do was to help save it.

"Where are you going," Gunning asked, "back to Washington?"

"Of course not, do you think I'm some sort of turncoat? I'm joining Dr. Grange at a field hospital; I've cleared it with the powers at Chimborazo."

"Impossible," he blurted. "I can't let you do it, how could Dr. Grange even think such a thing?"

"He doesn't know, in fact, he forbade it. But once I'm there—I hope I'll be able to change his mind."

Knowing that the new plan for the invasion of the North would commence at the end of May, Gunning felt a stab of fear for her. He adored his niece and the idea that she might be putting herself in jeopardy—he tried repeatedly to dissuade her but she just smiled her sweet determined smile.

"I can't explain why I've got to go, but with every beat of my heart I know I must, it's that strong in me. Uncle Gunning, I don't have your convictions, I've lost sight of who's right and who's wrong. All I see are the dead and the dying, and if I can ease the pain of just one soldier…"

Thoughts of Geary robbed him of speech, but he finally managed, "Since I can't persuade you, let me at least give you a going-away present?" He reached into his pocket and handed her the vial he'd intended to give to Romance.

Her eyes widened; "Morphine? How? Oh, thank you."

"Don't thank me, thank—well, all I can say is that this courageous man has proven to be a staunch fighter for the Confederacy. If he were caught, his career, even his life would be forfeit. Understand?" and smiled knowingly.

She took his cue; "This man is someone I know, isn't it?"

He nodded; but didn't dare tell her that the medicines had been smuggled into the South by John Wilkes Booth.

Chapter 32

LIKE A great scythe wielded by the God of War, the Confederate army began its sweep northward: Brandy Station, Newtown, Middletown, one Union stronghold after the other fell. Lee's victory at The Wilderness had emasculated Hooker and he was impotent in the face of the new Rebel offensive.

The Balloon Corps flew sporadically, but Thaddeus Lowe no longer led the aeronauts. In May, weeks before the Rebel offensive started, Lowe had resigned from the corps over the army's refusal to provide him with new equipment, to pay his expenses, and to act on the aeronauts' information.

Lee's army slogged on and by June 15 they'd recaptured Winchester, Virginia, along with huge stores of supplies. In effect, the Union was now supplying the Rebels with the tools of war. Days later, the Rebel army flung pontoon bridges across the Potomac, forded the river and invaded Maryland.

Once again hysteria gripped Washington, legislators and citizens alike fought to get on departing trains. But forewarned of the capital's formidable defenses, Lee swung wide and continued north, further confusing the Union generals. No one knew where the Gray Fox might strike next; in Baltimore, unionists erected breastworks against the anticipated invasion, and during the night, secessionists tore them down.

When it became apparent that Lee wouldn't stop at Maryland, the panic spread to Pennsylvania. With the conflict now so freewheeling, encompassing sections of northern Virginia, Maryland, and southern Pennsylvania, there were no clear battle lines. The Union High Command degenerated into a Tower of Babel, and conflicting orders confounded everyone. By the third week in June, the balloons and all the supporting equipment had become so derelict that the army dismissed the corps as a viable unit.

"Don't know what the hell we're supposed to do," Forrest confessed. "No orders, no one knows anything. Looks like we've fallen through the cracks."

"Great," Tim Aikens whooped, "let's all go home."

Forrest angrily kicked a wagon wheel; "This is the most stupid, short-sighted—now's the time we should be flying, finding out exactly where Lee's heading." He paced about like a mountain lion; "No way I'm going to settle for this. Until I get an order from Comstock telling me otherwise, or assigning us to a new outfit, we're still aeronauts."

"But Forrest, how? And with what? Lookit this junk."

"Whatever there is, we'll make it fly."

With a lot of Yankee ingenuity and backbreaking work, Forrest and his crew repaired and improvised, swore and prayed, and in two days managed to piece together a craft: the patched envelope of the *Eagle*, the battered wicker gondola from the *Enterprise*, the bullet-pocked iron plate from the floor of the *Constitution*, and a hybrid portable generator made of spare parts salvaged from other defunct generators.

The crew circled their handiwork. Tim scratched his head; "Damned if this ain't the sorriest lookin'—?"

Forrest burst out laughing; "You're right, but I don't care what it looks like as long as we can get it up."

Tim twanged the guy ropes used to tether the balloon; "Lookee here, Forrest, these lines are frayed so bad—first strong gust and wham—you'll be twirling so hard, knock you ass over tea kettle."

"Then let's start splicing these ropes. Hop to."

They continued north, ostensibly to rejoin their division. A Union command post had been set up near Frederick, Maryland, but Forrest bypassed it.

Alarmed, Tim howled, "Ain't you gonna report in?"

"Not right now. I want to get closer to the action."

Tim smacked his head; "I get it, you're afraid that if you do report, they'll stop you. That's why you've avoided hooking up with anyone? Answer me this, all this information you're planning to collect, who are you gonna give it to? Or are we gonna take on Lee all alone?"

"If necessary. Look, Hooker's out of it by now, but maybe General Meade will listen to what we have to say. The size of the Reb army, where its moving—this isn't just another raid into northern territory. There's a master plan here, we've got to find out what it is and stop it."

"And you're gonna do it all alone with this—this bald *Eagle*? Oh Lordy, my sister's marrying a crazy man."

Forrest's eyes sparked with fanatical light. "I know the *Eagle*'s got only one or two flights left in her. But up there I can see in minutes what it'd take cavalry scouts days to find out. If they'd listened to us at The Wilderness, we wouldn't be in this fix. We're heading for a showdown—can't you feel it? All I know is—I've got to be there."

"And all I know is that for these past months, you've been taking so many reckless chances? I kept my mouth shut up to now but it's time for me to speak my piece. Happened ever since you got that letter about your cousin buying his plot. Forrest, m'boy, 'tweren't your fault. And getting yourself killed—that ain't gonna bring him back."

Forrest clenched his fists; "I joined this outfit because I had a dream that aerial reconnaissance could help end this war fast. I still have that dream, and nobody—not you or anyone else—is gonna take it from me. You can get the hell out any time you want. Go on, go join a new outfit. Or desert. I'm sick of listening to your complaints."

"You're crazy, you know that?" Tim shouted, but Forrest threw up his hands in disgust and stomped off.

The last week in June, footsore and weary, faces burned from the summer sun, Forrest's unit reached an area mid-way between Catoctin Furnace and Emmitsburg, Maryland, several miles from the border of Pennsylvania. They ran into occasional Union scouting parties, but they couldn't tell them very much about the position of the Rebels.

"Then it's time for us to find out," Forrest told his men. "If I discover anything, anything at all, I swear I'll bring it to the first commanding officer we meet."

They found a usable creek and began the laborious process of filling the *Eagle*'s envelope with hydrogen. With their remaining carboys of sulfuric acid and depleted trays of iron filings, where it once took four hours to inflate the *Eagle*, it now took eight hours. They worked by moonlight; they didn't dare light a fire, with the generator leaking and the gas so combustible, one mistake and they'd be blown sky high.

At last they were ready; Forrest checked the winches and the horses' harness. "If the Rebs start shooting and it gets too hot up there, you'll have to haul me down fast."

Tim nodded soberly, toed the ground; "Forrest, I know we've had our differences, but—don't suppose I could persuade you not to—?"

Forrest gripped Tim's shoulders, hugged him, then climbed into the gondola. The crew carefully played out the spliced lines. It was still hours before dawn and Forrest found this ascent in the darkness more thrilling than any of his other flights. With few visible reference points, only the peculiar sensation in his loins made him aware that he was rising.

…Rising slowly toward stars that beckoned. Suspended in the silent night, surrounded by stars, he could almost hear God's whisper on the night wind. How he wished he could share this with someone, mere words could never capture this awesome feeling of freedom. His father? Sure. Geary? Maybe. Then he thought, what a hoot if I could take Grandma up in a balloon! The idea tickled him; oh, she'd be kicking and screaming, cursing the man who'd invented such an infernal machine, but she'd go up. No doubt about it, the old girl would go up.

As the land took the lifting light of dawn, he couldn't help but remember God's command, 'Let there be light…'

Everything looked so peaceful that he shouted, "Why in hell are we fighting?" The predictable answers came to him, that the rebellion of a few must not be allowed to destroy the Union of many. But he realized it was much more than that. The country, the world, had reached a crossroads where no man could own another, or have the power of life and death over him. Every other question paled into insignificance beside this idea of freedom, the idea that all men were created equal, the idea that had given birth to this nation.

Forrest scanned the area with his telescope. Visibility was exceptional, he could see for miles. Below, the verdant Maryland countryside; to the west, the rolling hills of South Mountain. He saw the tiny figures of men on the move, their line of march converging north. Toward Pennsylvania?

Without warning there was a loud report as a spliced guy line snapped. Tethered to the ground by only two lines, the gondola swung crazily, pitching Forrest about. The craft gradually stabilized, but continued to swing in the sky.

The panorama of the Rebel advance became even more defined. No question, Lee was striking into Pennsylvania. He checked his map—what was in his path? Harrisburg, maybe? If they captured the capital of a powerful northern state it might undermine the North's resolve to continue the war.

In the distance, well behind the advance units, he made out ambulance wagons. Since both sides painted their field hospitals yellow he couldn't tell if they were Rebel or Union.

He'd been up for several hours and so intent on distant objectives, that he was caught off guard when the *Eagle* began to descend jerkily. He trained his telescope, searching, but only when he'd been hauled down 1,000 feet could he make out the team of horses and someone lashing them—it must be Tim—

Forrest stiffened—a cavalry unit was galloping toward the balloon emplacement. Rebs! Mesmerized, he watched the ant-like figures of his men fighting the superior force, but in short order they were captured or killed. And I led them into this, he thought, overwhelmed with guilt.

The *Eagle* hung in the air; then the Rebels took over the winch and Forrest began to descend again. His mind raced, they'll get the generator, the wagons, the balloon and me, and I'll spend the rest of the war in a Confederate prison.

"No way!" he spat. He grabbed his Bowie knife, leaned far out over the basket and slashed at the two remaining lines. The strands of hemp parted—and in that instant he spiraled up hundreds of feet in a dizzying ascent. The sun had warmed the gas in the envelope and without the umbilical tether, he rode free, swept along on thermal currents.

He'd never experienced free flight and the danger disappeared in his exhilaration. He wheeled over the fields of battle, traveling miles in one direction, then the other, saw toy soldiers in both armies pointing up at him. With luck he might catch a westerly wind and float back to the Union lines. Once on the ground he'd send out a search party for his crew.

But today the prevailing winds were sweeping in from the southeast, carrying him deeper over the Rebel line of march. He soared for what seemed an eternity and the briefest moment but was in reality, several hours. As long as the summer sun heated the gas in the envelope, the *Eagle* remained buoyant. But with the cooling afternoon wind he began a slow descent. Feverishly, he tossed all the ballast overboard, including the iron floor plate used as protection against enemy ground fire. The important thing was to stay aloft until the wind changed.

By late afternoon, with gas escaping through the rips in the envelope, the *Eagle* came within rifle range of Rebel soldiers. Miles away he saw field hospital wagons and tried to steer toward them, praying they might be Union. If they were Confederate—well, hospital personnel were less likely to be bloodthirsty than rank and file soldiers.

Then he heard the whine of bullets whizzing through the rigging. Suspended between earth and sky, he experienced a strange feeling of peace, a communion almost, and knew in his soul, that even if he was destined to die, everything was turning out exactly as it should.

A fusillade of bullets ripped through the gas envelope. It shuddered like a wounded beast and with a great hissing sound began to plummet. Now bullets were tearing through the gondola and through Forrest. One ripped away his ear; another tore into his chest. The deflating gas bag snagged on the limbs of a tree, breaking its fall, but mangled the gondola and Forrest. When Rebel soldiers hauled the Yankee out of the basket, they had every reason to believe that he was dead.

Chapter 33

BECKY GUIDED her horses along the lush country lane. Dr. Grange sat beside her on the ambulance wagon. When Becky had first appeared at his field hospital Dr. Grange had exploded in anger, but now, several weeks later, he confessed that he didn't know how he'd managed without her. Though they were well in the rear of Lee's advance units, they were also deep in Yankee territory; their wagons were clearly marked in yellow with yellow flags flying, but they'd still come under fire from Yankee scouting parties. Fortunately, they carried no wounded in the ambulance train; days before, all the wounded had been sent back to Virginia.

Around ten that morning the hospital wagons crossed into Pennsylvania and proceeded on for several more miles to a rendezvous point, where they waited for orders. In the afternoon, a courier arrived from Lee's field headquarters; they were to find a suitable location and set up a field hospital.

Dr. Grange told Becky, "It's a change in plan because they say there's a town nearby with warehouses full of shoes. Shoes that we need. So far our barefoot boys have marched a hundred fifty miles from where we started our offensive. Imagine how far we'll get if they have shoes?"

They came to a crossroads and Becky read the signs; "Chambersburg? Gettysburg? I've never heard of these places. Do you know where we are?"

"Between a rock and a hard place, I'd say."

"Why? We're winning, aren't we?"

"Up until now. But we're a long way from home. Remember how we fought for every inch of our home ground? Now the Yanks will be fighting on their territory; it makes a difference."

A short time later they found a choice spot. At the foot of a gentle knoll stood a stone farmhouse and a weathered red barn; the owners had fled before the Rebel advance. A nearby stream would supply them with ample water; behind the barn, a rolling meadow for pasturage. Dr. Grange dispatched a rider to inform Lee's headquarters of his hospital's location.

The cooks found a cache of vegetables in the root cellar, and that, along with the farm's livestock, promised ample food for several days. Living off land untouched by war, the Confederates were eating better than they had in years.

If a battle developed, Dr. Grange planned to use the barn as his Surgery, and Becky and several male nurses policed the place. Several hours later a flatbed wagon rumbled into the farmyard. A private and a sergeant carried a body into the Surgery. "This Yankee was flying one of them damned balloons? Looks more dead than alive to me, but if you can revive him, headquarters is anxious to question him, see what they can learn about their troop movements."

They laid the wounded man on the operating table; lanterns hanging from the rafters cast their light down on the drained and broken body. Then the soldiers left.

Silent communication flowed between Becky and Dr. Grange. Neither had to say anything about Becky's premonition many months before.

Dr. Grange knelt beside Forrest, searched for a pulse…so weak he could barely detect it. His trained eye took it all in: a bullet had torn away his left ear, his skull was fractured. A rib protruded from his chest, the entire area red with gore.

"Will he live?" Becky asked anxiously.

"Not unless we get this rib back in his chest, and maybe not even then." With a hacksaw, he gingerly sawed off the end of the protruding rib, popped it back into his chest, sewed up the laceration and bound his chest tightly. "His lungs aren't punctured, so that will heal soon enough. But that's the least of our worries."

He examined Forrest's head. "He'll never hear from this ear again. His skull is fractured, bad enough to cause a clot or the build up of fluids. Unless I release the pressure inside his brain pan, his head will literally explode."

As luck would have it, there were no Rebel wounded coming in, so they were able to give Forrest their full attention. "Strip him," Dr. Grange ordered, "and burn his uniform, there are maggots crawling all over it. "Then shave him."

Wielding a straight razor, Becky shaved Forrest's head. "All that beautiful blond hair…he looks so pink and naked. Like a newborn."

Dr. Grange strapped Forrest's head to the table and put a cloth gag in his mouth. Forrest moaned as the doctor made an incision in his scalp. He peeled back the flap and exposed the skull. Behind Forrest's closed lids, his eyes rolled in torment. Dr. Grange chose a small hand drill; it had a movable flange on the shank to prevent it from breaking through the cranium too quickly and plunging into the soft matter of the brain. As the drill bit into the bone, Forrest's body arched in agony and then he lay still.

Dr. Grange felt for a pulse. "He's still breathing. Quick now, before he regains consciousness."

Slowly, the drill cut into the skull. Dr. Grange moved the flange back a millimeter, then another, until the drill jerked ever so slightly, the signal that it had cut through. "Now I've got to drill another hole to equalize the pressure." The second hole drilled, Dr. Grange applied a suction cup to one hole and suctioned out every bit of fluid as he could. He then fit a small plate of galvanized steel over the drilled holes, scoring the skull to accommodate it. He closed the flap of skin over the plate and stitched it tightly in place.

"Scar tissue will form around the plate and hold it securely," he explained. "The first day will be crucial, the longer he lives, the better his chances. He'll hurt, and suffer from extremes of temperature, but even if he survives, given the extent of his injuries, and the fact that he may never regain his wits, death might have been kinder."

"No," she exclaimed sharply, "as long as he's alive, there's hope."

The operation had taken two hours. Becky moved Forrest to a tent and, and having burned his clothes, dressed him in a tattered gray uniform. Bone-weary though they were, Becky and Dr. Grange stayed with him through the night. Blessedly, Forrest remained unconscious most of the time; he woke once, his body writhing with such pain that Becky thought he was about to die. She quickly gave him a draught of the morphine that Uncle Gunning had given her. In a bit, Forrest retreated back to a dark, pain-free place.

As the hours passed, Becky couldn't help but wonder at the strange twists of events that had brought them here, even the odd way that she'd come by the morphine. Along with her wonder came a fear of how it would end. The family had lost Geary, now Becky vowed that she wouldn't lose Forrest.

During the next two days Dr. Grange and Becky fought for Forrest's life. One crisis after another developed, seizures, the threat of blood poisoning. Somehow, by constant care and prayer they managed to hold death at bay. Forrest remained in a deep coma. "Just as well," Dr. Grange said, "I don't think he could stand the pain."

The soldiers who'd brought Forrest in never returned and Dr. Grange stayed alert for an opportunity to transfer Forrest to a Union field hospital; he made inquiries to determine if there were any in the vicinity, but events moved too swiftly for that. That day, June 28, General Jubal Early entered the city of York and demanded $100,000, plus a king's ransom in food and supplies. The terrified citizens gave him all they had, including $28,000 in cash. General Early, implementing Lee's grand strategy, gathered his forces to strike toward Harrisburg while General Ewell, fighting in from the west, would join him in a two-pronged attack on that capital.

But on June 30, a minor skirmish occurred which changed the entire thrust of the Confederate invasion. The Rebel army, acting on reports about the warehouses full of shoes at Gettysburg, marched to capture the town. But they encountered several divisions of Union troops that had also moved into the area. Rebs and Yanks fought a brief but inconclusive battle.

The Confederate field hospital lay some four miles from Gettysburg and ambulance wagons began to cart in the wounded. Neither side wanted to fight there, the town had little strategic importance; yet somehow more and more forces on both sides were committed. Lincoln had by now replaced Hooker with General Meade who took a far more aggressive stance. When Lee learned that General Meade's army was marching up from Maryland he ordered Generals Ewell and Early to hold off attacking Harrisburg and join the major Confederate army massing around Gettysburg. If the Union army could be decisively defeated there, the road to Philadelphia and ultimate victory lay open.

By July 1, the lines were drawn and the roar of artillery began to reverberate throughout the field hospital, rattling anything not nailed down. The acrid odor of gunpowder drifted in from the battlefield. Then came the wounded.

Three surgeons worked at a breakneck pace; they'd just about finish with one wagonload when another ambulance would roll in. Given a choice, surgeons preferred to operate during daylight hours, but since most battles ended at dusk, they were forced to work through the night. All that first night the ambulances continued their run from battlefield to hospital. A low murmur wafted over the compound, punctuated by an occasional scream or a piteous cry for help. From these wounded men Becky gleaned what was happening at Gettysburg.

In all, 65,000 Confederate troops were ranged against the numerically superior 85,000 Federals. Prophetic names came from the soldiers' mouths, of Little Round Top, the Devil's Den, Cemetery Hill and Cemetery Ridge. A corporal with an ugly bayonet gash in his arm told them, "Been in this war since the very start but this is the bitterest fighting I've seen. Heavy losses on both sides.

But when General Lee arrived, we handed him Gettysburg. We whupped Billy Yank good and proper, 'spect they're retreating by now, so sew me up real tight, I want to be in on it tomorrow when we finish the job. Then on to Philadelphia."

But General Meade didn't retreat, instead he brought up reinforcements and consolidated his strategic position on Cemetery Ridge. Lee had ordered that vital site be taken the day before when Yankee defenses weren't in place, but the commanders had procrastinated and lost their opportunity.

Fierce fighting continued throughout the next day, July 2. Ambulances continued to rumble into the field hospital, and the wounded, mouths blackened from biting off the ends of the powder charges, spoke in hushed terms of how Billy Yank, now fighting on his own soil, was no longer a pushover. They whispered of the hand-to-hand fighting that created mountains of dead, and of the bloody stalemate that threatened to kill every last man in the field.

Becky searched the faces of the wounded, half-expecting to see Carleton's. The escalating casualties, the horror of their wounds tormented her, but she couldn't allow her despair to surface; the only way to survive was to remain numb.

"We've run out of tent space," she told Dr. Grange.

"Along with everything else," he muttered, as he probed for a bullet in a private's intestine. This type of injury usually meant an automatic death sentence, but he had to try. "We've no chloroform left, I've used the last of your morphine—damn the Union and its embargo!"

The private's body convulsed, death rattled from his throat. Nurses moved him off the table and another soldier took his place. Dr. Grange said to Becky, "Do what you can to find a place for the new wounded coming in. You'll think of something."

The nurses spelled each other at the operating tables, and during her break, Becky organized a work crew. The barn lofts were stacked with hay and she had orderlies spread the straw in the meadow to act as a blanket. She put the critically wounded close to the barn's operating area; the less seriously injured were laid out in the meadow. She lost count somewhere in the hundreds; by nightfall, acres of dead and dying lay in the meadow. She threaded her way through the rows, offering water to one, comforting words to another. She held her oil lantern aloft, terrified that one false step could ignite the straw and immolate them all. Ever so slowly, ever so silently, the North's golden hay absorbed the blood of Johnny Reb.

Whatever the horror in the meadow, Becky thought it minor compared to the scene in the barn's cavernous interior. Surgeons and nurses worked relentlessly, no time for lengthy examinations; if a man's arm or leg had been shattered by a Minie ball, the surgeons amputated. The only anesthetic, a slug of whiskey; the only concession to pain, a bullet to bite. Given the high risk of infection, experience had proven that immediate amputation was the best way to save a man's life. Those that died of shock—well, they wouldn't have had the strength to survive anyway.

Dr. Grange's rubber apron was splattered with gore and it looked like he was wearing dark red gloves. "More light," he ordered, and Becky trimmed the wicks of the lanterns and added oil to the reservoirs. The lamps burned a bit brighter, the harsh light illuminating the three trestle tables that ran red with blood. An emptied corncrib had been pressed into service and now a tangled mass of amputated arms and legs stuck grotesquely from it, as if reaching desperately for their owners. The smell of death hovered in the air and grew more fetid through the dark hours. Daylight seemed never to come, as if unwilling to shed light on the site, a barn no longer, but a charnel house.

As July 3rd dawned, everyone sensed that this Saturday would see the fateful battle. It had to be, neither side could sustain more casualties. Truth and rumor flowed in from the front and Becky listened, trying to separate the wheat from the chaff. She heard of Lee's anger over General Longstreet's indecision and of his despair that Jeb Stuart's cavalry had been so tardy in joining him, depriving him of vital information about the enemy's strength.

From a wounded major, Becky learned that the Federal army had massed along Cemetery Ridge, the Confederates faced them on the somewhat lower Seminary Ridge; the principal battlefield lay between. The previous day Lee had attempted to turn both of the Federal's flanks, but with no success. Today, Lee had decided on a direct assault, and the major cursed the injuries that prevented him from leading the charge for Lee, for the South, and for victory.

At one in the afternoon, a thunderous Confederate artillery barrage began and was quickly answered by eighty Union cannon. The shelling continued for two hours, then slackened. Lee, believing that the Federal line was weakening, ordered General Pickett's men to charge the very center of the Union defenses at Cemetery Ridge.

Down Seminary Ridge the Rebels streamed, 15,000 strong, their momentum carrying them up toward the crest of Cemetery Ridge where the entrenched Federals poured down their murderous fire. The line of Gray crumpled, regrouped, crumpled again, yet always moving toward the Blue, until they were locked in hand-to-hand combat. Men fired into each other's faces, bayonets thrust into flesh, saber strokes cut off arms and severed necks, men fell in grotesque heaps until there were mounds of dead.

The Rebels had sworn they'd follow Lee to hell itself, and this day they did. Again and again they charged into the withering fire. But Meade called up his reserves and the Federal line held. The resulting carnage decimated the Confederate ranks; Pickett's men were literally wiped out. Realizing his disastrous miscalculation, Lee buried his face in his hands and wept; "All this had been my fault, all my fault."

Lee had no other option; at dusk, his order went down the line. Retreat.

Chapter 34

THE NIGHT of July 3 and all the next day, the staff at the field hospital worked in a frenzy to load the wounded into the ambulance wagons. "Leave all unnecessary equipment," Dr. Grange ordered, "and the dead, no time to bury them."

"What are we going to do about Forrest?" Becky asked in a hushed voice. "If we leave him, he'll die."

Dr. Grange stared dumbly at her, three days of unrelenting hell and no sleep had left him on the verge of collapse. "I don't give a damn!" he exploded. "I hate every last one of these god-damned Yankees!"

She blanched at his assault then glanced around anxiously to make sure no one had heard.

Veins in his neck throbbed, "I could have saved some of our men—and theirs—if I had the medicines, if I had decent surgical equipment. How can you not hate these barbarians?"

She held him while his body shook with spasms of rage. "You're right, but we've got to save Forrest. He's family. What kind of monsters would we be if we denied one of our own blood? As evil as Cain, as evil as any Yankee. I beg you, we mustn't become like them."

Bled of tears and anger, reason slowly returned, and Dr. Grange murmured, "You're right, if we leave him, he'll die. Right now, everyone's forgotten that he's a Yankee. Somewhere along the line there'll be a prisoner exchange, we'll get him to a Federal hospital then."

They put Forrest in a wagon groaning with other Rebel wounded. Becky climbed into the driver's seat and Dr. Grange called, "God speed." She mouthed a silent amen, and at dusk, in a driving rain, moved her wagon into the line of march as Lee's army started its bitter retreat.

Wagons carrying the wounded and supplies left first, followed by artillery units and infantry, with Jeb Stuart's cavalry spearheading both the vanguard and protecting the rear. Bees and butterflies stirred in the summer haze, pollinating lupine and lily along the road and as the wagon train creaked by they'd swarm up in a flash of stained glass colors to settle again when the wagons passed. Watching their peaceful labors, Becky mused, "Of all God's many creations, has He given dominion over the Earth to the right one?"

The Union army dogged them half-heartedly, decimated as it was by its own awesome losses. Of the 85,000 Federals engaged at Gettysburg, 23,000 were killed, wounded or missing. The 65,000 Confederates had suffered 20,000 casualties. Two days later, the Federal cavalry, whipped on by the demands of Lincoln and Stanton, attacked. Though the hospital wagons were marked in bright yellow, little attention was paid in the melee; only Jeb Stuart's cavalry saved them from annihilation.

On July 9, at Beaver Creek, Federals again tried to destroy the wagon train, but a strong rear guard action by Jeb Stuart allowed them to reach the Potomac near Williamsport. The river was running high, too high to ford safely, and the Rebel army hastily fortified its position in a bend of the river and waited for the waters to fall. For five terrifying days they waited, trapped, while the river continued to rage, and the Union army pressed closer.

Each day Becky and the orderlies went through the ambulances, culling the dead from the living. Forrest's condition remained much the same; he'd taken no nourishment for a week and Becky wondered how he survived at all. Could it be that in times of deep trauma, with vital signs slowed to a minimum, the body slipped into a state akin to hibernation?

Lee tried to arrange an exchange of prisoners and wounded and Becky prayed it would come about. But Meade, knowing that this extra baggage slowed the Rebels, delayed and equivocated and no exchange was ever made.

On the banks of the Potomac the Rebels learned from gleeful Union pickets that July 4 had been a bleak day for the Confederacy. Not only had Lee been stopped at Gettysburg but on that same day Vicksburg had fallen to General Grant. Lee's invasion of the North had been thwarted and the South was now also cut off from the Trans-Mississippi's vital supplies.

Then came the worst news of all. Rebel scouts reported that the Union army was massing to deliver the killing blow. The river still ran at flood tide. Lee's Engineering Corps, aided by thousands of soldiers, worked furiously to build pontoon bridges. It came down to one thing, if it rained, the Potomac would remain swollen and they wouldn't be able to cross the river and escape. Lee's army would be crushed; the war would be over. As they felled trees and lashed pontoons together, men lifted their eyes to the sky and prayed.

It did not rain. The river receded a bit and on Monday, July 13, under cover of darkness, pontoon bridges were thrown across the Potomac. A test wagon crossed first, and when it reached the other side safely, the rest of the wagons began their slow, treacherous crossing. Campfires were left burning to make it seem that the Confederate army was still encamped.

Becky eased her wagon onto the bridge, holding the reins tightly as the skittish horses reacted to the swaying planks beneath their muffled hooves. It was absolutely imperative to keep the horses from veering to either side of the narrow causeway, one false step and the wagon would plunge into the river. A wagon full of wounded men sinking beneath the dark waters? No one would survive. She squinted to see the way, her head and shoulders aching with the effort, while the phosphorescent waters lapped dangerously around the wagon wheels. If only there was more light! If only she could see. She began to panic, clutched the reins in a death grip as tears of fatigue and despair blinded her. She knew she'd never make it.

Then for some unknown reason she thought of her mother…then her grandmother…both so different, yet hewn from the same bedrock, indomitable women, fierce in their beliefs. Yes, the women in her family had never given up, never.

She shut her eyes to force the tears out, then leaned forward, intent on the path. On the southern side of the Potomac she saw tiny twinkling lights, thousands of them beckoning to her. Am I hallucinating, she wondered? But as she got closer to the shore she saw them moving in their dazzling erratic patterns…fireflies, fireflies, fireflies! Such a host as she'd never seen before, beckoning, beckoning to her.

What seemed like an eternity later, she felt the wheels of her ambulance roll onto solid ground; a drover grabbed the reins and helped her up the bank.

All through that dark night Lee moved his men across the Potomac. Meade's army had maneuvered into position to deliver the deathblow at dawn. But the next morning, instead of an opponent, Meade found an abandoned camp.

Battered though the Rebel army was—they'd lost an additional 1500 men during the retreat to the Potomac—Lee blew up the pontoon bridges and held his position on the Potomac's south shore. This prevented Meade from crossing, and gave Lee time to transport the wounded back to Richmond.

Dr. Grange insisted that Becky return to Chimborazo. "I know you want to stay in the field, but unless Forrest gets real hospital care, we'll lose him. You're the only one who can see to that. You know I'm right."

She nodded but suddenly felt very frightened. "Do I keep up the deception that Forrest is a Southerner?"

"He is a Southerner, and he has the accent to prove it. We've gotten rid of everything that could identify him as a Union soldier. Give him a false identity from one of our own dead. At some point there'll surely be a prisoner exchange. Time enough then to tell the truth."

They both knew his plan made the most sense, and the following day it was with sinking heart that they said their farewells. He embraced her and she whispered, "I love you. If it hadn't been for you—all you've done for me and for others—you prove that life's worth living."

Neither could bring themselves to say what they truly feared, that they might never see each other again. With a final embrace, she broke free, and, sobbing uncontrollably began the long slow journey back to Richmond.

Chapter 35

REBECCA HAD been plagued with a dull headache for several days. Bittersweet had used every home remedy she could think of, but when the headache persisted, she told Rebecca, "I don't like this atall, I'm goin' to fetch the doctor."

"You'll do nothing of the kind, I've had these blasted headaches before and if I just grit my teeth, they eventually go away."

She unfolded the afternoon paper and cried out when she saw the blaring headline. "Have you seen this? Robert's tendered his resignation."

"Robert who?"

"The Robert, my Robert, the only Robert who's important, you ninny, Bobby Lee." She read the headline article aloud; "This newspaper has learned from reliable sources that on August 9, General Robert E. Lee asked President Jefferson Davis to be relieved of his command of the Army of Northern Virginia. After the South's crushing defeat at Gettysburg, southern newspapers were up in arms about the outcome, and Lee felt it his duty to resign. Unfortunately for the North, Jefferson Davis refused to accept Lee's resignation."

"What's so almighty important about that?" Bittersweet declared, "way you was yellin' I thought the war be over."

"It is almighty important. Two men are holding this rebellion together, Jefferson Davis and Robert E. Lee. If either of them falls, the war will be over in a week."

Rebecca sighed; "When I think how often Bobby Lee and Jeff have been in this house, broken bread with us—"

"If I'da known, I'da put ground glass in it."

"What did you say, dear? You must speak up, you've gotten into this terrible habit of mumbling."

"I said, did you ever hear from Mr. Gunning?"

Melancholy veiled Rebecca's eyes; "No; I don't even know if he ever got my letters. I suppose no news is good news. Incidentally, did you deliver my message to Bravo?"

"Third time you asked me that today, and for the third time, yes. Said he'd come to see you 'round about sixish."

"I don't know why he's avoiding me, I've asked him here twice this week—this package I sent to Forrest? With all the goodies you baked and the socks I knitted? Why was it returned? I must check the address. Or get his new one."

Bittersweet rolled her eyes; "And you told me that liken on to a hundred times."

"Do you realize, my girl, that as you get older, you're getting more and more testy?" The clock chimed six and Rebecca clapped her hands; "Time for our sherry." At Rebecca's invitation, Bittersweet joined her.

About a half-hour later, Bravo arrived. The moment Rebecca saw him her heart shriveled. His body was slumped forward and his face bore a look of such unutterable sadness it could only mean one thing.

She rose shakily; "Forrest?"

He swallowed hard; "Missing in action, but there's—"

She could barely make out the rest of what he said, barely heard Bittersweet's scream as she grabbed for her while she fell down and down into the abyss.

Rebecca hid in some dark corner of her soul, hid for a long time, her pain so profound she dared not face the truth. When at last she did surface, she became conscious of people hovering around her bedside, speaking in hushed voices.

The doctor was saying to Bravo, "She's had another stroke. Much like the one she suffered fifteen years ago when she learned that Suzannah had died."

"How serious is it?" Bravo asked. "Will she recover?"

"Too early to tell, it's only been a week. Her paralysis may be temporary, or it may be permanent. In so many cases the extent of the recovery is up to the patient."

"Then she'll pull through," Bravo insisted, "Ma won't give up, she's a been an ornery cuss all her life."

But though the stroke turned out to be mild, and Rebecca regained a good deal of her speech, she didn't get better. This despite Bittersweet's daily massages and Sharon urging her to get out of bed and try to walk. For weeks on end she just lay there, resisting all advice and in her slurred complaints, making life miserable for everybody.

"Oh, why didn't the good Lord take me?" she sobbed, trying to hide her twisted mouth.

Bittersweet, her nerves frayed, snapped, "Because He got enough trouble as is. The Devil don't want you neither, why should he? Long as you're doing his work right here."

"What do you mean?" she demanded in a gurgle.

"It's the truth, with your whining and complaining and making everybody wait on you when they could be doing better things? Like helping find Forrest 'stead of you feeling sorry for yourself. You'd think you was the one gone missing."

"How dare you—get out! Out of my house! I never want to see—" she tried to throw a book at her but it slipped through her fingers, "out!"

Bittersweet turned on her heel and hurried out of the room, leaving Rebecca trembling. She returned a short time later, a red bandanna tied neatly around her black curly hair, a cloth valise in hand. "'Bye now. Here's the house keys."

"Where do you think you're going?"

"Told me to get out, so I'm goin'. To my chilluns."

"You can't leave. You're the only one who understands what I'm saying."

"Don't forget to take your medicine, every four hours."

"Don't be so ridiculous. Besides, I wouldn't know where to find everything you've hidden in this house."

"Hidden? You means to imply that I'm stealin'? Can't stay here a minute longer, not with you actin' this way. Might as well be livin' in a lunatic asylum."

"How can you be so heartless? I loved him more than life itself. I raised him from a babe—"

"No you didn't, I raised him. You takes credit for it all the time, but who was the one cooked his meals, scrubbed his clothes, fixed his cuts, washed and bathed and nursed him from mah breast along with my own chillun? I was the one raised mah little boy!"

The two women glared at each other, tears coursing down their cheeks. Then Rebecca sobbed, "Oh, my dear girl—" She reached out with her good hand and Bittersweet fell to her knees beside the bed. The two women embraced and wept until both had no more tears left.

From that day on Rebecca made every effort to regain her strength. One thing impelled her, that Forrest might be alive, that she must find him. August burned into the breathless heat of September; by then she'd gotten out of bed, and leaning on Bittersweet, began taking her first tentative steps around the sitting room. By mid-October she'd relearned to negotiate the hall steps and could make her way downstairs for dinner. By October's end, her speech cleared up enough so she could be understood by all.

Still unable to write, she dictated frantic letters to Sharon, who sent them to every government department; Rebecca even wrote to Gunning and Becky in Richmond, hoping they might know something. But the underground mail system between Richmond and Washington had been severely compromised by Secretary of War Stanton's efforts and her letters never reached their destination.

*

On a vicious rainy day in early November, Bravo dragged his way to his mother's house. He poked his head into the kitchen where Bittersweet stirred brown sugar into a pot of bubbling blackberries she was putting up for preserves.

"Where's the patient?" he asked morosely.

"Upstairs, nappin'. Sit you, get the cold off before you wake her." She put the kettle on. "Had a busy day, she did, walked all over the house ten times, couldn't keep up with her. Where you been, Bravo, she's been asking for days."

She handed him a mug of tea; Bravo sat at the rough-hewn oak kitchen table and cupped his hands around the mug. "I've just come back from Pennsylvania."

Bittersweet sat down heavily; "You found out somethin', I hears it in your voice. Oh merciful Lord, afraid to ask."

He nodded somberly. "I've been trying to trace Forrest's movements, and a few weeks ago I heard reports of a balloon being downed late last June. So I went looking where it had been seen. I talked to every farmer I could, tracked every lead. Then a couple of days ago, I found the remains of a balloon, pieces of it still caught in a tree."

"Maybe it wasn't our boy's? Maybe—"

"It was his. All the other aeronauts had come back to Washington by then, Forrest was the last one flying. I never found his body, but it doesn't seem possible that anyone could have survived such a crash. I keep hearing Ma saying, 'What infernal killing machine did you invent today?'" He stared at his hands, "Wish I'd never..."

He stood up; "I've got to tell Ma."

Bittersweet seized his hand; "You dasn't! It would kill her. Almost killed me."

"How can I lie about something like this?"

"If you found his body it'd be different. But you didn't, so why rob your Ma of her one bit of hope? How much time she got left? This be the only thing keeps her alive. It's not like you're lyin', just don't say nothin'."

Bravo considered this, and when Rebecca wakened, he kept a brave front and said nothing.

*

In mid-November, Rebecca learned that Lincoln was going to Gettysburg on the 19th, to deliver a commemorative speech dedicating the battleground as a National Cemetery. Over the vigorous protests of her doctor and the rest of the family, she decided she had to go.

Bittersweet locked her in her room and wouldn't let her out until the last connecting train had departed.

The next day Rebecca read all the newspapers' reactions to Lincoln's address. A British correspondent declared, "It is the most inane, puerile speech ever given by a Head of State." One editorial labeled it, "Eminently forgettable," still another caviled at its brevity, "Only eighty-two words and the President took less than two minutes to deliver it? Shameful. Surely our honored dead deserve better than that."

Rebecca read the text aloud, "Fourscore and seven years ago our forefathers brought forth on this continent a new nation..." she thrilled to the soaring spirit inherent in Lincoln's biblical cadences, and with the concluding words, "we here highly resolve that these dead shall not have died in vain, that this nation under God, shall have a new birth of freedom, and that government of the people, by the people, for the people, shall not perish from the earth..." her tears fell, hot and blinding.

PART FOUR

PART FOUR

Chapter 36

SEVEN LONG months had passed since the carnage at Gettysburg, seven long months in which both sides paused to bind their wounds and stop the hemorrhaging.

Then on Tuesday, February 9, 1864, Richmond woke to the alarm of a terrifying tocsin. Church bells pealed without stop and the citizenry armed themselves for whatever new catastrophe threatened. Then they learned the terrifying news: Prison break in the heart of the city! Laboriously tunneling their way out of Libby Prison, 109 Union officers had escaped; 48 were recaptured, two drowned, but 59 eventually made their way to Union lines. A pall fell over Richmond; with over 10,000 Union soldiers incarcerated in the city, and guarded only by the flimsiest force, what if the damned Yankees were to rise up all at once?

*

News of the prison break electrified Washington. The escapees who reached Federal lines told tales of inhuman conditions and from across the nation came cries for Lincoln to "Do something!" An ambitious general in the Federal cavalry seized this outcry to advance himself.

In Lincoln's office at the White House, Bravo Brand listened to a spirited argument between Lincoln and Secretary of War Stanton, and Brigadier General Hugh Judson Kilpatrick. When Lincoln had asked Bravo to attend this meeting, he'd confided, "I'm wary of being swept away by Stanton's formidable passions, I need an objective opinion, I need to hear the voice of reason." Kilpatrick prowled the room, spurs jingling as he attempting to persuade Lincoln about a scheme of his, which Bravo experienced as the ravings of a wild man.

A wiry, undersized man, Kilpatrick wore knee-high boots with elevated heels. His red hair was slicked down and joined heavy side whiskers that grew like dewlaps, connecting to his moustache in an upside down U, leaving his chin bare. The design was his, meant to set him apart. His oversized head looked as if someone had pulled down on his jaw, elongating it and his nose. The joke in the Third Cavalry Division was that you couldn't tell Kilpatrick from his horse. Twenty-eight, and among the youngest generals in the army, ruthless ambition had earned him the nickname, 'Kill-Cavalry Kilpatrick.' At Gettysburg, acting with total disregard for his men, he'd ordered one of his brigade commanders to charge an impregnable Rebel position. The commander was killed, so were the majority of his troopers. The name 'Kill-Cavalry' stuck.

Lincoln interrupted Kilpatrick's diatribe; "I'm no authority on strategy but I do have serious reservations. Only the plight of our prisoners prompts me to consider your plan at all. How many casualties might you sustain? And is this really in our best interest?"

Stanton half-rose from his chair, his paunch jutting into the conference table; "Not in our best interest? I disagree most emphatically. I say use any means to stamp out this rebellion and bring that apostate Jefferson Davis to justice. He's nothing but a murderer and must pay for his crimes."

Everyone knew Stanton grieved for his son who'd been killed in the war and personally blamed Jefferson Davis for his loss. Nothing would assuage his grief save that Davis be brought to trial, convicted, and hung as a traitor.

Just then, Tad Lincoln burst in; "Paw! Maw says you must come quick; what do you want for your special supper tonight?"

Lincoln ruffled Tad's hair; "Tell your Ma I'll be with her shortly." After Tad left Lincoln apologized; "Forgive the interruption but after our Willie died, I find it hard to refuse Tad anything."

"Happy Birthday, Mr. President," Bravo said.

Lincoln nodded his thanks and remarked with a ruminative sigh, "Can I only be fifty-five? With all that's beset our Union, I feel more like Methuselah."

"Which is precisely why we should strike now," Stanton argued. "Our people grow weary, how much longer can we count on their support? Dare we forget that we face a presidential election only ten months from now?"

Lincoln sobered; "That thought haunts me daily. If the war isn't won by then and we're voted out of office, I fear that our Union is lost forever."

"Give me your approval and I swear the war will be long over before then and your re-election assured," Kilpatrick insisted. "I'll strike with a cavalry force of five thousand men and a few light cannon. We'll swing wide around Lee's army at Fredericksburg, ride hard and invade Richmond."

"Our spies report that Richmond is virtually undefended," Stanton added. "They've only a Home Guard made up of boys and old men. Their main army is many miles away at winter camp."

"What chance would a puny Home Guard have against our seasoned cavalry?" Kilpatrick demanded, the battle won even as he spoke. "Once in the city I'll make straight for Libby prison, set our officers free, then proceed on to Belle Isle where we'll do the same for our enlisted men."

Stanton peered over the rims of his steel-rimmed glasses; "Ten thousand of our men are imprisoned, dying in Richmond."

Kilpatrick rubbed his hands; "Those ten thousand, joined with my five thousand, gives us a force more than capable of conquering an undefended city."

"But Lee's cavalry is certain to respond," Bravo put in.

Kilpatrick shot him a disdainful look. "Already anticipated. I plan a diversionary strike at Charlottesville to draw Jeb Stuart off. Once I free our prisoners," he paused for emphasis, "I burn the Tredegar Iron Works to the ground."

"That alone would be worth any casualties sustained in the raid," Stanton interjected. "Kilpatrick would also destroy the Gallego Flour Mills which supplies ninety percent of the Confederacy's flour."

Kilpatrick exclaimed in jubilation, "With the city afire and all in confusion, we capture Jefferson Davis and bring him to Washington!"

Bravo blinked in disbelief. "General, Jeff Davis is a West Pointer, hero of the Mexican-American War. What makes you think he'd allow himself to be captured?"

Stanton pounded his fists on the table; "If Davis won't be captured so much the better, it will save us a long and costly trial. But one way or another he must be eliminated. Along with his cabinet, including the Jew, Benjamin. The head of the viper cut off, the rebellion must die."

Lincoln turned to Bravo, giving him leave to speak. If Bravo had his way he'd have booted both Stanton and this vainglorious high-heeled ass out of the White House, but politics dictated that he tread with caution. "Could you tell us more of your plan, General? When would you strike?"

"The last week in February, while Lee's army is still hibernating in winter camp. We'd be in Richmond by the twenty-ninth, March first the latest. By God, gentlemen can you imagine this war being over in less than a month?"

Bravo opened a velum folder and took out some maps and several pages of statistics. "President Lincoln asked me to gather some information about the Richmond area, so Joseph Henry and I poured through the Smithsonian's files. General, are you familiar with Richmond?"

"Enough to know that I can capture it," he snapped.

"Would it were that simple," Bravo replied equably. "Lee is about the best army engineer West Point ever turned out; during McClellan's Peninsula Campaign we discovered that Lee had ringed Richmond with formidable fortifications. Thus, a small Home Guard could hold off a much larger force."

General Kilpatrick cried in exasperation, "Surprise, sir, you forget the element of surprise."

"Your cavalry will have to ride through a hundred miles of enemy territory; sooner or later your objective will become clear. In February the weather can be abominable. Heavy rainfall, swollen rivers, mired roads—"

"Those conditions must also work in our favor," Kilpatrick insisted, "they'll impede pursuit by the Rebels."

"But you've got to get there first!" Bravo exclaimed in a flash of anger. "Your plan may seem fine on paper but it's a paper plan. One false step, one miscalculation and you put the lives of thousands of men in jeopardy. With all due respect, General, you haven't fully calculated the risks."

Kilpatrick stamped his high heel. "Yes, it is dangerous, yes, it is daring, but we're locked in a stalemate and daring is what's needed. Are we always to be stopped by the nay-sayers? Mr. President, hasn't your complaint always been that you didn't have a general who'd fight? I propose to fight and end this war in one bold stroke. The choice, sir, is yours."

A palpitating moment passed, then Stanton plunged into the breech. "Brand, your concern for our men is exemplary. Since you've studied the terrain, the weather conditions and the disposition of the Confederate forces, wouldn't it make great sense if you accompanied General Kilpatrick?"

Kilpatrick grimaced and Stanton added hastily, "In an advisory capacity only, of course; military decisions would be left solely in the General's hands. I'd sleep easier with you along, I'm sure the President feels the same way."

Bravo knew Stanton's statement for what it was, a crock, but in one bold stroke his insidious lawyer's mind had put the burden on his shoulders.

Taking his cue from Stanton, Kilpatrick adopted a conciliatory tack; "Brand, Stanton's idea has merit. Consider this; from my main force of five thousand, I plan to handpick five hundred troopers and have them operate as a separate cavalry unit. They'll enter Richmond from the south, over the Manchester Bridge, which gives direct access to Belle Isle. Once there, they'll free our prisoners and join up with my main force in Richmond. Colonel Ulric Dahlgren will command that cavalry unit. You could ride with Dahlgren's advance guard and give him the benefit of your knowledge."

Bravo's mind scrambled at the mention of Ulric Dahlgren. Rear Admiral John Dahlgren's son, about Forrest's age. He'd read about him recently, wounded at Gettysburg, but wasn't there something else…?

Stanton peered at Bravo; "As a father who's lost a son, I know how you must feel with your own boy missing in action. But what if unbeknownst to us he was a prisoner? And what if you were destined to be the instrument of his release?"

For an instant hope sprang in Bravo. Instead of Forrest lying in some unmarked grave, might he be in a Rebel prison? But that seemed very remote, he'd checked and rechecked every prisoner list posted by the War Department and Forrest's name had never been on any of them.

Bravo looked to Lincoln but his weary face remained impassive. He knew the President was under tremendous pressure from abolitionists to end the war swiftly, and had to investigate every possibility. That this scheme had come via his Secretary of War, one of the most powerful men in the Republican War Party gave it ponderous weight.

"I'm meeting with Ulric Dahlgren tomorrow," Kilpatrick told Bravo, "the Long Bar at Willard's, four o'clock. Why not meet us there? Gauge the man, make up your mind then."

Lincoln spoke up; "Bravo, I'd be obliged if you would meet with Dahlgren, then let me know what you think."

Then Lincoln pinned Kilpatrick with a hard stare. "Even if I should say yes to your raid, I want it understood that my objectives are as follows: To destroy all war installations, particularly the Tredegar Iron Works. To distribute our leaflets with our amnesty proposal. Finally, and dearest to my heart, the release of our soldiers held prisoner."

Bravo noted that Lincoln made no mention of Kilpatrick's intention to capture Jefferson Davis.

Further discussion was cut off when Tad burst into the room and began pulling his father toward the door. "Maw says you must come now. You must choose a cake…" Tad's importuning grew fainter as Bravo left the White House.

The following afternoon, Bravo waited at the Long Bar at Willard's. Officers four-deep lined the forty-foot mahogany bar. Clinking spurs announced Kilpatrick's arrival; he removed his rakish campaign hat, gauntlet gloves and military cape with a flourish worthy of an Italian tenor. He and Bravo got a table; Kilpatrick never drank, Bravo nursed a bourbon.

Colonel Ulric Dahlgren came in a bit later, propelling his body forward with two canes. Bravo's heart sank; now he remembered. While pursuing Lee's army from Gettysburg, Dahlgren had been wounded in the foot. He refused to leave the field and finally collapsed from loss of blood. His leg had to be amputated below the knee.

Bravo studied Dahlgren: Tall, thin, handsome, twenty-one or thereabouts. He had a sensitive face, light thinning hair and a blond moustache and goatee. His head appeared small for his lanky frame, which made Kilpatrick's head seem that much bigger. His voice rang clear and youthful, in fact, everything about him shouted youth. During their discussion Bravo gleaned some disturbing qualities about him. Dahlgren was impulsive, dominated by a need to constantly prove himself. For good reason; his father, inventor of the 11-inch naval gun that had been used on the *Monitor*, was so revered that Ulric had spent his life trying to measure up. The loss of a leg only made him more determined.

Dahlgren saw Bravo glance at his canes and rapped on his hollow wooden leg; "Walking is a bit difficult but I can ride as well as any man. Nor has my aim been affected, or my brain, and I'm determined to bring the Rebels to heel."

So this is the man Kilpatrick's chosen as his second in command? Bravo thought. A callow, one-legged hothead desperate to prove himself? Would Kilpatrick have made the same choice if Ulric's father hadn't been an admiral with powerful connections in the War Department?

The men talked for an hour, each man trying to get the measure of the other. Kilpatrick used his considerable energies to persuade Bravo to join them. Bravo wasn't taken in, he knew his compliance might go a long way toward eliminating some of Lincoln's reservations.

Finally Bravo stood up; "I've several things to discuss with the President. I'll let you know tomorrow."

Bravo walked over to his mother's house. When Rebecca saw him her hope sprang, but he shook his head as he'd done for so many months, and watched her hope die.

"I may be going away for a few weeks. Don't ask where, what you don't know—"

"Ridiculous to think that I would ever say anything."

"Not only would you say it, you'd print it for everybody to read," Bittersweet declared, as she entered the drawing room with a tray of cider and sandwiches.

"Whose idea was it anyway to abolish slavery?" Rebecca sniffed. "I say bring it back, along with leg irons and the lash." Then she turned to her son, her eyes soft and pleading; "Does this have anything to do with Forrest?"

He hesitated, then said, "In a way." For despite his overwhelming misgivings about the mission, Bravo had decided that if Lincoln approved the Richmond raid, he'd ride with Kilpatrick and Dahlgren. His reasons were many, to offer as much help as he could; Ulric Dahlgren was so young, so impetuous, he'd need all the help he could get.

But he had deeper reasons. Ever since Forrest had been listed as missing and presumed dead, Bravo had slipped into a slough of despond. There were days when he felt it really didn't matter much if he lived or died. Then Stanton, in his conniving, self-serving way, had given him hope.

There always remained a glimmer that Forrest might be alive in some Rebel prison. Yes, the raid was dangerous and yes he might not come back. But if there was the slightest chance that his boy might be a prisoner in Richmond, not only would he have stormed Richmond, he'd have battered down the gates of hell itself.

Chapter 37

ON FEBRUARY 26, Bravo entrained from Washington to Brandy Station, Virginia, winter quarters for the Union's Army of the Potomac; 100,000 men were camped in a 10-square mile area. An aide of Kilpatrick's, a Sergeant McLernan, met the train. They then rode three miles to Stephensburg where Kilpatrick and his Third Cavalry Division were bivouacked. They were challenged repeatedly by pickets and Bravo commented, "Kilpatrick runs a tight outfit."

McClernan grunted; "The Rebs've hit us too many times to count. First thing they go after is horses."

"Guess losing Vicksburg and all those herds from the Trans-Mississipi hurt them real bad."

The camp clanked and clamored; a herd of remounts had just arrived and blacksmiths kept the forges roaring to shoe the horses. The pungent odor of fire, sweat and manure hung over everything.

"Know what we're paying for a decent horse?" McClernan asked, "a hundred fifty-nine dollars. Gotten so in this here army, a horse's life is worth more than a man's."

Bravo found Kilpatrick in conference with Dahlgren. The general greeted him with far less enthusiasm than he'd shown in Washington. Why not, Bravo thought, he's gotten Lincoln's approval, he doesn't need me anymore. Kilpatrick filled Bravo in on their progress; Bravo noticed that Dahlgren continually fiddled with a leather writing case that never left his hands.

"The Rebs know we're up to something," Kilpatrick said, "we're twenty-five miles from Fredericksburg where Lee's quartered, so there's no way to hide our build-up. To throw them off, Sedgwick will strike east and engage Wade Hampton. Fanny will attack Charlottesville to draw off Jeb Stuart's cavalry."

Bravo's forehead creased. "Who's Fanny?"

"Brigadier General George Armstrong Custer. We called him Fanny at West Point. He had all this long blond hair? Pretty as a debutante and twice as vain. Since there's no telegraph line along our route to Richmond all we need is a few hours head start and Fanny's raid will give us that."

"When do we ride?"

Kilpatrick stood on tiptoe; "Been meaning to talk to you about that, Brand. We'll be riding hard, seventy-five miles in two days, then back. Under enemy fire. Every man here is a seasoned soldier, and young. No offense, but at forty-five, you're twice the age of most of my troopers."

"No offense taken. Don't worry, I'll keep up."

"Really, Brand, I must insist, I can't jeopardize—"

"General!" Bravo barked, "you have your orders, I have mine. From your Commander-in-Chief—and mine. Now when do we ride?"

In the tension that followed Ulric Dahlgren cleared his throat; "We go the day after tomorrow. We've divided—"

Kilpatrick overrode him; "I've divided our force into two units, A and B. I'll command Force A, with three thousand five hundred men, Colonel Dahlgren will lead Force B, with five hundred men."

"The most extraordinary luck," Dahlgren put in eagerly, "We put out the word that we were looking for guides—would pay well, and this young nigger showed up. Claimed he was born in Richmond, knew the city like the back of his hand—"

"Can you trust him? Can I talk to him?" Bravo asked.

"Time enough en route," Kilpatrick replied irritably, "he'll be going with Dahlgren's unit. Requisition a uniform, a private's. Can't have you in civilian clothes, if you're captured, you'd be shot as a spy. Now Brand, Dahlgren and I have a mountain of details to work out. Dismissed."

Smarting with Kilpatrick's rudeness, Bravo left. Then he realized he'd forgotten his map case. He walked back, rapped on the door, waited, then entered. Kilpatrick looked like he'd been caught with his hand in the till; Dahlgren scrambled to cram a small black notebook into his writing case.

"Damn it, man, we're busy! Get out!" Kilpatrick shouted.

Bravo retrieved his map case, then left. Outside, he fought to control his anger. Under normal circumstances he'd have taken this high-heeled brat across his knee and taught him some manners. But that disturbed him less than the two men's patent guilt. Something was going on.

Knowing Stanton and his perpetual grab for power, Bravo wouldn't put it past him to have given Kilpatrick wide discretionary powers. Lincoln had been explicit about the raid's objectives, but far from the White House and in the heat of battle, Kilpatrick could easily broaden its scope. Whatever it was that made Kilpatrick and Dahlgren look like conspirators, the secret lay in Dahlgren's writing case.

Sunday, February 28, under cover of darkness and dense fog, Bravo watched Colonel Ulric Dahlgren, crutches strapped to his saddle, ride up and down the line of his 500-man force. The troopers, all veterans of the field, had been chosen from the First Maine, the First Vermont, the 5th Michigan, and the First and Second N.Y. Volunteer Cavalry.

A trooper's mess kit clanked and Dahlgren cursed, "God damn it, man, secure all equipment. You're making enough noise to wake Jeff Davis in Richmond."

A shudder rippled along the length of the column. After weeks of speculation, this was the first inkling the troopers had of their objective. "Richmond?" Sergeant McClernan swore, "we might as well be riding into hell."

Dahlgren raised his saber and in his clear piping voice called, "Forward yoooo!" The seasoned troopers looked at him as if he was a child playing with new toy soldiers.

The column headed south toward Ely's Ford at the Rapidan River. Kilpatrick had given Dahlgren's unit a two-hour head start; they were to ford the river and capture any Rebel pickets patrolling the southern shore. Bravo rode just behind the advance guard. He pulled his collar up against the cold penetrating fog; if they were lucky the fog would mask their movements, at least until they'd crossed the Rapidan.

Bravo saw a Negro lad, about twenty, riding up ahead and swaying precariously on a piebald, much to the troopers' amusement. Bravo moved up and steadied the lad's horse.

"Thankee, suh," the lad said, "ain't hardly used to horses, likes a mule mahse'f. Not so far to fall."

"What's your name, boy?"

"Martin Robinson, suh, mos' evabody calls me Robby." His smile was dazzling as he proudly proclaimed, "I'm a Lincum man, ah is." He pointed to Dahlgren; "The man with the wooden leg? I's takin' him all the way to Richmond. Born and raised dere I was. Promised to pay me, he did. My folks be in Richmond, colonel promised me he's g'wan free dem all."

"Do you know how far it is to Richmond?"

The dark eyes rolled in confusion and Bravo's heart sank. Barefoot and dressed in homespun, the lad didn't look like he'd last the night in this weather, let alone the seventy-odd miles to Richmond. Bravo was about to question him further when Dahlgren cantered up. "Cut that chatter."

Bravo fell back in line; nothing much he could do now anyway, the wheels were in motion. Later, when they stopped for a break, he'd question Martin Robinson more intensely.

As they reached Ely's Ford the fog began to lift and a hazy moon emerged. The men cursed their luck; if the pickets spotted them fording the Rapidan their gunfire would sound the alarm, the Confederate cavalry would move to intercept them, and the raid would be over before it began.

There'd been a heavy accumulation of snow and the Rapidan was running high. Scouts crossed first and signaled the all clear. The troopers eased their mounts into the icy rushing waters. Bravo saw Robby clutching his piebald's neck with a death grip; he grabbed the lad's bridle and allowed his own mount to lead them. At last they reached the far bank. The advance guard, with their horses' hooves muffled, rode out to reconnoiter. Ten minutes later they'd captured the dozen Rebel pickets patrolling the river. No one had escaped to sound the alarm and Ulric Dahlgren could barely contain his elation. He gave the order to ride on and didn't object when Robby fell in beside Bravo.

Branches and brambles lashed them as they moved deeper into impenetrable thickets. Bravo wrinkled his nose at a sickly smell...decaying flesh. It stayed with them for miles. Teeth flashing in the dark, Robby mumbled, "Ghosts be in dese parts, folks swears dey still hears dem fightin'."

Bravo's mount stumbled on something; he saw a skeletal rib cage arching out of the ground, farther on, a skull. This must be Chancellorsville, where Lee had defeated Hooker in May of 1863, some ten months before. The dead hadn't been buried very deep and the frost had thrown up the bones of those who stirred in uneasy sleep. Bravo passed in silence, remembering that Forrest had fought in this bloody battle.

They skirted Spotsylvania and continued on toward Mount Pleasant. There, Dahlgren's unit would angle off southwest while Kilpatrick would head due south. Dahlgren's unit was now deep in enemy territory, without the protection of Kilpatrick's larger, more heavily armed cavalry.

An hour later Bravo rode up to Dahlgren. "Colonel, bad news. We're being dogged. Probably Rebel scouts."

Dahlgren nodded curtly; "I'm aware of that, but without any telegraph lines, the only way they can alert Richmond is for them to get there before us. So we'll just have to ride harder. We're going to be in Richmond on Tuesday,

March first or die in the attempt." So saying, he ordered the troopers forward at a more punishing pace.

Chapter 38

ALL THE next day, Dahlgren's force struck deeper into enemy territory. After they'd crossed the Pamunkey River, Bravo studied his map; if they continued in a southwesterly arc it should bring them to the James River, about twenty miles upriver from Richmond. He showed the map to Robby; "Can you point out the best place to cross to the south bank?"

"Jude's Ferry," Robby answered promptly, "can't read, so I don't know it on no map, but I'll know it when I sees it."

Bravo searched the map but Jude's Ferry wasn't marked. "Have you ever crossed in the winter? The truth now."

"Yassuh. You gets wetter, but I'se crossed."

At dusk, while still in the saddle, the weary troopers ate their meager supper of hardtack and jerky. Robby cocked his head, listening to the moaning wind. "Animals be hidin', liken to be a storm comin'."

Dahlgren twitched impatiently; "Storm or no we must be in Richmond by ten tomorrow morning. Kilpatrick will be waiting for our signal to attack."

Once more Bravo went over the plan in his mind. They'd cross the James River at Jude's Ferry; skirt around Richmond, slash through the town of Manchester and enter Richmond through its southern back door. While Dahlgren struck up from the south, Kilpatrick would attack from the north. It had to be timed precisely so the two forces would join up in Richmond. Everything depended on Dahlgren getting across the James River at Jude's Ferry, freeing the prisoners held at Belle Isle, then attacking Richmond.

With darkness the wind picked up and the temperature plummeted. Bravo threw Robby a poncho; "Can't have you catching pneumonia before you get us across the river."

A wind-driven rain began to fall; it grew to an assault and the troopers rode in misery. Just when Bravo thought it couldn't get worse it turned into stinging sleet and snow. By midnight the horses could barely slog through the drifts, troopers caked with snow fell asleep in their saddles. They'd been riding for thirty-six hours without a break.

Dahlgren knew he had to call a halt or his men would collapse. They took shelter in a forest, huddling under hastily pitched lean-tos. After an hour the wind died. Though Bravo could have slept for days he forced himself to get up. He went to check on Dahlgren and found him laboriously transcribing information from his notebook onto Third Division stationery.

"Get any rest?" Bravo asked.

His guard momentarily down, Dahlgren shook his head and massaged his leg ruefully; "When I close my eyes...this damned stump, sometimes it feels like the leg's still attached, that the surgeon's still sawing. Anyway, I had to copy out these Orders of the Day. I'll read it to the troops at dawn, just before we attack Richmond. This will fire the men up; when they hear this—well, you'll know for yourself soon enough."

The moment of camaraderie evaporated, Dahlgren shoved the Orders of the Day back in his case. "Mount up," he ordered, "the storm's cost us a lot of time, we're cutting it close."

Robby couldn't get on his horse and Bravo gave him a leg up. He heard a trooper mutter, "Nigger lover," and barked at him, "You stupid son-of-a-bitch, if you had any brains, you'd realize this boy is our passport to Richmond."

Robby inclined his head toward Bravo; "Minds if I asks you sumpin', suh? You a Southren man?"

Bravo nodded and Robby grinned, "Thought you might be, you ain't like de rest of dese here Yankees."

The storm settled into a penetrating mizzle. Dawn found them lost in a heavily wooded area. A trooper climbed into the limbs of a leafless oak, peered through the snow flurries and called down, "There's the James River, dead ahead."

Bravo studied his map; "I figure we're maybe twenty miles from Richmond. We'd best be crossing the James soon." He turned to Robby; "How far are we from Jude's Ferry?"

"Ain't rightly sure, but I'll knows it when—"

Dahlgren shouted, "Sergeant, when we've crossed the river, assemble the men, time for the Orders of the Day."

They broke free of the woods and followed the roiling river. Trees along the banks showed where high-water marks had once reached and the river was fast approaching that flood level. Bravo's pulse began to race; he checked his watch; 8:30. In an hour and a half they <u>had</u> to be in Richmond.

They reached a bend in the James where it narrowed considerably and Robby slid off his horse and did a jubilant jig. "Dis be it, dis here's Jude's Ferry!"

Thundering water rushed past, spuming high against the riverbank, upending sawyers as it swept them downstream, creating such an impassable barrier it drowned Bravo's heart.

Dahlgren turned bloodless and brought his crop across Robby's head, "You lying bastard, this can't be the place!"

"Dis be it, suh, ah swears."

Dahlgren shouted, "Sergeant, have one of your men test the river, see if we can get across."

A wiry Michigander volunteered and spurred his roan into the rushing river. The horse balked, then plunged in and began to swim. But the current proved too treacherous and man and horse were swept away. Some troopers galloped downstream and barely managed to save their half-drowned comrade.

Dahlgren bulled his horse at Robby; "You nigger bastard, show me where the real crossing is or I'll have you hanged."

Robby fell back before the onslaught, blubbering, "This be Jude's Ferry." Several troopers chuckled at the boy's fright, and one sniggered, "The colonel sure is scaring hell out of that booger."

"Sergeant, bring me a rope," Dahlgren ordered.

Terror lit Robby's eyes and he began to babble, "Dis be it, I'm a Lincum man, please, you don' mean to hang me? You're funnin', right? We're gonna free mah folks—"

Sergeant McLernan brought the rope and Dahlgren knotted it into a noose. "For the last time, you lying Rebel spy—"

Bravo cut in, "Colonel, it's not the boy's fault that we hit a storm, you can see yourself this is all fresh run-off—"

Dahlgren tossed McLernan the rope. "Hang him."

The troopers stirred uneasily; one called, "Leave him be, Colonel, he can't control the weather," while another called, "Hang him and be done, spy or no, he's only a stupid coon."

Apoplectic, Dahlgren shouted, "I'll court martial the next man who opens his mouth. Now hang him!"

McLernan moved half-heartedly toward Robby but Bravo spurred his horse between the lad and the sergeant. "Colonel, call your man off."

Dahlgren drew his sword; "I'm in command here, stand aside." Bravo didn't move and Dahlgren cried, "Arrest him."

Two troopers pinned Bravo's arms; one of them whispered, "Careful, if you cross the colonel he's liable to hang you too, and he'd have the right."

Robby writhed in fear as troopers lifted him onto his piebald; McLernan knotted the noose around his neck.

Bravo fought to get free, all the while shouting at Dahlgren, "You crazy bastard, don't do it. He's only a harmless boy. He's not responsible for your mistakes, don't do it!"

Dahlgren slapped Robby's horse with his saber, the piebald bolted forward, leaving Robby clawing at the rope, slowly strangling...until at last he hung still.

"Move out," Dahlgren ordered, "we've got a war to fight."

The two troopers released Bravo; "Sorry, but orders—"

Shaken out of self, Bravo stared at Robby hanging before his eyes...so young...Forrest's age.

The column advanced down river but couldn't find a place to cross to the south shore. Fast running out of time, Dahlgren had no option but to force his way into Richmond along the north bank of the James. But on this side of the river General Lee had fortified the access to the capital with a series of entrenchments; even a handful of old men and boys could hold off hundreds while inflicting punishing casualties. Dahlgren fearlessly led the cavalry in charge after charge against the harassing Home Guard; they'd chase the guard off, only to run into another entrenchment a short distance away.

Precious time was lost; already they were already three hours late for their rendezvous with Kilpatrick. Then the troopers' spirits soared when they heard a series of cannonades in rapid succession.

"That's Kilpatrick!" Dahlgren shouted, rallying his men, but Bravo muttered to a sergeant, "Remind the colonel that Kilpatrick carried only five small field pieces with him, those shots were fired too fast to be anything less than twenty guns. That's Rebel artillery."

Two miles from Richmond they met with stiffer resistance. Sharpshooters circled them, picking off stragglers. From the diminishing sounds of cannon fire it became apparent that Kilpatrick's attack from the north had also failed. Facing immanent disaster, Dahlgren was forced to break off the engagement and flee for Hungary Station, ten miles north of Richmond, the place that Dahlgren and Kilpatrick had chosen as a rendezvous in the event that anything should anything go wrong.

Bravo tried to figure the odds against them. By now, units of the Rebel cavalry would be riding hard to intercept them. But we still have a chance, he told himself, if we can hold together until dark, maybe we can fight our way out? As they rode and fired and fought to get to Hungary Station, he had an oblique, almost laughable thought, Dahlgren had never gotten to inspire them with his precious Orders of the Day.

His anger against Dahlgren, against Kilpatrick, against Stanton, against himself, for getting hornswoggled into this benighted raid, soon gave way to an even more pressing fear. Never had he felt so afraid. This wasn't like fighting an enemy who might not be as brave or as smart as you, these were fellow Americans, your equals, and better than equals, because they were fighting on their own soil.

Darkness brought another heavy fall of snow, soon changing into an ice storm. Every so often Bravo saw Dahlgren shudder; he was suffering terribly, not only from his amputated leg, but also from the greater pain of his failure. Bravo couldn't bear to look at him, every time he did he saw Robby, eyes popping, tongue protruding as he strangled.

To reach the rendezvous they had to cross the Chickahominy, Pamunkey and Mattaponi Rivers. They battled their way across the first two, only the Mattaponi was left. By now the troopers were so exhausted they rode like corpses propped in their saddles. Horses stumbled into ditches, broke legs, others died from exhaustion and riders had to double up. In the driving storm, the cavalry column lengthened and rear units of Dahlgren's force separated from the lead body and more than 300 men disappeared. Of the 500 troopers who'd started for Hungary Station only 100 reached the Mattaponi.

Dangerously low on ammunition, despair and disappointment blurred their reason. They had only one thought, to get to Kilpatrick's large force, and safety. Without sending out advance scouts, Dahlgren led the sorry remnants of his cavalry unit in a thundering gallop across the swollen stream.

Right into a Rebel ambush. Believing he only faced a small force, Dahlgren drew his gun and charged, screaming, "Surrender, you damned Rebels!" The thickets erupted with gunfire and five bullets smashed into him.

Midst the curses of the wounded and dying, the shrill whinnying of horses and bloody entrails, Bravo's horse went down, throwing him. He crawled to where Dahlgren lay and confirmed what he knew in his gut. The boy-colonel was dead.

Bravo checked his ammunition, three rounds left, the other troopers were in much the same fix. Many surrendered, to tired to fight on, others slipped into the brush to try and escape. Head pounding, Bravo struggled to get his wind and wits back. Kilpatrick had been right, he was too old.

He inched forward on his belly, a dozen times he came within yards of the Rebels…twice he heard troopers challenging him and lay still and the slashing storm obscured him.

After hours of crawling he broke free of the ambush. He stood up and ran. I'm going to make it! He shouted inwardly, and ran right into a platoon of Rebel soldiers.

Chapter 39

THROUGHOUT THE night and all the next day Richmond's church bells rang out their alarm, calling its citizens to arms to fight off the Yankee invaders. Gunning Brand galloped from one post to another gathering intelligence to determine the strength of the Federals. In the next twenty-four hours Rebel cavalry not only killed or captured most of Dahlgren's 500 troopers, they also forced Kilpatrick's 3500-man cavalry division to turn tail and flee for their lives.

Flushed with victory, Gunning returned to the Customs House to report to Jefferson Davis and found the President's office in an uproar. Davis, Judah Benjamin and Major William Norris, head of the Signal Bureau and the Confederate Secret Service, were pouring over a small black book, shouting and cursing, disbelief and anger patent on their faces.

Davis said crisply, "I still can't believe it. Early this morning a lad from the Richmond Home Guard found these documents on a Yankee raider, identified as Colonel Ulric Dahlgren." He pushed them to Gunning; "See for yourself."

Gunning began to read: "You have been selected from brigades and regiments as a picked command to attempt a desperate undertaking—an undertaking, which, if successful, will write your names on the hearts of your countrymen in letters that can never be erased, and which will cause the prayers of our fellow-soldiers now confined in loathsome prisons, to follow you and yours wherever you may go. We hope to release the prisoners from Belle Island first, and having seen them fairly started, we will cross the James River into Richmond, destroying the bridges after us and exhorting the released prisoners to destroy and burn the hateful city; do not allow the Rebel leader Davis and his traitorous crew to escape. The bridges secured, and the prisoners loose and over the river, the bridges will be burned. The men must keep together…and once in the city it must be destroyed and Jeff Davis and Cabinet killed."

"Good God!" Gunning shouted.

President Davis repeated, "Jeff Davis and Cabinet killed." Grinning wryly he turned to his Secretary of State, "That means you, Mr. Benjamin."

"How you can be so sanguine about this?" Benjamin grumbled. "I've warned you repeatedly about threats to your life and you pay no heed. In January an arsonist sets fire to the White House—in the midst of a reception— and you laugh it off? Now this? These orders are written on stationary of the Third Cavalry Division, these are no longer idle threats, but reveal murderous Federal policy against us."

"What do you make of it, Brand?" Davis asked.

"I agree with Benjamin totally; the war's suddenly taken a treacherous turn, one of extreme personal danger to you. Not only must we redouble our efforts to safeguard you and your Cabinet but we must think in terms of retaliation."

"Exactly," Norris exclaimed, "I've been trying to impress that on His Excellency but he chooses to make light of it."

"How can we be sure this Ulric Dahlgren wasn't acting on his own?" Davis pondered.

Norris interjected vehemently, "Four to five thousand men attacked Richmond. Such a large force must have had the approval of their commanding officers."

"Absolutely," Gunning declared. "I'd wager this order originated in Stanton's War Department, if not the White House itself. If these barbarians are capable of denying our wounded medicines, refusing to exchange prisoners, they're capable of anything. These documents are damning evidence against the Union; we must do everything to safeguard them."

"I've already had them photographed," Norris said. "The originals will be kept here under lock and key."

"Do we know how many men they lost?" Gunning asked.

"So far we estimate three hundred troopers and a thousand horses," Norris answered. "We've captured a hundred thirty men, including thirty-eight Negroes. I'm holding them at Libby Prison for interrogation."

"I should be there when they're questioned," Gunning said. "We've got to find out where these orders originated."

Davis turned to Benjamin; "Do you concur with this?"

"One wants not to believe that these people, once our countrymen, could act so, but the evidence points otherwise."

Davis drummed his fingers on Dahlgren's black book. "Report back to me after you've interrogated the prisoners."

Gunning and Major Norris left and proceeded to Libby Prison, at 20th Street and the James River, at the foot of Church Hill. Before the war, the three connecting red brick warehouses had been leased to Luther Libby, a ship's chandler. When war broke out, the buildings were commandeered and it became known as Libby Prison. A large, tin-roofed, three-story structure going to four stories as the land fell away to the Kanawha Canal, the outside walls had been whitewashed to make it easier to spot any attempt at nighttime escape.

Supply rooms occupied the ground floor; the next floor housed enlisted men, the top floors were reserved for officers. Each of the upper floors had nine rooms, 102 feet long, by 45 feet wide, with seven barred windows on each side looking out onto the city; 1,000 Union officers were crammed into the facility, 110 men to a room.

Lieutenant David H. Todd, Mary Lincoln's half-brother, had been in charge of the prison but he'd been reassigned. The new commandant, Major Thomas Pratt Turner, a slight twenty-three-year-old, told Gunning that the captured Yankee raiders had been locked in the basement dungeons. Gunning and Norris stamped their way down the steps to scatter the rats. Each of the squalid cells, fifteen by ten feet, held fifteen prisoners; as punishment to the Yankees, Negroes and Whites had been thrown into the same cells.

Norris split the prisoners into two groups; he'd interrogate the captured officers, Gunning the enlisted men. One by one they were brought into the respective offices. After several hours Gunning had gotten down to the last of the men. A private was brought in, older than the rest...Gunning looked up to stare into the face of his brother.

Gunning jumped to his feet—Bravo fell back. Impossible to tell who was more surprised.

Gunning called to the guard at the door; "This man may speak more freely if we're alone. Wait outside." The moment the guard left Gunning shut the door and growled, "What in God's name are you doing here?"

Bravo shot back, "I could ask you the same thing."

Gunning waved Bravo to a chair. "You look like hell. Are you wounded? Have you been mistreated?"

He shook his head; "No to both."

They stared at each other, strangers ill met, caught in an impossible situation. Not only of this moment, but in the accumulated grit of a lifetime. As a boy, Bravo had idolized his older brother. But Gunning had grown up hating him, constant proof of his mother's infidelity to a father he'd worshipped. And when his father, Zebulon, had died, victimized by those circumstances…there was no way to resolve their feud, it ran too deep in the blood.

Gunning hovered over Bravo, sometimes confronting him, sometimes circling behind his chair. He forced his questions to be impersonal. "You were with Dahlgren's raiding party?"

Bravo stared straight ahead and matched Gunning's military tone; "I went along as an observer for Lincoln."

"In a private's uniform?"

"General Kilpatrick insisted. If I was in civilian clothes and captured, he thought I might be hung as a spy."

"There's a strong possibility that will happen anyway."

"Oh? Has the Confederacy taken to hanging combatants?"

"Yes, when their goal is as dastardly as Dahlgren's. Extraordinary, that you who've always professed such high moral standards should show no shame."

"For what? After seeing the conditions in this pest hole, I'd risk my life ten times over to free our men."

"Don't you take the high road with me," Gunning snarled. "All Stanton has to do is renew our prisoner exchange and every last Union prisoner would be freed."

Bravo's voice rose a notch; "Stanton will do that when you stop treating captured Negro soldiers as escaped slaves and sending them back to their masters."

"You've such high regard for Negroes? Then who was that young black boy we found? He was wearing a Union army poncho so he must have been with you; why did you hang him?"

Still tormented by the memory of Robby twisting in the wind, Bravo told Gunning of Dahlgren's dementia. Whereupon Gunning kicked the table; "That's how you abolitionists plan to free the Negroes—by hanging them? And if you believe the prisoner exchange broke down over slaves you're a bigger fool than I thought. Admit it, Stanton's aim is to deny us our soldiers so they can fight again; for that he's willing to consign his own men to this living hell, even death."

Bravo's breath came in rapid gasps, he couldn't contradict Gunning, in this he believed he was right.

"See how cleverly you've sidetracked us onto the prisoner issue," Gunning snorted, "another example of Yankee duplicity. Let's see you wiggle out of this." He shoved the copy of Dahlgren's orders into Bravo's hands. "This is the kind of murderers you chose to lie down with." Gunning watched Bravo intently and saw the shock register on his face; it seemed genuine but then in war men learned very quickly to dissemble.

Bravo rubbed his temples; "I knew Dahlgren was headstrong, I knew he was fiercely ambitious, I didn't realize he was also stupid."

"Are you suggesting that he wrote this on his own? A junior officer? Without the approval of his superiors?"

"I can't answer for Dahlgren or Kilpatrick, but I know Lincoln never authorized Davis' assassination."

Gunning asked softly, "How can you be so sure?"

"Because I was in Lincoln's office when he gave Kilpatrick his orders. Lincoln was absolutely clear, our prisoners were to be freed, and—and that's all." He thought it best not to mention the destruction of the Gallego Flour Mills or the Tredegar Iron Works.

Gunning shook his head in exasperation; "Will you never learn? Here you are in a grown man's body but you might as well be the simpleton of your youth. Don't you understand? Lincoln is unscrupulous. He'll say anything, do anything to defeat us. How do you know he didn't secretly conspire with Kilpatrick and Dahlgren and just kept you in the dark?"

"Impossible," Bravo blurted, but Gunning's salvo had hit below the water-line and suspicion began to trickle in.

Gunning circled Bravo; "You've put me in an impossible position. When our people learn what you planned they'll demand that every last one of you be hung. By all rights I should just stand aside; you've sown the seeds, now reap the whirlwind. But for the sake of family—for Ma—I'll do what I can. But only if you cooperate, you must tell the truth about the Union plot to assassinate President Davis."

"I have told you the truth."

"We both know you haven't. I'll be back tomorrow. Think about this carefully. Your life depends on it."

Gunning called for the guard who started to lead Bravo away. At the door Bravo turned; "One last thing, we were all devastated when Geary died. I'm sorry, truly sorry."

Gunning didn't look up from his papers.

For the next several hours Gunning and Major Norris compared their interrogation reports. They could only come to one conclusion, Dahlgren and Kilpatrick had intended to burn Richmond to the ground and assassinate President Jefferson Davis and the entire Confederate cabinet.

Gunning went home and found Judah Benjamin. "Judah, spare me ten minutes, I need the benefit of your thinking."

Gunning recounted all he'd learned about the raid, and hesitating only for a moment, included Bravo's participation. Benjamin accepted it all with his usual equanimity. "As far as your brother is concerned, we must do something."

"I don't want any special treatment for him, he's as guilty as the rest of Dahlgren's murderous swine."

"I wasn't thinking so much of him, but more of our own protection. It would bode us ill if Miss Rebecca declared war on the Confederacy." Benjamin's Mona Lisa broadened to a full smile. But when it came to how the Confederacy should respond to the assassination plot, Benjamin's demeanor changed drastically. Gone the self-effacing man, gone the hedonist with French tastes, he became the consummate, brilliant strategist, and he and Gunning plotted far into the night.

And the next day, March 5, newspapers all over the South screamed about the raid. At breakfast Gunning and Benjamin poured over the papers. *The Whig* editorialized, "Are these…soldiers? Or are they assassins…thugs who have forfeited…their lives? Are they not barbarians redolent with more hellish purposes than were the Goth, the Hun or the Saracen?"

The Richmond Examiner fulminated, "To the Washington authorities, we are simply criminals awaiting punishment…In their eyes, our country is not ours, but theirs. The hostilities they carry on are not properly war, but military execution and coercion…What then would we suggest? Retaliation!"

The Richmond Sentinel cried, "Let Lincoln and Kilpatrick remember that they have bidden their subordinates give no quarter to the Confederate chiefs…No disguise will prevent a just and stern vengeance from overtaking them."

Benjamin folded the papers; "The outrage is unanimous, the call for vengeance more Old Testament than New."

"But if we hang the raiders the Union will surely retaliate and hang some of our men," Gunning pointed out.

"That must be avoided at all costs. Let's to work and see what the day brings."

Gunning spent the morning firing communiqués off to the Union High Command, demanding an explanation. As he expected, the Union insisted that Dahlgren had acted without their authorization. Later in the day, came the Union's outrageous claim that Dahlgren's Orders of the Day had been forged by the Confederacy.

That evening, a telegram arrived at the Confederate War Office. It had been sent from Washington to the Federal outpost in Virginia and then by galloping courier to Richmond. Davis immediately showed it to Gunning who was stunned by its contents. After conferring with Davis, Gunning rode off to Libby Prison and had Bravo brought up from his cell.

"Well, brother, it seems that your State Department wants to know if you were captured. If so, they're anxious to arrange an exchange; they'll parole any general we name in return for you. I'd no idea you'd become so important."

"Neither had I."

"Could it be that Lincoln's anxious to get you back before you spill your guts about the raid?"

"I've already told you—"

"—Yes, yes, that Lincoln's a saint, beyond suspicion, above reproach—"

"Damnation, you're a miserable cuss. You wouldn't be so hard-nosed about Lincoln if you knew what he did for Geary."

Gunning reacted as if he'd been punched in the gut. "Geary? What's Geary got to do with this?"

Haltingly, Bravo told him the circumstances surrounding Geary's hospitalization and death. "You know Ma has no love for Lincoln, never has, probably never will. But in this instance she says he acted like a decent human being."

"Decent human being?" Gunning shouted, "if he were a decent human being he'd have left us alone to work out our own destiny and Geary would still be alive!"

"And if it weren't for Jefferson Davis trying to protect this obscene, immoral institution of slavery, then Forrest would be alive!"

Gunning stopped short. "What? What did you say?"

Bravo hung his head. "Missing in action. Presumed dead." A long moment passed, then Bravo went on, "That's why I agreed to ride with Dahlgren. I felt from the start that this raid was doomed but when they told me they were going to free the prisoners…I know it sounds stupid, but I was out of my head, desperate to grasp at anything."

"Not so stupid," Gunning answered softly. "I can't tell you how many times I've replayed Geary's life in my mind. If it was God's design to take him, how I wished I could have been there for a final goodbye."

Gunning wanted to know about Geary's last days and Bravo told him. "You'd have been proud of Kate and Sharon, Bittersweet too. But the real surprise was Ma, she turned into a tigress, even took on Lincoln. If love could have saved Geary then he'd still be alive. But…God had other plans."

Gunning swallowed hard; "And your own boy?"

Bravo stared off into the distance; "It's been eight months…I have this awful fear that he's lying in some unmarked grave, that I'll never find him."

"I'll check here, see if I can turn up anything."

Bravo nodded his thanks. Then Gunning said, "Did you know those two rapscallions came all the way to Alabama to see me?" Remembering, a smile lit his face, making the pain and the years roll away. "What a pair of cut-ups they were. Drank me under the table they did, and there wasn't a female in town safe from them. Those two, they were really something."

Bravo's voice cracked, "Forrest loved him, thought of him as his brother." His voice dropped to a whisper, "Oh God, Gunning, what have we done, what have we done?"

Gunning started to say something then turned his face away. After a moment he managed, "No matter, it's done and these are the mistakes that can't be recalled. All we're left with are words like honor and duty…and those must sustain us for the rest of our lives."

Gunning's voice caught, then he cleared his throat; "As to the matter at hand, Jeff Davis is an honorable man, if you tell him you knew nothing of this assassination attempt, he'll take you at your word and order your release."

"I can't answer for anyone else but I came to free the prisoners. This I swear, on the memory of my son, and yours."

Gunning nodded then smiled ruefully; "To bad you chose the wrong side, we might have made a good team."

"It strikes me that we've been on opposite sides all our lives. And knowing our pig-headed Brand dispositions, we'll probably be on opposite sides until the day we die. But that doesn't mean I love you any the less."

They faced each other for a long moment, neither daring to make the first move, then with the binding memory of their sons, they impulsively embraced.

Then the moment passed…the war resumed.

Chapter 40

"GUNNING, you can't cancel," Romance pleaded. "You told me to get involved in the war effort and I've been preparing this divertissement for weeks. It's meant to bolster our morale. I've rehearsed with the musicians; our guests are due any moment. What will everyone think if you're not here?"

"Romance, be reasonable. I've been summoned to a meeting with President Davis—"

A strangled scream tore from her throat and he gripped her shoulders to keep her from spiraling into one of her uncontrollable episodes. "Darling, I'm sure this meeting will end early, I'll come back as soon as I can."

She tore free from his grasp; "Don't bother to come back at all. Ever!" and shoved him out the door.

Gunning groaned, long and low. Not even Job could have put up with her. Of late, all they did was fight, the only common ground they shared was the battlefield of bed.

He loped the two blocks to the White House. He got there only two or three minutes late but Davis, punctilious to a fault, showed his displeasure with a curt nod. The windowpanes rattled under the bluster of March winds; Judah Benjamin drew the heavy curtains while Major Norris went about the room turning up the lamps. Burton Harrison, Davis' secretary, usually took notes at all of the President's meetings but tonight Davis had dismissed him; the men had decided that it would be best if there was no official record of this meeting.

Davis, wrapped in a heavy shawl Varina had crocheted for him, inched closer to the dying embers in the fireplace. Judah Benjamin moved to throw on a small log but Davis stayed him with a trembling hand. "I must save it for the nursery, the children suffer so from the cold."

Benjamin nodded, commiserating; "It will be spring soon, and with wood five dollars a log it can't come soon enough."

Norris cautioned, "Spring will also bring the new Yankee offensive. Our spies in Washington report that Lincoln's about to name a new commander for all the Federal armies, none other than Ulysses S. Grant, butcher of Vicksburg."

Gunning tallied the Union commanders on his fingers; "McDowell, McClellan, Burnside, Pope, Hooker, Meade. Now Lincoln's scraping the bottom of the barrel. Bobby Lee will make short work of Grant also."

Davis nodded absently; "Can you believe that the Union cavalry got within two miles of this very house? I should have been able to defend our capital better."

"Your Excellency, it wasn't your fault," Benjamin told him for perhaps the tenth time. "If not for your efforts Richmond would have fallen long ago."

Davis wouldn't be comforted. His assumption of guilt had literally felled him with yet another debilitating illness and all government business had been moved to the White House.

Their heads turned at the timid tapping at the study door. Shepherded by Varina, who was seven months pregnant, the children trooped in to say goodnight. Maggie, nine, seven-year-old Jeff Jr., Little Joe, the President's precocious five-year-old, and the toddler, Billie. They were scrubbed clean, bundled in flannel nightshirts and nightcaps. Each received a kiss from their father, then left.

But Little Joe escaped from Varina and knelt at his father's knee. Davis placed his hand on the child's head, the boy closed his eyes and said his prayers, "Dear Lord, please bless my brothers and sisters, bless my Mama, bless all the soldiers of the Confederacy, and God, please protect my Papa."

With a radiant smile, Little Joe skipped from the room. Davis said, "Gentlemen, forgive the intrusion, but Little Joe claims he cannot sleep unless he says his prayers with me."

The children acted like a tonic on Davis and the strain on his face eased. God bless Jeff Davis indeed, Gunning thought, whatever his other frailties, he was still doing his duty to produce little Rebels for the Confederacy. He felt a pang of envy, then abruptly dismissed it; Romance was right, their own situation, and the times, were too uncertain to bring a child into the world. Still...

Davis cleared his throat; "To the business at hand."

Gunning allowed Major Norris to take the lead in their report about Dahlgren's raid. He knew Davis often thought him hotheaded and he didn't want that to ruin the strategy that he and Norris had worked out. Norris finished, "The top level of the Union government, including Stanton and Lincoln, must have approved Dahlgren's plan to assassinate Your Excellency."

"What say you, Brand?" Davis asked.

Gunning chose his response with care; "As you know, my own brother was in this raid. I cannot apologize enough—"

"No apologies necessary," Davis interrupted, "the war's ruptured so many families; Jeb Stuart attacks the Union cavalry and is opposed by his own father-in-law. Even Mr. Lincoln's house is divided." He smiled at his little joke.

Gunning went on, "My brother claims Lincoln knew nothing of Dahlgren's plot, but Bravo's a novice in the cutthroat game of politics. I agree with Major Norris, Lincoln not only knew, Lincoln not only approved, but Lincoln would have been ecstatic had the raid succeeded in all its objectives."

Norris picked up the attack; "We can't let this dastardly act go unanswered. Does this raid merit retribution? Should a similar fate be meted out to the highest Union officials?"

A look of abject horror crossed Davis' face and Gunning put in quickly, "Not assassination, Your Excellency, nothing so foul as their intent. But Washington is a Southern city, filled with Southern sympathizers." He paused, felt his heart pounding as he said, "With a well-conceived plan, we believe Lincoln could be kidnapped and brought to Richmond."

President Davis and Benjamin exchanged sharp glances.

Gunning pushed on, "With Lincoln as hostage, at the very least we could negotiate the exchange of our prisoners, at the very best we might negotiate an end to the war. Every sign indicates the North hungers for peace. With Lincoln in our hands, I believe that their will to fight would wither away."

Davis didn't respond, caught between his own bitterness over the raid and his personal credo that such actions were unworthy of a West Point officer and a Southern gentleman.

Benjamin cleared his throat; "We do have ancient injunctions in the Bible that have guided men for millennia, 'An eye for an eye,' or, 'Fight fire with fire.'" Davis still remained silent and Benjamin asked Norris and Gunning; "Put the case that His Excellency gave you leave to investigate the possibilities of such an undertaking. How would you proceed?"

Norris said, "The operation would be top secret, handled through the Signal Bureau. All aspects would be strictly compartmentalized; no one would know our true purpose until we were ready to strike. Gunning would act as a verbal liaison between my department and yours, hence there'd be no paper trail, nothing could ever be traced back to the Presidency."

"A most unpleasant undertaking," Benjamin mused, "but we must ask ourselves the most pertinent question; have these monsters in Washington not brought down this retribution on their own heads?"

Davis' gray-blue eyes took on the mien of an avenging prophet. "My own life is of little import, but to invade our land, kill our sons, deny our wounded medicines—and now this? Does their treachery know no bounds? If all of you are of the same mind, that the capture of <u>that</u> <u>man</u> might aid our cause, then investigate the possibilities. Remember, he's to be kidnapped only, nothing more, or he loses his value to us."

"You may be certain of that, Your Excellency," Norris responded eagerly, "and nothing will go beyond this room. The plan will need a name, one that we four will recognize."

After worrying several names, they chose one with a biblical ring. So in March 1864, in Davis' study in the Confederate White House, was born "Operation Come Retribution."

Gunning returned to Norris' office at the Signal Bureau and they sifted through a list of operatives. Who might be best qualified to lead such a daring exploit? From its humble beginnings that long ago night in Montgomery, Alabama, the Confederate Secret Service now included 10 captains, 20 lieutenants, 30 sergeants, and 100 enlisted men.

This new effort would be double-edged; Norris and Gunning would choose a point man in Richmond and another in Washington who could assemble an action team to actually kidnap Lincoln. Washington was already the hub of a thriving Confederate spy network. After careful culling, they agreed to contact one man, someone who wasn't an army regular, which was to the good; if he was apprehended, he couldn't be traced back to the Confederacy. Gunning said, "He's already proven his loyalty to the South a hundred times over. Most important, because of his profession, he can travel anywhere in the North without arousing suspicion. No one would ever suspect him."

Major Norris transcribed a message into code. Judah Benjamin's personal courier, John Surratt, would carry the coded letter to Montreal then swing down to Boston where the man was presently engaged. When decoded, the message would read: "Urgent we meet. Advise city and date."

The communiqué sent, Gunning felt a mixture of relief and apprehension; relief that the wheels were finally in motion, apprehension in their choice of the man. Dedicated, to be sure, but flamboyant, perhaps even a bit notorious? Somehow Gunning felt that the outcome of the war was inextricably entwined in "Operation Come Retribution." And in the spy he'd chosen to act as the operation's point man in Washington.

Chapter 41

TWO WEEKS LATER, Tuesday, March 22, a weary, disheartened Bravo Brand arrived back in Washington. It had taken this long to affect his parole and he couldn't shake the suspicion that Stanton had purposely delayed it. After being released from Libby Prison he'd been taken to City Point and boarded the truce ship that plied between that Rebel river port on the James and Washington. He docked at the Navy Yard and went directly to the White House. Recalling the stench of Libby Prison he gulped great breaths of the quick March air.

Worrying questions resounded with his every step. How can I persuade Stanton to change our policy about prisoner exchange? Is Lincoln strong enough—politically, morally—to stand up to him? How do I find out the truth about Dahlgren? Those thoughts plagued him as he bounded up the flight of stairs to the President's office.

Lincoln's craggy face wreathed in smiles when he saw him. "Thank you for securing my release, Mr. President."

"I got you into that mess, the least I could do was get you out. I need you; the Union needs you. I've read Kilpatrick's report about the raid—incidentally, he's been shipped off to a remote post in the Carolinas—but I'm anxious to hear what really happened."

Bravo gave him a detailed account, then screwing his courage, said, "Mr. President, this is very difficult for me, but Colonel Dahlgren's orders, did you know about them? Did you know what he planned?"

Lincoln stared out the window at the lawn where the first shoots of fire-green grass were spearing through the loam. "Admiral Dahlgren came to see me when we first learned the news. He was convinced the papers discovered on his son's body had been forged by the Confederacy. You tell me that you saw him writing something, but can't swear to its contents?"

"The letter my brother showed me appeared to be in Dahlgren's hand. Sir, I'm sorry about my brother—"

"No apology necessary, with four of my own brothers-in-law fighting for the South, no one knows better than I the pain of divided loyalties. The end of Dahlgren's terrible disaster is that whatever happened I must take responsibility; on my shoulders the burden, in my heart the pain over the deaths of our men, including Dahlgren's. And that poor innocent Negro lad."

He looked so crestfallen that Bravo felt the need to comfort, protect him. "Mr. President, it may be that the Rebels will try to retaliate. Precautions should be taken—"

"If I lived my life behind a wall of guards, would I be able to fulfill my duty as President? If any man is willing to trade his life for mine, there's little I can do about it."

He grasped Bravo's hand; "The only consolation I have is that you've returned safely. Now we must press on to finish the task before us. Two days hence there'll be a meeting in this office that may well be the most important of my entire Presidency. General Grant is off conferring with General Meade at Brandy Station; he's also been to Nashville to see General Sherman. Grant claims he has a grand strategy for winning the war; he's done a masterful job in the western theater, but then he wasn't facing Lee. You know Lee, you also served with Grant in the Mexican American War, and you must have some opinions about him. I need to hear as many informed views as I can. After the Dahlgren debacle, you'd have every right to refuse me, but I'd be very grateful if you'd attend."

Bravo couldn't tell if Lincoln really valued his opinion or if he was just trying to placate him. Gunning's warning came back to haunt him; "He'll use you like he's used everyone else,"...And in truth, Lincoln had never really answered his questions about Dahlgren.

It was dark when Bravo left the White House. All he wanted was a decent night's sleep. But at his house he found a note. "Where are you? It's been a month since I've heard from you. Beside myself with worry, come see me the instant you get home, no matter what the hour. Ma."

Thinking that his mother might have taken ill again, he walked the few blocks to her house. He saw the lamp on in her bedroom, let himself in and went upstairs. He found her writing furiously in a journal. At the sight of him she cried out and quickly jammed the book under the covers.

"What a fright you gave me," she declared, her joy at seeing him quickly masked by petulant queries. "Where have you been? Why did you leave without telling me?" Along with a myriad of other mother questions.

Bittersweet ran upstairs in her nightclothes and interrupted Rebecca's harangue; "Leave the poor man be, can't you see he's walking in his sleep? Fix you sumthin' Bravo?" and hurried off to the kitchen. She returned a bit later with a plate heaped with sliced meats, corn bread and a strong bourbon and branch.

Bravo told his mother about the raid, leaving out details that might upset her. She seemed genuinely relieved that he was safe but then reacted with a vehemence he hadn't expected.

"I've never heard of such a stupid enterprise in all my life. Whatever possessed you to take part in it? What's to become of our country when one political leader can plot the assassination of another?"

"Ma, Lincoln had nothing—"

"Spare me the administration's official line, but I assure you, Rebel Thorne had something to say about that. I wrote, 'Ignorance is no excuse, if Lincoln didn't know about Dahlgren's plans then he should have, that's what being Commander-In-Chief is all about.'"

"Ma, I think it's wonderful that you have all the answers, even when you don't know what you're talking about."

"I suppose you do? I petitioned the War Department for a passport to go to Richmond, and as an objective reporter, find out the truth about the raid. Naturally, Stanton refused. One good thing's come out of this; it's absolutely ruined any chance of Lincoln being re-nominated. The Republican convention is only three months away and there's a groundswell among the party big-wigs to replace him with Salmon Chase."

"That's got to be about the dumbest—can you imagine those three vindictive esses, Salmon, Sumner and Stanton in control of the South's destiny? Salmon Chase would incinerate the South if he could. Stanton's already declared that he'd hang all the Southern leaders as traitors. And Charlie Sumner's introduced a bill in the Senate to cut the South up into eleven districts, with a military dictator at its head and the Bill of Rights suspended. Is that what you want to see happen to your beloved South?"

"Do you take me for some idiot?"

"Then wouldn't a moderate Lincoln be the best choice?"

"Your entire argument is moot; there isn't one Republican in all America who can possibly win the Presidency," she declared emphatically. "Look what their war's done to us? Geary, Forrest—"

To keep her from falling into that endless morbid argument, he said quietly, "I saw Gunning."

A miraculous sea change swept over her. "Why didn't you tell me that first?" In her excitement her lip twisted a bit, the last vestige of her stroke. She demanded to know everything, no detail was to be overlooked. How did he look? Was he well? Was he still with the Connaught bitch? Did he ask about her? After Bravo told her everything he knew, she insisted that he repeat it again.

Bravo felt a gnawing ache; where Gunning was concerned nothing else mattered to his mother...her first-born son, forever a problem, the favored one who'd always command her attention.

Shortly thereafter he went back to his own house. Drifting off to sleep, he wondered, what was she writing about so furiously? And why did she hide it? Another one of her articles, no doubt, one that would get the whole family thrown into leg irons.

*

Two days later, Bravo sat in Lincoln's office, along with Secretary of State Seward, Secretary of War Stanton, and several other officers of the Union High Command. Stanton barely acknowledged him and Bravo got an irrepressible urge to give him a swift kick in his big fat ass.

General Grant arrived, looking like he'd slept in his uniform. Fifteen years had passed since Bravo had last seen him. Outside of the reddish beard and the normal aging, he hadn't changed much. Still spare and slight of frame, five foot eight, about 130 pounds. Unprepossessing, slightly confused, as if about to ask, What am I doing here, Mr. President? You've chosen the wrong man.

The cabinet members treated Grant with fawning deference. After three long years of horrifying bloodshed they needed to believe that Unconditional Surrender Grant, the conqueror of Vicksburg, could defeat Lee and bring the Rebels to heel.

Bravo congratulated Grant on his promotion and reminded him that they'd served together in the Mexican War, even got rip-roaring drunk together. Grant was friendly enough but Bravo could tell he had no recollection of their carousing; it had happened a long time ago and since then Grant had gotten rip-roaring drunk with lots of people.

Cordiality dispensed with, everyone listened intently as General Grant stood at a large roller map of America and outlined his plan. "Up to now the Union armies have been divided into nineteen departments. These various armies acted separately and independently of each other. I'm determined to stop this. My general plan is to concentrate all the force possible against the Confederate armies in the field.

"I'll mount four simultaneous blows: Ben Butler will lead an army up the James River. Franz Sigel will advance in the Shenandoah Valley. Sherman will strike out from Chattanooga and capture Atlanta, an important rail hub that feeds Lee's army. Finally, Meade will lead the Army of the Potomac, one hundred ten thousand strong, directly against Lee. Wherever Lee goes, Meade will go, and I will go there too. Tomorrow, I'll join Meade and with the first sign of decent weather all our armies will go on the offensive. Mr. President, I promise you that I will not stop until the Rebels are defeated."

Cabinet members burst into spontaneous applause. Here was a commander unlike the others, for despite his diffident manner, an odd determination emanated from him. Lincoln, charged with excitement, made it clear that Grant was to be given everything he needed; money, munitions, men, nothing would be spared in this one final assault.

Lincoln declared emphatically, "This rebellion must be crushed before the next election or the Union will be lost."

Grant nodded; "We're armed, our divisions are at full strength and ready; at the first sign of spring, we strike."

Chapter 42

As APRIL drew to a close, moderating weather brought mixed blessings to Richmond's citizens: no longer did one have to shiver before a meager fire, but crocus and violet did signal the onset of the killing season.

At noon on the last day of April, Gunning, Judah Benjamin and Jefferson Davis were closeted in the President's office at the Customs House. Davis had just shown them a batch of telegrams, including a plea from General Lee for reinforcements. "Lee is convinced that Grant is about to launch his spring offensive," Davis told them. "If only I had those reinforcements to send."

Gunning jammed his fists on Davis' desk; "Your Excellency, it makes "Operation Come Retribution" that much more vital." Davis shrugged uncomfortably but Gunning went on, "Major Norris and I have chosen the man to head our operation from the Confederate side, Captain Thomas N. Conrad."

Davis nodded his approval; Conrad, originally a lay reader in the Methodist church in Washington, had been imprisoned in 1862 for expressing his Southern sympathies. He'd been paroled and now served as chaplain of the Third Virginia Cavalry. His labors for God were second only to his efforts for the Confederate Secret Service; he'd gone on many spying missions for the South with outstanding success.

"Have you decided on your point man in Washington? The one who'll do the actual kidnapping?" Benjamin asked softly.

"We've someone in mind," Gunning replied, "but I want to talk to him—face to face—make sure he's our man. He's in Boston and will be for several weeks. If it meets with Your Excellency's approval, I'll go there immediately."

Davis exhaled deeply; "I still have serious doubts about this enterprise." Before he could expand on this the clock chimed one, followed by the arrival of Varina Davis, laden down with several covered dishes and eight months of pregnancy. Davis, afflicted with a dyspeptic stomach, often neglected to eat his mid-day meal and to entice him, Varina brought him his favorite dishes from the White House kitchen.

Savory odors filled the office and Gunning wondered, would Romance ever do this for me? He doubted it, people usually brought things to her. This past week she'd taken to her bed claiming female problems, and from the look of her she wasn't lying. This loveless stretch had frayed tempers and made life very difficult for both of them.

Just then a Davis household slave burst into the Customs House, tears streaming down her face; "Come home quick, there's been an accident. Little Joe—"

They all rushed from the Customs House to the White House. Amidst the shrieks and tears they learned that Little Joe had been playing on some construction materials on the south portico. The five-year-old had lost his footing and plunged fifteen feet to the courtyard below. He'd broken both legs and fractured his skull.

Jeff Jr., Little Joe's brother, kept repeating in a daze, "I've said all the prayers I know how, but God will not wake Joe." The boy died before the doctor arrived. Varina collapsed and in her piteous hysterics they feared she might lose the child she was carrying. Catherine, the children's Irish governess, had to be forcibly restrained from doing herself harm. What Gunning found most heartbreaking was Davis' efforts to contain his grief. Little Joe, who couldn't fall asleep unless he said his prayers with his papa, Little Joe, the brightest of the brood, Jeff Davis' hope, yet Davis didn't dare lose control, not even for a private moment of grief, not while an entire nation depended on him.

As Davis dragged his way upstairs Gunning heard him murmur in a litany, "Your will, oh lord, not mine, Your will…"

On May 3, all Richmond turned out for the funeral of Little Joe Davis. The children of the city began raising money to buy him a tiny headstone.

Whatever mourning period Jeff and Varina Davis had hoped for was cut short, for the next day, the Army of the Potomac crossed the Rapidan River and struck with full fury at The Wilderness. The ferocity of the attack threatened to overrun Lee's out-manned, outgunned army. Every man, every rifle was needed and Gunning postponed his trip North.

To prevent Lee from being reinforced by troops from the Western Theater, General William Tecumseh Sherman struck south from Chattanooga with the intention of capturing the vital rail hub of Atlanta. Though opposed by a considerable Confederate army led by General Joe Johnston, Sherman met only sporadic resistance, but then he was facing a man who'd proven all too often that he would rather retreat than fight.

The battle around The Wilderness escalated and Richmond held its breath as Grant poured tens of thousands of troops into the carnage. When a war correspondent asked Grant about his strategy, Grant responded, "I'm feeding the battle."

Gunning went into the field to interrogate captured Union soldiers, trying to unearth what Grant's next move might be. He thought he was inured to the horrors of war, but this new onslaught chastened him. In the fierce bombardment, men were mangled beyond recognition; the woods caught fire, and he watched helplessly as the wounded from both sides burned alive where they'd fallen, their screams seared indelibly into his brain. It forced him to wonder, was States' Rights worth it?

General Lee, with a canny knowledge of the terrain, inflicted such terrible casualties on the Federals that on May 7, Grant was forced to break off the engagement. Gunning told Lee, "You've done it again, general. Information from our captured prisoners leads me to believe that Grant will have to retreat."

But instead of retreating, as every other Union general had done after such catastrophic losses, Grant moved his army south, attempting to turn Lee's right flank at Spotsylvania. Lee moved to intercept him and when Grant reached Spotsylvania he found the entrenched Rebels waiting. Once more the Army of the Potomac suffered staggering casualties and once more Grant attempted another flanking move, this time taking him to the North Anna River.

On May 12, the Confederates sustained a loss they could not afford when General Jeb Stuart was mortally wounded. When Lee heard the news, he said, "Jeb Stuart was my eyes and ears. He never brought me a piece of false information. I can scarcely think of him without weeping."

Colonel Carleton Connaught, riding with Stuart, took a bullet in the left leg and another tore through his right palm. His men caught him as he fell from his horse. An ambulance took him to a hospital in Fredericksburg where overworked, over-zealous surgeons prepared to amputate Carleton's leg and hand.

Another battle, another Union defeat, another flanking attempt by Grant, which brought him to Cold Harbor. With uncanny accuracy, Lee had anticipated every one of Grant's moves and had beaten him, inflicting casualties high as three to one. Though severely mauled, Grant remained unperturbed and simply wired Lincoln for more men—and got them. Cold Harbor stood only twenty miles from Richmond.

Lee couldn't replenish his losses; his men hadn't eaten in days and were weak from hunger. Pressing his advantage, Grant decided to strike with all his strength at Cold Harbor. Both armies sensed that this would be the decisive battle in Grant's campaign. If he smashed through here, Richmond would fall, and with it, the Confederacy.

June 2, the night before the battle, Gunning watched as soldiers wrote their names on slips of paper and pinned them to the inside of their uniforms so that if wounded or killed, they could be identified. Then they went back to digging trenches as they'd been doing for several frantic days.

Lee had ordered a maze of enfilading entrenchments dug on the seven-mile front; these fortifications crisscrossed each other so that withering fire would cover every possible approach by an attacking enemy. Buoyed by Lee, guided by Lee, swearing by Lee, the Rebel army had turned the terrain around Cold Harbor into a deadly labyrinth.

Grant, still supremely confident, hadn't taken the time to inspect the battle area and ordered the attack. It proved to be a disaster never before witnessed on the American continent. Nothing could withstand the rain of death coming from the Rebel guns and in the first eight minutes of fighting 7,000 Union men fell. Confederate loses were minor in comparison, only 1500. The bloodshed continued unabated and in two scant days of fighting at Cold Harbor, Grant lost 17,000 men.

Grant finally wept. But sidled his way south once more, trying to cut the supply lines between Petersburg and Richmond. By June 18, Grant got as far as Petersburg, 20 miles south of Richmond. There he was stopped again. Decisively. Rebel fortifications around the vital rail hub, created a veritable no-man's land. Not even Grant dared to sacrifice any more men. In six of the bloodiest weeks of the war, the Union had suffered more casualties than in the preceding three years. Grant's men nicknamed him, 'The Butcher'.

The appalling fatalities created a firestorm in the North, with demands that Grant be replaced. In the midst of the turmoil, and against all odds, the unexpected, the unthinkable happened; The Republican Party nominated Lincoln for a second term. Buoyed by this, Lincoln refused to remove Grant from command. At last he'd found a general who'd fight.

President Davis went into the field to inspect the battleground and Lee told him, "Grant has settled in for a long siege. If he can't take Petersburg by a frontal assault, he'll try to starve us out, the way he did at Vicksburg."

"Then our objective is clear," Davis said firmly, "we must hold until November when Lincoln is defeated at the polls. We're confident that the new Democratic administration will call a halt to this bloodbath and be anxious to negotiate a peace granting us independence. We must hold till then."

"Then we'll hold," Lee said simply.

The two exhausted armies lay panting before Petersburg. Every time Gunning questioned one of the youthful prisoners, it ate away at his soul, for the information he extracted could only serve to annihilate more men. The ancient biblical armies had done it better, predicating victory on a battle between two men. More and more he became convinced that "Operation Come Retribution" was the slingshot that would bring down the Goliath.

The fighting degenerated into the grinding stalemate of trench warfare and Gunning's presence at Petersburg served little purpose. He returned to Richmond where he and Major Norris revitalized their plan. The man he'd intended to meet had left Boston and was travelling between New York City and the oil fields of Pennsylvania, where recent oil strikes had produced a liquid gold rush. He held a large stake in the oil fields, which promised to make him a very rich man; he'd already given a great deal of his profits to the Confederacy. Gunning made arrangements to meet him in New York City.

"Now comes the hard part," Gunning muttered to himself, "telling Romance I've got to leave." When he got to her house he found her lying on the chaise looking wan and melancholy. She opened her arms and embraced him. But when he moved to become intimate, she pushed him away.

"Still feeling badly? It's been weeks now, why won't you let me send for a doctor?"

"I don't need a doctor, I know what's wrong. It's the way you treat me, taking me for granted. As long as we're not married you can come and go as you please and what recourse do I have?"

"Darling, we've been over this a hundred times, you know that Kate won't give me a divorce."

"Always that same tired excuse. If you really wanted your freedom you'd get it. Spouses are known to die—suddenly, unaccountably—mine did. But because Kate the Cow still breathes, I was forced to have an abortion."

The blood rushed from his face; had she knifed him in the heart, shot him in the groin—

"What else could I do?" she asked plaintively. "In Richmond, where blood line counts for everything, they would never have tolerated a bastard—or its parents."

He stroked her cheek; "I'm so sorry. Are you all right?"

"I'll never be all right. A horrible, tawdry affair, a violation such as I've never experienced, while you men walk away Scot free." She pummeled weakly at his chest; "I hate you for having so compromised me."

"Why didn't you tell me?"

"How many times have I begged you to leave Richmond? And what was your answer? Country and honor first. Who am I to have the temerity to compete with your duties?"

Abortion…boy or girl…he'd never know.

A faint clink of chains grew louder as Montgomery came up from the basement with an armload of firewood; he stored it in the wood bin then retreated back to the cellar.

"Why do you still keep him shackled?" Gunning asked.

"I like the sound, it's comforting, it let's me know he's still here."

He pressed her hand to his lips; "I'll make it up to you, I swear, the moment I get back—"

She bolted upright; "Get back? But you've been away. For weeks."

"President Davis ordered me into the field again—"

"You're lying! Every officer I've spoken to has told me that the front is quiet. Where are you going?"

"You know I can't tell you."

"Yet you want to know everything that I do. If I'm not at your constant beck and call—"

"Romance, that's not the same thing. Whenever I don't tell you something it's for your own protection."

"Take me with you."

"It's too far and far too dangerous."

"What if I told you that it was far more dangerous for me to remain here, alone…where such thoughts lurk in every corner of my mind? I must go with you, please, oh please."

He tried to soothe her; "I'll be gone a week at most, and when I get back…"

His voice droned on but she argued no more. If he chose to cut her out of his life, so be it. For years, Sean had been pressing her to send him any and all information about the Confederacy. She'd always refused, but the moment Gunning left her house she composed a long letter to her bother. In it, she detailed every bit of gossip she'd gleaned from loose-lipped officers about the size and disposition of Lee's army. She'd pass the letter on to Monsieur Alphonso Paul, the French Consul in Richmond, he'd forward it to the French Embassy in Washington. In a matter of days, Sean Connaught would have her letter in his hands.

Chapter 43

JUDAH BENJAMIN had insisted that Gunning have a knowledgeable guide to see him safely through enemy lines and had assigned Gunning his best courier, John Surratt.

"At this rate we could walk faster," Gunning grumbled to John Surratt. They'd taken the train from Richmond to Milford Station, doubting each moment that the wheezing old locomotive would make it. "We just don't have the factories to produce rolling stock," Gunning said, "the engines we have left are held together by bailing wire and prayer."

Surratt clasped his hands; "Then I'd best say one," and with twinkling good humor launched into a Hail Mary.

"You're Catholic, then? My wife's Catholic, my children were raised in the faith."

"And you, sir?" Surratt asked.

Gunning chuckled; "As my sainted spouse would have the world believe, a sinner fallen so deep into fiery the pit, not even the long arm of the Lord can reach me." His smile turned rueful; "Perhaps she's right."

At Milford, horses awaited them, arranged by Major Norris. Now they were entering territory held by the Union. Travelling only at night, they soon reached the Potomac River. A farmer, one of many Virginians who operated along the river for the Confederacy, ferried them across. "Twilight's best," he told them as they bent their backs to the muffled oars, "shadows from the Virginia hills reach clear across river, Yankee pickets can't hardly see a small boat."

The boat bumped against the far shore and Gunning stepped onto the soil of Maryland. This tidewater region was fiercely loyal to the South and only the presence of Federal troops had prevented Maryland from seceding. They'd landed near the town of Port Tobacco; thirty miles due north lay Washington.

When they reached the outskirts of the capital, Gunning and Surratt parted; Surratt went to his mother's boarding house and Gunning proceeded to Union Station. Soldiers doing spot passport checks heavily patrolled the railway station and Gunning didn't breathe easy until his train left.

At Camden Station in Baltimore, the railroad cars were drawn separately by teamster wagons through the streets to the Calvert Street depot, where they were then hooked up to another locomotive. Four years before, when President-elect Lincoln had journeyed to his inauguration, this was where the Baltimore Blood Tubs and other secret societies had plotted to assassinate him, only to be foiled by Detective Pinkerton.

What if Lincoln had been assassinated then, Gunning wondered, would the outcome have been different? His mother had said that the schism between North and South went back too far—far back as the founding of the nation—for any one man to have caused or prevented it. She was probably right.

Fields waving with ripening crops passed before him, so rich, so fecund under the July sun. How different from the ravaged lands of Virginia whose only crop was blood and bone.

He hadn't been in New York City since 1834, thirty years before, and the change astonished him. Now the largest city in the nation, it had grown outward, it had grown upward, buildings seven and eight stories tall! And paved streets and trolley lines and streams of people bustling about. Compared to New York, Richmond looked like a provincial village. His appointment wasn't until evening and he took the day to walk the sun-baked streets, to gauge the mood of the people.

Across the East River, a forest of ship's masts bristled the Brooklyn Navy Yard. Along open railroad tracks on Park Avenue, he watched as freight and troop trains rolled past. The North was in the throes of creating an invincible juggernaut. Bravo's words came back to haunt him…"Modern wars are fought with material, with weapons…"

"My God," Gunning breathed, "if the South had only a tenth of these supplies."

Could the South with its limited industrial capacity and limited manpower, ever hope to win a war against this giant? Absolutely, Gunning exclaimed inwardly, but only through the most daring of actions.

He stopped at a neighborhood bar, bought a pail of suds for a group of day laborers, and while munching on free hardboiled eggs, listened. Arguing in their polyglot of foreign accents, Gunning heard smoldering resentments;

against the war, against the slaves who'd caused this. They talked of the riots that had ravaged New York City last summer. Strong resistance to Lincoln's draft, the first draft in the nation's history, had erupted in rage against the Negroes. Hapless free blacks had been shot, hung, beaten to death, and a Negro orphanage burned to the ground. Horace Greely, editor of the Abolitionist newspaper, *The Tribune*, had barely escaped with his life.

Union troops had been rushed to New York to restore order, but not before millions in damage had been done and hundred of Negroes killed. So much for the North's sanctimonious preachments about abolition, Gunning thought. In the dissatisfaction of the war-weary common man, in his fear that cheap black labor would undercut his own livelihood, ah, Gunning mused, there lay the South's hope for a negotiated peace. And Lincoln would be the means to bring it about.

The sinking sun warned him it was time for his meeting. He took a carriage to the St. Nicholas Hotel, a quality establishment on a beautiful tree-lined street in Greenwich Village. The pimply-faced desk clerk told him, "Got to wait, mister, someone's up there with him."

Minutes later, an attractive woman with sparkling eyes and a flushed face hurried down the stairs and out the door. The clerk stared after her enviously; "He's got them coming and going all day long; that one's Annie Horton, his favorite. Wish I knew what tonic he was using, I'd drink a gallon."

Gunning went upstairs and knocked. He heard a resonant voice call in a commanding tone, "Enter." He opened the door and stood face to face with John Wilkes Booth.

Handsome, charismatic, strong sexual magnetism; dark curly hair, moustache, fine chiseled features, about five nine, though his posture made him appear taller, a muscular one hundred and fifty pounds. Gunning had never seen Booth perform but knew he was one of the premiere stars of the American Theater and the darling of southern audiences. The men liked each other immediately. Here's a man I could drink with, Gunning thought, a friend I could go out whoring with.

"Brand, you say?" Booth asked, "I have the acquaintance of a Miss Rebecca Breech Brand in Washington."

Gunning hesitated, then decided that at least in this small matter, he'd trust him. "My mother."

John Wilkes beamed in delight; "Then you're more than welcome here. An extraordinary woman. She's well, I hope?"

"I haven't seen her since the war began. The occasional letter only, from which I gather that she's fine."

"This calls for a celebration." They drank the first toast, "To the Confederacy," the second, "To Bobby Lee," and the third, "To Miss Rebecca." Gunning noted Booth's prodigious consumption of alcohol but it didn't seem to intoxicate him. Booth went on extolling Rebecca's virtues; "As Rebel Thorne, she's the bane of Stanton's existence, as Rebecca Brand, she sets the finest example for Southern womanhood."

Gunning shook his head, extraordinary how everybody got on with his mother—except her children. Tentatively, he maneuvered to the business at hand. "Thank you for the last shipment of medicine, it did much to alleviate suffering. And very astute of you to secret it in those horse collars."

Booth acknowledged the compliment deferentially.

Probing, Gunning led him into a discussion of the political scene. "Everywhere I went today I saw posters offering hundreds of dollars, and citizenship, to foreigners if they'd enlist. It seems the North will stop at nothing."

"It's the unwisest move this country has yet made," Booth agreed. "The suave pressing of hordes of ignorant foreigners, buying up citizens before they even land."

"President Davis alerted the Vatican that Union recruiters are going to Germany and Ireland, bribing poor Catholics to enlist in the Union armies. The Vatican tried to stop it but droves of immigrants are still arriving and are still being impressed into the Union army."

John Wilkes struck a pose, raising his clenched fist; "It's a thing Americans will blush to remember one day when the Irish coolly tells them that he won their battles for them, that he fought and bled and freed the nigger. The time will come, whether conquered or conqueror, when the braggart North will groan at not being able to swear they fought the South man for man. If the North conquer us, it will be by numbers only, not by native grit, not pluck, and not by devotion...So help me holy God, my soul, life, and possessions are for the South!"

"Why not fight for her then?" Gunning goaded him. "Every Marylander worthy of the name shoulders his gun."

Booth's face eloquently expressed his passion; "I have only one arm to give, but my brains are worth twenty men, my money worth an hundred. I have free pass everywhere, my profession, my name, is my passport; my knowledge of drugs is valuable, my beloved precious money—oh, never beloved till now! Is the means...by which I serve the South."

Gunning felt an irresistible urge to applaud. "I find it a piece of poetic justice that you have Grant's pass."

"He's given me freedom of range without knowing what a good turn he's done for us. Not that the South cares a bad cent about me—mind, a mere pere-grinating play-actor."

Gunning considered long and hard. Booth had given much of his wealth to the cause, had risked his life smuggling medicines into the South. Had he been caught, he would have been hung. Yes, Gunning thought, this could be the man with enough dash and daring in his soul. "Suppose I told you that a group of reputable Southern men had a plan that could end the war in one stroke, would such an enterprise interest you?"

John Wilkes gripped Gunning's arm; "Yes, and again yes."

"I must warn you, it could mean your death. But if successful, your name would be revered throughout the South."

Gunning could see that such a venture thrilled Booth, appealing not only to his patriotism, but to his need for the dramatic. He went on, "It requires cun-ning and a fair amount of deceit, you'd have to appear to be what you're not."

"I deal with that daily in my profession."

"You'd also have to be available at a moment's notice, you couldn't contract out for another theatrical season."

"A minor sacrifice. I'd be willing to free myself of any other distractions for such an opportunity."

"You'd have to live in Washington for several months."

"It's a city familiar to me, one in which I used to feel eminently comfortable. Not now, never now," he swore, working himself into a wine-induced rage, "make no mistake, Washington is now ruled by a virtual dictator."

"We'll never let that stand," Gunning answered grimly.

Booth sprang to his feet; "No, by God's mercy, never. This benighted fool has been made the tool of the North, to crush out slavery by robbery, rapine, slaughter and bought armies. This man's reelection—it would become a reign! Never!"

Listening to these tirades from a wild heart, Gunning made his decision. He'd recommend that John Wilkes Booth be their point man in Washington. He'd assemble the action team that would kidnap Lincoln and spirit him to Richmond. Jefferson Davis, Judah Benjamin and William Norris would have to approve his choice, but they knew of Booth's service to the South and Gunning had little doubt that they'd agree.

Gunning rose; "You'll be contacted when to meet me in Washington. Till then, say nothing, do nothing that would call down any suspicion on you." They shook hands firmly.

The next day Gunning took the train back to Washington. If he had any qualms that John Wilkes might be a bit too flamboyant in his approach to

"Operation Come Retribution," he buried them. When Gunning's train pulled into Union Station, he found the place in pandemonium. Mobs of people pushed and shoved to board any train heading North. "What's happening?" he demanded of a white-faced, dithering station guard.

"Rebel army's attacking Washington, they're only five miles away!"

Chapter 44

"HITCH OLD GLUE to the shay," Rebecca shouted to Bittersweet as she pulled her out of the kitchen. "General Jubal Early's attacking Washington; he's reached Fort Stevens, can't you hear the guns?" she demanded all in one breath.

"You sure that ain't thunder?" Bittersweet asked. About two that afternoon, a storm had drenched the area, but now the sky was cloudless. The booming continued. Bittersweet began to shudder. "I'll get the carriage, best get away from here. We'll go to my chilluns in Anacostia."

Rebecca climbed into the shay; "I'll drive." She flicked the reins and Old Glue ambled off at her notion of a trot.

"You goin' the wrong way to Anacostia," Bittersweet said then cried out, "no you don't! I ain't goin' to no Fort Stevens, you crazy old lady, you be eighty-four years old!"

"Eighty-two. You're as young as you feel and right now I feel as young as I did when I reported the British attack on Baltimore during the War of 1812. This is the chance every correspondent dreams about. Every other reputable reporter in Washington is off at Petersburg-Richmond front. I'll scoop them all. The newspapers will dig deep in their pockets for such an exclusive. Help me get there and I'll give you ten percent of whatever I earn."

"Where'm I gonna spend it, the graveyard?"

"Fifteen percent, and I'll put your name in the report. Have you ever seen your name in print? You know any other maid who's gotten her name in print?"

"Twenty percent. Bold print."

"Done," and handed her the reins.

They drove north on 7th Street; many panic-stricken citizens were heading in the other direction, alarming Bittersweet even more, but Rebecca's excitement propelled them on. She began jotting notes for her piece; "To take pressure off Richmond, Lee sent Jubal Early with an army of 14,000 men to attack Washington. Time and again the Federals claimed that they'd stopped him, but today, July 11, his army and his cannon stand at the very gates of the capital."

Five miles later they reached Missouri Avenue, continued north then turned left onto Quackenbros Road. As they got closer to the line of battle the thunder of cannon became more distinct. Bittersweet slowed the shay; "Twenty-five percent."

An army sergeant darted from behind a breastwork and grabbed the reins. "Get back you fools!"

Rebecca thrust her press credentials at him. "I'm here with the expressed approval of President Lincoln. Unless I'm permitted to pass, you'll answer to him."

The sergeant bumbled, "You're with the President's party too? He's here already, First Lady also, that's their carriage parked near the fort's sally port. Get this heap over there now before you're blown to smithereens."

"My nerves," Rebecca whispered to Bittersweet, "I never expected that the Lincolns would be here."

Bittersweet eased their rig behind an earthen barrier. Here they were somewhat safer from the occasional cannon ball that thudded into the wall, or flew harmlessly overhead. Rebecca trained her telescope on the terrain and spied Lincoln's party in the fort; sure enough, Mary Todd was there—along with Sean and Veronique Connaught.

"Oh to be a Rebel gunner," Rebecca muttered, "one cannon ball, dear God, just one."

Bittersweet took the telescope from her; "You always tellin' me not to lie, right? But you lied about Lincoln."

"You are not supposed to lie. I, on the other hand, being old and white and rich, can say anything I want. It's one of the small compensations that God's bestowed on me for forcing me to live this long." She snatched the telescope and trained it on the fort. "My nerves, Lincoln's climbed up on the breastworks, he's sticking up like a flag pole. Oh! Bravo's with him! What is my fool of a son doing here? He could get killed." Moments later she saw both men duck their heads down.

The fighting grew heavy and continued until dusk. Unable to penetrate the Union's defenses, the Rebel army withdrew. When Lincoln and his entourage emerged from the fort, Rebecca stood waiting for them.

Bravo stopped dead in his tracks. "What in blue blazes—Ma, are you crazy coming here?"

"Are you?" she retorted.

"It's my job."

"Mine too," she said, waving her foolscap. "Tell me everything. How did the Rebels get so close? Who—?"

As Lincoln got into his carriage he remarked wryly, "Better tell her, Bravo, else the entire report will be garbled in the press, including that Washington was captured."

Bravo turned on Bittersweet; "Why did you let her come here? I thought you had more sense."

"Knew it'd turn out to be my fault."

"Bravo, you heard your President," Rebecca interrupted, "why not just tell me what happened and we can all go home?"

Bravo cursed under his breath. "I guess Lincoln's right, you might as well hear the truth. Last night we got news that the Rebs were advancing again. So we drove out to inspect the defenses and give our men moral support. You saw the rest."

"That is the most inane, boring—you'll never make it as a reporter. Did Mary Todd and the Bitch come along to man the barricades?"

"You know Mary Todd, she's not happy unless she's in the President's hip pocket. She turned the whole thing into an excursion. Best dresses and all."

"Who was the military genius who allowed Lincoln to expose himself the way he did? Some Democrat, no doubt."

Bravo grinned in spite of himself; "That did give us all a turn. An angry young officer shouted at Lincoln, 'Keep your damned fool head down or you'll get it shot off.'"

"Don't suppose you had the wit to get the officer's name? Rank? The state he's from? The little important things?"

"Massachusetts. Wounded three times. A captain, and only nineteen years old. Lincoln liked his vinegar, thinks he'll go far. Name's Oliver Wendell Holmes, Jr. The important thing is that the forts we built to protect Washington have held. I don't think Lee will ever try this again. So, Ma, write your article and I hope you'll be fair about it?"

"I'm always fair. It's my trademark."

*

Two days later Bravo stormed into Rebecca's house and threw down a newspaper. "You call this piece of tripe fair?" His anger startled her; she picked up the paper and read her article aloud; "Three months ago, Grant began his campaign to take Richmond. Lee defeated him at The Wilderness, at Spotsylvania, at Cold Harbor. Grant's lost sixty-five to seventy thousand men—more than Lee had at the outset. Losses of other Northern armies since the first of the year bring Union casualties to one hundred thousand. What have we to show for this staggering carnage? Stalemate at Petersburg; stalemate in the west and Jubal Early rampaging through Maryland to the very outskirts of Washington. Is it any wonder that good and decent men all across the nation are asking, Just exactly who is winning this war?"

Rebecca folded the paper; "Where have I been unfair? Where haven't I told the truth?"

"This kind of negative reporting does nothing but encourage the South to resist further. Every word you write can mean a soldier's life."

"How dare you! I'm not alone in these sentiments." She grabbed other newspapers; "This from *The New York World*, 'Who shall revive the withered hopes that bloomed at the opening of Grant's campaign? Stop the war! All are tired of this damnable tragedy…'"

"The *World* is a Democratic paper, what did you expect?"

She flared back; "This next editorial is from Horace Greely, your own arch abolitionist! 'Our bleeding, bankrupt, dying country longs for peace, it shudders at the prospect of further wholesale devastation, of new rivers of human blood.'"

Her breathing became rapid and shallow; "Open your eyes, Bravo, every responsible person knows the nation is wild for peace. My own grandchildren—" She broke off, sobbing.

"I'm sorry for your pain, mother, but you haven't exactly cornered the market on grief. The whole country is grieving. Believe it or not, Mr. Lincoln most of all. It comes down to this, do you or don't you believe in Union?"

"Andrew Jackson—"

"Don't bore me with Jackson again! I've no time for the creaking meanderings of your mind, we've more important work before us. Lincoln's being attacked by radical Republicans for being too conciliatory toward the South, attacked by Democrats pressuring him to drop emancipation as a condition for peace negotiations. Anyone with any brains can see he's trying to hold a moderate position. I thought you knew better, Ma, I never imagined that you'd join the pack of ravening politicians." Without another word he strode from the house.

Furious with him, Rebecca responded by coming down with that most dreaded of ailments, a summer cold. She took to her bed, muttering, "Creaking meanderings of my mind, is it? Well! When he comes to see me I'll pretend nothing's wrong, I'll just cough a lot."

During that week, friends congratulated Rebecca on her article and letters of praise poured in. Yet amid all the adulation, Bravo's denunciation rang loudest in her ears. Nothing in the news commanded her interest, not even reports that on July 17, Jefferson Davis had removed Joseph Johnston from command of the Confederate Army of Tennessee. Davis claimed Johnston had constantly retreated, instead of engaging Sherman while they were still in the Great Smoky Mountains where he held the tactical advantage. Sherman was closing in on Atlanta, but with General John Bell Hood now opposing him, Southern resistance stiffened and the Union offensive stalled. Still Bravo didn't come to visit and with each passing day Rebecca grew angrier. "I could've died for all he cares," she complained to Bittersweet, "it's as if he's not my child. They must have switched babies on me when I gave birth."

Bittersweet nodded; "Never thought of that before, but you must be right. Bravo's much to nice to be yours."

She threw a pillow after the scurrying maid. Her anger, like her summer cold, gradually dissipated. But not her confusion. She was far too astute not to realize that Bravo had challenged her on one of the most important of her beliefs. The Union: how could it best be served? Only one person could clarify that, and so Rebecca swallowed her pride and wrote to Lincoln requesting an interview. After her last article, so critical of his leadership, she had little hope of a response, so she wasn't surprised when his curt note said he was unavailable; pressing affairs kept him busy during the day; in the evenings he wasn't in the city.

Rebecca knew that Lincoln spent nights during the hot summer months at the presidential cottage at Soldier's Home, three miles outside of Washington. Plucking up courage, she wrote him again, saying she'd be pleased to ride out there. She also not so subtly implied that such an interview might do much to gain Rebel Thorne's support. With all pens raised against him, he needed all the help he could get.

Two days later she received a note from John Nicolay; Lincoln would see her the following evening.

Late the next afternoon, Rebecca rummaged through her file, took out an old newspaper article and with a good deal of trepidation set out for Soldier's Home. Bittersweet drove.

The complex had a quaint air; ornate gingerbread trim framed the roofline and windows of all the buildings. Above the main building rose a crenellated, medieval-looking tower, which had been used as a lookout point during Jubal Early's invasion. Off to one side, and surrounded by lush planting, sat the President's three-story cottage.

Bittersweet joined the help in the kitchen; Rebecca went to see Lincoln. Contrary to her expectation, he greeted her with his usual odd brand of frontier courtliness and told her that Mary Todd Lincoln and Tad had gone off to the mountains to escape the stultifying heat. Rebecca did not miss them.

He sat tilted back in his rocking chair, his size fourteen feet propped on a footstool. She studied him in the light of the whale oil lamps. At Fort Stevens she'd caught only a glimpse of him but now she could see every line in his haggard face. Dark circles under his eyes whispered of sleepless nights, the eyes so wounded, as if the death of each soldier had scored a line of suffering on his face. But as sympathetic as she felt, she'd come here this evening not to bestow pity, but for solutions.

She began on a conciliatory note; "Mr. President, I know we've had our differences, I also know that you probably don't like me, or those in my profession."

"Hold right there," he interrupted. "I've nothing but the highest regard for the written word. It's humankind's greatest gift. It enables us to converse with the dead, with the absent, with the yet unborn."

A bit disarmed, she plunged on; "In the midst of war, we face yet another time of trial, a new election for President. Are you aware that of the past fifteen presidents, nine owned slaves? Since the founding of our nation, slavery has been a way of life—even at the very top level of power. You do understand then, why Southerners feel so strongly?"

"But isn't it also true that the South has exerted disproportionate pressure in the choice of our Presidents? Virginia alone claims five. So then, a small minority of rich planters determined who'd be nominated, and in many cases, who'd be elected. Soon it became a vicious, self-fulfilling prophecy. But no more, all that has ended."

She'd never quite thought of it that way, and was both impressed and annoyed by his political acumen. Behind that diffident, cow-chip-kicking manner, lived a consummate politician. She'd have to proceed cautiously. "Admittedly, I do hold some prejudice for the South, I am a Southerner."

"But Miss Rebecca, I'm a Southerner also, at least by birth. From Kentucky, as is Jefferson Davis. I've often wondered, what if as a child, the Davis family had moved to Illinois, and the Lincoln family to Mississippi? How would that have shaped our lives? Might Jefferson Davis now be President of the Union, and I the President of the Confederacy?"

"A pretty speculation, fit for party chatter perhaps, but hardly the issue. What is pertinent is that our exhausted nation hungers for reason, for humanity. Yet you and Davis both appear so—so inflexible."

He set his feet down with a bang. "Between him and us the issue is distinct, simple and inflexible. It is an issue, which can only be tried by war and decided by victory. If we yield we are beaten, if the Southern people fail him, he is beaten. We have more men now than when the war began. We are not exhausted, nor in the process of exhaustion. The public purpose to reestablish and maintain the national authority is unchanged and as we believe it, unchangeable. It is that strength of will in the North which ultimately will be the cause of Confederate defeat and Union victory."

"But must it be a battle to the death? There's a strong feeling among many legislators that if you'd drop your Emancipation Proclamation, the South might come to the bargaining table much more quickly. In some curious way, you and Jeff Davis aren't so far apart in your feelings about Negroes."

He bolted forward in the rocker, body tensed, his voice tight. "By what odd reasoning can you possibly say that?"

"Why, from your very own words. Jeff Davis has always sought to advance the Negro, but like you, sir, he doesn't believe Blacks can ever become the White man's equal."

She handed him the article she'd brought along; he'd written it several years before, "Address on Colonization to a Deputation of Negroes." Lincoln had urged Negroes to leave the U.S. and colonize in Central America. To a group of Negroes who'd come to see him on August 14, 1862, he'd said, "You and we are different races. We have between us a difference greater than between almost any other races...your race suffers very greatly...by living among us, while ours suffers from your presence. Even when you cease to be slaves, you are yet far removed from being placed on an equality with the White race. On this broad continent, not a single man of your race is made the equal of a single man of ours. But for your race among us, there could not be war...It is better for us both, therefore, to be separated."

Lincoln stared at the ceiling; "I did say those things, and how they've come back to haunt me. But—I said them more than two years ago. Those two years have been like two hundred in the way my thinking has changed, as I hope yours has, for an open mind is a signpost of any sentient human being. But you're right, if I dropped emancipation, I'd stand a better chance of being elected. All about me, people cry out that I must do just that. I may bend, but I won't break under this pressure. The Emancipation Proclamation has promised freedom, and the promise being made, must be kept. I should be damned in time and in eternity if I were to return to slavery the Black warriors who had fought for the Union. The world shall know that I will keep my faith to friends and enemies, come what will."

The determination in his voice, the set of his face left no doubt that the issue was closed. She left shortly after that, more confused than ever. Had he really changed in those two years, she wondered? Had she?

Chapter 45

BECKY TOSSED and turned on her cot; there was a spot deep within her so weary that even sleep couldn't reach it. Her fatigue was further compounded by her menstrual cycle. From the core of her being came the melancholy whisper, another barren month, another missed opportunity. Would Carleton ever come back? Was he alive? Would she ever bear a child, or had her spirit been twisted beyond repair? Oh, this damnable war that held life hostage.

At five A.M. she dragged out of bed into a dawn that already felt like hot tar. These last weeks of July had been brutal and the *Farmer's Almanac* predicted worse to come. She dressed and went immediately to look for Forrest. She found him, eyes glazed and blank, slowly mopping his ward; though still an invalid and a shadow of his former self, in the past year he'd regained some strength. But he still had no recollection of who or where he was. She made certain he was all right then began her rounds.

She fielded the usual rash of complaints from staff and patients; ordinarily she could cope, but when Sour Soup came snooping around, dogging Forrest as he had for weeks, she took a broom after him. "Get out of here, git, you damned hospital rat," she yelled. Forrest stared at her, trying to comprehend her anger, and even that annoyed her. Having to hide his identity for so long had taken a grinding toll of her. Each day she lived with the fear that at any moment he might regain his memory and give everything away.

What would happen to all of them then? She began to tremble and a plate slipped from her fingers to shatter on the floor. Matron Phoebe Yates Pember noticed her distress and ordered crisply, "Becky dear, you haven't had any time off in months. Take the rest of the day, get some rest. I need you as a nurse, not a patient."

Mortified by her weakness, Becky ran to her quarters and fell into a fitful sleep. Hours later she surfaced slowly and imagined that Carleton Connaught was sitting by her bed. When he whispered, "Hello," she seized him lest he be some trick of her mind and slip away. He felt real enough, but so thin—how could anyone be so thin? His hair and moustache were shot with gray, adding years to his face. Seeing that he had difficulty getting to his feet, she helped him up. One of his legs moved so stiffly, she feared it might be wooden.

His voice sounded weary and wounded; "The surgeons wanted to amputate, swore I'd be dead within the day if I didn't. I told them I'd shoot the first man who touched me. They cursed me up and down but finally left me alone. I think they were a little disappointed when I didn't die."

"Why didn't you write? Why didn't you let me know?" She squeezed his hand but quickly dropped it when he winced. His fingers were clawed from a bullet wound in his palm.

"Not very pretty, is it? I couldn't write. In fact, the surgeons referred to me as Humpty Dumpty. Can't squeeze a trigger, hold a sword, or ride a horse, but your pity would have been the deadliest wound of all. I'm unfit for combat duty, so if ever I get strong enough, I've been given a choice of a desk job in Danville or one here in Richmond."

"But that's wonderful," she exclaimed.

He averted his gaze; "Becky, I've decided it would be best for both of us if I left."

She searched his face, trying to reach beyond his words. What was he really trying to tell her? That he didn't love her anymore? How could he, given the drudge she'd become? And why should he when he could have his pick of any of Richmond's beauteous heiresses…her tears fell then.

His eyes were brimming also. "Before I left, I needed you to see the mangled thing I've become. I know how loyal you are, but I can't let you throw your life away—"

She turned on him; "Is that why?" He began to list the reasons why she had to forget him and she clapped her hand over his mouth. "Say another word and I'll personally finish what the Yankees couldn't." She brought his wounded palm to her lips. "Wherever you go…unless—you must tell me—is there someone else?"

"I told you once, I tell you again, there's only one Becky for me, there'll never be another." His tentative smile lit hers; then he asked, "Do we still have our secret castle?"

She nodded, and without a word they left the hospital grounds and began the long walk down the winding trail of the Chimborazo bluffs to their tiny loft apartment in the abandoned warehouse near the James River.

"It's the way I remember it, so welcoming," he murmured.

"I kept the place ready, waiting for you. Sometimes I'd just come here…and remember."

For the longest time they just held each other, as if the war had so frozen them they might never thaw. But body warmth accomplished just that and soon they were out of their clothes. His wounds forced them to be inventive and inventive they were, making love with tenderness and then with an abandoned passion that left them in exhausted wonderment.

She nudged him in the ribs; "Your doctors are crazy, I'd say you were very fit for active service," then blushed furiously at her forwardness. She rested her head on his bony chest; "How I prayed to God, swore I'd never ask for anything else ever again if only He brought you back. But now I do want something else. I want to have a child, our child."

"As soon as the war's over," he whispered, "as soon as the world is sane again."

They drifted off to sleep; she woke once, trembling with fright that it had all been a dream, then feeling him next to her, wept with joy that she could be so blessed.

The next day Carleton informed the War Department that he preferred the post in Richmond. They told him that when he'd fully recovered, they'd try to find a place for him.

Revitalized, Becky breezed through her hospital chores. One day while she was washing up and singing "I'll Be a Soldier's Wife Or Die an Old Maid," Sour Soup accosted her.

"Somebody's feelin' purty frisky," he leered, "I saw you goin' off t'other day with your fancy colonel. 'N you always actin' like a prissy old possum with a sewed up poontang."

She whooped aloud and cracked him on the head with a ladle. He rubbed his noggin; "What's more, there's somethin' fishy goin' on with that dim-witted private you're always coddlin'. I axed him what he did in the army and he said something about flying eagles? Whatever that means. I got a nose for such things and my nose smells somethin' fishy—"

Feigning glee, Becky chased him down the hall, whapping him repeatedly on the head. But her fears about Forrest intensified. That night, though she'd sworn to herself that she wouldn't involve Carleton, she blurted out the truth. "I've got to get Forrest out of Chimborazo before he regains his memory. If they send him to Libby Prison, or Belle Isle, he'll never survive. Months ago I tried to smuggle a letter to my grandmother—with her contacts in Washington I thought she might be able to help, but I doubt the letter ever reached her. I can't let Forrest die, I just can't."

"Becky, if you're caught aiding and abetting the enemy—"

"He's my kin! Haven't we killed enough people in this damnable war? Everyone says that no matter who the Democrats nominate for President he's sure to beat Lincoln. Then we can negotiate an end to the war. It's only a few more months. All I've got to do is keep Forrest hidden till then."

She began to weep softly and he took her in his arms. "You're right, we have killed too many. I've killed too many. Bring him here, we'll take care of him together. I'm still waiting for the War Department to find a place for me, and in their disorganized state, that may take months, if ever."

"Are you sure? Your career is at stake."

"Career be damned. If he's your kin then he's my kin. But how will you manage it? Won't Forrest be missed?"

"We've processed so many dead and wounded, fallen so far behind in our records that I think I can cover-up his disappearance. I'll just have to wait for the right moment."

That moment soon presented itself. On July 30, a bizarre battle erupted at the siege of Petersburg. Attempting to break the stalemate that had dragged on and on, the Federals dug a 510-foot tunnel from their trenches to a key fort in the Confederate line, packed that end with 8,000 pounds of gunpowder and ignited it. The explosion blasted a crater 300 feet deep and 200 feet across, and instantly killed more than 250 Rebels. Waves of Federals poured into the crater, and climbed up the other side, about to overwhelm the Rebel defenses. But a combination of Yankee ineptness and Rebel courage turned the tide. Lee counterattacked, and trapped the Federals in the crater—they'd forgotten to bring ladders to climb out—and it created what one Reb called a turkey shoot. In a few hours, 4,500 Yankees lay dead and dying. But the Confederates had also suffered 1,500 casualties, and a great many of the wounded were rushed to Chimborazo.

Once the wounded were treated, Becky alerted Carleton. They took advantage of the turmoil, spirited Forrest out of the hospital and hurried him to the loft. But the commotion had jogged Forrest's brain and recognition flickered in his eyes…"Becky?"…Staring at Carleton's gray uniform, he sprang at him, "Watch out, Becky, he's a Reb!" and might have overwhelmed Carleton if Becky hadn't intervened.

She and Carleton wrestled Forrest to the floor. Becky hissed at him, "Listen to me you stupid fool or I'll kill you myself." Cowed by her vehemence, Forrest stopped struggling. Quick as she could, she explained what had happened.

Forrest kept shaking his head in disbelief. She hauled him to the window; "If you don't believe me look outside, see where you are."

Across the river he saw the Confederate flag flying from the ships in the Navy Yard, watched soldiers in Rebel gray guarding the huge ammunition dumps. Chastened, struggling to make sense of it, his fingers drummed on the metal plate in his head. "I've been in a Reb hospital all this time? Nearly a year? It's—dishonorable—got to escape—"

His moment of clarity burst in a stab of pain and he fell back into his unknowing comatose state. He curled into a fetal position, his patched brain unable to cope with either his nightmare memories or his new reality.

"What are we going to do with him?" Becky asked, her voice edged with despair. "If he acts this crazy every time he regains his memory—"

"Take heart," Carleton said, "I see it as a good sign, he's opened the door a crack, he'll open it wider next time."

"Do you really think so?" She gazed at her cousin; "Oh my poor beautiful Forrest, he was the kindest, the brightest, he was our hope…the doctors told me that he may never recover. They don't know how much of his brain was damaged."

"Let's pray that there's enough left so he can build new memories, maybe even lead a decent life."

Chapter 46

"HAVE YOU ever seen the stars quite so bright?" Rebecca murmured. She and Bittersweet were sitting in the back garden, their melancholy reminiscences about Geary and Forrest frequently interrupted by a spate of tears.

"Look up there!" Bittersweet pointed to the fiery trail of a shooting star. "Be an old saying among my people that shooting stars are God's tears for the evil that men do."

"What a compelling thought," Rebecca sighed. "I once read about an ancient Indian legend that says stars are the souls of the good that the Great Spirit set in the heavens."

"Umm, like that one better, to think that everybody we ever loved be up there looking down on us? It's a comfort."

Rebecca started to cry again; Bittersweet put her arms around her and rocked her back and forth. She helped Rebecca to her feet. "Come on, time for our evening constitutional, best get your blood flowing back into yo' head."

After a few turns around the garden, Bittersweet said, "You're walkin' a bunch better, no limp at all." Rebecca didn't respond and trying to pry her out of her mood, Bittersweet whispered the juiciest piece of gossip she knew.

Rebecca stopped in her tracks; "I don't believe it! Somebody tried to assassinate President Lincoln?"

"Don't you go tellin' nobody, supposed to be the biggest secret in Washington."

"Then how, pray tell, did you find out about it?"

"Miz Lincoln told her seamstress, Miz Keckly, and Miz Keckly told Senator Sumner's maid and the maid told me."

"Oh, pardon me, I didn't realize the Federal Secret Service had a Maid's Division. How in the world do I verify this?" She snapped her fingers, "Bravo. Lincoln can't burp without calling Bravo in for a conference."

"Bravo ain't been around much since that there mean article you wrote about Lincoln."

"Around much? He hasn't been here at all. You'd think he'd have the decency to apologize but he's so damned stubborn, I can't imagine whom he gets it from. I suppose I'll have to make the first move. And I've the perfect excuse."

She sent a note around to her son; "I realize that pressing affairs of state keep you from your family obligations but a situation's arisen that demands your attention. Sharon has become quite serious about this Yankee soldier, Samuel Somethingorother. I've tried to alert Kate but she's wrapped herself in a cocoon of prayer and platitude and is simply not equal to the task. With Gunning gone, it falls on you to put a stop to it. Sharon and he are coming to supper tomorrow, I'm sure Mr. Lincoln can forgive your not holding his hand for an hour or two? I'll expect you at six. Your Loving Mother."

Promptly at six, Sharon and Sergeant Samuel Stockwell arrived at Rebecca's. She cringed when she saw the sappy look on her granddaughter's face; puppy love, no doubt about it. Stockwell was what Rebecca called a Medium Man: medium height, medium build, medium features, so nondescript she could have lost him in a crowd, and at this moment, wished she could. If only to rid herself of his ghastly New England twang.

Nevertheless, she was determined to be gracious, above all, fair, convinced that this Medium Man would soon hang himself. Her smile couldn't have been more engaging, her accent more honeyed as she asked, "Have I ever told you how Andrew Jackson handled South Carolina's threat to secede?"

Sharon rolled her eyes; "At least a hundred times."

"Thank you very much, Miss Snippy, just remember that one day you may be old and forgetful. I hope your grandchildren treat you with a little more respect."

Stockwell said soberly, "I'll see that they do, ma'am."

Rebecca bristled; "Have I just heard some young man taking liberties? In my day you'd have been horsewhipped."

"But Grandma, we're engaged."

"Put that right out of your mind. There'll be no talk of engagement, at least until I've met his parents. Radical abolitionists, no doubt."

Sharon answered defensively, "And what if they are? Anyway, I've told you, Herself said yes, providing we bring the children up in the faith."

Rebecca waved her hand airily; "You still need my approval, I'm the important one, I've got all the money."

Sharon pealed with laughter; "Grandma, if I let you tell the story about Andrew Jackson will you put me back in your will?"

Rebecca tried to look stern—but gave it up and laughed along with them.

Bravo arrived late, and full of apologies. "Lincoln and I were at the War Department hoping we'd hear some news from the Democratic convention in Chicago. Nothing yet."

"Does it really make any difference who they nominate? Any Democrat will beat Lincoln handily," Rebecca declared.

"I'm not so sure of that," Sam Stockwell countered.

Rebecca waggled her finger at him; "Young man, I assume you read the same war dispatches I do? Republicans all over the country are praying for the tiniest military victory so they can hold onto the Presidency. But Bobby Lee still has Grant confounded at Petersburg and Sherman's been stopped dead at the outskirts of Atlanta. Stalemate, nothing but stalemate, and stalemate means defeat for Lincoln."

Before they could come to blows, Bittersweet yelled, "Supper's here." She whispered to Rebecca, "If you can't remember how to be a lady, then remember your blood pressure."

Much to Rebecca's surprise, supper went tolerably well, though Bravo appeared not to remember their last altercation, which annoyed her no end. He was much too busy discussing military and political strategy with Sam Stockwell.

"I've talked to a lot of men in my department," Stockwell told them, "and most of them are leaning toward Lincoln."

"Then you and your men obviously have the survival instincts of the lemming," Rebecca cooed. "Even Lincoln knows that he's going to be defeated. He's told any number of his friends, 'I am going to be beaten, and unless some great change takes place, badly beaten.'" She turned to her son; "Isn't it true that on August 25, he wrote a blind memorandum and asked all his cabinet members to sign it, sight unseen?"

"Damnation, are there no secrets left in Washington?"

"Should there be? The people deserve the truth."

"If he loses the election, then the Union's lost forever," Bravo retorted, "is that what you want?"

"I want my grandsons back!"

"Dessert!" Bittersweet fair shouted, proffering a peach cobbler. Afterwards, Bravo and Sam Stockwell retired for cigars, brandy and what Rebecca hoped would be the finish for the twangy Yankee. Sharon fidgeted while the men were gone but sighed with relief when they returned, smiling. Which threw Rebecca into a snit. Shortly thereafter Stockwell announced, "Much as I've enjoyed the evening I've got to be back by Taps," and he and Sharon left.

The moment they were gone Rebecca demanded, "Well, what happened?" and began pointing out all of Stockwell's faults.

Bravo held up his hands; "Hold on, Ma, there's a lot more good in that young man than bad, a little rough around the edges I admit, but I liked him. He's got a responsible position in the War Department—"

Bittersweet shouted from the kitchen, "That proves it, that Yankee is a spy. Don't say I didn't warn you."

Bravo groaned then went on, "What's more, he's not a bit intimidated by you or the Brand name, which is refreshing."

"And here I was hoping to come off like Lady Macbeth. But seriously, he's so ordinary, so—medium."

"Ma, has it ever occurred to you that Sharon might also be—medium? Not that there's anything wrong with that, Lincoln claims that common men are best, that's why the Good Lord made so many of them."

"How comforting that we're quoting from Honest Abe's Homilies. Do you think he'll replace Plato and Aristotle? Oh what's the use, no one listens to me anymore." Whatever hopes she'd had of persuading Sharon to pursue a career had vanished in the girl's vision of pots and pans and dishes and diapers.

Bravo stood up; "I've got to get back to the War Department, we may have some news from the convention by now."

"One last thing," Rebecca began innocently, "I'm planning to do a piece on the attempted assassination of Lincoln—?"

Bravo stopped dead; "Where did you hear that?"

"Why, everybody's maid Washington knows. To keep peace in this family—did you know I came down with a dreadful cold when you were so rude?—I need to be certain of my facts."

"Ma, if you print that, you may put the idea in every other madman's head. Is that what you want?"

"Of course not, but the First Amendment—"

"Damn it, must you reporters always hide behind the First Amendment? We both know freedom of speech isn't the issue here. Why can't you exercise discretion? Aren't you part of this nation, or is personal glory always to be more important than the common weal?"

"He's the President, everything that happens to him—if you don't tell me the details, someone else will—"

"Lord save us from ferreting gossips who call themselves reporters. But you're right, someone else would confabulate a tale straight out of Grimm's. All right, Ma, here's what I know and it comes straight from the two men who were there, Lincoln and a Private John Nichols, Company K, 105th Pennsylvania Volunteers. Nichols was assigned to guard Lincoln's summer cottage. He was on duty a few nights ago at Soldiers' Home, Lincoln was expected shortly. Nichols heard a gunshot followed by rapid hoof beats. Lincoln came galloping in alone, without his hat. Nichols searched for the hat and finally found it; there was a bullet hole in the crown."

Rebecca's hand flew to her heart; "Merciful heavens!"

"Lincoln insisted that the shot came from some foolish hunter, that it wasn't meant for him. He ordered absolute secrecy, but he told Mary Todd, and in her hysteria, she told friends. Stanton began an investigation but nothing's come of it. Lincoln's bodyguard, Ward Lamon, threatened to resign unless he agreed to an escort at all times. Lincoln gave in and now never rides alone. Now Ma, if you feel you can't exist without printing that, then go ahead. But if you've got the slightest bit of decency, if you don't want to place the President in greater jeopardy—oh, what's the use?"

He started for the door but Rebecca caught his arm. "You're right, this shouldn't be made public, at least not before the election. For a variety of reasons."

Pleasantly surprised, he beamed at her; "What a relief to discover that you've inherited some of my good sense."

"Bravo, think. You've known Lincoln long enough to realize he's the canniest of politicians. Was this really an assassination attempt? Or did he concoct the entire incident in order to gain sympathy for his reelection?"

He shook his head in disbelief; "You won't be satisfied until he's dead, will you?"

"That is so unfair. I just find it hard to believe that any assassin could be so stupid. After all, he need only wait two more months and Lincoln will be voted out of office."

"I give up," Bravo shouted and stormed out.

Rebecca hardly slept that night, anxious to know whom the Democrats had chosen. Though she'd fully expected it, she was dismayed when they nominated General George McClellan. She'd always regretted giving the pompous twit such flattering coverage in her early articles.

But the choice of McClellan brought rousing cheers from every Democrat, North and South. McClellan was not only running on a Peace Platform, he also loathed Lincoln, and told the press, "I've been called on once more to save our bleeding nation from the corrupt policies of this Black Republican administration." Everyone knew McClellan's not-so-hidden agenda included repudiating this coarse, incompetent rail-splitter who'd so heinously wronged him by taking away his army.

The Democrats left Chicago in wild elation convinced that nothing could stop them from capturing the White House.

Three days later, on September 2, telegraph wires tapped out the electrifying news, "Sherman Captures Atlanta!"

Chapter 47

SWEPT ALONG on the crest of these turbulent events, Gunning Brand stole into Washington in late September. Travelling with him, Captain Thomas Conrad, the former Georgetown lay minister converted to Confederate spy, now operating the Richmond end of "Operation Come Retribution."

As they crossed the Long Bridge, Conrad observed, "Amazing how simple it is to get in and out of Washington."

Gunning nodded; "The pickets are even more lax than they were last time, it works to our advantage."

The men proceeded to the old Van Ness mansion on 17th St. and C where they were being given refuge. Now the home of Thomas Green, married to Anne Lomax, whose brother was the Confederate general, Lindsay Lomax; the Greens had long been members of the Rebel spy network in Washington. To avoid bringing undue suspicion down on the Green family, all clandestine meetings were to be held elsewhere.

John Wilkes Booth had been summoned and was staying at the National Hotel. Booth suggested they meet there but Gunning vetoed that; it was far too public; both Conrad and Gunning were known in Washington. Booth then urged that they meet at the home of his favorite mistress in Washington, a young prostitute named Ellie Starr. She lived in a House of Delight run by her sister, Nellie Starr, at 12th and Pennsylvania, in the southeast quadrant of the city. That area, frequented by cutthroats, slatterns and pimps, had a reputation so dangerous that the law rarely ventured into it, not even the Union's Secret Service. Gunning agreed to the rendezvous.

Gunning and Conrad entered Nellie Starr's emporium disguised as paying customers. They walked past rooms where pleasure was being bought and sold, then climbed a flight of stairs to Ellie's room. They interrupted Booth who was reading Marc Anthony's funeral oration in *Julius Caesar* to Ellie. Booth bounded to his feet, embraced Gunning warmly and with playful pats goosed Ellie out the door.

Gunning took it all in: rumpled bed, rumpled man. It made him uneasy though he couldn't imagine why; in years past he'd operated in much the same fashion. Maybe he'd come to realize that self-indulgence had little place in this war—or maybe you're just getting old and envious, he told himself.

Gunning plunged right in; "The fall of Atlanta has been a blow for the South, not only militarily but politically, it's given Lincoln's election campaign new life."

Booth's dark eyes flashed; "It is a setback, but not fatal. I view it more as a test of our resolve."

Gunning thought he might be listening to Jeff Davis. On September 20, Davis had left Richmond for Georgia, convinced that his presence could reverse the South's military defeat in Atlanta. With Sherman's supply lines stretched thin, Davis was determined to recover Atlanta, drive Sherman out of Georgia and destroy the Federal army. But Gunning had no such confidence in Davis' magical presence; if the war continued on this way it was only a matter of months before the South suffered total collapse.

"We've got to do everything we can to defeat Lincoln at the polls," Gunning told Booth. "We're funding Democratic newspapers in the North to speak against him, we plan to raid a few Union prisons and free our soldiers, sabotage civilian targets. To that end, I'll need you to go to Montreal—"

Booth interrupted anxiously, "In November, my brothers, Edwin, Junius and I are performing in *Julius Caesar* at the Winter Garden Theater in New York. It will be the first time ever that the three of us will appear on the same stage."

"Damnation!" Gunning swore, "didn't you agree to cancel all engagements?"

"It's a benefit, one night only. We're raising money to erect a statue of Shakespeare in Central Park."

Somewhat mollified Gunning growled, "You'll be going to Montreal in mid-October, it won't interfere with your plans."

Booth sighed with relief; "Excellent. But why Montreal when our important work is here?"

"We're planning something in Vermont that will bring the war home to the North. It will prove that as long as Lincoln remains in the White House no one's safe. In Montreal you'll register at the Hotel St. Lawrence where you'll be contacted by two of our agents, Patrick C. Martin and George N. Sanders; you'll give them the orders you'll be carrying. You must be in Montreal no later than October seventeenth."

"You can depend on it." Then Booth's expressive face reflected his confusion; "Why not kidnap Lincoln right now, as we'd planned? Then there'd be no need for an election."

"I agree, but politics got in the way. The consensus among the High Command is that if Lincoln can be repudiated at the polls, by his own people, it will best serve our purpose."

Booth glowered; "But what of retribution? What of punishment for crimes committed against the South? And what if he is reelected?"

"That last possibility is why we're here; Conrad and I will stay in D.C. until the election's over. Five weeks should give us enough time to establish a solid base of operation. If by some perverse stroke of fate Lincoln does win, we'll be fully prepared and we then move ahead with the kidnapping." He added emphatically, "But not before, is that clear?" Booth nodded glumly and Gunning continued, "What progress have you made putting together your action team?"

Booth came alive; "True patriots whom I trust with my life, men ready to sacrifice all for our cause. Four so far, but I can enlist as many as we need."

"Four's enough for now; the fewer who know our plans, the less chance of a leak. Don't underestimate Colonel Lafayette Baker; that swine rules the Union's Secret Service with an iron fist. If we're caught, he'll hang us first and question our corpses later. When can I meet your team?"

"I can assemble them in a matter of days. I'll contact you as soon as they're all here." Gunning prepared to leave and Booth said, "When next you see your dear mother please give her my very best regards."

"I've no intention of seeing her, it's far too risky."

"If it were my mother, nothing could stop me. But I keep forgetting that you don't have the same freedom in Washington that I do. I'll call on her myself—"

Gunning lunged at him and grabbed his shirt. "Not on your life! I don't want her implicated in any way."

Booth fell back before Gunning's assault and swore that he wouldn't try to see Rebecca.

When Gunning and Conrad left Nellie Starr's, Conrad said, "Booth's an odd one, isn't he? Are you sure he's reliable?"

Gunning grunted. "Sometimes I get the feeling that our operation is nothing more than play acting to him. God knows he's dedicated enough, but he is something of a loose cannon. I can't be here all the time to keep tabs on him;

I'd feel a whole lot better if we had our own man on the inside, someone we trusted to keep us posted on Booth's progress."

"What about John Surratt?" Conrad suggested. "He's a sensible lad, with a good head on his shoulders. And he travels between Washington and Richmond regularly."

"Excellent idea. I've trusted him—with my life—to lead me through the Federal lines and so far he's never failed me. He may be just the leavening touch Booth needs."

For the next several days Gunning and Conrad took turns spying on the White House. Lafayette Square, just north of the mansion's entrance, proved an excellent vantage point. A pattern soon emerged; Lincoln usually left Washington in the evening, riding in his carriage out 14th Street to Columbia Road then across to the higher elevations of the countryside to Soldier's Home. An armed escort always accompanied him.

Gunning thought the country road a good place to waylay him. They'd have to dispatch his guard but once Lincoln fell into their hands, it would be simple enough to head for the lower Potomac and cross the river into Maryland. There, as the Confederate Secret Service was arranging, a regiment of General Mosby's Raiders would be waiting to spirit Lincoln to Richmond.

Several days later, John Surratt came to Washington, and Gunning took him to meet Booth. Gunning's hope that they might get on was more than realized; Surratt treated Booth with just the right amount of hero-worship to charm him, yet he still retained his own cool wit.

By week's end, Booth and Surratt were thick as thieves. Booth became a frequent visitor at the boarding house run by John's mother, Mary Surratt, at 604 H Street, near the corner of 6th. A three-story, inconspicuous brick building, with bona-fide boarders, Gunning recognized its potential as a safe house; John Surratt, eager to please, urged that they use it as a meeting place and Gunning and Conrad accepted.

Surratt's sisters were a-twitter about their brother's famous friend and fair swooned when Booth presented them with signed *Carte de visites*. Like many actors who sought to keep their names before the public, he'd had a collection of photographs taken in a variety of striking poses and handed them out freely. Gunning thought it yet another crazed anomaly of this war that in the midst of their top-secret mission, one of their principal conspirators should be so notorious.

In due course Booth informed Gunning that the action team he'd recruited had come to Washington and Gunning and Conrad went to meet them at Mary Surratt's boarding house. The conspirators gathered in John Surratt's bedroom where Gunning took their measure. Two men from

Baltimore, boyhood friends of Booth's, Michael O'Laughlin, 24, and Sam Arnold, 29, seemed solid, intelligent choices. But warning signals went up when Gunning met George Atzerodt, a dissolute German jack-of-all-trades from Port Tobacco who drank recklessly. But Booth assured him that he could control Atzerodt, and Atzerodt did own a boat and knew secluded places along the Potomac where they could cross with their prize. The fourth conspirator was David Herold, a local pharmacist's clerk who looked a bit dim.

Booth took center stage and mesmerized the band, detailing their glorious mission, how their names would be inscribed on all Southern hearts. Slavishly devoted to Booth, they responded with unbridled enthusiasm.

Watching this, Conrad took Gunning aside. "What do you think of this team?"

Gunning worried this. "It's a start, but what's lacking is someone with military experience. It's time we got a seasoned operative assigned to Booth's team. Someone trained in guerilla warfare, maybe an officer from Mosby's Raiders?"

"I'll check with General Mosby, he recruits only the most fearless men, he should be able to provide someone tough."

After the meeting disbanded, Gunning stayed behind to talk to Booth; he'd gotten the distinct impression that Booth wanted Lincoln to win the election, for only then could he become the hero of his own imagination. He tried to impress on Booth the need for caution, for team effort. He then gave Booth last minute instructions about Montreal.

Booth looked vaguely bored as he drained the dregs of his wine. "Since this is my last night in Washington, I'm off to make my Starr twinkle, why don't you join me? You seem overly nervous and Dr. Booth prescribes the tonic of horizontal refreshments. I've always found it the best way to drain off my own dark humors."

Gunning considered, then declined. He'd come to an odd place in his life; the act would have little meaning without Romance. If anyone had ever told him that he'd stay faithful to one woman for four years he'd have laughed in his face. Yet he had. He felt responsible for her, wanted to protect her…was that love? He wondered what she was doing this evening? She'd recovered enough from her abortion to resume her whirl of social activities: Was she at the gaming tables with Judah Benjamin? Or out with some gallant war hero? They were always lurking in the wings…A wave of uncertainty washed over him…of anger, of jealousy…was <u>that</u> love?

In this mood he tramped the streets, then, even though he recognized the danger, strode to his old house where his wife and daughter still lived. He had no desire to see Kate, she was a good woman and he bore her no ill will, but he'd never understand why he should be forced to spend the rest of his life with her just because she was a Catholic. But he hungered for a glimpse of Sharon.

He watched the house from a safe distance; after a time he saw a Union sergeant enter and a short time later come out with his daughter. He followed them discretely; once clear of the house they embraced with an abandon that cut across Gunning's heart. Was this the moppet who with tender kisses had sworn she'd never love another except her Dada? How old it made him feel, as if he must seize time or be left behind. At that moment he vowed that when the war was over he'd take Romance off to a far corner of the world and start a new life—yet how to explain that he still felt the tug of the old? He studied the soldier with all the concerns of a dutiful father.

He followed them to his mother's house, saw Rebecca greet Sharon at the door, unreserved love flowing between them, and Rebecca's cool, correct behavior toward the sergeant. Whatever he felt about his mother, he couldn't fault her where her grandchildren were concerned; he almost pitied Sharon's beau, he'd have to pass Rebecca's muster.

Long after Sharon and her beau had left Gunning remained, watching his mother's house. He felt an irresistible urge to see her, at her age, anything might happen. What a pity if she died before he got a chance to tell her how much he adored her. And he did, despite all of the difficulties throughout their lives. Or perhaps because of them. They seemed to be people who needed constant confrontation, always testing, always redefining themselves. But as much as he wanted to, he couldn't risk seeing her now, not when so much was at stake. If he saw her chances are that sooner or later she'd tell Bravo. And since Bravo had been involved in Dahlgen's raid on Richmond, he might easily put two and two together.

Recalling that his mother had consistently spoken out against Lincoln's Administration, he wondered if she'd be willing to help in the upcoming election? After much soul searching he wrote a long letter and the next evening sent John Surratt around to his mother's house deliver it. From a hidden spot, Gunning watched as Surratt eased through the gate, stealthily climbed the front stairs and shoved the note under the door.

As luck would have it, Rebecca chanced to be at the window, saw the intruder and ran outside. Surratt vaulted over the wrought iron fence and fled, pursued by a flood of blistering invective from Rebecca.

Chapter 48

"AND IF I ever catch you here again I'll take my shotgun to you!" Rebecca shouted.

Bittersweet came running to the door brandishing the fire tongs; "What's going on? Whozat?"

Rebecca waved the note angrily; "I'm sick and tired of these Yankees plaguing us with their hate mail. But this time I got a good look at that young scoundrel. I'll have the constable around tomorrow and give him a description."

"What's the note say?"

"Probably nothing they haven't accused me of before."

She adjusted her spectacles and read, "Dear Rebel Thorne, Time runs out for our bleeding world. We must end this war. The simplest way to do that is for Lincoln to be defeated on November 8. Had he allowed the South to go her own way, solve her problems in her own fashion, might hundreds of thousands of young Americans still be alive, including your own grandsons? Since you've consistently spoken out against Lincoln's administration, everyone expects you to endorse McClellan. I beg you, don't disappoint them. By all you hold dear, by all that's holy in the human heart, I implore you, speak out against these black Republicans, let honor and reason and peace return to our land."

She took off her glasses and they fell from her trembling fingers. She whispered dully, "It's from Gunning."

Bittersweet helped her to the settee. "Lord a' mercy, just look at you looking like you died yesterday. Take your medicine, quick."

Rebecca dutifully swallowed a teaspoon of digitalis and Bittersweet ventured, "Think maybe you a little mixed up in the head again? Didn't look to me like no Mr. Gunning running off."

"He didn't deliver it himself," she retorted irritably, "he sent it by that young man. It's so curious, this letter doesn't sound anything like Gunning—could he have changed that much? But it's his handwriting; I know it like my own. What am I going to do?"

"Tell Mr. Bravo right away. I'll go fetch—"

Rebecca seized her arm; "You mustn't! Swear you won't tell him. Or anybody else, not even Kate or Sharon. If Gunning is here I mustn't put him in jeopardy. Swear," she pleaded.

Bittersweet put her arm around her; "Hush, I won't say nothin'. Umm, why not look at the bright side? Leastwise we knows he's alive. Come on now, I'll help you to bed. Come mornin', things will be clearer, you'll know what to do."

But when tomorrow came, Rebecca still didn't know. Conscious that time was running out—less than four weeks until Election Day—she decided she could no longer sit on the sidelines. "I'll simply have to choose the lesser of two evils." But which one was that? Intellectually, she sided with the North but her blood coursed for the South. Whose heart wouldn't go out to such a brave people? If only her countrymen didn't have such misguided notions about slavery! She agonized over it; started a piece supporting McClellan, tore it up, wrote one against him, and shredded that also.

One evening Sharon brought Sam Stockwell over. Rebecca took her granddaughter aside; "I've just gotten word that your father is all right." Sharon screamed with delight and pressed for details, but Rebecca claimed not to know anything more.

Within moments of sitting down to dinner, Rebecca and Sam plunged into their ongoing battle over the election. "If you young nincompoops took the time to learn our history," Rebecca instructed, "you'd realize that the odds against Lincoln are overwhelming. No President since Andrew Jackson, as far back as 1832, has served a second term. William Henry Harrison and Zachary Taylor died in office and James Polk chose not to run, but Van Buren, Tyler, Fillmore, Pierce and Buchanan were all booted out of office by an irate electorate."

"Guess I didn't realize that," Sam Stockwell conceded.

"I'm convinced the same fate awaits Lincoln, particularly since McClellan is so respected by the men in the army."

"Maybe you've got more historical perspective than I do, but being in the army I'll wager I know the mind of the enlisted man better; it's McClellan who says we respect McClellan."

Rebecca started to object and Sam said, "Don't know why we're even arguing this, it's not as if women can vote."

"That does it!" Rebecca cried. Goaded to madness by his laconic misguided
Yankee logic, male logic, she argued and fumed and at one point got so
incensed she threatened not to attend their wedding.

When the couple left, Stockwell paused at the door; "I'll give the rebellion
another thump this fall by voting for Old Abe. I can't afford to spend three
years of my life holding this nation together then turn around and give the
Rebels all they want."

"I shall scream," Rebecca called after them, "I hate anyone who has to have
the last word!"

But with sober reflection she realized that her argument with Stockwell not
only gave her exactly the theme for which she'd been searching, it also afforded
her the opportunity to agitate for her own life-long cause.

In her article for the newspaper, eagerly awaited by the powerbrokers in
Washington, Rebel Thorne began: "I understand there's a movement in
Congress to give the Negro the vote? If all literate citizens are to be considered
equal under the law, this seems to be entirely appropriate. Under. When may we
expect that this right will be extended to the women of this nation? Or must we
fight a civil war for that also?

"I've been asked to voice my opinion about the candidates. When this government allows me to express my choice via the ballot box, then I'll say that
freedom has at last come to this land. Until that time, all I can do is point out
certain facts for your consideration.

"We Americans have always had a love affair with our generals and for their
service to our nation have elevated them to our highest office; witness George
Washington, James Monroe, Andrew Jackson, William Henry Harrison, and
Zachary Taylor. But those generals won their battles, while McClellan lost his.
Now I ask you, where in the annals of history has a loser been chosen to lead
his people?

"Our Little Napoleon insists that the soldiers of the Army of the Potomac,
which he once commanded, are totally with and for him. Well, why not let
them speak for themselves?

"With so many men in the armed forces, the soldier vote will be crucial,
perhaps even the deciding factor. Absentee voting has become a bold experiment in democracy, pioneered by both sides since this war began. And now in
1864, 18 of 21 Northern states allow soldiers to vote in the field. Just three
states refuse to do so; Illinois, Indiana and New Jersey, all controlled by
Democrats. Why? Do they fear how their soldiers will vote?

"When this war began, 50% of the men who went into the army were Democrats. Is this still true? You men in the service, you're the ones fighting and dying. So tell us your choice, tell us by casting your ballot, so that we will know once and forever the will of the people. Put down your guns long enough to vote!"

The article, written with such strict objectivity, offended very few voters, except the misogynists in the government, and, of course, McClellan. The Republican Party had tens of thousands of Rebel Thorne's article reprinted and distributed throughout the Union armies. Absentee balloting was scheduled to begin the last week in October giving soldiers in the field two full weeks to cast their ballot.

The afternoon of October 20, Bittersweet came tearing into Rebecca's study; "The Rebel army just invaded Vermont!"

Rebecca rolled her eyes; "After all I've tried to drum into you, have you still no sense of geography? Vermont is near Canada, there's no way the Confederate—"

Bittersweet thrust the special edition of the newspaper in front of Rebecca. Her mouth fell open as she read: "Yesterday, October 19, a band of 25 Rebels invaded St. Albans, Vermont, 15 miles from the Canadian border. They held the town hostage for a day, robbed three banks of $200,000 then escaped back across the border. Other acts of such daring sabotage have been reported throughout the North."

Rebecca exclaimed, "This has got to hurt Lincoln's chances. He can't even protect his own northern states."

Then November 8th was upon them.

"Can it be four years since we last waited for these results?" Rebecca asked Bittersweet. "Sometimes it seems like four minutes, other times like four hundred years. Our young people killed, our family torn apart, and for what? Because men couldn't reason with each other? Perhaps this Charles Darwin is right, that we're all descended from savages, and that killer instinct still lurks in all of us."

"You for sure," Bittersweet hummed under her breath.

By evening, Rebecca was beside herself with nerves. "I can't stand just sitting around here, let's gird up our loins and go to the War Department. Bravo will probably be manning the telegraph station. If Stanton's there I'm sure he won't let us in but we can wait outside." They bundled up against the brisk autumn night and went.

A large crowd had gathered outside the building, cheering or groaning every time the results were announced. By midnight, reports indicated Lincoln was being beaten in Delaware, Kentucky and in McClellan's home state, New Jersey. New York, with its huge block of electoral votes, was too close to call.

But as the soldier vote came in a turnaround began; though 50% of them had once been Democrats, only 20 to 25% voted the Democratic ticket. In the 12 states that counted soldiers' votes separately, 78% voted for Lincoln. When the final results were tabulated, Lincoln got 54% of the total popular vote and carried all but three states, New Jersey, Delaware, and Kentucky.

Rebecca was astonished with the landslide; the soldier vote had been the deciding factor. She told Bittersweet, "Even if the southern states had remained in the Union and voted in this election, their ballots wouldn't have made a difference, Lincoln had enough popular and electoral votes to win without them. This time, the judgment of the majority—including the men fighting and dying—couldn't had been stated more emphatically."

In the wee hours of the morning, responding to a serenade of well wishers in front of the White House, Lincoln came out on the portico. Rebecca listened as he addressed the crowd. "The election results will be to the everlasting advantage, if not to the very salvation of this country."

For all her fears about the man, Rebecca somehow believed him and his proclamation declaring the last Thursday in November as a national day of Thanksgiving seemed entirely appropriate. She decided she'd observe it, for in her mind, it did mark the very preservation of the Union.

PART FIVE

Chapter 49

THE SNARLING December ice storm slashed at the windowpanes in the Snuggery, the tiny library on the main floor of the Confederate White House. Members of the High Command, General Lee, Major Norris, Secretary of War Seddon, he'd replaced John Randolph who'd resigned after a bitter feud with Davis, Judah Benjamin and Gunning Brand, waited for President Davis to join them. With Lincoln's reelection, Davis had been felled with a host of ailments and once again all government business had to be conducted from his home.

Judah Benjamin, with his customary legerdemain, had procured a small log and a timid fire burned in the grate. The talk was subdued, touching on Sherman's rampage in Georgia that was threatening Savannah, but the hypnotic bombardment in the distance always brought their conversation back to the battle on the Petersburg front. For Gunning, who'd spent the last several weeks there, it conjured up a scene from hell.

Immediately on returning from his mission in Washington, President Davis had sent him to the Petersburg front. There, he'd risked the fire of sharpshooters as he galloped up and down the thirty-mile line, interrogating captured Union soldiers, trying to determine where Grant might try to punch through next. Only in that way could General Lee move his ever-thinning forces to head off the new Federal threat.

Never had Gunning witnessed such desolation; not a tree left standing, soldiers endlessly building fortifications, redans, abatis, chevaux-de-frise, anything to protect them from an enemy charge. Inside the trenches they huddled in bomb-proofs made of wicker gambians filled with dirt and roofed over with heavy logs; but nothing could withstand a direct hit. Every two minutes the enemy siege guns spewed out their message, not only to kill, but to prevent them from sleeping. They lived a horror beyond imagining and Gunning felt guilty for being in Richmond with a roof over his head.

At last Jeff Davis shuffled in on the arm of Burton Harrison; Lee rose and gave Davis his seat near the fire.

Gunning avoided meeting Davis' gaze, afraid his profound disappointment would show; incontrovertible now that so many of the President's ailments were self-induced. Where is the man I once idolized? Gunning wondered. After four long years, Davis' imperious manner, and his need to always be in the right, had eroded Gunning's faith. In every branch of government envious men no longer praised his iron will, but whispered, "Jefferson Davis would rather be right—than win the war."

When Davis dismissed his aide everyone tacitly understood that he considered this meeting top secret. He began in a wispy voice; "We're at a perilous place in our war for freedom. With that man's re-election we can no longer hope for a negotiated settlement, we can depend only on our own resolve." He turned to Lee; "General, what have you to report?"

"Discouraging news only. The Federal army now numbers a hundred and twenty thousand and grows daily. We can only field fifty-seven thousand men but our desertions are alarming. With this foul weather all fronts are relatively quiet but that won't last, we've perhaps three months until spring, then Grant will resume his offensive."

Davis' voice caught; "If only the deserters would return, if only the states would send us their militias, if only—dear God, can we hold at Petersburg?"

Lee's "No," sounded like a death knell. "In trench warfare, Grant's superior power must eventually overwhelm us."

Davis' jaw set; "Any recommendations? Anyone?"

General Lee said, "I believe our success lies in a new military strategy. We've proven again and again that on our own soil and in the open field we can out-fight…Those People. As painful as this will sound, I'm convinced our only hope is to break free of the enemy's siege and engage him on our own terms. It means we must abandon Richmond."

There it is, Gunning thought, the dreaded words spoken at last, but the earth hadn't opened nor had the sky fallen.

Secretary of War Seddon, a native of Richmond blurted, "It means we'll lose our capital—and the Tredegar Iron Works."

"What does it profit us to try and save Tredegar but lose the war?" Lee countered. "General Gorgas has accomplished miracles establishing ordnances elsewhere in the South. Unless we make this sacrifice for the greater good—"

"In the open field," Davis repeated slowly, "yes, there we'll show them our mettle." He stood up, a surge of hope restoring some life to his ashen face. "Let us use this relatively quiet time to regroup our forces, lay in new stores. Then before Grant can begin his spring offensive, our armies will slip away from their imprisonment at Petersburg. General Lee, you will march to join our army fighting in the Carolinas, and thus reinforced, engage Sherman and defeat him. That accomplished, you then turn on Grant."

Lee didn't respond and Davis said, "Come, sir, don't look so pained, I have every confidence in your success. Our cause will prevail, for God knows we are in the right."

"My pain is for Richmond," Lee answered, "I fear it will be destroyed like Atlanta. After all our people have sacrificed, they deserve better."

Davis began to ramble on about God's will, and loath to become mired in another interminable discussion, Lee claimed pressing military matters and left.

"Lee's point is well taken," Gunning began, "Richmond's been the backbone of our cause and it deserves our fullest protection. There is a way to do just that." All eyes fixed on him as he said, "Operation Come Retribution. We were going to use it to effect prisoner exchange? Why not also use it to save our capital? Kidnap Lincoln, hold him hostage to insure that Richmond won't be raped the way Sherman raped Atlanta."

A heated argument erupted about the plan's efficacy; Davis still wasn't persuaded that it could succeed, but in desperate time's men do desperate things. The plan to kidnap Lincoln, which had begun after Dahlgren's raid in March of 1864, now became an integral part of Confederate strategy.

Gunning left the White House feeling slightly euphoric and very nervous, for the responsibility weighed heavily. By the time he reached Romance's house, mania won out for he hadn't seen her in weeks and was literally pulsing with need. His mood proved infectious and with each goblet of wine, Romance became alternately coy, shy, virginal and sybaritic, intoxicating him with her wild mood swings.

He chased her through the clutter of exquisite antique furniture that crowded her drawing room, all purchased for a pittance from destitute families. When he caught her she asked breathlessly, "Do you believe that cities have souls? Paris has the wistful soul of a gamin; London, that of a penurious merchant; Washington, since it was planned rather than evolving naturally, has no soul at all. But Richmond, ah, here's a city that's entering the dark night of its soul."

"What's all this soulful prattle about?"

With a deft motion she sat astride him. "Simply that we must whip our mounts and flee this doomed city." She slapped him hard across his flanks; "Listen to Grant's cannon, night and day, like the heartbeat of some monster moving ever closer to devour us. We must flee before we're eaten!"

"Too late," he cried, upended her and carried her into the bedroom where he became the devouring monster.

Her fevered hand closed around his fevered body. "It's been ages since I've seen you in such good spirits. Have I missed something? Has your precious Confederacy won the war?"

"Ask me again in six months."

She pealed with laughter and tightened her grip on him; "Beast, how dare you have good news and not share it with me? Lord knows I've suffered with you through all the bad."

"Indeed you have, and you're right. I want you to leave Richmond. If you want to return North and visit your family for a bit, I'll have Judah Benjamin issue you a passport."

"You'll do no such thing, I'll leave when you leave."

"You must leave before that," he insisted. His eyes swept around the bedroom gorged with more precious antiques. "Dispose of everything, I don't want you to suffer any financial loss. That includes Montgomery. Go see Harmony Lumpkin, he'll give you a good price for the slave."

Her eyes widened as she tried to penetrate his meaning. "Are you telling me that you plan to abandon Richmond?"

"Are you mad? We'll never give up our capital."

Once more she gave way before his exploring mouth, knowing all the while that he'd lied. In the throes of their driving passion, part of her mind was already composing a letter to Sean, while another part scrambled with the problem of how best to deal with the mass of ebony muscle that lay shackled in the basement.

*

All that next week Gunning and Major Norris worked long hours in the Signal Bureau's office, moving "Operation Come Retribution" forward. "Once Booth and his men have kidnapped Lincoln, how long do you think before it's discovered?" Norris asked.

"If we're lucky we may have a few hours, but more than likely it will be known almost at once." Gunning went to the large wall map; "The Union will react with full force. We can expect cavalry from Grant's right wing to come pouring across Booth's escape route to intercept him, so we must make sure he has enough protection to reach Richmond with the prize."

"General Mosby is ready to deploy his cavalry on our command. Every one of his troopers has been handpicked; they're the best we have. We'll position units along the entire escape route, from the Potomac all the way to our railway station at Milford. When the Federals start their pursuit, our counter force will engage them. Meanwhile, other units of Mosby's Raiders will meet up with Booth's team and will escort them and Lincoln to Richmond."

In a rare moment of candor Norris asked, "Brand, do you really believe our military situation is salvageable?"

"I don't know, but I do know that unless we get out of Richmond we're lost. But we've got to insure that when we do return as victors that our cities and land haven't been laid waste. Grant and Sherman are as vicious as the Huns, but with Lincoln our hostage we'll force the North to be civilized. Now for our last problem, as I've mentioned, I'm apprehensive about Booth, not his loyalty or commitment, God knows with all the money he's given the Confederacy he's certainly proven that. It's just that he's so—volatile, so impulsive. Have you spoken to Mosby about detailing a seasoned army man to help Booth?"

Norris nodded; "It's in the works right now. Mosby's going to dispatch one of his best men to stiffen Booth's spine, that should keep him in line."

*

In late December, companies of Mosby's Raiders, C, E, F, and G, were quietly moved out of Fauquier and Loudon Counties to the Northern Neck of Virginia, just across the Potomac from Washington. Other cavalry units were stealthily deployed in the area between the Potomac, Milford and Richmond.

On January 13, one of Mosby's Raiders, Private Lewis Powell, Company B, Forty-Third Battalion, entered a Union encampment at Fairfax Courthouse; using the alias Lewis Paine, he requested asylum. Since droves of Rebel soldiers were deserting, his story was accepted without much questioning. Powell, alias Paine, was sent to Alexandria where he took the Federal oath of allegiance and was released. Once free, he went to Baltimore and joined Booth and the two boyhood friends Booth had already recruited. The band then returned to Washington with a formidable arsenal of weapons.

By mid-February, the Confederate High Command had finalized its plans to sacrifice Richmond; the government secretly began to move its archives to it's new capital, Danville, Virginia. As for Lee's army, their abandonment of

Petersburg and Richmond depended entirely on the weather; they'd slip away as soon as the roads became passable.

In late February, John Surratt returned to Richmond from Washington and told Gunning the thrilling news that Booth and his action team was poised to strike. Since Davis planned to abandon Richmond by April 10 at the latest, the die was cast. Lincoln had to be in Confederate hands by the end of March or the very beginning of April.

Chapter 50

Bravo Brand was at a meeting with Lincoln, reporting on the development of several new weapons when Colonel Lafayette Baker, the head of the Union's Secret Service interrupted them. "Sorry to barge in, sir, but I've urgent news."

A hulking, dark-haired man in his late thirties, Baker's bushy sideburns connected to a full moustache that framed an avaricious mouth. An unsavory schemer with an unsavory reputation, he'd gotten his position by toadying to Stanton, and like his mentor, self-importance oozed from him. Bravo considered his methods more befitting a member of the Inquisition than an officer of a democracy and detested him.

With pride oozing from every pore, Colonel Baker addressed Lincoln; "This has been a great day for me. These letters were sent by the French consul in Richmond to their ambassador here in Washington, but I intercepted them."

As Lincoln read each of the letters he handed them to Bravo, much to Baker's chagrin. Most of them contained the usual diplomatic parlance with nuggets of news about the hardships in Richmond. But one letter snapped Bravo to attention; it was from Romance Connaught to her brother, Sean. In it, a hint that Jefferson Davis might soon abandon Richmond, and another veiled hint that there could be a plot brewing against Lincoln.

During Lincoln's first term in office he'd received some eighty written threats against his life but had dismissed them all as cranks letters. But Bravo took Romance's note seriously; her affair with Gunning could easily make her privy to such information. He turned to Baker; "Do you have any other evidence that could corroborate this letter?"

Baker spoke pointedly to Lincoln, "Our agents report that an unusual number of Rebel guerrillas have been spotted along the Virginia and Maryland
shores of the Potomac. We believe they're units of Mosby's Raiders, the Gray
Ghosts. Exactly what they're up to, we just don't know."

"Mr. President, might it not be wise for you to increase your protection?"
Bravo urged. "Assign more bodyguards?"

Lincoln demurred; "It would never do for a President to have guards with
drawn sabers all about, as if he fancied he were an emperor. Ward Lamon
insists I have such an escort for my inauguration but I refused. Nor will I coun-
tenance such royalist pretension in any of my public duties lest it appear that I
fear my own people." He leafed through his appointment book; "A case in
point, in a few days, I've been invited to a matinee performance of a play to be
given for our wounded men at Campbell's Hospital. If I arrived with a cavalry
guard, would it inspire confidence in my leadership? Let's talk no more of
plots, as Secretary of State Seward has so eloquently stated, assassination is not
the way of a democratic people."

Lincoln dismissed Baker then said to Bravo, "Progress on our new weapons
is excellent. Now I've a personal request, do you know if your mother plans to
attend my inauguration? It would please me if she would." Bravo blinked in
surprise and Lincoln continued, "I've never thanked her for her editorial about
the soldier vote, in that, she was surely on the side of the angels—and of the
Union. I've been in Washington four years, she's lived here more than eighty;
since she's viewed as something of an institution, her presence might go a long
way toward healing sectional wounds in our capital. If it will help persuade
her, tell her I've reserved two seats."

"I'll do what I can, Mr. President, but I think you've already noticed that my
mother has a mind of her own."

After Bravo left the White House he stopped off at his mother's and
repeated Lincoln's invitation.

She reacted sharply; "If I go it will be viewed as tacit approval of his policies
and I do not approve of so many of them; suspending the Writ of Habeas
Corpus is a crime against our Constitution. And the North's refusal to
exchange prisoners—that, even you must admit, is an abomination."

"Then play the political game, Ma. Who knows, you may need a favor from
him someday? Besides, you've been to every inauguration since Washington
became our capital. You know you're just dying to go—if only to complain."

"There's absolutely no way that I'm going to attend."

Saturday, March 4, dawned as dismal a day as Rebecca could recall.
Bittersweet clucked, "With your rheumatiz acting up, you're crazy to go out in
this mean miserable weather."

"You're right," Rebecca sighed, "but I must be politic. I've simply got to make this sacrifice for Bravo."

Bravo picked her up and they joined the procession to the Capitol. Torrential rains had flooded Pennsylvania Avenue and anyone who couldn't swim was warned to beware of the hip-deep quagmires at every intersection.

Bravo told her, "The army engineers considered building a pontoon bridge all along the avenue for the inaugural parade but they found that the bottom was too spongy."

When they reached the Capitol, the place was a madhouse, 30,000 people had jammed the stands built on the east front of the building. Rebecca nodded to several acquaintances, then spied a man seated several rows behind her, waving furiously.

"Bravo, my sight isn't what it used to be; who is that?"

"I think it's John Wilkes Booth. So it is."

A slight blond young man was sitting with Booth. Rebecca squinted, had the uncomfortable feeling that she'd seen this young man before but couldn't quite remember where.

John Wilkes Booth clambered nimbly down the stands and took a seat directly behind Rebecca. He leaned close to her, out of earshot of Bravo. "So we're met to see the anointing of King Abraham the First?" His tone sounded so good-humored that she smiled, but her smile froze when he added, "Let the tyrant beware for the Ides of March are hard upon us."

"That young man you're sitting with? He looks so familiar. Who is he?"

"A dear friend of mine, John Surratt by name."

As Lincoln came out on the portico the crowd cheered, their shouts floating up to the just-completed Capitol dome, crowned with its Statue of Freedom. Chief Justice Salmon Chase, appointed by Lincoln to keep the fanatic Republican from sabotaging his policies, administered the oath of office.

Rebecca listened raptly to the thirty-five words that bound the man to the nation and the nation to its destiny. Starting with Thomas Jefferson, she'd heard fourteen Presidents take this oath, "I do solemnly swear that I will faithfully execute the office of..." and never had the vow seemed as important as this.

Just as Lincoln was about to speak the sun burst forth in all it's meridian splendor and the crowd gasped. Then in his clear, high-pitched voice, Lincoln read his address. "...Yet if God wills that the war continue until all the wealth piled by the bondsman's two hundred and fifty years of unrequited toil shall be sunk, and until every drop of blood drawn with the lash shall be paid by another drawn with the sword, as was said three thousand years ago, so still it must be said, the judgments of the Lord are true and righteous..."

Rebecca felt Booth grip her shoulder, heard his tremulous whisper, "Hear how he loathes the South."

She glanced quickly at Bravo, afraid that he and Booth would come to blows, but thank God Bravo hadn't heard. From what Lincoln had just said she tended to side with Booth; but what the President said next sent hope coursing through her.

"…With malice toward none; with charity for all, with firmness in the right, as God gives us to see the right, let us strive on to finish the work we are in; to bind up the nation's wounds, to care for him who shall have borne the battle, and for his widow and his orphan; to do all which may achieve and cherish a just and lasting peace, among ourselves, and with all nations."

These words held no rancor whatever, his voice was compassion itself and Rebecca found herself deeply moved.

A battery of howitzers fired a final salute and the crowd began to disperse. Rebecca blotted her tears. Booth, his wounded eyes laden with his own sadness murmured, "Yes, Miss Rebecca, we true patriots have reason to cry. Mark me well, he'll use this ill-gotten election to crown himself king."

He clenched his fist passionately and stared at the podium where Lincoln had stood. "So close, I could have reached out and struck the tyrant down."

Bravo whirled at this but Booth had already disappeared into the crowd. "What was that Booth said?" Bravo demanded.

"Twaddle," she responded quickly. "Just John Wilkes being his usual melodramatic self. You know actors, they're full of sound and fury, signifying nothing."

As Rebecca and Bravo joined the receiving line to congratulate President Lincoln, Rebecca caught sight of Booth rejoining the young man he'd been with. At that moment she recognized John Surratt as the man who'd shoved Gunning's letter under her door. She stumbled and clutched Bravo's arm for support, overcome by a preternatural fear.

Then the President was shaking her hand. "Miss Rebecca, could you come to the White House early next week? There's something important I'd like to discuss with you."

She nodded absently, her thoughts still with Booth and Surratt. Shall I tell Bravo, she wondered? But if I do tell him my suspicions, might that not implicate Gunning? Instead she asked, "Bravo, why does the President want to see me?" He hunched his shoulders and she asked, "Will you be there?"

He shook his head; "I'm leaving Washington within the hour, I'll be away for a few weeks—don't ask me where—"

"I know, I know, it all has to do with some silly top secret plan or invention. Well, whatever Lincoln has up his sleeve, I'm sure it will astonish."

Chapter 51

REBECCA'S SCREAM rent the drawing room; she collapsed onto the settee, the letter she'd just received via the Confederate underground dangling from her trembling fingers.

Bittersweet came tearing into the room; "What's wrong? Quick, take your medicine," and gave her a spoonful.

"Merciful God," Rebecca coughed, and thrust the letter at Bittersweet. "I'm not sure, but does it say what I think it does? Oh please, please, say it does."

Bittersweet snatched the note. The words had been cut out of a newspaper and then pasted onto a scrap of paper. She read it, read it again, studied it as if it foretold the resurrection. Written in July of the previous year, it had been lost, retrieved and finally smuggled into Washington. But if the letter was to be believed, Forrest was alive. Somewhere in Richmond. It was Bittersweet's turn to scream.

Rebecca struggled to get up from the settee; "Oh pray God this isn't some cruel hoax."

Bittersweet kissed the note; "Got me a feelin' it's real; whoever wrote it went to lots of disguising trouble."

"It's from Gunning, I know it is. I must tell Bravo—" then Rebecca recalled that he'd left for parts unknown.

All through that night Rebecca wandered the house, with Bittersweet trailing after her. "I'll never be at peace—never—until I know for certain if Forrest is dead or alive." And a desperate plan began to form in her desperate mind.

Early the next morning Rebecca walked to the White House. The waiting room was filled with all manner of applicants and supplicants; Lincoln wasn't a dedicated churchgoer and often used Sundays to hear petitions. One of Lincoln's secretaries, Nicholas Hay, placed her at the head of the line and in short order she entered the inner sanctum. To her surprise and delight she found young Nettie Colburn there.

"Miss Nettie was just about to leave," Lincoln said, "but I thought you two might enjoy a brief visit."

Rebecca knew that Nettie had been in Washington since December holding spiritualist meetings. Rebecca hadn't attended any, voices from the 'other world' no longer seemed so vital; Lord knew she'd had enough trouble enough with voices from this world. "Nettie, dear, I hope you had nothing but wonderful things to tell our President?"

"Only what our friends on the other side had already predicted, that he'd be elected for a second term." Nettie's gentle face grew somber; "But they also reaffirm that the shadow they've spoken of still hangs over him."

"You've already told me," Lincoln said, escorting her to the door; "I have letters from all over the country from your kind of people, mediums, I mean, warning me of some dreadful plot against my life. But I don't think the knife is made, or the bullet run, that will reach it. I cannot bring myself to believe that any human being lives who would do me harm."

"Therein lies the danger, Mr. President," Nettie murmured, "your overconfidence in your fellow man."

The old melancholy look came over his face; "Miss Nettie, I shall live till my work is done and no earthly power can prevent it. Then it doesn't matter, so that I am ready—and that I ever meant to be."

With a deep curtsy, Nettie left. Lincoln seemed unnerved by his interchange with Nettie and paced the floor, head bent, massaging his fingers, swollen from shaking hands with thousands at the inauguration's Open House.

Once again Rebecca was struck with his unrelenting homeliness. But somehow she'd grown accustomed to it. He looked up and smiled and such a radiance transformed his features that she thought, If saints of old had ever had the time or inclination to smile, this is how they might look.

"Mr. President, I must reach Bravo, can you help me?"

"That may be difficult; he's traveling to several cities, but I'll do my best. Is there a special message?"

"That he's to come home at once. There may be some news about his son."

"Good news, I hope?"

"I don't know, that's why I need him here." She said no more, not daring to admit that she'd been in contact with the enemy.

Realizing her dilemma, Lincoln didn't press her. He said, "Miss Rebecca, let me cut to the bone. You're in a position to do our cause some good. I understand that you're an old and good friend of Jefferson Davis'? And of Judah Benjamin's? The way Benjamin's kept the South going—that man is the brains of the Confederacy."

Before Rebecca could answer the door flew open and Tad Lincoln skittered in. "Paw? Maw needs to see you right away. Which dress shall she wear to the ball tomorrow?"

"Tell her I'm working, I'll attend her as soon as I can."

Lincoln led his son to the door and closed it. He then fixed Rebecca with a hard stare. "Do you believe in dreams?"

Caught off balance, she said guardedly, "Sometimes."

"Since becoming President, I've had this recurring dream, it's a wonderful dream, and I've come to embrace it as I would a welcome visitor. I see an enemy ship, sailing away rapidly, badly damaged, and our vessels are in close pursuit. Then as so often happens in a dream landscape, I see a furious battle on land, the enemy being routed, and our forces in possession of vantage ground of incalculable importance. I've had this dream just before the battle of Antietam, before Gettysburg, and before Atlanta."

I wonder if Jeff Davis had similar dreams about Manassas, Chancellorsville and Cold Harbor? Rebecca yearned to ask, but held her tongue. She had an odd feeling that Lincoln truly believed what he was saying, and having had several unnerving prophetic dreams in her own lifetime, she listened intently.

"These past weeks I've had another recurrent dream, I see a beautiful city in flames, terrible explosions, people fleeing, screaming. I walk through streets blackened by fire and then I enter the White House of the Confederacy and find myself sitting in Jefferson Davis' chair. But I feel no joy, for all about me, Richmond lies in ruins."

Rebecca felt her skin crawling, Gunning, Becky—perhaps even Forrest? Her loved ones were in Richmond.

"If this can be avoided, it must be done at any cost." He added softly, "For all practical purposes the war is lost to the South, yet Davis persists in continuing the fight."

"Mr. President, couldn't you send emissaries?"

"We have, Francis Blair went to see Davis in January. Davis appointed a peace commission, and I met them aboard the *River Queen* in February, but it was only a political ploy. Davis insists that any negotiations be between the 'two separate nations', which is totally unacceptable since it's the very reason we're fighting this rebellion. He must be told that my call for an additional five hundred thousand men is no idle threat. And our men will be equipped with the latest in weapons. Bravo tells me our new Gatling machine gun spews out hundreds of bullets a minute, imagine, a <u>minute</u>? Our 'Gat', as we call it, is more terrible than anything seen before. But Davis lacks everything, men, money, munitions."

"Mr. President, what does all this have to do with me?"

"You see the truth all around you, the build-up of our troops, our weapons. Would you consider writing an article or several if you prefer, documenting what I've just told you? I've asked several other reporters to do the same, but if Davis and the South heard these truths from a friend, one they know is trustworthy, who's spoken for both sides and from the heart—? That, in addition to everything else that presses in on him—we must do everything we can to persuade him that his cause is lost and the shedding of more blood an unholy sin."

She was so startled by his proposal that for several moments she couldn't speak. She posed her next question with care, "What of the Southern leaders? Can I ask them to give up their fight when so many of the Northern newspapers, including *The New York Times*, demand that they be hanged?"

"You heard my inaugural address, vengeance is farthest from my mind. I seek reconciliation, without lengthy trials and recriminations, which can only breed further hatred. In that light, if the Southern leaders felt they might better prosper in some foreign land; there's so much coastline to cover, I doubt they'd ever be captured."

"I have your word on that?"

"Yes, but not officially, for I must also keep the more rabid elements in my own administration in check. As everyone in Washington knows, Stanton blames Davis personally for the death of his son, he'd shoot him on sight. But you may hint strongly at my thoughts on emigration."

He pressed on; "Your neutrality in the last election puts you in a perfect position to speak objectively. I've witnessed your eloquence and your compassion first hand. Might you not use those qualities now to save lives?"

This is a fool's errand, she thought, and clearly he's using me for his own ends. But if he had his agenda, she had hers and that revolved around her family in Richmond. Did she dare pass up any opportunity to insure their safety? "Mr. President, may I now cut to the bone?" He nodded and she continued, "I've little hope for such an enterprise. Jeff Davis is far too strong-willed to be swayed by the pleas of an old woman. You and I both know that."

"But Miss Rebecca, if you recall, there was that one final straw for the camel's back?"

She studied his face, trying to decide…then was overcome with an unbidden memory of his poignant moment with the young Confederate boy, Johnny X. Perhaps Lincoln was right, perhaps every single last thing had to be tried and since wise men had failed so miserably, perhaps it was time for fools. "Mr. President, these last several years I've petitioned you repeatedly for a pass to Richmond; you've always refused."

"Given the circumstances, I thought it best."

Her voice grew stronger with each word; "My son Gunning's presence on Davis' staff would undoubtedly have created problems. Now you've asked me to help, and I will. I'll get your message to Jeff Davis, but in a far more effective way than writing an article. I want to go to Richmond myself."

His eyebrows lifted in shock; "You know that's impossible—for any number of reasons. First of all, you're a woman—"

"Which works in my favor. Being gray-haired and doddering, I doubt that soldiers on either side would shoot me. Frankly, I'm not worth the bullet."

"I realize you're still a slip of a girl at heart but there is the problem of—don't think me disrespectful—"

"My age is an obstacle, I admit, but I don't intend to <u>walk</u> to Richmond. Can I prevail on you for passage on one of the Union boats that sail regularly to City Point? That's fifteen miles from Richmond; less than an hour by carriage."

"But you'd be in a war zone; the danger is considerable."

"Grant and Lee are held fast in the grip of this endless winter. The campaign won't start again until the weather moderates and from the frost on my window panes this morning, that's not likely for a few more weeks."

He shook his head; "The responsibility is too heavy. I know you've been ill, what if something should happen to you? It would be on my conscience for the rest of my life."

"If I don't go, then something dreadful will happen to me. Not knowing if my children and grandchildren are alive or dead—who can live without knowing? I'd go mad in a matter of days. The only thing that sustains me is that I may be of some small help to those I love. Though I'm under no delusion that I'll be able to accomplish anything, at least I'll have made the effort and can go to my Maker in peace. I won't stay in Richmond long, two or three days at most. Which will give me a chance to relay your message to Jeff Davis directly."

She broke off as the door flew open again and there stood Tad, twitching with the importance of his message. "Maw says that you must come instantly. Her dress—come, come!"

Lincoln muttered under his breath, "Will that woman never cease? Will she never understand me?"

Rebecca rose; "If I've done anything to deserve your consideration, then find it in your heart to do this for me. If you're concerned about my well being, as I am, then make my journey easier. But I must tell you this, with or without your help, I'll find a way to get to Richmond."

Chapter 52

"YOU'RE GOING WHERE?" Bittersweet shrieked.

"Richmond," Rebecca repeated. "Tomorrow."

"Say there, you know my name?"

"Silly goose, of course I know your name. Whatever's the matter with you?"

"'Spects you be having one of your fits again. Like the night you woke up and thought I was my own grandma? Kept calling me by her name, 'Letitia, Letitia, I gotta go to Texas to bring back my Suzannah.' And now it's Richmond?"

"Tomorrow. Help me pack."

"No. 'Cause if I did let you go, Bravo would kill me."

"By the time Bravo gets back, I'll have been to Richmond, seen Gunning, discovered the truth about Forrest and returned home. And Bravo will bless me for going."

"Miz Rebecca, case you haven't looked lately, you ain't no spring chicken. You're a winter chicken."

"Letitia—I mean Bittersweet—don't mix me up! It's not as if I'm going to China, Richmond's only a hundred miles from here."

"But you're eighty-five years old, just had a stroke."

"What a nerve! I've just turned eighty. What's the worst that can happen, that I'll die? Small loss, I know a few people who'll dance on my grave. But if I can do some good before I go to my Maker—hurry, help me pack."

"No, never, not me, never."

Rebecca huddled in the cabin of the boat as it chugged along. Armed with her press credentials and a fair amount of money in gold coin, her plan to bribe her way aboard one of the packet boats transporting supplies to City Point had met with success. Had someone in high places intervened for her? She asked no questions, she just embarked.

They'd been traveling a full day; the boat had left from the Washington Naval Yard, steamed down the Potomac to Chesapeake Bay, around Hampton Roads, then up the James River. Bittersweet huddled beside her, miserable with seasickness.

"Will you stop carrying on as if we were in a tempest?" Rebecca grumbled, "can't you see the river's perfectly calm?"

"Only person supposed to be on water is Jesus."

When Bittersweet couldn't stop her mistress, she went with her. Rebecca had objected vehemently and was still objecting; "I must have been insane to let you come, we're going into slave country and you're an escaped slave."

"We both gonna get killed, so what's the difference? Had me this terrible dream? We got shot twelve times, one for each Confederate State."

"There are only eleven Confederate States."

"One for good measure."

As they steamed into City Point, Rebecca gaped at the docks teeming with activity. Never had she seen such a concentration of ships, men, munitions, horses, as if all the wealth of the God of War had been funneled to this one place. Upon disembarking she paid a king's ransom for a wagon to take her close to Rebel lines. Under a flag of truce she was then transferred to gawking, disbelieving Confederate officers. But on learning of her connection to Gunning Brand (and a large bribe) they ordered a flatbed to take her to Richmond.

Shell craters pocked the countryside…stands of trees splintered by gun-fire…farm houses leveled to rubble, the land looked as if it had been mauled by prehistoric beasts, and everything Lincoln had asked Rebecca to tell Jefferson Davis gained greater import. As the church spires of Richmond slowly took shape, hope and fright and the unknown thumped hugely in Rebecca's bosom.

"I'll drop you at the Spotswood Hotel then go directly to see Jefferson Davis," she told Bittersweet. "He's sure to know where Gunning is and Gunning will help me find Forrest."

"I'm goin' with you."

"It's too dangerous. What if some bounty hunter starts asking questions? You've still got that slave brand on your shoulder. Best stay out of sight. Ah, there's the hotel. What's in your bag? It feels heavy as lead."

"Never you mind. Be careful now, don't go angrying up too many people. You're not Miss High-and-Mighty here."

On arriving at the Customs House, the Rebel driver and his flatbed returned to the front; Rebecca was directed to President Davis' office on the third floor. Had she passed him on the street she'd never have recognized him, he looked that dreadful; there wasn't a trace of blond in his gray hair, and nanny goat whiskers elongated his already gaunt face.

He, on the other hand, couldn't have been more amazed to see her. Blind in one eye, he inclined his head toward her when he spoke. "Miss Rebecca, how wonderful to have you here in the bosom of our nation. You have my deepest sympathies on the death of your grandson, Geary. I can tell you that the Confederacy lost a dedicated fighter for freedom."

She felt a saber slash across her heart—Geary would have been the first to challenge that piece of self-serving propaganda—but she managed to murmur her thanks.

"But as for your son, Gunning—"

Rebecca girded her loins for another blow—

"—He's one of my finest officers. In the field, he's my eyes and ears, at headquarters, my rod and my staff."

Has the world stopped turning? Rebecca wondered, or is it just fatigue addling Jeff's brain? Or mine?

"Jeff, I must see Gunning; it's most urgent."

"He's at the Petersburg front, conferring with Lee but I expect him back this evening. Will you do Varina and myself the honor of dining with us tonight? Hopefully Gunning can join us."

"That would be wonderful."

"Why not come early, spend some time with Varina, I know she'd love to see you." The amenities dispensed with, he fixed her with his good eye, his probing expression more eloquent than words: Why have you come? What do you want?

She burned to give him Lincoln's message then and there, but dared not, not until she'd seen Gunning and learned the truth about Forrest. She left his office soon after.

Though her heart thumped dully with fatigue, Rebecca tried to hire a carriage so she could drive to Chimborazo and find Becky, but with every horse requisitioned by the cavalry, there was absolutely no transportation available. With her rheumatism acting up, it was much too far to walk; she'd collapse before she got there. Perhaps Gunning could help.

When Rebecca returned to the Spotswood she was atremble. "Forrest is alive, Bittersweet, I know it. He's right here in Richmond, I can feel it."

Bittersweet sighed hugely; "Suppose this means we got to stay till we finds him? Knew somethin' like this would happen. Good thing I brought this along," and pulled a smoked ham from her bag. "'N your extra medicine. I'm goin' out now, try to find us some food besides this ham, greens and things. You best take a nap before you go see Miz Varina."

Rebecca lay down and had just drifted off when Bittersweet rushed back into the room. "I just seen him!"

Rebecca bolted up hopefully; "Who? Seen who?"

Trembling, Bittersweet locked the door and drew the curtains. "Lordy, lordy, Harmony Lumpkin is who. Bringin' a passel of slaves to work right here in this hotel."

"Nonsense, you're just imagining it. Stop shaking, will you? Even if it was this Lumpkin creature, he'd never recognize you; it's been thirty years. Stay in the room, don't open the door for anyone. Now I'd best get over to Varina's."

Ever so slowly Rebecca made her way through the streets and then up the steep hill to the White House. She gave the doorkeeper her calling card and waited in the elliptical entrance hall. The house, with gray paint flaking from its exterior and interior, appeared shabby and forlorn.

Varina Davis rushed into the entryway; "I can't believe—mercy, it is—Miss Rebecca!" and embraced her.

Rebecca winced at the change four long difficult years had wrought. Childbearing had thickened Varina's figure to matronly proportions. She was what, in her mid-thirties? Yet looked a decade older. What had happened to the ebullient, party-loving creature she'd once known? "Dear Varina, so wonderful to see you. Jeff suggested that I come early—"

"His Excellency sent word to me," Varina responded, emphasizing his title. That piece of protocol established, Varina led Rebecca to the Snuggery for an afternoon of, as she put it, catching up. "I'm mortified that we can't put you up, but we've only three guest rooms; Sister Margaret is in one, His Excellency's secretary has another and my personal maid occupies the third."

"I'm quite content at the Spotswood, not one bedbug so far. Remember my Bittersweet? She's traveling with me."

"You're taking all your meals with us, I insist. The fare will be meager, not what you're used to in King Abraham's Babylon, I'm sure. Bittersweet can eat with our slaves. My housekeeper, Mrs. O'Melia, will arrange it. Now tell me—"

Rebecca interrupted, "Varina, I'm eager to see my granddaughter Becky; I believe she's still at Chimborazo? Might there be a horse available? I swear on everything I hold holy, I promise I'll return it."

Alas, Varina confided, one of their horses had been stolen; His Excellency was using the other. Rebecca had little recourse except to fretfully mark time until Gunning arrived.

"This is a wonderful house, Varina. In many ways much more of a home than the White House in Washington."

Fiercely proud of her reputation as a homemaker, Varina apologized profusely for the house's shabby state. "Help is hard to get, harder to keep. The Emancipation Proclamation of Abraham the First has deluded every slave into believing that he's free—they just run off—can you imagine? There's no loyalty whatsoever—and after all we've done for them."

Best not to get mired in that swamp, Rebecca thought.

"At first we so loved this place; my Willie and Winnie were born here. But the house was never intended to withstand thousands of muddy boots, nor the stream of petitioners from all over the South. Congress appropriates such a paltry budget it's gone in the snap of a finger. If those drunkards gave us a hundredth of what they spend on whiskey—yet I'm expected to keep an Open House for the people, but when I do, the newspapers complain that I'm being profligate. How they've turned against His Excellency and me."

One thing about Varina hadn't changed, Rebecca noted, her penchant for instantly voicing her grievances.

From Varina's conversation Rebecca gleaned a picture of conditions in Richmond; unless her eyes and ears deceived, things were even more desperate than Lincoln had portrayed it. At the same time she kept thinking, Where would Forrest have gone? Is he hiding? How can I find him? Gunning will know.

After a bit Varina led her out to the colonnaded portico running along the south side of the house. Rebecca looked down some fifteen feet to a charming hillside garden. "It looks so bare now," Varina noted sadly, "but it's lovely in summer, with horse chestnut trees and the gayest flowers. I grow poppies, as do all Southern ladies. To extract the opium. I honestly believe so many of our men, and the North's, would be alive today if we'd had the drugs to treat them. But the embargo, even on medicines! That man is the devil incarnate!" She pinched a dead leaf from a plant. "Jeff and I love to putter in this garden while the children play all about us—" she broke off, eyes welling; "it was from this balcony that my Little Joe fell."

The two women held each other and wept, death drawing them together in a way that life never could.

Jefferson Davis came home at dusk with the disappointing news that he'd been unable to contact Gunning. In honor of Rebecca's visit they dined in the State Dining Room, directly to the left of the entrance hall. A generous room, about 20 by 30 feet, made airy by the 14-foot ceiling and the floor-to-ceiling windows that opened onto the south portico. Above the mantel hung a portrait of George Washington, festooned by two Confederate flags, a tacit reminder that the South considered Washington, a Virginian, a slave owner, and father of his country, to be the godfather of the Confederacy.

There were twelve at table, some of whom Rebecca knew, others only by reputation. A broad strip of gray canvas had been laid under the dining chairs to keep the maroon and green floral Brussels carpet from wearing out. Jeff and Varina sat at opposite ends of the long table, Rebecca at Jeff's right, next to her, the indefatigable Judah P. Benjamin.

In the midst of the meal, Judah Benjamin raised his wineglass; "May I propose a toast to our dear Miss Rebecca? Who comes to us looking younger and more vital than ever."

"You sir, are a rake and a liar, but charming as ever."

Benjamin, dark eyes twinkling, asked, "Miss Rebecca, have you come to deliver Old Abraham's surrender?"

"Now you've gone and ruined my surprise. But there are conditions; one obstacle and one only stands in the way of peace, you must become Confederate minister to Washington."

Benjamin grinned; "Knowing those tight-fisted Yankees, Lincoln doubtless wants free legal advice. Well, we shall certainly instruct him on Constitutional Law. No charge."

Rebecca returned a smile in kind, but neither fooled the other. She recognized his badinage as probing; he was too astute not to realize that she'd come on some mission. Rebecca debated whether to take Judah into her confidence; he might be a valuable ally. But feminine instinct warned her to wait.

Responding to repeated urging from Judah Benjamin, Davis held forth about the war. With knives, forks, and salt cellars, he illustrated on the plain of the table just how Lee had beaten Grant in the last eleven months.

Benjamin interjected, "What our too-modest President neglects to tell you is that Lee rarely makes a move without first consulting him. Even now His Excellency is formulating strategy that will change the entire course of the war."

Rebecca's encouraging smile belied her sinking heart. "Pray tell, what? We could all use some good news." Davis made a non-committal gesture, but Rebecca could tell that he considered it important. As the conversation continued, she noticed that Benjamin buoyed spirits, told humorous anecdotes, all designed to place the diners in a mood merry enough to forget the horror without. Even Jefferson Davis was seen to smile occasionally. Yet what was it about the evening, and Benjamin's manner, that so disturbed her?

After dinner, the men repaired to the main drawing room for cognac and cigars, once again provided by the cornucopius Benjamin and the women to the adjoining ladies' parlor. Both rooms were decorated in the modish en suite style with maroon and black carpet, maroon and black flocked wallpaper, and couches and chairs upholstered in glistening black horsehair, all frayed and tattered. At last, Rebecca thought, I've found the perfect decor for my mausoleum.

Varina held forth over sassafras tea sweetened with gossip. By nature outspoken, years of being First Lady had given that quality even freer rein and she punctuated her restless conversation with trenchant witticisms. Laughing at Varina's sallies, Rebecca thought, she's clever, but far too eager for approval, especially from these Virginians who'd never really accepted her. In the rarified circles of the F.F.V., they'd marked her as "a western woman," and as the Confederacy's fortunes declined, it had become "a coarse western woman." Which made Varina work all the harder to be gay and brilliant.

In her most bizarre imaginings, Rebecca could never have envisioned a situation where there'd be two First Ladies in America. Both wielded such undue influence; both were adored by their husbands; both were Southerners; both were extremely protective of their titles; both had lost children while living in their respective White Houses.

Of the two, Varina was more intelligent, more adept in her role; she wasn't called Queen Varina for nothing. But Mary Todd held a far more chilling fascination for Rebecca, for she'd witnessed flashes of madness in her behavior that made it impossible to predict what she'd say or do.

Varina wasn't mad in the least; she bore the trials of the Confederacy in a way that Mary Todd never could and supported her husband with a strength that would have made Lincoln envious.

"Ladies, do you know whom we have in our midst?" Varina asked conspiratorially. "None other than the bane of Abraham the First's existence, the formidable Rebel Thorne."

Oh, what a patter of polite applause greeted that, with trilling cries of, "I loved your piece about—" "When the Washington papers are smuggled in, I look first for—"

"Dear Miss Rebecca, if only I could write like you," Varina sighed. "But it's in drawing room conversation that I find my genius, only to have it lost when the last guest leaves. What a pity I don't have an amanuensis to follow me about. Will you be my Boswell? Oh, say you will."

In the genteel titter that followed, Rebecca wondered, am I going mad? Witnessing mass hysteria? What is the matter with these people? Do they believe that if they talk loud enough, laugh loud enough, they can drown out the sound of cannon from the front? The March wind moaned and shrieked and she prayed, dear God, let Forrest be someplace safe tonight.

A short time, later groups of officers and their ladies came to pay their respects to the President and his Lady.

Suddenly from across the room Rebecca heard a voice call, "Ma! What in the hell—?"

She turned to face her son Gunning, and the stunning presence of Romance Villefranche Connaught.

Chapter 53

ROMANCE STOOD framed in the doorway, her billowing lavender gown an exquisite foil for her luminous eyes and midnight hair, her artless pose worthy of a Fragonard.

Gunning bolted toward his mother; "What are you doing here? How are you?" his questions charged with shock and concern and unrestrained joy at seeing her.

For a moment Rebecca forgot this Jezebel behind him and rejoiced that he was safe. But with the intuition that only mothers have, she felt a subtle but compelling fear. Four years since she'd last seen him…his red hair looked frostier, he'd lost weight, and though the lean look gave him more character, it wasn't his outward appearance that distressed her. She pulled her thoughts back to the urgent question and whispered, "Gunning, I got your note about Forrest—"

He stared at her blankly; "I didn't send you any note. Bravo told me he was missing in action and presumed—that's the last I heard—"

Rebecca paled and would have fallen but Gunning supported her. She whispered, "But I thought you'd written me—"

Like a wraith, Romance moved to Gunning's side and he said, "Mother, may I present Romance Villefranche Connaught?"

Rebecca replied softly, "No, you may not."

Gunning reacted as if she'd run a sword through his gut.

If Romance had taken offense she gave no sign. Her face remained a mask of hauteur, her kohl-lined eyes revealing nothing, signifying everything. Her expression of disdain was so redolent of her mother's, that Rebecca could barely resist the urge to pull out every hair in her head.

Instead she said, "Gunning, I'm at the Spotswood, could you spare me some time tomorrow? I've some news about your wife and children. Do you know if Becky's still at Chimborazo? If so, how does one get there? I've no horse—"

"She's still there, I'll take you tomorrow."

Rebecca saw the slightest arch of Romance's eyebrows.

"Ah, *mon chere*," Romance breathed, her ungulate fingers stroking her temple, "*suddenment, j'ai mal a la tete.*"

"I'll take you home. I've an early day myself."

"I wouldn't dream of it. You must attend your dear mother who's traveled so far to see you. Major Bix will see me home, he's offered so many times before."

Gunning grasped Romance's arm firmly then turned to Rebecca; "Wonderful to have you here, Ma. See you tomorrow morning." Then he escorted Romance from the room.

Rebecca tried to hide her distress—if not Gunning, then who had sent her the note? Becky? That seemed unlikely. Had the letter indeed been a cruel hoax? She knew Gunning wouldn't come to her hotel tomorrow morning, there'd be some excuse, Romance would see to that. Perhaps her headache would disappear the moment he was ready to leave and Rebecca knew her son well enough to know what his choice would be.

Really, sons were such ingrates, and as a breed, men were asses. But for Gunning to be so taken in—? Yes, Romance was beautiful, astonishing beautiful, Rebecca was honest enough to admit that; and no doubt fascinating and accomplished. Yet everything about her whispered of some inner decay. In a city where grief lived in the face of every citizen, Romance remained untouched, as though she feasted on disaster.

By nine o'clock Jeff and Varina were bidding the guests goodnight. War was an early game and the officers had to get back to their units. Judah Benjamin remained until the end, his jocular laugh resounding as he entertained Jeff Davis.

"Doesn't Judah have the most remarkable capacity for life?" Varina said to Rebecca. "How I wish some of it might rub off on His Excellency. Judah works harder than ten, the State Department's the most efficiently run office, yet still he finds time for pleasure."

"Do you know that Lincoln calls him the brains of the Confederacy?"

"Oh no," Varina shook her head vigorously, "Jeff is—"

"—I think of Jeff as being more the heart of the Confederacy, don't you?"

"Heart <u>and</u> head," Varina insisted, not giving an inch.

"Of course you're right," Rebecca agreed, surprised at her sudden acquisition of the oleaginous gift of diplomacy. Then abruptly she realized why she hadn't taken Judah into her confidence; he had that gift and used it masterfully. She recalled that in the past four years there'd been eighteen changes in the six-man Confederate cabinet. Davis found it almost impossible to delegate power, so was always trapped in details and internecine battles. But through all the changes, and despite the insidious anti-Semitism in the government, Benjamin had leapfrogged from Attorney General, to Secretary of War, to the most prestigious post of all, Secretary of State. How? Everything he'd said tonight had been to bolster Davis. Others might voice an opinion opposed to Jeff's, but never Judah. Clearly, Jeff was nourished by this support and had assigned more and more power to him. Benjamin wasn't a sycophant, he did have the brightest mind in the government but he'd never jeopardize his security by risking any disagreement with his protector. Benjamin was lost to her; she'd have to cope with Davis alone. When Judah rose to leave he looked at her expectantly but she gave him no sign to stay.

A short time later Rebecca sat in Davis' study on the second floor. Though his demeanor remained courtly she detected a distinct wariness. "Your Excellency," she began, then suddenly she forgot all she'd rehearsed and blurted, "Jeff, we must have peace before our land is bled dry."

He sat erect in his chair, his bearing that of a southern gentleman and President of the Confederacy. "The only way to peace is for the enemy to withdraw. The Confederacy is, and will remain, a separate and independent nation."

"How in the world can two peoples with the same language, the same heritage and separated only by an imaginary line, live at peace with each other? From a practical point of view wouldn't regional disputes always arise? Wouldn't both sections fall victim to a constant round of bloodshed?"

In response, he declared as if by rote, "For decades, the sole aim of the North has been to subjugate the South."

She tamped her exasperation; "I know for a fact that Mr. Lincoln has no wish to subjugate us. If you've read his inaugural address you must know that he'd welcome us back and forgive all the loss and bloodshed."

"He forgive? The invader forgive? The unmitigated gall of the tyrant! When Colonel Dahlgren was killed in his attempt to burn Richmond we found papers on his body authorizing him to assassinate me, and members of my cabinet. So don't be deceived by the deceiver, his interest is only in crushing our armies and exterminating us."

"Your Excellency, brutal as this may sound, isn't that nearly accomplished anyway? Grant has shut us up in Richmond; Sherman's taken Savannah and lays waste to the Carolinas. The Union's blockade strangles us. The Confederacy appears to be at the end of its resources. Wouldn't it be more humane to accept honorable terms while we can, and retain as much of our prestige as possible and save our Southern people?"

He looked at her in utter disbelief as if to imply, How can you—how can anyone disagree with me, President of the Confederacy? He addressed her as if she might be some errant heathen who must be brought to the light; "Miss Rebecca, you do not understand the situation. Lee still commands his intact army and holds Grant at bay. As for Sherman, any tactician will tell you that the farther he goes from his base of supplies, the weaker he'll grow and the more disastrous his defeat will be. What Lincoln doesn't know is that we are about to implement a new strategy that will send the North reeling." He pressed his fist to his chest; "The Confederacy is more than a nation, it is an ideal, one worth living for—and dying for."

Dear God, Jeff, she cried inwardly, have you so lost touch with reality that you can't see the horror around you? She felt unutterably sad for this man, this lonely, tragic hero, and if she could have turned his 'ideal' into a reality she would have, but not at the price of one more life.

His voice swelled passionately, "But if we were without money, without food, without weapons—if our whole country was devastated and our armies crushed and disbanded, could we, without giving up our manhood, give up our right to govern ourselves? Would you not rather die and feel yourself a man, than live, and be subject to a foreign power?"

No! she wanted to scream. It's not a foreign power you fight but your own countrymen. Do I really care that you think my grandson Geary was a good soldier and died for your holy cause? Give me back his life instead. All this she wanted to shout, but managed to control herself until diplomacy could fashion another avenue to reach him. Dear Lord, she prayed, give me the strength to open his mind.

"I know first hand that Lincoln's about to call up a half million more men. His re-election's given him an overwhelming mandate to prosecute the war to its conclusion. His resources are endless. Ours are severely limited. Daily our soldiers desert, our own newspapers call for peace at any price before the South is totally annihilated. We know the North is willing to pay an indemnification for every slave. Why not leave it to our people, let them vote on the issue of war or peace?"

"By 'the people', you mean the majority, don't you?" he demanded. "But we seceded to rid ourselves of the rule of the majority and this would only subject us to it again."

"In any democracy surely the majority must finally rule."

"If I agreed to that, I'd be hung within the hour."

"Why? You allow the majority to rule in a single state, why not let it rule in the entire country?"

"In our country, yes, the Confederacy."

"And if any one of your states disagrees with the majority of the Confederacy, then she's free to go?"

"With our blessing. It is their sovereign right."

"Jeff, Jeff," she murmured, lapsing into the familiar without realizing it, "that's so far removed from political reality it's ludicrous. A breakdown of our nation into weak city-states—at the mercy of the large powers? Even now, see what France does in Mexico, putting Maximillian on the throne, something that she would never have dared unless we were at war. And how long before England, operating from Canada, begins to gobble up these isolated states and incorporates them back into her own empire? Is this what our Founding Fathers saw as America's destiny? Under such dissolution could we ever take our place in the world as a power for democracy? And that, dear Jeff, I believe is our ultimate destiny."

His face turned bloodless; a tense moment passed and she prayed, Am I reaching him? "Jeff, you speak of your honor, your pride, as though you'd been personally affronted. Think instead of our nation, the United States of America, with a glorious future ahead of it. And it can be glorious, if only we can resolve this dreadful dilemma slavery's brought us to."

"Slavery was never the issue," Davis cried ardently, "slaves are guaranteed under the Constitution. The issue is the right of a state to determine its own destiny."

"No matter what abstract name you give it, the real point is that a small percentage of men who own most of the slaves in the South are fighting to protect their privileged way of life. At a horrifying cost to everyone else. You've heard our soldiers grumble, 'Rich man's war, poor man's fight?'"

He brushed that aside; "The Negro isn't ready for emancipation, he must be guided carefully into our civilization or he'll founder and die. Our concern for these child-like people is Christian in the extreme. As for this being a rich man's war, you're very much mistaken. We could never have gotten this far if the people weren't behind us."

"In the beginning, yes, in the euphoria of Fort Sumter and Manassas. But walk the streets of Richmond now, listen to the starving populace. All of us are Americans; we're tired of killing each other no matter what the reason. Every state in the South—except South Carolina—has already sent a regiment, or more, to fight for the Union. You must see for yourself that secession hasn't worked. The reluctance of the individual Southern states to give up their power to your central government—that inherent flaw has been your own worst enemy. And daily our situation grows more perilous."

As if to punctuate that truth, they heard the distant booming of cannon. Davis' gray hair, his Confederate gray suit, blended with the pallor of his face. He said through bloodless lips, "What did Lincoln promise you to come here?"

She rose slowly, quivering with distress. "He promised me a great deal. Peace for one. And an end to senseless bloodshed. He promised me the lives of my remaining children and grandchildren. Your Excellency, what can you promise me?"

"Not one drop of blood shed in this war is on my hands," he said fervently. "I can look to my God and say this. I tried all in my power to avert this war. I saw it coming and for twelve years I worked night and day to prevent it but I could not. And now it must go on till the last man of this generation falls in his tracks, and his children seize his musket and fight his battle, unless the North acknowledges our right to self-government. We are not fighting for slavery. We are fighting for independence—and that, or extermination, we will have!"

He stood up, dismissing her, and unable to resist the final word, said, "If you thought to overwhelm me with your tales of doom, I assure you, we are not in extremis. With our new strategy about to be implemented, I promise you that within six months, you'll see the North suing us for peace!"

Rebecca left Davis' study weighted with misery, praying that she hadn't alienated him beyond recall. When she got back to the Spotswood Hotel, she told Bittersweet about her confrontation with Davis.

Still trembling with aftershock, Rebecca said, "Tonight I saw a totally different side of Jeff Davis. I keep remembering what President Zachary Taylor once told me, that Jeff had been the chief obstacle in Congress to a compromise about slavery. Come to think of it, Sam Houston wasn't too kind about him either; if I remember correctly, he said, 'Jeff Davis is as cold as a lizard and as ambitious as Lucifer.'"

"You believe that?" Bittersweet asked softly.

"I don't know what to believe, but in spite of all his disclaimers about not wanting to be President of the Confederacy, he did wind up being President. And between Abe Lincoln and Jeff Davis our children are being slaughtered."

She sat down and began to cry softly. "The worst thing of all—I saw Gunning tonight."

Bittersweet cried out in joy but Rebecca sobbed, "He swears he didn't send the letter about Forrest. This whole trip, it's turning out to be nothing but an exercise in futility brought about by a stupid old woman."

Chapter 54

"WHY SO surprised to see me, Ma?" Gunning asked, "didn't I tell you that I'd pick you up this morning?"

Rebecca couldn't have been more astonished when Gunning appeared at the Spotswood. In the matter of women, especially Romance, was her son finally showing some backbone?

He'd brought her a broken-down shay with a broken-down mare. "I told Judah Benjamin you needed transportation and somehow he produced this. Though I'm afraid this old nag's just about ready for the glue factory."

"So is this old nag, we can keep each other company." She drove the shay; Gunning rode beside her on Baal. The temperature hovered in the forties but some precocious snowdrops and violets in search of spring had already poked their brave heads above ground.

They'd ridden about half way to Chimborazo when Gunning asked, "Would it pain you to talk about Geary? I read your letter a hundred times and Bravo told me a great deal."

She told him, recalling the vivid details as if they'd happened yesterday. "He died the way he lived, making us laugh." By the time she'd finished, including Geary bequeathing all his imaginary slaves to Harriet Beech Stowe, Gunning was roaring with laughter and sobbing all at once.

"The big surprise was Lincoln," she murmured. "In the midst of all the Yankee horror he was kindness itself. That's when I began to see him in a different light."

"How can you? He's responsible for every—"

"Gunning, he believes in the Union. And so do I."

He threw up his hands in a hopeless gesture. Then he asked after Sharon. When Rebecca told him about Sam Stockwell he fired his questions with the speed of a repeating rifle. "Who is he? What are his prospects? Do you like him?"

"He's from Massachusetts and you know what sanctimonious prigs they can be. But Sharon likes him—loves him—so there must be some good in him. I'm delighted that you're exhibiting a father's normal concerns for his daughter."

"I know you've got a very jaundiced view of my life but I do happen to love my children."

She put forward her next question with utmost care; "What about you? The war can't last forever. What will you do then?" and added hopefully, "come home to Washington?"

"I don't know; I do know that my life with Kate is over." She started to object but he cut her off. "I'm sure all your burning questions revolve around Romance. The last time you and I traveled down that road it turned into a disaster. I don't want to fight now, I'm just that pleased to see you."

"About Romance," Rebecca mused, "you're right to tell me that it's none of my business, you've got to work out your own life and your own happiness. But because I love you—no matter what you think I do love you—all I ask is that you be careful. Remember, Connaught and Villefranche blood flows in her beautiful veins; call it woman's intuition, or a mother's fears, but I think she could be a very dangerous woman."

"Dangerous doesn't do her justice. But she's more than that, including being quite mad. I must be a little crazy myself, else why do I remain her partner in this mad dance?"

Unable to resist, she blurted, "Why do you?"

"The obvious reasons…she's beautiful, desirable, I've never felt quite so alive. Also, at one point I believed I was getting even with all the Connaughts and with Veronique as well. But those are the easy answers. The truth is…we're both trapped and we don't know how to break free. Much like the North and South in this war. We've got to play it out to its bitter end."

His matter-of-fact tone sent shivers through her. "Gunning, you said you didn't write me about Forrest, but I did get a letter from you last fall? Were you in Washington then?"

He shook his head but instinct told her that he was lying. She knew that he held some position in the Confederate government, in Intelligence, she thought, Bravo had intimated as much. That he'd stolen into Washington, risked his life—God! it was all too much for a mother to bear.

"Ma, how long do you plan to stay in Richmond?"

"I don't know, for a while at least."

"But why? Why did you come here at all? For your own safety I want you to leave immediately. I can't say more but you're a bright woman, draw your own conclusions."

She looked at him blankly; "Apparently I'm not as bright as you think. What are you implying?"

"Listen to me. You must leave—"

"I can't, I've got to find Forrest—"

"—If you don't go on your own I'll have you taken forcibly—" He turned abruptly in his saddle; "Forrest? But Bravo told me he was missing in action— presumed dead."

He listened as the story tumbled from her in fever pitch. "Can you help me find him?" she pleaded, "please?"

"Do you realize what you're asking? Even if I did find him I'd have to turn him over to the authorities."

"How can you be so heartless? He's your nephew, your own blood! Doesn't that mean anything to you? Or will you carry your grudge against Bravo to the grave?"

At her outburst Baal shied, rearing and pawing the air. Gunning fought to control the beast and finally calmed him. A pall descended over them and they rode the rest of the way in silence. When they reached Chimborazo, Gunning said stiffly, "I've got to leave you now."

"Gunning, let's not part this way. I didn't mean—it's this damnable war, it's all my fault. Please. When can I see you again? This evening? I promise—"

"I'll be away for a few days," he answered gruffly. "I should have left at dawn but I did want to see you. Because Ma, though you may not believe it, I do love you too."

"Where are you going?"

His lips parted in his delightful off-center grin; "Why I'm off to Washington. To check on this Sergeant Stockwell and make damned sure he's good enough for Sharon. Then as long as I'm in the lion's den, I'm going to spirit Honest Abe off and talk some plain old Southern sense to him."

"Can't you be serious for once?"

He leaned toward her; "All right, I will be serious, deadly serious. Get out of Richmond as fast as you can."

He wheeled Baal and cantered off. She reached for him, aching to call him back, to make everything right between them. She needed so desperately to do that with all her children, and before she was called to her Maker. But he'd disappeared down the hill.

At Chimborazo's administration building Rebecca waited while a slave went to fetch Becky. When she appeared, Rebecca thought she might faint; it was as if she was looking at her daughter, Suzannah. Years of living on the Texas frontier had changed Suzannah from a demure Washington debutante to a compassionate, indomitable woman. It was a quality one could only earn and now Becky had earned it. And something more. Adversity had burned every vestige of timidity from her, revealing an inner strength that made her incandescent and Rebecca's spirit soared with pride.

Without a word they embraced, clinging to each other, drawing strength from each other. "Somehow, I always knew you'd come," Becky murmured.

"We must talk," Rebecca began, only to be interrupted by a steward with a question, followed by a surgeon with a complaint. The hospital bustled with people who were always interrupting them. "Is there someplace quiet we could go?" Rebecca asked. "Gunning's given me a carriage."

Becky looked at her lavaliere watch; "I've two hours before I start the dinner meal. I know a place."

Rebecca climbed into the shay; Becky grasped the nag's bridle and led them down a path so steep and torturous Rebecca thought they would surely overturn.

"Pity I no longer have my horse," Becky said, "but he was requisitioned long ago by the Confederate army."

A dozen times Rebecca started to ask her granddaughter if she knew anything about Forrest, but each time Becky motioned for her to be silent.

Soon they'd reached the base of Chimborazo cliff and a bewildered Rebecca was drawn deep into a seedy wharf area. Across the James River, the remnants of the Confederate fleet lay anchored at the Navy Yard. At an abandoned warehouse, they secreted the horse and shay in the stable, then up precipitous flights of steps that left Rebecca's heart pounding. Into a tiny room where she came face to face with a vaguely familiar man, one leg stiff from a wound, his right hand clawed.

When she did recognize him she turned on her granddaughter and with voice rising, demanded, "Why did you bring me here? What makes you think I've any interest in seeing Carleton Connaught?"

To Rebecca's complete shock her granddaughter clamped a hand over her mouth. "Not so loud. No one must know we're here. We owe Carleton a great deal. He could have left Richmond, gone someplace safe, but he stayed here to help me."

Becky drew her to a tiny alcove. Lying on a thin pallet Rebecca saw the gaunt and drained form of Forrest. In all her life she'd never experienced such a feeling as swept over her, as though she'd been touched by God's grace.

She sank to her knees beside him. Forrest stared at her without recognition, eyes dull, sallow skin stretched tight over his skull. She called his name softly, trying to rouse him but he remained silent.

"What's wrong with him?" Rebecca moaned, and listened in stunned silence to a tale of balloons, capture, operations, loss of speech and memory. She pressed her hands to her pounding temples; "Why won't he talk?"

"He hasn't spoken in a long time," Becky told her. "He's been through so much, it would have killed a lesser man. Now it's as if he's hiding. The important thing is to help him get his strength back. Can you help us?"

"How? Anything," Rebecca sobbed.

"Stop crying. We've no time for that. If he had decent food he might have a fighting chance. We've kept him hidden here for almost four months; it's been a battle everyday. I've got to keep working at the hospital, to avoid suspicion."

Carleton picked up the tale; "I've been mustered out of the army, with these wounds I'm more of a hindrance than a help. I go out foraging for food every morning but I can't stay away too long, Forrest slips into these deliriums, and his screams might alert somebody. Squads of General Winder's Plug Uglies are scouring Richmond for spies, escaped prisoners and deserters, if Forrest is found and captured—"

"I'll get the food," Rebecca promised. "Bittersweet brought along a smoked ham. When that runs out I'll find more. I don't know how—but I'll get it."

Becky instructed her on the best way to get to their warehouse from the Spotswood Hotel. Carleton handed her a revolver; "Do you know how to use this?"

"I used to be a fair shot, before my rheumatism and my cataracts. Now I'm probably a hazard."

"This is a rough area," Carleton cautioned, "a horse is really valuable, so be on your guard. When you come here wear old clothes, no jewelry, not even your gold wedding ring."

Becky checked her watch again; "I've got to go." The two women left. Rebecca wanted to give Becky a ride back to the hospital but she shook her head; "The hill is too steep, that horse would never make it."

Then she said softly, "I know you've never liked Carleton, you probably still don't. But if it makes any difference, Forrest would be dead by now if it wasn't for him." With a final embrace Becky left.

Rebecca followed the towpath along the riverbank to the Spotswood; she imagined that anyone who looked at her was about to steal her horse and kept one hand on the revolver. The instant Bittersweet saw Rebecca, she knew and started to weep for joy. "The Lord be smilin' on us today."

"Listen to me, my girl," Rebecca said resolutely, "we lost Geary, we mustn't lose Forrest. I swear before God, I'll die first."

*

The smoked ham was gone sooner than Rebecca anticipated. Drawing strength from some hidden reserve, she set out to find more food. Thank God she had fifty dollars in gold coin left and that supplied provisions for several days. When the money gave out she went to Gunning's to borrow some, only to learn that he hadn't yet returned. She pawned everything she owned including her wedding ring.

Most evenings, though exhausted from the hunt for food, and tending Forrest during the day, Rebecca made a point of making an appearance at Judah Benjamin's, for no one must suspect. Several times she managed to filch food from the Benjamin larder and secret it in her carryall.

Bittersweet threw herself into the effort. The chef at the hotel had taken a shine to her and through promises made and some kept, allowed her into the kitchen. She'd spend hours picking bird carcasses clean, grinding the bones and boiling it all in cheesecloth and rendering it into a hearty broth.

Rebecca expressed astonishment at her ingenuity and Bittersweet shrugged; "No trick to it a'tall, most poor folks live this way. The trick was to sweeten up the chef. Lordy, the things I do for mah family."

Then there came the day when Rebecca found she had no money left; she'd pawned everything she owned. She wracked her brain, rummaged through her bags, then cried, "I do have something valuable."

"You dasn't," Bittersweet cried.

"I must," she answered simply.

She went to an apothecary on Broad Street and carefully placed several vials on the marble-topped counter. The last of her supply of digitalis.

The pharmacist sniffed, tasted, then began counting out an enormous stack of Confederate notes.

She shook her head vehemently; "Gold, only."

He argued, swore, but finally gave her the gold. As she pushed the money into her purse he noticed her trembling hands and asked, "Are you sure you don't need it yourself?"

She flashed him a radiant smile; "There are other, better medicines for the heart."

Rebecca had arrived in Richmond on the sixth of March, found Forrest on the seventh, and in ten short days of lavish care, Forrest had gained enough strength to sit up, even take a few steps.

The booming of cannon at the front increased in intensity. Remembering Gunning's warning—"Get out of Richmond as fast as you can,"—Rebecca fretted over Forrest's slow recovery. Nor could she overcome this feeling of impending disaster.

Chapter 55

THE SURRATT boarding house in Washington lay in darkness. Gunning looked around furtively to make sure he hadn't been followed from his safe house at the Thomas Green's, then went inside. He climbed the creaking steps past rooms where Mary Surratt's boarders lay asleep, up to the top floor where a sliver of light shone from under John Surratt's door. He knocked and entered. John Wilkes Booth sprang at him, dagger in hand, and another man caught him in a crushing headlock.

Booth slumped with relief; "It's all right, Paine, he's one of us." The man released Gunning and Booth introduced them. "Meet Lewis Paine, the agent General Mosby's sent us."

Gunning rubbed his wrenched neck. Paine was a powerful twenty-year-old, handsome in a farm-boy sort of way. From his faithful-dog manner Gunning intuited that Paine, rather than being in control of Booth, had fallen under the matinee idol's peculiar spell.

The rest of Booth's action team sat ranged around the room; the Baltimore bookends, Michael O'Laughlin and Sam Arnold; David Herold, slightly lost in his simplemindedness; George Atzerodt, his heavy German accent made more incomprehensible by drink; and cool, clever John Surratt.

Booth clapped Gunning on the shoulder; "Sorry for the rough greeting but we didn't expect you for another day."

"I found it easier to get here than planned. The Federals are getting complacent, security's lax at the checkpoints and that fills me with hope. If we can just spirit Lincoln out of Washington and get across the Potomac to Mosby's Raiders—"

"We can do it," Booth interrupted. "I'm developing a plan, but don't ask what it is, it's very complex and I don't want to reveal it until I've worked out every last detail. To that end, tomorrow night we're all going to Ford's Theater—"

"The theater?" Gunning repeated incredulously, "Booth, we don't have time to waste on that sort of nonsense."

"Trust me," Booth said urgently, "I beg you, trust me. Through friends at Ford's management I've procured four seats in the presidential box, the very seats that Lincoln uses when he goes there. To make it look like an ordinary outing, John Surratt and Lewis Paine will escort two young ladies, boarders of Mary Surratt's. The rest of us will buy separate orchestra seats; make sure you familiarize yourselves with the theater's layout. After the performance we'll meet at Gautier's Restaurant; by then I'll have worked out every detail of my plan."

What in blue blazes can be in his mind? Gunning wondered. Despite the danger of being recognized in such a public place, Gunning decided he'd better go. The next evening he waited until the play had begun, slipped into the theater, scooted up to the mezzanine and stole into the presidential box where Surratt, Paine and their dates were already seated. During the play, a pseudo-classical drama titled *Jane Shore*, Gunning scanned the audience with his opera glasses and started when he spied Sean Connaught. Gunning fell back into the shadows.

During intermission he watched as Sean talked earnestly to a bullish, dark-haired officer whom Gunning recognized as Colonel Lafayette Baker, head of the Federal Secret Service. Was their presence coincidence? Was it planned? Whatever the truth, it unnerved him. Gunning left before the final curtain and went to Gautier's where he rendezvoused with Booth in a private room. The rest of the action team arrived shortly thereafter—Surratt and Paine had dropped off their dates.

Booth had ordered a tub of oysters and champagne and had already consumed a good deal of both. Voice throbbing with excitement, he said, "Now for my plan; everything's falling into place, just as I hoped. This afternoon I went to Ford's Theater and broke the lock on the door to the presidential box; knowing Ford's management, they won't get around to repairing it for months. Lincoln's night bodyguard is a heavy drinker and during all performances visits Tueteval's Tavern next door. This leaves the box accessible and unguarded. Next time Lincoln goes to Ford's Theater, we strike!"

The men listened, dumbfounded, as Booth acted out his scenario. "O'Laughlin will turn off the main gas valve plunging the theater into darkness. Paine and I burst into the box and wrestle Lincoln into submission. Arnold, waiting in the wings, rushes onstage and Paine and I lower the bound and gagged Lincoln to him. We then leap from the box onstage—it's only twelve feet—and help Arnold carry Lincoln out to the alley where Herold will be waiting in a carriage. We throw Lincoln into it; Arnold guards our prisoner while Herold drives the carriage off. We all join up with Surratt and Atzerodt at the Navy Yard Bridge—it's the quickest, shortest way out of Washington—and they'll take us to Port Tobacco where Atzerodt has his boat hidden. Once we cross the Potomac Mosby's Raiders will be waiting, then on to Richmond!"

Is the man mad? Gunning thought.

Flushed with champagne and his bravura performance, Booth looked around for approval and instead met a firestorm of protest. Arnold's shouts rose above the rest, "Trying to kidnap the President from a crowded theater with guards all about? It's insane. I want no part of it. If this isn't concluded within the week, I'm out."

Fire flashed from Booth's eyes; "Any man who talks of backing out now ought to be shot."

When Booth got no support he grew so inflamed that a fistfight threatened. With the entire operation looking like it was about to fall apart, Gunning stepped in. Clearly, Booth was a loose cannon, but there just wasn't enough time to assemble another action team, Richmond was scheduled to be abandoned in three weeks. If the operation was to succeed, he'd have to keep a very tight reign on Booth.

"Gentleman, we're all stretched tight," Gunning began, "but we've got to put aside our differences for the sake of the greater goal. Come Booth, we owe our friends an apology."

When tempers cooled, Gunning pushed an idea forward; "Can we think of some event where there'd be fewer people about? Where the chances of escape would be better? At a private party, or an outing—?"

Booth bounded to his feet; "I have it! We actors give benefit performances for convalescing soldiers at various hospitals, some in the city, some in the country. The papers always announce when Lincoln's going to attend. It will be easy to find out from my colleagues when he's expected—"

Booth went on excitedly, formulating a plan even as he spoke; "I grant you it would be simpler to waylay Lincoln on a lonely country road and carry him off from there. We'd be long gone before the alarm was sounded."

This new plan met with enthusiastic approval and Gunning breathed a bit easier. No question, Booth was quick-witted, but he needed iron-fisted guidance. If he had that, he'd do just fine. The band then broke up, once more charged with the conviction that their daring might yet save the South.

As Gunning exited Gautier's he caught sight of Sean Connaught; even though the restaurant was a popular after-theater rendezvous, this time Gunning knew that Sean's presence was no accident. Sean had been a great help in setting up a Confederate spy network in Canada, but was the two-faced bastard playing a double game?

The next day, March 17, it appeared that luck had finally smiled on the conspirators. At noon, Booth received word that the Ford Theater Company would give a performance of *Still Waters Run Deep* at Campbell's Hospital that very afternoon and that Lincoln planned to attend. The information reached Booth only an hour before the time appointed, but so perfectly had he worked out communications with his team that by one o'clock they were in their saddles and galloping hard to a rendezvous point near the hospital.

As they rode, Booth shouted to Gunning, "I've sent David Herold with my buggy to take our cache of arms to the old Surratt tavern in Surrattsville; it's ten miles south of the Navy Yard bridge. He'll be waiting for us with enough weapons to fight a war: two double barreled shotguns, two Spencer carbines, pistols, ammunition, a dirk, a sword, an ax, and a monkey wrench. The ax to fell trees to slow pursuit, the monkey wrench to repair our carriage if we have an accident." He finished proudly, "I believe I've covered everything."

Campbell's Hospital was located far out on 7th Street, near Soldiers' Home. Arnold and O'Laughlin arrived at the meeting place first, then Atzerodt and Paine, and finally Surratt, Booth, and Gunning. They hid in a stand of trees that bordered a sharp bend in the road. Gunning could barely control his excitement; "God damn, this looks like it's going to work. In minutes, Lincoln could be in our hands!"

Booth said excitedly, "When Lincoln's carriage appears, Surratt and I will ride out and seize the reins. Paine, you follow close behind, jump into the carriage and subdue Lincoln. Arnold, O'Laughlin and Atzerodt, you'll dispatch any escorts that Lincoln has with him."

Soon they heard horses approaching. Booth cantered to the center of the road and signaled frantically that an unescorted carriage was coming. Surratt joined Booth, and feigning nonchalance, they moved slowly down the road toward the hospital. They allowed the carriage to come abreast of them and then Booth wheeled closer and peered inside. To his dismay, instead of Lincoln, he saw Chief Justice Salmon Chase.

The carriage continued on to the hospital and Booth and Surratt galloped back to the grove. The conspirators fell into another furious argument. Surratt and Arnold were convinced that the government's Secret Service was aware of their plot and had sent a decoy carriage to force the kidnappers to tip their hand. "The damned cavalry is probably charging down this very road to capture us," Surratt swore.

Booth tried to calm them; "I swear my information is solid, if you'll just be patient, Lincoln will be along."

"Enough of this guess work," Gunning rasped. "Let's find out for certain if Lincoln is expected."

Booth grudgingly agreed and the two men galloped to the hospital. There, Booth met an old acting crony, Edward L. Davenport, who'd stepped outside to smoke a cigar.

"Hallo, Ned," Booth called with forced jocularity, "who's in the audience today, anyone important?" Davenport named several distinguished guests, including Chief Justice Salmon Chase. Booth asked, "What about the Old Man? Did he come?"

"Promised he would, but Governor Morton of Indiana persuaded him to go to another function. Seems his 140th regiment captured a Reb flag at Wilmington, North Carolina; there's going to be a grand parade and then the flag will be presented to Lincoln. You can make a lot more political hay from a captured Rebel flag than from a theater matinee."

With an oath, Booth wheeled his horse, and Davenport shouted, "What's your hurry? Stay for the second act."

When Booth and Gunning told the others the news they scattered, Arnold and O'Laughlin headed back to Baltimore, vowing that they were through with Booth's reckless schemes. Atzerodt agreed to stop off at Surrattsville to let Herold know that the plot had failed, from there he'd return to Port Tobacco. Paine, Surratt and Booth rode hard for the Surratt boarding house, fearing that they were about to be arrested.

The next night Booth was scheduled to appear in a one-night benefit performance of *The Apostate* at Ford's theater. It had been announced weeks before, but Booth, suffering from a severe case of nerves, refused to go on.

Gunning grabbed him by his lapels; "Do you want to wreck this entire operation? The only way to avoid suspicion is for you to go about your normal routine. Now do it!"

Shamed, Booth did go on but critics reported that he seemed disconnected and unsure of himself.

The conspirators then learned that Lincoln planned to go to City Point in a few days—and under heavy guard. In those circumstances, kidnapping him was virtually impossible. Booth's mood got worse and when he insisted that he had to get away for a few days, Gunning agreed. In this condition Booth was not only useless, but also dangerous. Tuesday, March 21, a very agitated Booth boarded the 7:30 train to Baltimore, then went on to New York where he checked into the St. Nicholas Hotel and into the arms of his favorite New York prostitute, Annie Horton.

Given Booth's erratic behavior, Gunning's misgivings about "Operation Come Retribution" had grown. But Booth wasn't his only concern. There was something cowardly about kidnapping Lincoln, an admission that the South couldn't fight the battle man for man but had to resort to the same foul chicanery as Dahlgren's raid on Richmond. Though Gunning had originally pushed hard for the plan, the deeper he got into it, the more it rubbed against his grain.

But what was the alternative? Even if there was only the slimmest chance of success, Gunning was prepared to challenge heaven and hell to make it happen. The destiny of Richmond, the destiny of the South, depended on it.

Late one night Gunning was returning to his safe house at the Thomas Greens' when he spotted two men lurking near the grounds; one was Colonel Lafayette Baker, whom Sean Connaught had been talking to at the theater; the other, younger man, looked oddly familiar. Gunning increased his pace, only to hear footsteps running after him. He turned the corner and as his pursuer rounded the building, Gunning caught him in the solar plexus with a hard right. In that moment he recognized Sam Stockwell, Sharon's beau. Surprise held Gunning immobile.

The youngster scrambled for his gun. Gunning hit him again and he fell; but he knew the lad had gotten a good look at him—could identify him. He heard Baker running—he'd be on them in moments—Gunning aimed his gun at the lad—but recalling Sharon's passionate embrace, and his mother saying 'Sharon loves him'—he dashed off. He ran, pursued by the grim certainty that Sean Connaught was behind this. How in the world had Sean known that he was in Washington? Gunning ran faster, trying with every stride to run from the truth.

With his safe house denied him Gunning took refuge at the Surratt boarding house and for days didn't venture out. Booth returned to Washington on Saturday, March 25, refreshed and bubbling with new ideas of how to kidnap Lincoln.

Gunning told him somberly, "Lincoln left two days ago for City Point. That means Grant's about to begin his spring offensive. I've had a piece of bad luck; I've been recognized by a Federal agent. The High Command thinks that if I remain in Washington, not only will I jeopardize our plan, I might compromise our entire spy network here. They've ordered me back to Richmond. Surratt is going to guide me through enemy lines, and then he'll join you back here. So now it's up to you. Stay alert, when Lincoln returns to Washington, another opportunity is bound to present itself. Your orders remain the same. Lincoln is to be kidnapped. Kidnapped only. Remember, his value to us is as a hostage. Alive."

Chapter 56

WHEN REBECCA left her room at the Spotswood Hotel this Saturday evening, April 1, she had every reason to be cautiously optimistic. Forrest had made steady progress and was even walking around the loft. Another week of decent food and he might be able to travel. Though his mind remained clouded and he still hadn't spoken, she clung to the hope that rest and care would restore his senses.

"Don't dawdle," she urged Bittersweet, "I want to get to Judah Benjamin's early, that way I may be able to snaffle off a bit of extra food."

Bittersweet glanced around; "Got to make sure that Harmony Lumpkin ain't lurkin."

"Are you still obsessed with that silly notion? Really." Passing through the lobby Rebecca clutched Bittersweet's arm. "That young man standing at the desk? Isn't he the one—?"

"Slipped Gunning's letter under our door," Bittersweet moaned. "Oh Lordy, g'wan murder us in our beds."

Rebecca waited until the man left then hurried to the desk clerk. "I believe I know that young man but I've forgotten his name, could you spare me the embarrassment?"

The fussbudget of a clerk thumbed through the register. "Checked in on Wednesday, March 29, name's Henry Sherman. Oh, Mrs. Brand, there is the matter of your overdue bill?"

"Later, I'm due at the White House for dinner," she lied. She rejoined Bittersweet; "That's not the man's real name, John Wilkes Booth introduced us at Lincoln's inauguration. Oh, why can't I remember anything?"

To spare the horse, Rebecca rode while Bittersweet walked alongside, leading it. "If we knows him, he knows us, things gettin' too thick for honest folk. Best we pack up Forrest and leave, 'n' before this old nag dies."

When they arrived at Judah Benjamin's, Bittersweet stabled the horse and visited with the coloreds; Rebecca joined Judah in the drawing room. "What news?" she asked.

"Lee is still holding at Petersburg."

"And what of my errant son? Has Gunning returned yet?"

"He got back yesterday," Benjamin confided. "His Excellency sent him immediately to brief Lee at the front."

Though she could have bitten off her tongue she suddenly blurted, "John Surratt! Oh dear, forgive me, I just recalled someone's name." She couldn't help but notice that Benjamin colored visibly, and all at once she realized where Gunning had been. Keeping her tone casual but intent on Judah's reaction, she asked, "Gunning's been in Washington, hasn't he? I pray it was in the cause of peace?"

Whatever Benjamin's true feelings, they were camouflaged by his enigmatic smile; "I can assure you, dear Miss Rebecca, our ultimate aim is, and always has been, peace."

Other guests began to arrive and while Benjamin was occupied, Rebecca managed to secret two finger sandwiches in her reticule. All the while she kept thinking...John Surratt delivering Gunning's letter...Surratt and Booth at Lincoln's inauguration...Booth's invective against Lincoln...she filed that information in a musty corner of her mind, trying vainly to put the puzzle together, to make sense of it all.

Rebecca said to Judah Benjamin, "I've just heard the most startling rumor. That Varina and the children left Richmond yesterday; sent away by Jeff Davis. Can this be true?"

Benjamin nodded; "Varina begged to remain here with Jeff, but his concern was for the children. He gave Varina his pistol, taught her how to shoot so she might take her own life rather than be captured by the Federals."

A furor of questions swept the room and a matron cried, "Is Richmond lost? Should we all not leave?"

Everyone looked to Benjamin; clouds of cigar smoke clouded his Cheshire smile. "I'll admit that the city's fate does look uncertain, but Richmond is not the entire Confederacy. His Excellency is determined that we will fight on until we're victorious."

"What a pile of horse shit," Rebecca muttered under her breath. Since her bleak interview with President Davis she hadn't been invited back to the White House, nor did she expect to be. Just as well, for she'd come to the chilling conviction that Davis was now so far removed from reality that rather than face the dishonor of surrender, he'd immolate his entire world, and the South along with it. If he'd ordered his family to leave, the situation must be perilous. Her heart began to thud, Bittersweet was right, even if Forrest was still weak, they should get out of Richmond now.

She left Benjamin's soon after and was thrilled to discover that Bittersweet had filched some rice. They drove out to the Rocketts wharf area. Forrest lay in deep sleep but Carleton promised he'd feed him when he woke up.

On the way back to Richmond, Bittersweet commented, "I like that there boy, Cotton, he's got a good heart."

Rebecca frowned; "*Et tu*, Brutus? I'm too tired to argue, all I can say is, he's a Connaught."

"Here you been tellin' me this life is for learnin' and so what have you learned? Chased your daughter Suzannah from you 'cause you was set in your ways, now you be doin' the same thing with your granddaughter? No fool like an old fool. Oh lordy, lordy, lordy, there's Harmony Lumpkin!"

Harmony Lumpkin emerged from an alley alongside the Spotswood Hotel leading a coffle of slaves. He stopped and stared at Bittersweet; "Don't I know you, nigger? Never forget a face—been watching you for days now, tryin' to think, where...? N'Orleans? 'Bama? Mississip? That's it, Mississipp! You're the feisty bitch who scarred my face!" and grabbed her.

Rebecca cracked him over the head with her cane; "Are you mad? This is my slave and I've the papers to prove it," and swung at him again as she hurried Bittersweet off.

Harmony Lumpkin shouted after them, "Soon's I deliver these slaves, we'll see what the law has to say. She's a runaway. The bitch will have my brand on her shoulder."

Rebecca and Bittersweet didn't sleep that night. "Don't worry," Rebecca soothed, "I won't let anything happen to you. If necessary, I'll buy you back from that cretin."

"He won't be satisfied with that, long time ago he tried to bed and breed me and he still got that look in his eye."

"Over my dead body," Rebecca swore. "Just stay out of sight, we'll be leaving tomorrow or the next day."

The next day, Sunday, April 2, Rebecca attended services at St. Paul's Church, more in the hope of keeping abreast of events than from religious conviction. She spied Jefferson Davis alone in his pew, number 63, looking immaculate in his gray Prince Albert coat. The church was abuzz with the news that Varina and the children had indeed left Richmond.

The choir finished singing, "Jesus, Lover of My Soul," Rector Charles G. Minnigerode mounted the ornate brass and wood pulpit and began his sermon. At a commotion in the rear, all heads turned to watch the sexton, Mr. William Irving, a large Scotsman in a faded gray coat, hurry down the center aisle to the President's pew. He handed Davis a note.

Jefferson Davis read it, turned bloodless, crushed the note in his fist, then hurried out of the church.

The ominous news swept over the congregation; Grant had breached Lee's defenses at Petersburg. The government must evacuate Richmond. Immediately. Today.

A woman moaned, "They'll burn Richmond the way they burned Atlanta." With that, the worshippers ran for the doors while Minnigerode tried vainly to recall his flock.

Outside, Rebecca gathered up Bittersweet, and most importantly, the horse and shay. "It's the only way we'll get Forrest out of the city alive," she panted. "No point going back to the hotel, I've nothing there, I've pawned everything; no money left to pay them anyway. Can you believe that in my dotage I've come to this? Running out on hotel bills?"

By 3 o'clock, panic had spread throughout Richmond. Streets were clogged with people fleeing the city, the affluent drove carriages heaped high with their belongings, others pulled carts loaded with their possessions, while the mass of the population shouldered their burdens. Wagons broke down, hysteria sounded in the shouts and shrill curses, and always in bass counterpoint, the growing growl of cannon.

It took Rebecca and Bittersweet until late afternoon to fight their way through the crowds and reach the old warehouse in the Rocketts wharf area. Becky and Carleton were there.

Becky told them, "We've been moving the wounded out of Chimborazo all day. The entire hospital's been abandoned. We were ordered to leave, to save ourselves."

"We must get out of here," Rebecca began but Becky interrupted, "Grandma, you saw for yourself, it's bedlam out there. For the moment, this is the safest place."

Rebecca fretted, but saw the wisdom. The setting sun streaked the James with its molten golden glow, then dusk descended. With darkness came a gnawing sense of doom.

Chapter 57

GUNNING SPURRED Baal and the ghostly gray fought his way through the throngs of people in the twilight streets of Richmond. A frantic man tore at Gunning's leg, trying to unseat him and he lashed him across the head; nothing must stop him from delivering Lee's message to President Davis.

Coming directly from the front lines, he'd gone first to the Customs House, only to learn that Davis had already left for the Richmond-Danville Depot. He'd galloped the two blocks to Romance's to make sure she'd gotten off safely; the house was locked and shuttered so he assumed she was waiting at the station for him, as planned.

Back down the hill then to 14th and the street that led to the depot. Mobs fought and bit and clawed to get on the last of the six trains leaving the beleaguered capital. Great piles of food and ammunition lay heaped on the platforms; the vital supplies had been intended for Lee's army but had been removed from the boxcars so that government records could be shipped to Danville.

In the turmoil, Gunning spotted Harmony Lumpkin leading a gang of twenty shackled slaves along the tracks; he was trying to climb aboard one of the trains, but no one would let him on. "This is radickalos," Harmony bleated. "Got me twenty thousand dollars of my life's blood in these hyar slaves, ya gotta let me aboard. Give ya one for free?"

As he moved past the slaves, Gunning searched their ranks for Romance's slave, Montgomery; Romance had said that she'd sell him to Lumpkin, but the buck wasn't there.

A platoon of Naval Cadets, no more than boys, loaded the chests containing $500,000 in gold bullion aboard the train that would carry the President and the cabinet to Danville, Virginia. The gold represented the last of the Confederacy's treasury.

Gunning felt a flood of relief when he saw Judah Benjamin on the platform—Davis couldn't be too far away. He rode to Benjamin and above the din of hissing steam and belching black smoke, shouted, "Where's Jeff?"

Judah pointed to the passenger car; "Safely inside."

"Have you seen Romance?" Gunning yelled.

"No. Perhaps she left on an earlier train?"

Gunning doubted that; she would have waited for him. His apprehension for her began to grow. He entered the railroad car and found Davis calmly writing a letter to Varina. Gunning heaved for breath; "You Excellency, General Lee reports that Grant has cut off his escape to the south. He's retreating west along the Appomattox River."

"West?" Davis interrupted. "But then how can he hope to join up with our army in the Carolinas?"

"Lee had no choice. Our army has only one day's supply of food. Lee begs that provisions be sent immediately to Amelia Courthouse where he'll try to make a stand."

Davis ordered an aide to report this to General Ewell; he was in charge of Richmond's defenses and had access to its supplies. But given the turmoil and the lack of transportation, Gunning had little hope that the supplies would ever reach Lee's army.

"Incidentally, Brand, this is something that you should know. While you were at the front, I understand that our Torpedo Bureau has instituted new plans concerning those monsters in Washington."

"What plans are those?" he asked, confused and suddenly apprehensive.

"Time enough to tell you when we're safely away."

"When exactly do we leave?" Gunning asked.

"As soon as the train's loaded and repairs made to the locomotive," Davis replied crisply. "The engineers estimate about nine o'clock, but eleven may be closer to the mark. Have you seen to the disposal of your own records? You understand that nothing must fall into the enemy's hands?"

"My records have been destroyed, but I've still got some unfinished business."

"See to it with dispatch. I'll have the engineer sound the train whistle fifteen minutes before departure. Don't be late, this will be the last train out of Richmond."

Gunning nodded and left. He went first to the Spotswood Hotel to check on his mother, but the place was abandoned and he assumed that she'd left. He galloped back to Romance's house. His concern for her was mixed with other thoughts…somehow he had to get a message to John Wilkes Booth, warn him not to proceed with Lincoln's kidnapping. With Richmond lost and Mosby's Raiders cut off from Lee's army, there wasn't a hope in hell that Lincoln could be successfully kidnapped.

Romance's house was as he'd left it earlier. He pounded on the door and when he got no answer, kicked it in. He ran to the drawing room—the scent of her perfume lingered—then bounded upstairs to the bedroom. Where was she? A series of explosions shuddered through the city and he dashed to the window and flung open the shutters. At the Navy Yard, the remaining ships of the Confederate navy were being blown up. He knew Davis had also ordered that the tobacco and cotton warehouses be torched and with these strong winds the flames might spread and immolate the entire city.

Taking the stairs two at a time, he went downstairs and barged into Romance's study. An oil lamp burned on her desk—had she left him a note? There was a letter, held in place by the jeweled letter-opener he'd given her ago when they'd first begun their love affair. He snatched up the note only to discover that it was addressed to her brother.

"Dear Sean, Of necessity, this must be brief. Gunning wants me to leave for Danville where the Confederacy plans to establish its new capital. I've just learned that Secretary of War Breckenridge—yes, Davis has yet another secretary, he changes them as one might change underwear—and other members of the High Command, have ordered the Confederate Torpedo Bureau to dispatch an explosives expert to Washington. The man's name is Sergeant Thomas Harney and his orders are to blow up the White House. Preferably when Lincoln and his cabinet are in it. With the administration decimated, the Rebels hope to create panic and thereby gain enough time to reform their lines and continue the war—"

The letter broke off here. Gunning's brow knitted, Was this information true or just more of Romance's imaginings? He had no knowledge of any such mission of the Confederate Torpedo Bureau, but it could have been formulated while he was in Washington, or at the front. And Jeff Davis had mentioned something about new plans.

His despair at learning of this stupid suicidal mission was matched by an even greater sense of betrayal. What he'd suspected for months was now undeniable; Romance had been sending information to Sean all along. He started to rip up the letter when he heard the cellar door creak open. Romance emerged.

He froze when he saw her. Her chemise hung from her, ripped, stained with blood. One breast was exposed. Yet she appeared unhurt for she had the barest smile on her lips. She looked right through him until he caught her arm, then with the shock of recognition, melted into him.

"Montgomery," she moaned, "horrible. I unchained him, thinking he'd help me pack, you weren't here, you're never here, I needed someone to help me, no one ever helps—"

He shook her; "Stop babbling. Tell me what happened."

She pointed toward the basement door. He drew his revolver and made his way down the steep steps into the darkness; she followed behind, continuing to ramble on in an incoherent singsong. He struck a match, lit the hanging oil lantern and glanced around. He saw him then. The young slave lay on his back, eyes staring at the rafters. A stream of blood ran from his slashed throat. He was naked.

Romance moved into the cone of light cast by the oil lantern. Gunning thought he heard her murmur something—something about the Nile? But he couldn't be sure. Scores of questions crowded in on him but deep in his gut he knew the answer to the horror that lay before him.

He brushed by her and went climbed up out of the basement. Romance followed him. As he gathered his belongings to leave, she stood at the window, alternately watching him and the ships burning in the James River. "Where, oh where, are you going my lad?" she hummed.

"The last train will leave Richmond shortly. Jefferson Davis will be on it. So will I."

"To go where? Can't you see that the war is lost?"

"Maybe, but I'm still responsible for Davis' safety."

"Nor must we forget your responsibility to your precious Ma-ma," she sneered. "I hear she's still in Richmond, stealing food from everyone's table like a common thief. Surely the dutiful son must see to his thieving mother's well being?"

"I stopped at the Spotswood, she's gone, but that's neither here nor there."

With slow deliberate motions Romance ripped off her chemise and stood naked at the window, the glow of distant fires bathing her skin with luminous light. "The Confederacy is doomed. Stay with me." Her voice rose passionately, "We'll go off to a new country, someplace where no one knows us, we'll marry, I'll give you what you've always wanted, children, beautiful, gifted, extraordinary children. We'll start tonight, right now, I won't take precautions."

But he saw the blood all over her, knew where it had come from, knew she'd gone mad, mad beyond reason, mad beyond redemption. And suddenly the caul of enchantment was ripped from his eyes. He saw her for what she truly was, not only one of the most glorious creatures God had ever fashioned, but also a poor wretch trapped in the whirlpool of her own making, a woman descending into the sink of her own soul, a woman who'd drag anyone who tried to save her to his destruction.

"Goodbye, Romance."

"Goodbye?" When his intent dawned on her, her face twisted with rage. "Goodbye is it?" she repeated, her voice rising in hysteria, "where is that fabled empire you promised me? And what of its capital that was to bear my name? Are you like all the others, spewing lies just to ensnare me?"

Then mercurially her mood changed to an angelic calm. "My darling, I care nothing for that, only you—"

From the direction of the railroad depot, the insistent shriek of a train whistle rent the night. He started for the door and she screamed, "Didn't you hear me? I said I'd bear your children!"

His glance flicked to the basement, then back to her. "How could I ever be sure that they were mine?"

He yanked open the smashed door, dimly hearing her snarl, "You dare leave me? No one ever leaves me."

She flew across the room and as she passed the desk, scooped up her jeweled letter opener and with full fury plunged it into his back. He staggered forward, hands moving behind him in a futile effort to pull out the blade, then slumped to his knees.

He struggled to get up and she hit him on the head with the oil lamp. The burning oil fountained all over her and she screamed as the flames ignited a tendril of her hair. She panicked and ran screaming around the room, arms flailing to beat out the blinding flames, screaming again and again, "Gunning, help me!" but he lay gasping for breath, his lung punctured.

The damask curtains caught fire, fell to ignite the Aubusson rug and one by one all the precious antiques she'd so religiously collected during Richmond's years of trial began to go up in flames.

Red and orange and yellow and blue, the room turned into an inferno. Gunning choked, and with every gasp, the pool of blood around his body widened. He moved his fingers trying futilely to write in his own blood, "Booth—" all the while seeing the blood beginning to bubble from the intense heat until blood and fire were one.

Romance stood like a pillar of fire then crumpled to the floor. The ceiling collapsed in on them, then the roof, and they were buried beneath the burning debris, their mad dance ended at last.

Chapter 58

IN THE abandoned warehouse at the Rocketts, Rebecca and her little band sat forlornly in the darkness.

"We're caught in a dilemma," Becky mused. "When Richmond falls, Forrest will be safe, but Carleton and I—"

Carleton limped to her and put his hands on her shoulders. "Becky, the war's over, only a fool would fail to see that. It's time to go home, time to rebuild our lives."

Rebecca shuddered at the thought of them being together, she'd have to do something to stop it, but before Rebecca could object, Bittersweet pointed out the window, "Mercy me, look!"

Across the river, fires had started to burn throughout the Navy Yard. Carleton said, "President Davis ordered our fleet burned to keep it from falling into the Union's hands."

A ship blew up, spewing flaming ammunition in every direction. Other ships were put to the torch until the river ran red. Then a deafening blast trembled the entire district as the Navy's ammunition dump exploded with apocalyptic fury. Impossible to contain the fires springing up everywhere, igniting wooden shacks and warehouses on both sides of the James.

Rebecca screamed as something crashed onto their roof.

"Must be a spent shell," Carleton told them. Another thud; and in short order they smelled the odor of burning wood. Carleton limped out to the landing and saw the roof afire. "Everyone out," he ordered, urging Rebecca and Bittersweet downstairs. He and Becky shouldered Forrest under his arms and managed to get to the alley just as a section of the roof collapsed. Bittersweet led the horse out of the stable and Carleton and Becky eased Forrest into the shay.

Becky motioned to Rebecca; "Grandma, you drive."

"It's too heavy a load. I'll walk. You lead the horse."

The hill up to Chimborazo was too steep for the nag, the streets to the east where the naval warehouses had stood were a wall of fire, their only escape lay west along the river, back toward the center of town. The horse whinnied in terror and Carleton tied his handkerchief around its eyes.

After a block Rebecca could go no further. "You go on without me," she gasped, fighting for breath. But Carleton and Bittersweet pushed and pulled and cajoled her along. They'd walk a bit, rest, start out again. Block by block, hour after hour with the fire pursuing them through the night, the tiny band struggled back to the Shockoe District in town.

Only to discover that where they'd expected to find safety, pandemonium reigned. Tobacco and cotton warehouses at the Canal Basin had also been put to the torch, casting a hellish glow over everything. There wasn't a constable in sight, or any soldiers and the mob ruled; fierce crowds of skulking men and women had broken into vacant shops and houses and were plundering them. The order had been given to destroy the army's entire supply of liquor, casks were staved in, whiskey ran ankle-deep in the gutters, while half-drunken men and women and even children fought to dip up the alcohol in pans and buckets. They gulped it down, splashed it over their heads in bacchanalian abandon, adding yet another insane note to the city gone mad.

There'd been several prison breaks from the municipal jails and packs of feral criminals roamed the streets. A band of them spotted the horse and shay and with whoops and howls descended on them. Carleton drew his revolver as the gang warily circled the carriage.

"Looks like you got a lame hand there," the leader grinned, "whyn't you just give us the horse and carriage?"

Becky's first shot took off the criminal's ear. "The next one will be between your eyes."

The gang slunk off in search of easier prey.

Then shortly before dawn the unthinkable happened, a quick capricious wind spread the fire from the warehouses to the Arsenal at 7th and Canal Streets; 25,000 artillery shells were stored there along with countless rounds of ammunition. With a blinding flash that turned night into day, the entire city seemed to erupt. With firelight and fear reflecting on their faces, Rebecca and her band stared in numbed horror as one after the other the magazines exploded. Columns of smoke rose followed by deafening roars. An immense store of cartridges ignited, sounding like thousands of rifles being fired. The ground rocked as hundreds of shells detonated in the air and spewed down their iron spray. The entire Shockoe District along the river front clear up to Main Street seemed to burst into flame simultaneously, a thousand buildings burning, tens of thousands fleeing, screaming.

"We've got to get away from the waterfront," Carleton shouted, "someplace where the fire can't reach us."

"Capitol Square," Becky choked. The Capitol with its twelve-acre lawn might act as a firebreak. She started to lead the horse up the steep hill, its hooves scrabbled for purchase on the cobblestones, then with a long whinny it sat down and died. Rebecca laughed in rising hysteria until Becky slapped her; "We've no time for that!" Once more Carleton and Becky shouldered Forrest, leading him up the hill, while Bittersweet, her arm around Rebecca's waist, urged her on.

At last the exhausted band reached the square and took refuge. From the top of the hill they looked down into the burning pall. "Oh my poor Richmond," Rebecca sobbed; "Gunning where are you?" Then she fell to her knees and collapsed.

Chapter 59

ALL THROUGH the dark hours Rebecca's little band huddled together, terrified that the fire would reach the square and overwhelm them. Finally dawn broke, the early light grayed by the pall of smoke from Richmond's ruins. Trapped by the still-burning fires, Rebecca and her group were forced to remain in Capitol Square. A short time later, they watched as Federal troops marched into the city and headed to the Capitol Building. At 8 A.M, Monday, April 3, the Stars and Bars that had flown over the Capitol Building for four years came down and the Stars and Stripes were run up.

Richmond wept. And braced herself for further Yankee atrocities. But the city's fears weren't realized; not only were the Federals highly disciplined, they quickly quelled the criminal elements and restored order. Then they went about saving the rest of Richmond from the ravaging fires.

All roads from the city were clogged with troops and military transport so Rebecca and her kin had no choice except to wait until the crush eased. Thinking that he might beg some food from Romance, Carleton walked the three blocks to her house only to discover that it had burned to the ground. Impossible to get close, it still glowed with embers.

Shaken, he returned to the square and whispered to Becky, "I didn't think the fire got that far. What's even stranger, Romance's house was the only one on the block that burned."

A frightened look passed between them, then Becky said, "Could a cinder have started it, or an exploding shell? Best not tell Grandma right now, we've got enough to worry about without her getting hysterical."

By evening, the Federals had contained the remaining fires and also distributed food. Rebecca and her family went to sleep that night in a conquered city, but more secure than they'd felt in weeks.

Early the next afternoon, Wednesday, April 4, while trying to figure how to get back to Washington, Bittersweet gripped Rebecca's arm and pointed. "Lookit there." A crowd of dancing, singing black people were trudging up the hill; rising above them, the towering figure of Abraham Lincoln.

The President and 12-year-old Tad had arrived in Richmond aboard a small barge. Accompanied only by a handful of guards they'd walked through the smoldering city. A sea of joyous Negroes surrounded Lincoln. Former slaves knelt before him, straining to touch his hand. "I know I'm free," cried one, "for I have seen Father Abraham and felt him."

Lincoln helped the man to his feet; "Don't kneel to me. You must kneel to God only and thank him for your freedom."

Rebecca said resolutely, "Lincoln will help us."

Carleton and Becky stayed with Forrest while Rebecca and Bittersweet chased after Lincoln. But because of the crush of jubilant blacks, they were unable to get close.

Lincoln headed to the Confederate White House; when he sat down at Jefferson Davis' desk the troops watching him from the garden burst into cheers. Rebecca finally managed to get to the White House, only to discover that to avoid the crowds, Lincoln had already slipped out the back door.

Using her press credentials and lying outrageously, Rebecca finally located an officer who'd help. A near-empty ambulance wagon was returning to City Point and the officer allowed her and her band to ride back on it. At last they were on their way out of the desolate city, still pungent with the odor of fire. They saw families sifting through debris trying to salvage what they could while squads of Union soldiers kept order and worked to clear the thoroughfares.

"I never thought I say this," Rebecca sighed, "but thank God for the Yankees, they saved Richmond from being totally destroyed—and by her own citizens."

"Lookit, lookit," Bittersweet cried, and pointed to a naked tarred and feathered man stumbling along the road and babbling insanely, "This is radickalos, ah'm worth thousands in slaves. Lemme on the train and I'll give ya one for free?" As they passed him, Bittersweet raised her fist in triumph.

Soon they were in the countryside; all along the 15-mile route to City Point the desolation stayed with them, barren meadows crisscrossed with trenches bore mute witness to the horror of the past four years.

Hours later they reached City Point. After boarding a steamship, they heard several passengers gossiping about the bitter argument that had erupted between Mary Todd Lincoln and Julia Dent Grant, wife of the general. Mary Todd, in one of her flashes of unreasoned anger, had accused Julia Grant of coveting the White House. It left such bad taste that the two women no longer spoke to each other.

The little band slept during most of the boat trip back to Washington. When they docked, Becky asked Carleton tentatively, "Will you be going back to your plantation?"

"That life is over for me." His eyes searched hers. "Remember you once said...when the world is sane again?" She nodded and he gripped her hand; "Becky, will you marry me?"

Rebecca felt her head grow light. She realized that without Carleton they probably wouldn't be alive. But he was a Connaught, and could a Connaught ever change?

Becky drew Carleton's crippled hand to her lips. "I married you a long time ago but if you want to make it legal, I'd consider it a great honor to be your wife." She added airily, "We'll have to find a place to live, then get to a Justice of the Peace. And as quickly as possible."

Rebecca exclaimed, "Put that right out of your mind—"

With deadly determination, Becky confronted her grandmother; "Grandma, no matter what you say it won't do any good, I love Carleton, I intend to marry him."

"I don't care one whit," she retorted. "I'll need at least six months. There are arrangements to be made, caterers, dressmakers, a hope chest. I never had a proper wedding, your mother eloped, denying me the joy of giving her a proper wedding; I simply won't be cheated again. And no nonsense about looking for a place to live, you'll stay with me, at least until Carleton's well enough to get about. In the meantime, I'll draw up the guest list. Oh dear— Carleton, I suppose we'll have to ask your family? They're not out of the country by any chance, are they? No, I didn't think so. But I'll need six months, at the very minimum."

"Grandma, in six months the reasons for my having to get married will be all too obvious."

At first her meaning didn't penetrate but when Carleton yelled, "What?" it dawned on Rebecca and she cried out, "My nerves!" and smacked Carleton on the head. "Wounded indeed! Your limp, your hand—the entire thing's been a hoax."

But when she turned to Becky, tears brimmed in her eyes; "Oh my darling, how wonderful. For you, for Carleton, for me, for my first great-grandchild. A new life, a new beginning."

Chapter 60

WHEN REBECCA got back to Washington she went immediately to see President Lincoln but was told that he hadn't yet returned from Richmond. She left him a long letter detailing her conversation with Jefferson Davis.

Two days later, Becky and Carleton were married in a simple ceremony in Rebecca's drawing room. Rebecca and Bravo gave the bride away; Sharon was maid of honor, and Forrest, though still mute, acted as Carleton's best man. Because Becky and Carleton had both served in the Confederacy, Rebecca thought it prudent not to invite any government officials. Particularly since Sam Stockwell confessed that he'd indeed been an agent for the Secret Service assigned to spy on Rebecca; all that had gone by the board when he'd fallen in love with Sharon.

"I should horsewhip you," Rebecca declared, "but since this is one of the happiest days of my life, I forgive you. Even though you are from Boston and speak appalling English."

An invitation had gone out to the Connaught estate but Veronique and Sean declined, claiming pressing family matters in Richmond concerning the disappearance of Romance. The absence of the Connaught clan didn't deter the festivities. Everyone agreed that the bride looked radiant, but that the old lady stole the show after a couple of belts of bourbon and a spirited two-step around the stiff-legged groom who jumped a foot when she pinched his bottom.

Rebecca went to bed happy, but couldn't seem to recover from the Richmond ordeal. She slept fitfully, reliving events; once she dreamed that

Gunning came to her wearing a flaming shroud and she woke in terror. "Why is it taking me so long to come to myself?" she complained to Bittersweet.

"Can't imagine, seeing as how you're only eighty-five."

"I freed my slaves long, long before Mr. Lincoln did, so there's no need for you to be impertinent. And, for your information, I'm only seventy-nine."

"Ah, you are getting better."

But she wasn't; at times she felt so lightheaded she had to sit for fear of falling. Once, her arm went numb and flashing lights blinded her. She attributed it to euphoria at Becky's salvation and Forrest's return to the living.

On April 9th, Palm Sunday, Washington woke to rumors, rumors that grew to a groundswell and in late afternoon erupted into reality. Newsboys raced through the streets hawking the Extra Edition, frantically run off by the newspapers: "Lee Surrenders to Grant at Appomattox!"

Rebecca hurried to the avenue and bought a paper. She scanned it, her entire being pulsating with joy. A curious item buried in the text caught her eye. Wilmer Mclean, whose farm had been the battleground at First Manassas, had then moved a 100 miles deeper into southwest Virginia to escape the war, only to have Grant and Lee sign the terms of surrender in his house at Appomattox. It all seemed so ritually right, that Rebecca took it as a sign that the war was really over.

She clutched the paper to her breast and breathed deeply. The air still had an edge to it but spring undeniably held sway. Rampant flowers sprouted everywhere, trees were bursting to bud and people too were bursting, with joy, laughter—when had she last heard unrestrained laughter in the capital?

Washington celebrated far into the night. Quipped one wit in the *Washington Evening Star*, "Any man caught sober on the streets will be arrested."

On Tuesday, April 11, Rebecca learned that President Lincoln intended to give a short speech at the White House, and she and Bittersweet joined the crowd on the South Lawn.

"My nerves," she whispered to Bittersweet," there's John Wilkes Booth, and what's worse, he's seen us. Here he comes."

Booth was with a tall young man she didn't know and he introduced her to Lewis Paine. Sheer brute energy exuded from Paine and Rebecca's skin crawled with intimidation. When Lincoln came out on the portico, she wasn't unhappy when Booth and Paine moved to get closer to the President.

Lincoln spoke about his plans for reconstruction, about giving the vote to the Negro, and healing the nation. Rebecca thought the speech conciliatory, figured with mercy, and her heart beat a bit easier for her beloved, beleaguered South.

The President concluded to ringing applause, except, Rebecca noticed, for Booth and Paine, who were arguing violently. Then the two men stomped off. Rebecca remarked, "Mercy, but isn't John Wilkes acting stranger and stranger?"

The next morning, Wednesday the 12th of April, Bittersweet entered Rebecca's sitting room, her face wreathed in smiles. "The President be downstairs, he wants to see you"

Thinking it might be the president of the bank, or of the orphanage, Rebecca asked, "Which president?"

"The President, the real President, the only President," Bittersweet announced, "my President."

Rebecca got up from her chaise as fast as brittle bones would allow, inspected her face in the vanity mirror and pinched her cheeks in despair; "I look a fright."

"Complainin' night and day of aches and pains," clucked Bittersweet, "but let a pair of pants come callin'—don't rush down them steps. Last thing we needs is a broken hip."

"Will you shut up?" Rebecca hissed, then swept into the drawing room as if she were leading the cotillion.

In the smaller confines of her home, Lincoln appeared even taller. "Welcome home, Miss Rebecca. Bravo told me the wonderful news about your grandson, and we're grateful to the Lord for that." She nodded her thanks and he went on, "I've studied your letter but I wanted to hear about Davis first hand. I've also come to apologize."

"Whatever for?"

"I should have preventing you from going to Richmond. Not a day went by that I didn't feel deep concern for you."

Bittersweet bustled in with a tray of cider, cookies, and freshly cut fruit. With a curtsey worthy of a cupbearer to the Gods, she set it down before her President while Rebecca furtively motioned for her to get out. Finally she said in exasperation, "My dear, I know you've mountains of chores."

Bittersweet left but not before she stuck out her tongue.

Rebecca shook her head; "Help these days."

Lincoln resumed; "When you spoke to Jefferson Davis, did he say anything that I should know? Think carefully."

She massaged the pith of her neck; "Just what I've already written you. I reasoned with him, called on his better instincts, and he has so many. But Jeff sees this conflict in a different light from other men. He's not like other men."

Lincoln nodded; "Never have I come across a man with such an unbending will. Even now with his principal armies surrendered and the South in ruins, he still calls for the rebellion to continue. But for all practical purposes, the war is over. With Lee's surrender, the rest of the South's generals must soon follow. We know that Davis and some members of his cabinet have fled as far south as Georgia. But will he head for the coast to try and escape to England, or strike inland to Texas and continue the fight?" He looked at her pointedly.

She hunched her shoulders in bewilderment; "I don't know. I promise you, I really don't know. Are you still of the same mind, that it would be best if the Confederate leaders sought refuge in foreign countries?"

"There's such an unrelenting cry for revenge in the North that they'd be safer out of the country. When peace is fully restored and cooler heads prevail, hopefully they can return and lend their talents to rebuilding. There's so much to be done. Now that the Union is safe, we can do it."

To be sure, she thought, and if they leave the country, then you won't have to worry about any court battle over the Constitutional right of a State to secede.

"I must go," he murmured.

Yet he didn't move, his face bemused with such melancholy that it unnerved her. Finally she asked, "Is anything wrong?"

"No, nothing…and yet everything. I feel as if I've wakened from a nightmare, one that's lasted for four years. Miss Rebecca, you strike me as a wise woman, someone with a wealth of life experience, experience from which we can all benefit. Do you recall my asking if you believed in dreams?"

"Indeed I do, and in the case of Richmond being consumed by flames, that dream of yours certainly proved prophetic."

"I had another dream several nights ago, so vivid it disturbs me still. I made the mistake of telling it to Mrs. Lincoln and it upset her greatly. Ever since our little Willie died she's been so vulnerable."

"I've lost a daughter, a grandson, and perhaps even my son Gunning. I'll dream of them until the day I die. Be easy with your wife, there's no greater pain than losing a child, it contravenes everything in God's design—that a child should outlive a parent. Sometimes the only way to ease the pain is to seek refuge from this world that's caused it."

"You're kind to see it in that light. I'm sure that's what prompted Mrs. Lincoln to hold those seances…if I could have found comfort in them, how much happier I'd have been."

He paused and Rebecca thought he might not continue. She said, "Sometimes it helps if we talk about our concerns."

"You're most generous to indulge me." After a long pause he began, "Several days ago I retired very late. I couldn't have been in bed very long when I fell into a deep sleep, for I was so very weary. I found myself in a dream. All about me there was a death-like stillness. Then I heard sobs, barely audible, as if a number of people were weeping. I left my bed and wandered downstairs. Here too, everything was silent, save for the same pitiful sobbing, but everywhere I looked, I saw nothing, the mourners were invisible. I drifted from room to room, no living being was in sight, only the same subdued weeping met and followed me as I passed along…The rooms were lit, and every object in them was familiar to me, but where were all the people who were grieving as if their hearts would break?

"My puzzlement gradually gave way to fear, a cold, unnatural fear, for I could find no earthly meaning for any of this. Determined to find the cause of this state of things, at once so mysterious and so shocking, I kept on drifting until I came to the East Room, and I entered it. I was met with a sickening surprise. Before me stood a catafalque, on which rested a corpse wrapped in funeral vestments. Around it were stationed soldiers acting as guards; and there was a throng of people, some gazing mournfully at the corpse whose face was covered, others weeping piteously.

"Who is dead in the White House? I demanded of one of the soldiers. 'The President,' he answered. 'He was killed by an assassin.'"

Though she could have cut off her tongue, Rebecca blurted, "Tenskwatawa!"

"Then you also know the curse? That every President elected in a year ending in zero will die in office?"

"But surely that legend is only a superstitious tale."

He said with wry humor, "Let's hope so—for my sake. I slept no more that night and I've been haunted by it since."

"It is a very unnerving dream," she breathed.

"My apologies if I've caused you any distress." Then he smiled; "But it is only a dream, so let's say no more of it."

He rose and she accompanied him to the door. "Mr. President, might it be prudent for you to have a stronger guard? As Rebel Thorne has written so often, Washington is a southern city."

"Which was borne out quite forcibly this week; our Secret Service arrested a Confederate explosives expert, a Sergeant Thomas Harney who intended to blow up the White House."

She gasped and he nodded ruefully; "Can you imagine such a thing? I pay little mind, for I believe that when my time comes there's nothing that can prevent my going." He paused, then murmured, "This has been the most cataclysmic time in our history. Preliminary reports indicate that more than six hundred thousand men, from North and South, have perished, a dreadful toll. As I've said, and believe even more fervently now, whatever man's plans and purposes have been, the Almighty had His own purposes; He gave to both North and South this terrible war."

"I wonder," Rebecca mused, "or has the Good Lord just left us to our own devices? Who's right? Those who clung to the strictest interpretation of the Constitution? Or those who believed in a higher law? I have a feeling that Americans will argue that question for generations to come."

His response was measured, but commanding; "When they do argue that question, it will be as citizens of the United States. The preservation of the Union, that and that alone was the guiding angel of our battle. And the Almighty saw fit to preserve this great nation. And as you once wrote, it is divided no longer, but beats with one heart."

"Amen," she whispered.

"This Friday I'm arranging a small theater party. I've invited General and Mrs. Grant, and seeing as how Rebel Thorne and I have often been at odds, I believe it would do a great deal for peace in our capital if she agreed to be my guest. Could you persuade her to attend? Of course you're invited also."

Rebecca scrambled for a polite way to refuse; she'd sooner submit to thumb screws than spend an evening with Mary Todd. "Mr. President, I've reached the age, and so has Rebel Thorne, that when the sun goes down, so do our eyelids. What would it profit you to have two old ladies, Rebecca and Rebel Thorne, snoring in your box? But I do so appreciate the invitation. Incidentally, I have it on excellent authority that with peace, those two old biddies will be more than anxious to retire and leave the battlefield to the victor."

Chapter 61

SHORTLY AFTER the President left, Rebecca and Bittersweet strolled to a dry goods store on Pennsylvania Avenue. They were shopping for fabric to sew a layette for Becky's baby.

"Nothin' like new life to bring joy into a house," Bittersweet hummed. "The way Becky's carrying, high and low, wouldn't be surprised if she birthed twins."

"Wouldn't that be wonderful? There'd be one for each of us to spoil. Have I thanked you for all you did in Richmond?" Bittersweet nodded and Rebecca said, "I want you to know I'm leaving you a great deal of money in my will."

"Umm, could I have it now?"

"You may not. Since I'm leaving you a thousand dollars for every year you've been with me it's to your advantage to keep me alive as long as possible. I'd love to see Becky's baby born, so please try not to aggravate me to death?"

"Me aggravate you? Miz Rebecca, you so ornery you'll see us all into our graves. You discovered the secret of long life—the more you complain the longer God lets you live."

Scowling, Rebecca said, "I can change my will any time at all," then gave it up and sang out with laughter.

As she paid the bill she had an uneasy feeling that she was being watched. Am I really getting senile, she wondered? Next, I'll be finding Republicans under my bed.

When they came out of the shop, they were suddenly accosted by John Wilkes Booth. Rebecca was taken aback by his wild appearance and by the reek of alcohol all about him.

"Miss Rebecca, if I could have a word with you alone?" Booth slurred, dismissing Bittersweet with a sidelong glance.

Fearing to create a scene Rebecca said, "Bittersweet, I'm sure John Wilkes will be kind enough to walk me home."

"He's dead drunk," Bittersweet grumbled. Booth's eyes blazed with anger and Rebecca gently nudged Bittersweet off. Bittersweet crossed the avenue but kept a wary eye out for her mistress as she kept pace with them.

"What did he want?" Booth demanded.

Rebecca looked at him, bewildered; "What did who want?"

"Abraham the First." Then Booth recounted a lurid tale of tracking Lincoln from the White House to the War Department and then to her house. "With that stupid excuse for his new bodyguard, Mr. Crook, trailing after him like a hound dog."

"John Wilkes, are you telling me that you're following the President about? Don't you have better things to do?"

She strained to hear his garbled reply, trying to make sense of his demand to know why she wasn't excoriating the administration with her pen as she'd done in the past. "You heard him yourself last night on the White House lawn? My friend Paine and I stood in the rain, falling like God's tears they were, for what that criminal plans to do. He said he'd give the vote to the slave and I told Paine, 'That means nigger citizenship! I've no country left.'"

"John Wilkes, you're talking absolute nonsense. The war's all but over. It's time to rebuild, to heal—"

He interrupted, barely coherent; "This war will never be over, not as long as Confederate armies are in the field. Campbell's Hospital may have been a fiasco, but take heart, a decisive blow will be struck. But where are the experts they promised me? Must I depend on myself alone? Then so be it. The actions of one man will yet save the South. And this time in my forum, so the world can bear witness that as long as true Southern men draw breath, tyranny can never triumph!"

He hiccuped mightily, reeled, collided with a tree, then lurched off. She stared after him, certain that he'd be run over by a carriage as he staggered across the intersection. But with the luck of the drunk he made it across safely.

Bittersweet hurried back to Rebecca and took her arm.

"You all a'tremble. Never seen him such. What'd he want?"

"I couldn't make sense of it. Just another drunken Southerner pouring out his grief at the South's defeat. After all that braggadocio about one Rebel being worth ten Yankees, losing the war must stick in their craw."

That evening, Bravo came to Rebecca's to see Forrest. Since his son's return, Bravo was a changed man, concerned, loving, and charged with optimism. He spent every free moment with Forrest, talking about the past, trying to ignite his memory. Afterward Bravo sat with Rebecca in the drawing room.

"Did you notice any improvement?" she asked hopefully.

"Perhaps a bit. I think Becky's right, it's as if Forrest is hiding, afraid that if he dares to show himself, something awful will happen again."

She squeezed her son's hand. "He'll come out of it, I know he will. He's his father's son. He's a Brand."

After a while, Bravo rose to leave and she said, "Bravo, I almost forgot. The next time you see Mr. Lincoln would you ask him if Campbell's Hospital has any significance for him?"

Bravo grasped her arms; "What do you know of Campbell's?"

"Nothing. That's why I asked you."

Bravo knew that Chief Justice Salmon Chase had reported an unusual incident the afternoon he'd substituted for the President at the veteran's hospital, but Lafayette Baker and his Secret Service operatives hadn't been able to unearth anything. "Ma, what made you ask about Campbell's?"

She hesitated, for Booth led to Surratt, and Surratt inevitably led to Gunning. She was loath to say anything to jeopardize Gunning; she still nurtured the hope that he might be alive.

"Ma, please, this is vitally important. It could be a matter of life and death. Who told you about Campbell's?"

His question sounded with such urgency she couldn't resist him. "I ran into John Wilkes Booth today and he mumbled something about Campbell's, but he was so terribly drunk."

"What else did he say?"

"Nothing sensible, really. Why are you so upset?"

Bravo swallowed hard; "When we captured Richmond, we learned from an enlisted man in their Torpedo Bureau that an explosives expert had been sent by the Confederate government to blow up our White House. Luckily, we captured him two days ago, a Sergeant Thomas F. Harney. Harney's confessed; he planned to blow up the mansion using an entrance on the War Department side of the White House. And preferably when all the cabinet members were at a meeting. That would wipe out any semblance of government, throw the North into confusion and allow the South to regroup."

She clutched her throat; "The President mentioned that. Thank God you caught the man. But surely this can't have anything to do with Booth? He's only an actor, not a combatant."

"Harney had to have a contact in Washington but we don't know who it was. And his contact may still be operating in Washington. We need to investigate every possibility. I'll get this information to Stanton and Baker—for all the good those two idiots have ever done." With a somber nod, Bravo left.

Chapter 62

FOR THE next twenty-four hours, Rebecca worried. And worried some more. Imagine the Confederacy sending someone to blow up the White House? She couldn't believe, didn't want to believe, that Jeff Davis had ever given such an order.

She struggled to recall what Booth had said…hadn't he mentioned something about…'Where are the experts they promised me?' Were Booth's enigmatic ravings merely the ravings of a drunk or did they have greater significance?

Bits of information she'd gleaned in Richmond—Jeff Davis insisting that all wasn't lost; Judah Benjamin commenting that major events were about to happen; Booth introducing her to John Surratt, then suddenly seeing Surratt in Richmond—all formed a patchy, indecipherable mosaic that grew more frightening. But her brain wouldn't work fast enough to make the proper connections and she cursed herself for being an addled old fool.

The next day, April 14, Good Friday, Rebecca read in the society column of the newspaper: "The President will attend a performance this evening of *Our American Cousin* at Ford's Theater." Reminded of his invitation, she felt a comforting contentment; how good it was to be at peace with him.

Rebecca napped in the morning and wanted to nap again in the afternoon but Bittersweet insisted they go for a walk. "Do you good to get out in the fresh, keep the blood flowing into yo' head, make you less forgetful."

Four in the afternoon, fine weather. A horseman sitting his horse like a centaur came cantering along Pennsylvania Avenue. Faultlessly dressed in the height of fashion, buff jacket, fawn trousers, elegant riding boots with slender steel spurs, plain to see this was no common man. He wore a soft felt hat, the brim cocked low to set off his matinee-idol face. He knew every gay young blade on the avenue and they returned his high-spirited greeting.

"You'd never know that be the same drunk who scared us half to death on Wednesday," Bittersweet grumbled.

"Now don't go frightening him off," Rebecca cautioned, "I want to pick Booth's brains, find out what in heaven's name he was talking about." She waved gaily; "John Wilkes?"

John Wilkes Booth turned at Rebecca's call and trotted to her. He swept off his hat in a greeting worthy of a cavalier then chatted Rebecca up in his usual debonair fashion. He apparently had no recollection of their meeting earlier in the week, for he showed no embarrassment whatever.

Rebecca jockeyed for an opening to question him but before she could, a carriage rolled by and Booth exclaimed, "Hallo, there goes Unconditional Surrender Grant."

Rebecca turned to see Grant and his wife, Julia, riding in an open barouche, heading toward the train station. Rebecca tapped her forehead; hadn't Lincoln mentioned that the Grants would be his guests at the theater that evening? Obviously, Mrs. Grant was having no part of Mary Todd either.

Rebecca turned to Booth but he now seemed preoccupied, and with an abrupt wave, galloped off. She was more than a little miffed; "You'd think the devil was after him. I didn't get a chance to ask him anything at all."

Rebecca spent the rest of the day snapping at anyone who came near her. The sun set with unusual splendor, mists from the river and distant lowlands blended in the dim horizon, soon creating a dark overcast evening that obscured the stars. Rebecca retired early, planning to bring her journal up to date but she couldn't concentrate. On the night air came the melancholy strains of the "Miserere." Good Friday...Catholics and other Christians throughout the city were observing Christ's crucifixion.

She put out the gaslight, only to be hounded by Booth's cry—"This time in my forum, and for all the world to bear witness that as long as true Southern men live—"

Unable to sleep, she lit a candle, her eyes fixed on the clock...she imagined the crowd filing into Ford's theater. Curtain time...with each passing minute her heart thumped louder, drawing her irresistibly to she knew not what. She eased out of bed, then woke Bittersweet.

"What you be doin' wanderin' about? You all right?"

"I can't manage the shay alone, you must take me—"

"Straight to the doctor," Bittersweet exclaimed, genuinely frightened by Rebecca's appearance.

"Yes, all right, but first stop at Ford's Theater—"

"You crazy? You can't—"

"Don't argue with me, just take me!" Unable to make her fears understood, she burst into tears. Bittersweet obeyed. Rebecca thought she'd jump out of her skin waiting for the shay to be brought around but at last they were on their way.

Urged by Rebecca, "Faster, faster!" Bittersweet drove the carriage to Ford's Theater on F and NW Tenth Streets. They arrived about ten minutes to ten.

Once inside the theater Rebecca heard unrestrained laughter and slumped with relief; clearly everything was fine, she'd just been a worrisome old wretch. Gradually her eyes became accustomed to the dark; she saw the Presidential Box, draped with national flags and emblems. A portrait of George Washington hung from the front of the box, festooned with flags that fell in graceful folds to the stage.

Rebecca could make out President Lincoln, Mary Todd and their guests. She thought she recognized Major Henry Rathbone and his fiancée, Clara Harris.

On stage, the frothy English comedy of manners bubbled along. Rebecca had her eyes fixed on Lincoln and barely heard the character of Asa Trenchard say about the offstage villainess, "Don't know the manners of good society, eh? Well, I guess I know enough to turn you inside out, you sockdologizing old man trap!"

In the burst of laughter that followed, Rebecca saw a shadowy form enter Lincoln's box, she tried to raise her hand to point to the danger, but it remained immobile at her side. She opened her mouth to scream, but nothing came out; she'd suffered a stroke that left her conscious, but paralyzed.

In a blur, she heard the gunshot, saw President Lincoln slump forward, saw the man vault over the railing of the box, catch his stirrup in the draped flag and fall to the stage. For a moment he stood in the glare of the footlights, derringer in one hand, dagger in the other, and giving his most chilling performance, John Wilkes Booth shouted, "*Sic semper tyrannous!* The South is avenged!"

Then dragging his broken leg, Booth hobbled offstage.

Screams, cries, confusion swirled about Rebecca, she saw guards clear a path through the hysterical crowd and carry the body of the President out of the theater. She knew the wound was mortal. In that instant all the pieces of the mosaic fit together in blinding clarity, and then she sank into oblivion.

Chapter 63

FOR DAYS Rebecca hovered near death. Bravo, Becky and Sharon tended her continually while Bittersweet kept the household running. During the night, when everyone else was asleep, Forrest would come into her room and spend hours just sitting by her bedside. When Rebecca regained consciousness and it became evident that she could understand them, the family took turns reading to her from the newspapers. With that part of her brain still functioning, she struggled to comprehend the fragmented, horrifying details of Lincoln's assassination.

Booth's bullet had entered the back of Lincoln's head, torn through his brain and lodged behind his right eye. Too critically injured to be taken to a hospital, he was moved from Ford's Theater to a Mr. Peterson's boarding house just across 10th Street, where he died the next morning.

Mary Todd suffered a total breakdown and was locked in her room under heavy sedation. She was unable to attend the funeral.

Cries of "Conspiracy!" redounded through the outraged capital with suspicion falling on the leaders of the Confederacy, particularly on Jefferson Davis. Details of a plot were uncovered; John Wilkes Booth did have a gang and they'd planned other assassinations. Private Lewis Paine, assigned to Booth's team by General Mosby, was to kill Secretary of State Seward, who was bedridden, recovering from a carriage accident; Paine would have succeeded but Seward's neck brace blunted Paine's knife thrust. George Atzerodt, assigned to shoot Vice President Andrew Johnson, got cold feet and got drunk instead.

With all these officials murdered, the Union would have had no chief executive, no leadership, which would have given the South a chance to regroup its
forces and fight on.

Other conspiracy theories abounded; with Lincoln, Johnson and Seward
dead, Secretary of War Stanton would have undisputedly held the reins of
power and many believed him to be the evil genius. He'd been responsible for
Lincoln's safety; why hadn't the broken lock on the door to the theater box
been discovered and repaired? Why did Lincoln's bodyguard leave his post to
go drinking at Tueteval's tavern?

But ultimately the smoking gun pointed to the Confederacy. Booth's room
at the National Hotel was searched, incriminating letters were discovered along
with the secret Confederate cipher decoder. Booth had clearly been sending
and receiving messages to and from the Rebel spy network in Montreal, New
York, and Richmond. One message when decoded, read, "Operation Come
Retribution."

The co-conspirators were apprehended and imprisoned, including Mary
Surratt, David Herold, George Atzerodt and Lewis Paine. John Surratt, who'd
fled to Montreal after Richmond fell, escaped to Europe. Under questioning,
Lewis Paine revealed that just before the assassination, Booth had told his
team, "'Our country owes all its troubles to Lincoln. God made me the instrument of his punishment.'" Then Paine added, "They ain't caught the half of
them that planned this."

Rebecca struggled to make sense of it all. Where was God in all this? Had
Booth been the instrument chosen by a higher power to work out some grand,
mysterious end? As the Bible so vehemently insisted, "Without the shedding of
blood there is no redemption." Without a sacrificial lamb, humanity could
have no atonement. In one stroke Lincoln had passed from a vilified President
to a martyr for the ages.

And what of Gunning, she wondered? How deeply had he been involved?
All his life he'd been someone who'd drawn the lightning…had a vengeful God
at last struck him down? As the days passed Rebecca became convinced that
she'd never see her son again.

On April 26th, Rebecca listened to Becky and Carleton discussing in hushed
tones how Booth had been cornered in a barn, how it was set afire to flush him
out, and when he aimed his pistol at the Union soldiers, was shot dead. The
other conspirators were awaiting trial. Given the cries for revenge they were
certain to be hung.

Then during the week of May 10, Rebecca heard newsboys hawking the latest extras outside her windows; each day held news of momentous events.

"Jefferson Davis Captured Near Irwinsville, Georgia!"

"Judah Benjamin Escapes, Probable Destination England!"
"President Andrew Johnson Orders Jefferson Davis Imprisoned at Fortress Monroe!"
"Stanton Accuses Davis of Involvement in Lincoln's Assassination!"
"War Officially Declared Over!"
"The Union Forever!"

Chapter 64

BECKY SAT by Rebecca's bed, sewing tiny cross-stitches on a baby's blanket. Though Rebecca hadn't spoken in almost a month, Becky kept up a patter of conversation.

"Carleton and I decided if it's a boy, we'll name him Jonathan, after my Pa; Jonathan Geary Brand Connaught. With a name like that he'll have to be famous. If it's a girl, would Suzannah Rebecca suit you? No two women I love more than my Ma and Grandma. Is that a tiny smile I see?"

Becky rested her hands on her stomach. "I never thought I could be this happy. Only one thing could make me happier, if you got well in time to hold your great-grandchild. Or great-grandchildren, because Bittersweet swears that I'm carrying twins. Mercy, twins, I'll never be able to manage them alone. Grandma, you've just got to get better."

That evening when everyone else had gone to bed, Forrest slipped into Rebecca's room, as he'd done every night since she'd taken ill, and took up the vigil. They gazed at each other for a long time. Locked in their own isolation, they were irresistibly drawn to each other, their silence signifying a communication that went far beyond words.

Rebecca's eyes slid to the night table. Forrest tried to decipher what she meant, and when she did it again, he opened the drawer and found Rebecca's journal. Recognizing it as something private, he hesitated to open it, but watching his grandmother's restless eyes, he had a simple thought. If he showed it to her, might it help restore her senses? He was also wildly curious;

he'd heard so many rumors about his grandmother's youthful indiscretions that the journal beckoned like some magical mirror to her past.

With one eye on his grandmother, he riffled through the pages, catching glimpses of familiar names and events. She blinked, and in their secret communication he took that to mean she wanted him to go on. He turned to the first page and began to read silently.

"This is the journal of Rebecca Breech Brand, the journal of a woman with a divided heart. All my life I've fought a battle within myself; I was blessed—or cursed—with knowing right from wrong, but often I was too willful to chose the right path, which led to the most dire consequences. Always too good for the people I chose, never quite good enough for those I truly loved.

"When I reflect on the truly important moments in my life, I can say my adult life began on October 13, 1792, the day they laid the cornerstone of the White House. That date had been chosen because it was the three hundredth anniversary of Columbus's discovery of America. I was thirteen years old and had come to the ceremony with my father, Mathias Breech; he'd been awarded the contract to supply bricks for the American Palace, as it was then called. Neither President Washington nor Vice President John Adams had come down from Philadelphia for the dedication; about a hundred locals had gathered in this rattlesnake-infested swampland, still the hunting grounds of wolves and bear. The Connaughts were there, they'd been Tories during our Revolution but they were still the richest, most powerful family in the district.

"Zebulon Brand galloped up with his usual dash, so brutally handsome it took one's breath away. And Zebulon's half brother—"

Forrest stopped reading and peered at the page. His mouth worked... "Grandma...I can't...make out this name, it's smudged."

Rebecca's mouth twitched as she tried to form the name, Forrest bent close and caught her whispered, "Jeremy Brand. Your grandfather."

He bounded to his feet; "You talked!"

And suddenly he realized that he'd spoken also. They looked at each other in wonder, their smiles and tears forming a bridge across generations.

Forrest continued reading, this time, aloud; "How could I have known that my involvement with these brothers, Zebulon and Jeremy, would bring such misery and passion and love into my life? How could I have known that I'd carry the sins of my youth into my old age? Even if I had known the outcome, would I have lived my life any differently? I doubt it, for all our destinies seemed to be entwined. For my sins, I've always been drawn to power, and the White House was fated to become the most powerful symbol in the world. How fortunate I was to be witness to it's beginnings, and to watch it become the beacon of hope and of freedom that it is today.

"It began that autumn day…"

As Rebecca lay immobile, listening, the transgressions and glories of her life flashed by…she imagined herself young again, budding with desire, anxious to fall in love…

The End…And The Beginning

CPSIA information can be obtained
at www.ICGtesting.com
Printed in the USA
LVHW102210050122
707981LV00013B/937

9 780595 272976